WAKING THE DEAD

D. B. SIEDERS

CITY OWL
PRESS

WAKING THE DEAD
Soul Broker, Book 1

CITY OWL PRESS
www.cityowlpress.com

Cover Design by Mibl Art. All stock photos licensed appropriately.

Edited by Amanda Roberts.

For information on subsidiary rights, please contact the publisher at info@cityowlpress.com.

Print Edition ISBN: 978-1-944728-13-7

Digital Edition ISBN: 978-1-944728-20-5

Printed in the United States of America

For my brother

PRAISE FOR D. B. SIEDERS

"A unique cast of characters drives this beautifully crafted tale that demands you keep a box of tissue on hand. WAKING THE DEAD is a soul-wrenching look into the decisions one must make about life and death, not only for one's self, but for a loved one. Ms. Sieders knows how to put words on paper that touch the heart, and invigorate the mind." - *4.5 Stars from InD'Tale Magazine*

"Revolution brews in the spirit world. Vivian and Lazarus encounter a vibrant cast of allies—among them mambo woman Bijoux Briggs and Vivian's sister Mae, who was disabled in life but is powerful in the afterlife —and develop a love connection despite their complicated past." - *Publisher's Weekly*

"D.B. Sieders is a unique storyteller. CROSSCURRENTS is a mix of science fiction and fantasy that is woven together perfectly. Ms. Sieders's characters are distinctive and the story is imaginative and fun." - *4.5 Stars from InD'Tale Magazine*

"For paranormal romance readers who are looking for something a little different, Lorelei's Lyric could be your first step into a whole new world." - *Romantic Reads and Such*

"Sieders delivers a well-written and intriguing supernatural world with a plot that pulls you in and characters that keep you turning pages until the very end in FIRESTORM." - *ARC Reviewer*

"In WAKING THE DEAD, there is an emotional, raw honesty in Vivian and her struggles to care for her sister, Mae. It's so rare to find a heroine, one we root for, who is not a saint but is desperately trying to do the right thing and is not always perfect." - *ARC Reviewer*

THE SOUL BROKER SERIES

BY D. B. SIEDERS

CHAPTER ONE

The sound of the crash struck her first.

Her tires screeched after she slammed on the brakes, barely missing the blue Sentra in front of her. It had one of those "Choose Life" stickers plastered on its left bumper, the smiling infant illuminated by the red of taillights.

The image still burned in her brain as she made a sharp left.

Her car fishtailed. She registered more squealing tires and the shriek of metal on metal signaling impact. Her heartbeat hammered above the clamor all around.

Breathe in, breathe out. The car stopped dead. But how?

Am I hit? Did I hit someone? Her airbag hadn't deployed, but the pain in her left shoulder let her know her seatbelt had gotten a workout. *Breathe, focus, look around!* Darkness had already swallowed much of the summer evening twilight's soft glow, but there was still enough light to make out her surroundings. *I'm off the road and half in a ditch, but I think I'm okay. I'm okay. I'm okay. God, what happened?*

There had been an impact. She'd felt it, heard it, but what had she hit? The car in front of her?

With a deep breath, she leaned forward with caution and peered into the ditch. The Sentra had landed in the narrow end of the gorge several feet away from danger. Its driver wrestled with his door, wedged against the side of the trench. When it didn't budge, he gave up, scooted over, and climbed out of the passenger door. Vivian's car teetered over a deeper part of the ditch. She couldn't see them, but knew jagged boulders lurked at the bottom below her front tires. She knew the road well.

It was close to home.

She managed to shift into park with a shaky hand, her right leg cramped from maintaining pressure on the brake. *Get up! Get out!* She turned off the ignition, wincing in pain, and shifted in her seat to remove her seatbelt. Unsure exactly how far her car lurched over the ditch's edge, she moved slow and easy, exiting the vehicle and closing the door. She clicked the automatic door locks and put her keys into her pocket out of habit. Shock and the surreal quality of the unfolding events kept her running on autopilot. The urge to move, to act, forced her to her feet. If she could breathe, she could move. If she could move, she could function. If she could function, she'd be all right.

Judging from the commotion further up the road, someone else involved in the accident was far from all right.

Her feet carried her away from her car and toward the small but growing crowd. The acrid stench of smoke, gas, and burnt rubber assaulted her. The glare of headlights hurt her eyes. She walked forward, ignoring the other spectators who ignored her in turn. Their chatter remained distant— conversations and comfort, tears and terrified mutterings, men and women speaking all around to one another.

No one spoke to Vivian. She spoke to no one.

Sirens wailed in the distance. She walked along the periphery of the crowd, grateful to go unnoticed so she could concentrate and just keep moving. A low rumble of dread gnawed at her gut, warning her to stop, but her legs refused to obey.

Time seemed disjointed, slowing, then skipping like a damaged film reel. She looked back at her car and realized she'd been inches from oblivion. *If I hadn't stopped when I did...if the guy behind me hadn't....* Any sooner, she'd have been rear-ended and launched full into the ditch. A moment later, her car would've been crumpled between the Sentra and the F-350 behind her. But she'd hit the Sentra, hadn't she?

No, no damage to the rear of the vehicle, and her front bumper remained intact, as far as she could tell from the distance. How had she stopped? Shifting her gaze to the F-350, Vivian saw it from the side now, the black truck adorned with a custom flame job painted across the doors and bed. The brawny owner inspected the body for damage. Flecks of dried mud and grime rose from the undercarriage and dulled the flares above. The vehicle's powerful bulk was adapted to rough terrain, like its owner. She and her sleek sedan were not. They'd all been going at least 35, maybe 40 miles an hour. She had to look away. Disaster had come so close.

I should've been knocked into that ditch. How did I miss it?

Shivering, she caught a flash of white in the periphery, but when she turned, it was gone, departing along with the warm breeze that swept in out of nowhere and chased the odd chill that surrounded her away. Infused with energy and a strange sense of urgency, she shook off the remnants of unease and continued.

She had to keep moving.

Another man lumbered across the street toward the crowd. He moved in the long shadows cast by the setting sun, looking from side to side and peering over his shoulder. He seemed as intent on his journey as Vivian was on hers, but unlike the other onlookers, he at least spared her a nod before moving along. Well, she thought he had. The dark green ball cap he wore shielded his eyes, and thus his intent, but he kept walking in the same direction. No one else paid him any mind.

When she turned back to face her destination, she saw what remained at ground zero of the evening's terror. The poor soul in that twisted and crumpled wreckage before her hadn't been so lucky. No one could walk away from this crash.

She took two steps closer. Smoke rose from the damaged engine, along with the occasional spark. Everyone around her stayed back. A man's hand emerged from the driver's side window, along with a soft groan. Another step closer and she heard his ragged breathing.

Vivian took one more step, close enough for her arm to brush the car's cooling frame. She met his stare through the window.

Oh dear God, no.

Her gaze burned a path from his face down to his torso, and then she had to look away from what remained of his body below the waist. The mangled steering column and dashboard covered much of the damage, but not quite enough. *He'll never walk again. He'll be paralyzed. If he took a blow to the head, he'll be a vegetable.*

Vivian's pulse raced. Her hands and fingers went numb.

He'd be better off dead.

Fighting the wave of revulsion, she took one more step toward the car. Every nerve in her body screamed for her to run away, to leave this *thing* that used to be a man and never look back. This was his nightmare, not hers.

She had already lived one of her own.

With palpable effort, Vivian reached for him with one trembling arm and took his hand in hers, gasping when she felt his skin.

Jesus, he's so cold!

The man's grip was iron and it caught her off guard. She hadn't anticipated the strength of it or the effect it would have on her. The bone-deep chill started where their hands joined and spread through her body. She flinched and tried to pull away.

The man squeezed her hand even tighter and tugged, pulling her closer. His brilliant green-eyed gaze was filled with fear, pain, and something she couldn't quite define. Was it anger? He closed his eyes after a moment and a shocking burst of heat traveled through her from their joined hands. His touch chased away the chill, soothing her from ragged fingertips to her battered palm.

When he opened his eyes again, the man's expression mirrored the sudden and inexplicable relief surging within her. No fear, no pain. These weren't her emotions. *They must be his.* But how was she able to experience them as if they were her own? Then a singular emotion reflected in his gaze suddenly pierced her with vivid clarity.

Regret.

Vivian swore she could *see* the gray light of this man's regret emanating from his very pores as it coursed through her.

His expression pleaded, and he spoke to her in a harsh rasp. "I'm...sorry."

"It's going to be okay," she whispered, even though it wasn't.

His chest heaved and his eyes dulled, rolling back as he gasped for air. Two more shallow breaths later, he stilled completely.

"No, please. You have to stay with me. Please, stay with me," she pleaded, shaking his shoulder with one trembling hand even as she felt his grip slipping from her other.

"Oh no, oh dear God, someone help him!"

"Ma'am, I need you to step away from the vehicle," a muffled male voice said from behind her.

"Where the hell did she come from?" asked another man.

"Easy, bro, she must've just wandered in before we put up the barricades."

"No, she didn't. She just popped up out of nowhere!"

Hands gripped her shoulders and tried to pull her away, but she struggled free, refusing to let go of the man in the car. He wasn't blinking. He wasn't moving. His pallor faded to ash even as she begged him to come back.

"Please, ma'am, let us help him."

She yelped when a second set of hands grabbed her around the waist and lifted her off the ground. She wailed in rage and agony when she lost contact with the man's hand. She kicked and clawed at her captor until he dropped her, then she spun around and lifted her hands, ready to fight.

"Jesus, lady, calm down. We're paramedics," one of the uniformed men said. "We're here to help. I'm Ed, and this is Abner." He gestured to taller man beside him. They stood between her and the wreckage. Both began moving forward with outstretched hands as she backed away.

"Why don't you come with us so we can check you for injuries?" Ed spoke in a soft voice, taking slow, measured steps toward her and holding out his hand.

"I'm not injured. I...I can't leave him."

"Were you in the car with him, ma'am?" Abner asked. His sharp tone carried a note of accusation, or perhaps suspicion.

No, not that. He was afraid of her.

"No," she muttered, confused. She shook it off, focusing instead on the overwhelming urge to return to the man in the car.

"What's your name, ma'am?"

"Vivian."

"And his?"

"I have no idea. I don't know him, I just—I saw the crash and I came over. And I need to get back to him. I—I need to help him. Let me go back to him."

"Shh, it's okay. Come on with us now."

Ed lurched forward and grabbed her wrist. She tried to pull away but his scream caught her off guard. He dropped her arm and stumbled back, clutching his hand against his chest and groaning as if in terrible pain. Looking down, she swore she saw a red spark flash out of her fingertips, but by the time she blinked, it was gone.

"Ed? You okay?" Abner stepped away from Vivian and turned his attention to his colleague.

"Jesus Christ, my hand is on *fire*. What the hell did you do to me, lady?" Ed groaned, arm still clutched to his chest and eyes wide with shock and fear.

"Let me have a look." Abner tugged on his buddy's arm. After a quick exam he said, "I don't see anything. Must've been static electricity or something."

"Static electricity, my ass," Ed muttered, wringing his hand and staring at Vivian like she'd sprouted a second head. He and Abner exchanged a few more hushed words before he turned his attention back to the mangled car and the man inside.

Abner spoke louder then, snapping Vivian back to attention. "As for you, you really should go over to the ambulance and let our team have a look at you. The police will want your statement too."

He didn't make any further attempt to touch her. Instead, he pointed to the ambulance parked behind the growing crowd of onlookers while inspecting her with a wary expression. What the hell just happened? Numb with shock and an inexplicable sense of loss, she willed her feet to carry her over to the ambulance, leaving the stranger to his fate.

She paused, glancing back over her shoulder. "Will he be okay?"

"We'll do all we can, ma'am. You just go on now and take care of you."

———

She made it home two hours later.

Vivian sat on the deck and looked out as far as moonlight allowed. The scent of early summer clover hung heavy in the air and almost masked the fading honeysuckle of spring. Lightning bugs twinkled in the dark while the heat of the day flowed off the land. It wasn't a boon year for cicadas, better known as jar flies in this neck of the woods, but they still sang loud enough to match the volume of the crickets. A few mourning doves cooed in their haunting altos, joined by mockingbirds from time to time.

Her cherished backyard paradise offered little respite from the evening's trauma, or the smaller terrors this night would no doubt offer.

She sighed and drew another long swallow from her glass of wine. Her late arrival back home earned her an earful from the home healthcare aide and a fifty-dollar penalty. At least she'd managed to get her car out of the ditch with the help of burly Mr. F-350 and one of the patrolmen on the scene. She could still drive her sedan, but the alignment was out of whack. She'd have to take it in for service tomorrow. What if she had to replace all four tires? Could've been worse. God only knew how she'd managed not to damage her last remnant of the good life. The way things were going, this car would have to last her well beyond its shelf life as a status symbol.

Not that she had any status left, or much of a life.

While still shaken, she wouldn't risk a stronger drink. She had to function. Her sister Mae was likely to have another bad night in spite of the new medications, so neither of them would be getting much sleep. Waiting was the worst. She could only afford about six more weeks off work, maybe eight if she pinched a few more pennies. Having burned through her vacation days and time allotted for family and medical leave, she still couldn't bring herself to return to work.

The irony wasn't lost on her. In the course of her work as a loan officer, she advised countless clients on the merits of financial planning, adequate insurance, and savings. So much for practicing what she preached. But Mae's condition was deteriorating fast according to the doctors, and Vivian couldn't bear to leave her. Besides, insurance only covered twenty hours of home health care per week, hardly conducive to a full-time work schedule.

But more time out of work would be time without pay, forcing her to use more of her scarce savings and dip into her retirement fund. Mae might live even longer. No one would have thought such a wreck of a body could make it thirty-two years.

Her passing would be a mercy for both of them, though the fact didn't offer any comfort, nor did the possibility that Mae might pull through. Guilt enveloped Vivian, wrapping around her like an old worn-out sweater stretched too far. She couldn't throw it out, and she wore it often these days.

Pushing those thoughts aside, she focused on the sights and sounds of her small patch of nature. A light breeze rustled through her favorite maple as its leaves showed their white underbellies. Rain's calling card, as if the heavy slate clouds and palpable humidity weren't announcement enough. A movement in the treeline caught her eye. A deer was always a treat. There weren't many left since the developers got busy in her little corner of the county. As it moved closer, she realized it was something bigger than a deer. No, not *something, someone* bigger. She stood and took a step closer to the door.

A man pushed out of the trees and onto the lawn. In the half-light, she saw his hat and heard his footfalls on the soft grass. He paused at the bottom of the stairs, looked up at her, then tipped his hat and raised a hand to wave.

"Evening, ma'am," came his low, gravelly voice. "Didn't mean to startle you." He stopped, perhaps waiting for her response.

"Good evening," she replied, clutching the cell phone in her pocket. "What can I do for you?"

"I just stopped by to see if you was all right after that big ruckus tonight."

She risked a step forward then leaned over the rail to get a better look at him. Yes, she remembered him now. Her visitor was the man who'd given her the nod at the crash site. The outdoor security light let her see him a little better now. He was definitely a local. Clad in well-worn overalls, a weathered John Deere cap, and dusty old boots, the clothes and their owner had more than a few miles on them.

"I'm fine," she said. "You did startle me when you came out of the trees. I didn't recognize you at first."

"You saw me," he said, almost to himself. He seemed to be chewing on some thought or another before he continued. "Oh yes, ma'am, I saw it. Shame too. That boy didn't make it."

"No, he didn't," she said, lowering her eyes. The images were still fresh and buzzed around in her aching head like a nest of angry hornets. Flashes of twisted metal and blood, but not a lot on his face. She'd done all she could for him, holding his hand and whispering words of reassurance. He looked to be about her age, a healthy man with years of life ahead of him.

Until capricious fate cut his life with sudden brutality.

Giving what comfort she could, she'd watched the life drain out of him. The medics had tried to console her that all was not lost. She knew the truth. He was gone. She winced at the thought, closing her eyes at the unexpected pang. Maybe it was just weariness with her own troubles. Death was an old if not welcome acquaintance. Should she try to find out more about him and talk to his family? What would she say? Of course, the police or paramedics would inform them, but the moment she'd shared with the man had been so personal, made her somehow...responsible for him. The voice of her visitor brought her back.

"Hey, now, you all right? I thought you might be pretty shaken up, watching that boy die." When she offered no objection, he took slow, steady steps up the stairs. Something about her visitor dampened the fear running beneath the surface of her civility. Any other night, she'd have run straight inside. It was as if his presence enveloped her in a cocoon of calm and safety.

Maybe she was just lonely.

Once he stood on the deck in front of her, he asked, "Is there someone I can give a holler for you?"

"No, I'll be okay, but it was nice of you to stop by. How'd you know where I live? Are you from the neighborhood?" He didn't look familiar. She'd lived here long enough to know most everyone. The realization should have set off alarm bells, but the warmth in his gaze and down home manner kept her at ease.

"Oh, I'm around here a bit." He smiled. "But I don't like the idea of leaving you all alone after what you been through."

"My sister's in the house, so I'll be fine. She's...she's not feeling well. I really should check on her." Retreating, she asked, "Did you know the man in the accident?"

"Not exactly, but I think we might have something in common," he said with a knowing smile.

His statement and smile poked a big hole in the cocoon of calm, giving Vivian a case of the creeps. Good down-home charm aside, she should never have let him get this close or stay this long. This wasn't like her, especially in light of the evening's stress. Time to end the conversation before the guy went all Jack the Ripper on her.

"Thank you for stopping by. I need to get back inside now. Rain's coming. You should get home before it starts. Good night, Mister...."

"Oh, you can just call me Ezra. It surely was a pleasure to meet you, Miss Vivian," he said, extending his hand.

She hesitated for a moment, but then accepted, tilting her hand slightly to hide the unsightly nails, chewed to the quick. His roughened skin and gnarled knuckles chafed her skin before the warmth of his grasp overwhelmed her.

The shock of it froze her in place, even as warmth suffused her fingertips and beyond—the same heat she'd felt with the wounded man in the car, only more intense and powerful.

When she didn't release his hand, Ezra pulled away gently. He tipped his hat and began his slow descent down the stairs as she stood dazed, still swathed in the pleasant warmth of his presence. Halfway down, he glanced over his shoulder and said, "I'll be seeing you soon. Get on in the house and rest easy now."

"Good night," she said politely, then nipped inside and bolted the door behind her with a sigh of relief and irrational regret.

She tiptoed down the dark hall to check on the shell that held her sister. Entering Mae's room with practiced quiet, Vivian listened. Her sister's breaths were shallow and still plagued by rasps and wheezes. Vivian stood over the narrow bed, regarding her sister with a mixture of love, pity, and resentment.

All of that time they'd borrowed and bought for her, and for what?

God, she was *loathsome* to think such things. What decent person questioned the value of life, especially the life of a loved one? Hell, Mae was the only family she had left since their parents were gone. Good people didn't think of their flesh and blood as burdens, especially someone like Mae. She hadn't asked to be born with her condition, and Vivian had long ago promised to assume responsibility for her should the time ever come.

Still, standing there in the dark, Vivian recalled the horror with which she first contemplated her sister's level of awareness. When she'd prayed as a child, Vivian had hoped God's mercy had spared Mae awareness. She didn't want to think of an intact mind trapped in such a body.

Without thinking, she stroked her sister's cheek and ran her hand over Mae's soft hair. Mae shifted and inhaled deeply. Vivian stiffened, bracing herself for a coughing fit or worse, Mae choking. Instead, Mae's breathing evened out and she drifted further into a peaceful rest. Stranger still, the air around them seemed warmer.

Perplexed, though relieved, Vivian left her sister and forced her own weary legs in the direction of her bathroom. Halfway there, realization dawned. She hadn't actually told Ezra her name.

Had she?

Then again, she'd given her contact information and statement to a half a dozen cops, medics, and even one firefighter at the scene. He'd probably just overheard it. A good chunk of southeast Nashville probably knew how to find her by now.

Still, she could have kicked herself for letting a stranger know she was more or less alone in the house, and for letting him get so close to her. The news and all of those crime dramas on TV tended to blur the line between healthy caution and paranoia. The events of the past few hours weren't helping either.

She didn't notice anything unusual with her hands while completing her nightly routine, other than the slight tremor running through them as she washed her face and brushed her teeth. And the raw skin and mangled nails, of course. Maybe she'd just zapped the paramedic and Ezra with a little static discharge, like the other paramedic had said. But she hadn't been wearing a sweater and it was such a humid night.

Oh God, she'd just touched Mae with that hand. What had she been thinking?

But she'd touched Ezra with it too, and his hot touch almost burned *her*.

What the hell? Static electricity didn't travel back and forth like a normal current. Since when had she turned into a battery?

She touched one tentative fingertip to the metal faucet fixture, bracing for a jolt.

Nothing.

Feeling foolish, she touched the brass-plated hoop that held her hand towel, her metal tweezers, and her scissors. Wet or dry, she felt nothing other than cold metal, which should have been a better conductor than flesh.

Vivian shook her head. Maybe things would look a little clearer in the morning.

"Go figure," she muttered, looking at her bottle of sleeping pills. She hadn't even realized she'd pulled them out of the cabinet, though it came as no surprise. Seemed her earlier brush with death had killed the mood.

She put them back with a little hesitation.

After all, they'd still be there tomorrow.

CHAPTER TWO

"The board has already reached a decision. I'm afraid you were not selected for the position." The assistant's words and their crisp, detached delivery drove another nail into Vivian's coffin.

She cleared her throat and fought to match the faceless administrator's detached tone. "I thought they weren't handing out promotions until August. All of the figures aren't in yet, and they still haven't calculated bonuses—"

"I'm sorry, Ms. Bedford, but their decision is final. Perhaps...when you return from leave you can apply for the next management position." Vivian bit back a retort, shoving two fingers into her mouth and gnawing what was left of her nails instead.

You mean if I come back, you cold-hearted bitch.

No, that wasn't fair. The woman on the line had no idea the hell she'd lived for the past half year, cramming fourteen hours' worth of blood, sweat, and reams of paperwork into six-hour days to close as many loans as her colleagues so she could get home and take care of her primary obligation. She didn't have to go out on repos, of course. None of the brokers did in her large firm. But she still checked in with the men who handled the tricky business of recovering property to make sure they were okay, be it after a grab under the cover of darkness or a mid-afternoon haul. No matter how hurried, harried, or sleep-deprived, she never, *ever* failed to call and make sure her guys made it back safe. And she always tried to work with delinquent clients first before calling in collections in an effort to avoid potentially dangerous confrontations.

Not many of her other colleagues bothered.

It cost her time, time she could've spent on solicitations and closings, but loyalty equaled return clients and kept her competitive. But that was before. And now that she'd been forced to take family leave, granted by her firm in compliance with the law if not out of concern for her situation, corporate had apparently passed her over for promotion in favor of another broker.

Because no good deed ever went unpunished.

"Ms. Bedford? May I assist you with anything else?"

"Yes, could you transfer me to human resources, please. I need some information about benefits. Denied insurance claims." She winced and bit her lip. *Shouldn't have added that last part.* God, it sounded like the beginning of a million and one conversations from her delinquent clients, behind on repayment and hoping for a miracle. Shame-covered desperation.

"Certainly. Please hold."

At least they had decent elevator music for the wait. She switched to Bluetooth mode, stuck her cell phone in her pocket, and walked down the hall to adjust the thermostat. The display read seventy-three degrees, but the sweat trickling down her back and heat in her cheeks suggested otherwise. The low hum of the air conditioner and cool bursts from the overhead vent were reassuring. Good. No need for an expensive service call.

She could take more money out of retirement, but for a hefty fee. And then if she got fired....

Shivers ran down her spine, leaving a trail of gooseflesh under beaded sweat. Was she coming down with something? Sudden shifts from hot to cold could mean flu, right? She'd been feeling it since last night, so it was possible. No, she couldn't get sick now. Who would take care of...things?

She yanked the phone out of her pocket and cursed. On hold for benefits more than twenty minutes. On hold for career advancement for the foreseeable future. She leaned back against the wall and stared at the rows of pictures facing her. Dusty frames filled with photos lined the wall, snapshots of laughter amid sunlight and sparkling wine, surprise and delight captured as she danced in blue satin. She'd caught the bouquet in her manicured hands that day, just over a year ago at a friend's wedding. He'd been with her then, the man standing next to her in another photo with his brilliant smile frozen in the glossy print. The tickle of dark stubble nuzzling her cheek that day sliced through her memory now, opening the raw wound. He'd left her heart as empty as her bed.

Pictures of beach vacations and ballroom dancing, scuba adventures and ski slope tumbles, the images assaulted her with memories of a not-so-distant past when she'd been alive.

She ended the call and shoved her phone back into her pocket. Red filled her vision and she reached out, yanked his picture down, and smashed it against the wall with all the force she could muster. It shattered in a shower of glass and wooden splinters. She slammed it again, hard enough to mutilate the glossy image of his face. Again, hard enough to dent the sheetrock, and again, with enough force to twist her wrist and bruise her palm. What did it matter? Black and blue would go nicely with her chewed nails and raw skin.

She heaved a few deep breaths and let the remnants of the past slip from her hand before stumbling down the hall to face the present.

There were promises, and then there were *promises*.

The whisper of promises made long ago urged her to extend a trembling hand, clasp the chipped faux brass knob, and open the door. She must have opened that door a thousand times by now, and yet the scent lurking behind it always threatened to shatter the thin veneer of calm that kept unfathomable despair and burning rage at bay. The piney sting of disinfectant waged war against the lingering tang of soiled cotton sheets and slow, progressive decay. A miasma that conjured her shattered innocence, her mother's grief, her father's absence.

Her current obligation.

She opened the bedroom door and slipped into darkness, willing her heart to slow, and listened for an unsteady jerk of limbs, a low moan, or a sharp cry indicating wakefulness, if not awareness. The wet gasp of labored breathing jolted her into action. She had promises to keep.

She flipped the switch on a corner table lamp. Its soft glow cast long shadows from keepsakes lining the dusty surface of a child's white bureau. Porcelain dolls clad in age-yellowed lace stared into the void with empty black eyes, faded cheeks jaded beyond blushing. Stuffed bears, bunnies, and the odd exotic beast in miniature filled the tattered ranks, keeping silent watch as she took up the mantle of care.

If they had any advice to offer, they kept it to themselves. It was just as well. They'd never served as objects of comfort.

She returned to her sister's bedside, wheelchair in tow. Mae's lashes fluttered as she unlatched the bedrail, but the gray-blue gaze didn't track with light or movement. The pupils constricted to pinpricks, suggesting sensitivity to light. The reaction was as good a reason as any to keep the lights off most of the time. Their mother always had. It was one more small way to honor her promise.

Temporarily shedding her cloak of misery to attend to the day's labor was another.

She ran a tentative finger along Mae's arm, feeling both relieved and foolish when nothing happened. No sparks, no shocks, no strange flashes. She still had no idea what she'd done the night before, but thank God it hadn't affected Mae.

"One, two, three, and here...we...go." Vivian groaned as she heaved Mae out of bed and lowered her dead weight into the wheelchair. How could someone so rail-thin be so heavy? Lifting her out of the bed seemed harder and harder each day.

Wheezing breaths rattled through Mae's chest and back, vibrations rumbling beneath Vivian's sore fingertips.

"We'll need to get you more asthma meds to go along with the new antibiotics." She stood and stretched her sore back muscles before checking her watch. The caregiver's shift didn't start for another twenty minutes, so she had time to call for refills before making the weekly pharmacy run, which would give her just enough time to meet her best friend for a much-needed sanity break. She just had to dig deep into her energy reserves and move faster.

"Think insurance will cover it all this time?"

Mae grunted. The guttural outburst wasn't a reply, of course, but she kept talking anyway. It wasn't like anyone else was around to listen.

"So your doctor thinks we need to keep you sitting at least four hours a day."

She squatted back down and shifted Mae's hips between the chair's customized seat pads. An involuntary kick knocked her on the chin. She caught Mae's other leg and deflected the second kick, which also saved her from stumbling backward and falling on her ass. It took two tries to secure the pelvic straps since Mae's legs kept twitching, making her body slide too far down in the seat. Vivian leaned back and shivered in spite of the sweat trickling down the back of her neck.

"He thinks it'll help you breathe better. Of course, *he's* not the one who has to get you in and out of this thing."

After latching the groin guard in place, Vivian captured Mae's legs one at a time, strapping each down before securing her ankles above the wheel-chair's footrests. It would have gone faster if she didn't have to dodge her sister's flapping arms too. Hopefully thicker socks and those new high-topped sneakers would cushion Mae's ankles against the tight straps. They'd cost a small fortune, but what other choice did she have? Free legs were a no go, and bruises were better than broken bones. Mae could injure herself kicking a wall or a piece of furniture. Her leg could catch on something while Vivian wheeled her around if she weren't completely secured. If she ever managed to get loose and slide out of her chair, the fall would probably kill her.

Vivian checked the straps a second time.

"Okay, let's see what's going on with your temperature."

She crossed the room, sidestepping a growing pile of dirty sheets so she could reach the bureau. After a pause to rub her aching chin and jaw, she rooted around in the top drawer through the stack of sterile wrapped tubes, syringes, and other random medical gear in search of the thermometer.

Thankfully, she was able to get a reading before Mae jerked her ear away.

"101.2, babe. You've got a little fever." It was probably just a cold or maybe a light stomach bug. Nothing the antibiotics wouldn't clear up. No reason to panic.

Maybe she should call the doctor's office again just in case.

God, I need a drink.

The kitchen timer beeped, snapping her back to attention.

"Want to keep me company while I finish dinner?"

Vivian wheeled Mae down the hall and into the kitchen, scuffing the wall again as she maneuvered the chair around one particularly sharp corner. Her home's narrow halls and doorways hadn't been designed for wheelchair access. There had been no need back when she'd bought the place.

She parked Mae beside the kitchen table, ran over to the oven, and turned off the timer before opening the door to retrieve her casserole. It put an end to the maddening cadence of beeps, but plumes of smoke that billowed out of the oven soon filled the kitchen and set off smoke detector, which set off Mae into a fit of high-pitched shrieks.

"Damn it!"

She slammed the charred casserole on top of the stove and rubbed her stinging eyes. After turning on the range hood's exhaust fan, she flung open the kitchen windows and the back door while trying to ignore the alarm, Mae's howls, and her own frayed nerves. The smoke began to clear, but not fast enough. It took balancing on a rickety kitchen stool and yanking out the batteries to finally silence the alarm.

But by then the damage was done.

Mae screamed and flapped her arms while twisting in the chair in full panic mode.

Vivian leaped from the stool and rushed over to the wheelchair, approaching from behind to avoid being hit, her reflexes oddly sluggish. The violent outbursts had been escalating in spite of Mae's physical deterioration, so Vivian had learned to brace for impact. She shivered. God, what was wrong with her? "It's okay, Mae-belle, it's okay," she whispered softly, stroking her sister's hair. "No more noise, sweet pea. It's all gone now. It's all gone."

Smoothing her fingers along Mae's cheek, the burst of heat from her sister's flesh alarmed her even as it eased her own chill. She needed to get that fever down and made a mental note to give her a dose of acetaminophen with dinner. Hot and cold, cold and hot, maybe they were both coming down with the flu.

Ten minutes of cooing and petting finally calmed them both down, but left little time to salvage dinner. She'd just warmed some leftovers when the doorbell rang, threatening to send Mae into another fit of shrieks. Vivian ran out of the kitchen and through her living room, banging a knee on the coffee table in the process, and then hobbled downstairs to the foyer. Yanking the front door open, she silently cursed the strange woman standing on the other side. Clad in neon pink scrubs that almost matched the highlights streaked through her spiky hair, the nurse turned her gaze to Vivian, looking her up and down while smacking the gum in her mouth with all the grace of a cud-chewing cow.

Great. Another new one.

"Whoa, sounds like World War Three in there." The nurse peered around the door frame, eyes wide with suspicion and apprehension as Mae's wails echoed from above.

"My sister has an SPD," Vivian said through gritted teeth. "The door-bell set her off."

"Hang on, I thought she was in a wheelchair?" she said between loud chomps. "I didn't sign up for ADD, lady."

Where on Earth do they get their nursing degrees? Wherever it was, the schools did a lousy job teaching medical terminology, not to mention compassion and sensitivity.

Vivian took a deep breath and exhaled audibly through her nose. "She doesn't have ADD, she has a sensory processing disorder that makes her sensitive to noise. The service was supposed to put that in her file so you'd know not to ring the doorbell."

She shrugged. "Nobody told me."

Vivian fought the urge to slam the door in woman's face. Instead, she took another calming breath and stood aside so the nurse could enter. "Okay, fine, I'm telling you now. Please try to remember that for next time, okay? And she is wheelchair-bound. I'm Vivian, by the way, and you are?"

"I'm Candi, with an 'i.'"

Of course you are.

"Okay, Candi. I just warmed up Mae's dinner. I'll give you a quick rundown for how to feed her before I head out—"

"Feed her?"

"Yes, *feed* her," Vivian said, no longer concealing her irritation. "Look, why don't you just come upstairs and meet her before I go over specifics."

Candi shrugged and then shuffled up the stairs. Vivian led her through the living room and to the kitchen, bracing herself.

God, she hated this part.

She knew the very moment Candi got her first look at Mae. The all-too-familiar gasp pierced her last thin layer of calm and squeezed her chest in a vise grip of dread. Through the lens of Candi's wide-eyed shock and revulsion, Vivian was forced again to regard Mae and her condition with aching clarity.

Being prone for the greater part of her life had ravaged her sister's body. Palsy and scoliosis left the thin limbs and spine twisted at unnatural angles. Though they could still deliver a wicked punch, those arms would never fully extend, wrists locked inward and elbows jutting out, even at rest. Years spent in a series of custom wheelchairs molded to fit the tortuous contours of her body hadn't helped. Forcing her upright had reduced the risk of pneumonia and spared her a feeding tube for years. But it had also accelerated the damage to her spine.

Mae's life was a series of trade-offs and time, endless hours and days.

And as long as she lived, so was Vivian's.

Clearing her tight throat, Vivian said, "Why don't you put your stuff down in the living room and get settled. I'll...I've just got to go grab her medicine from the back and then we'll get you situated."

She didn't wait for Candi's reply. Arms clutched tightly around her chest, Vivian ran to the bathroom in spite of the pain still shooting through her knee. She shut and locked the door, heaving great gulps of air before succumbing to sobs that shook her body and brought her to the floor. Rocking back and forth with hands over her head, she struggled for calm, breathing in through her nose and holding it before releasing shaky breaths through her mouth, repeating the process until her eyes cleared and she was able to stand again, though her legs still trembled.

She checked her watch. After a quick splash of water over her face, she opened the medicine cabinet and pulled out the three bottles she'd need to bring along to the pharmacy since she no longer had time for calling in the refills.

Her gaze landed on the bottle of sleeping pills, her own name displayed in bold block letters.

It would be so easy.

She slammed the door to the cabinet so hard it shook the mirror suspended on the front, cracking the glass and almost shattering it. Then she turned and went back out to the living room to fetch Candi and brought her to the kitchen for a feeding demonstration.

"The trick is lots of small bites. You have to give her enough time to swallow before you go for the next bite, otherwise she chokes," Vivian explained as she spooned a bit of puréed beef stew into Mae's mouth.

Vivian wound up doing most of the feeding.

Thirty minutes later, she dug her car keys out from under a stack of bills on the kitchen counter, checking her watch and hoping she'd have time to grab a few groceries before Candi's short evening shift ended. With more than a little reluctance, she left Mae and her caregiver in the living room in front of the television, reminding Candi a second time to keep the volume low and to keep one eye on Mae's respiration.

I'll only be gone a few hours. She'll be okay.

She walked out the front door and headed for her car. The warm rays of afternoon sunlight reflecting off her windshield were promising. Maybe there would be enough time for dinner instead of just a quick beer with Sue once she finished her errands. It would only take a few extra dollars for a small sliver of normal life.

And if that wasn't enough, the permanent solution was always close at hand. She squeezed her purse until the fabric molded around hard plastic. The muted rattle of pills reassured her that oblivion was only a few swallows away.

"No!" She slammed her hands against the steering wheel, relishing the rush of pain from palms to wrists, the physical manifestation of bone-deep rage, self-loathing, and spit-in-the-face-of-fate stubbornness.

No, she couldn't, *wouldn't* really do such a thing. True, she would never be the perfect, willing martyr or selfless angel of mercy, but she wasn't a coward.

And she knew better than most that it could be much, much worse.

But someday soon, perhaps on a day like this, promises might not be enough.

CHAPTER THREE

She should have made some excuse when Sue called and invited her out. With the trauma of the night before, not to mention the drama with the newbie home health aide, Vivian had every right to curl up in a ball and hide. And Mae was sick. Maybe she shouldn't have left her.

Catching sight of Sue, she almost believed she'd made the right decision.

"Hey, girl!" Sue's voice rang out from across the crowded, noisy bar. "Glad you made it."

Vivian smiled as the short blonde waved her over. She couldn't help it. With a megawatt smile and matching lust for life, Susan Carlson was Southern charm served with a side of humor that could probably brighten the day of a death row inmate. She'd only meant to have a quick chat, hoping a friendly voice could ease her. After half an hour of pleading though, Sue had worn her down and talked her into meeting at their favorite barbecue joint. They had two-for-one drink specials going, and Vivian had raided what was left in her fridge before coming so she could eat cheap.

Sue would offer to pick up the tab, but Vivian still had her pride.

"I'm impressed." Sue stood and held her in a bear hug before shoving a beer into her hand.

"Why?" She accepted the long-neck bottle, taking care not to let her fingers brush Sue's hand, and parked her butt on the neighboring barstool. "Did you think I'd stand you up?"

"After dodging my calls for three weeks? Nah, the thought never crossed my mind. But that's not what I meant." She looked Vivian up and down, waggling her eyebrows and letting out a low whistle. "I didn't think you'd actually listen to me when I told you to dress like you weren't going home alone, but damn, just look at you!"

"I will be going home alone," Vivian replied dryly.

Sue didn't mention Vivian's ex out of courtesy, or perhaps pity. He'd bailed as soon as Mae came to live with Vivian, citing the old "it's not you, it's me" line of bullshit. Whatever. He didn't want to deal with the burden, so he'd run off. And what with one thing and another, she hadn't had much time or inclination to start dating again.

Though she tried to make like it was no big deal, Sue was right on the money. Vivian *had* bothered to make an effort with the tight red tank top, tighter jeans, and high-heeled slingbacks, adding a little shimmy to her step. She'd tamed her auburn curls and left them trailing loose over her bare shoulders and had even put on some lipstick, remembering her mother's advice about an old barn looking better with a fresh coat of paint.

She almost felt like a woman again.

Too bad her conscience and wallet wouldn't let her hang on to the feeling.

"I can only stay for a little while, though. I went over my hours last night and had to fork over some extra cash to pay the caregiver service."

"How come?"

"Because I got in a car wreck and almost took a dirt nap."

"Come again?" Sue's head jerked back and her smile disappeared.

"There was this big, multi-car pileup out on Edmondson Pike that I missed by the skin of my teeth. And this one guy who was in it, he...he didn't make it. I tried to help him, I really did, but there wasn't much I could do except hold his hand—"

"Oh my God, Viv! You saw someone die, like right in front of you? Honey, are you okay?" Sue reached out, but Vivian pulled her hand away before she could grasp it.

"See, that's the weird part," Vivian began, trying to work out how to explain what happened next. She ran a fingertip around the rim of her beer bottle and chewed on her bottom lip, but then decided to hell with it. After sucking in a deep breath, she blurted out the whole story from her disoriented journey from her car and the heartbreaking and intense encounter with the dying man to her run-in with the paramedics and Ezra—scorching handshake and all.

Sue stared at her for a long moment while Vivian fidgeted. God, it sounded even crazier out loud than it did in her head. All of a sudden, Sue's arm flew out and she latched onto Vivian's right hand. Vivian yelped in surprise, quickly turning to panic when Sue's face contorted into a mask of pain. Her eyes rolled back in her head and she began to shudder as if in the throes of electrocution.

The scream lodged in Vivian's throat died at the sound of Sue's laughter.

"Goddamn it, that's not funny!"

Vivian leaped to her feet, her body now quaking with anger.

"Oh man," Sue said between fits of chuckles, "you should've seen the look on your face."

To hell with this.

Vivian grabbed a couple of bills out of her purse and slammed them on the bar, then stormed out the door with a curse. So much for a nice, relaxing night out. She was halfway to her car when Sue caught up with her.

"Oh come on, lighten up. I was just messing with you. Tell me you aren't seriously going to bail."

Vivian spun on her heel and got right up in Sue's face. "Look, I've had a really shitty week. No, scratch that. I've had a really shitty six months. The last thing I need right now is my best friend making fun of me."

"Jeez, I'm sorry, Viv. Look, I know it's been hard for you since you've got Mae—"

"No, you don't." Vivian cut her off, stepping back and running a shaking hand through her hair. "You have no idea. No one does. From the time she was two until my folks died, our mother spent every waking moment taking care of her. Feeding, changing, bathing—we're talking twenty-four seven. And that's not even counting the doctors' visits, the sleepless nights, the midnight runs to the ER. It never ended. She was tied down all the time. And now it's all on me."

"No one else in the family can take a shift?" Sue asked. She was probably trying to be helpful, Vivian reminded herself while working really hard to stop her fist from slamming through the windshield of her car.

"None of them live close to us and besides, I didn't ask."

"Why not?"

Vivian stopped, keeping her gaze fixed on the night sky above her. "My mom asked for help, but never got it. Not from family, friends, or all those sanctimonious people from their church. Oh, they just loved to talk about what a saint Mom was for taking care of little angel Mae. They were full of talk, but none of them bothered to come and sit for her, or bring dinner, or do anything to actually help."

Vivian paused to take a breath. She hadn't meant to unload all of that on her friend. This wasn't Sue's burden.

"Well, the folks at the church probably meant well. They didn't really see it every day," Sue said after a moment, sounding as awkward as Vivian felt. "But family and friends had some idea. It's okay to be mad at them. Hell, it's okay to be mad at me. I'm just as bad, aren't I?"

Vivian blinked a few times and looked away. "Being mad at strangers is easier. You're probably right, though. No one really knew what to do for us, and I never asked for help so I've got no business having a meltdown in the middle of a parking lot and taking this out on you."

Digging her keys out of her bag and shaking her head, she turned toward her car and muttered, "It's not your problem and I'm sorry I brought it up, so let's just forget I said anything, okay? I'll just go. I'm not fit company tonight anyway, and—"

A gentle palm landed on Vivian's shoulder and stopped her rambling. Sue tugged on her shoulder, turned her around, and pulled her into a fierce embrace. She waited until Vivian stopped struggling and then spoke in a very quiet voice. "You don't have to leave, and you can call me, anytime and for anything. I want you to call me. For a break or a night out, for a laugh, cry, primal scream, whatever. Promise me you'll call, okay?"

Vivian nodded against her shoulder. She didn't trust herself to speak. When she eventually let go, Sue just turned around, giving her some privacy and shielding her from view of the other patrons in the parking lot while she blotted her eyes with a tissue and took a few deep breaths. She was good like that.

Her back was still to Vivian when she finally spoke. "You know, in all the years I've known you, this is the most I've ever heard you say about growing up with Mae."

"I never talk to anyone about it. Well, unless you count the occasional head-shrinker. I learned to deal a long time ago." At least, she thought she had.

"Well, I'm glad you're talking now."

Vivian sighed and said, "I'm glad too."

Sue turned and gave Vivian the once-over. "Here," she said, grabbing the tissue and blotting Vivian's face.

"Now that we've fixed those raccoon eyes, how about we go back in, visit the powder room, and grab some grub?" Sue flashed a wicked grin and grabbed her hand. "Because the only thing shocking about you right now is your face."

———

Bean's wasn't a big place and it wasn't too flashy, but they made a mean brisket, Austin-style, sans sauce unless you cared to add it. After a quick trip to the ladies' room for a clean-up, Vivian enjoyed the company, food, and entertainment. The long-standing myth that you only get country music in Nashville? Not true. Bean's played The Stones, Fleetwood Mac, The Beatles, and featured great live acts several nights a week that rivaled anything downtown had to offer. Of course, you couldn't throw a stone in this town without hitting talent. But at least Bean's, unlike the Bluebird Café, had no moratorium on conversation in deference to swarms of singer-songwriters bent on scoring a big break.

The band of the night consisted of a nice-looking young couple armed with mandolin and guitar. After another beer and a few verses of "Me and Bobby McGee," she relaxed and even chimed in with the other patrons to the tune of "Jolene" crooned with such passion by the petite songstress that she damned near brought the house down. After the first set wrapped up, they took a stroll outside along Church Street on the way back to Vivian's car while Vivian filled her in on the rest of the previous evening's weirdness.

"So what exactly do you think's up with this Ezra guy? I mean, aside from having hot hands, he sounds like your average Good Samaritan."

"It's not just that. I got jerked around pretty hard last night, enough so that I should be sore and sporting a nasty bruise across my chest from the seatbelt, but I'm not. Not a single scratch or an ache this morning. And then there's Mae. I went in and patted Mae on the head after he shook my hand and I swear to God she just got still and stayed that way. All night. She never does that. Aside from the fever, she seems as well as she's ever been today. How do you explain that?"

"Maybe you got yourself a guardian angel," Sue said, trying her best to keep a straight face.

Vivian started giggling too. "Oh hell, it would be my luck to get some big old redneck for my guardian freakin' angel!"

"Well, whatever it is, I wouldn't worry too much about it. Just be glad his mojo is working for you. If he comes back, have him sit a spell. And you call me soon, otherwise I'm going to break down your door and kidnap you."

"Will do. Goodnight, Sue."

"Night, Viv."

She'd almost made it to her car when a man stumbling through the parking lot caught her attention. His unsteady gait grated against the gravel, and he had to brace himself on the hood of a car as he stumbled. Mindful of the darkness and distance from the bar, she figured it would be best to just ignore him and go about her own business.

The jangle of his car keys changed her mind.

"Hey, mister," she called. "You sure you're okay to drive?"

He didn't answer. After a few moments of fumbling, he managed to disengage the automatic door locks of a nearby black Corvette before dropping his keys. The idiot even hit his head on the side mirror when he leaned down to retrieve them.

"Seriously?" Vivian muttered. After last night, there was no way in hell she'd sit back while this fool got behind the wheel drunk enough to kill himself and God knew how many others.

She walked over to him, heart racing with anxiety and more than a little anger, something the sudden chilly breeze at her back did nothing to soothe. When she got close enough to smell the sickly sweet stench of liquor seeping from his pores, she tapped him on the shoulder.

"Sir, I think we need to call you a cab."

He turned around and gave her a scowl. The dark circles under his sunken eyes and hollows of his cheekbones added to the evil aura that seemed to emanate from him like wisps of dull fog. Between the sallow complexion and his dull gaze, he could've passed for a corpse.

"I don't need a fucking cab," he said, spitting what looked to be a wad of slimy tobacco on the ground. It almost hit her strappy sandal. He fumbled with his keys and opened the car door, turning his back to her and muttering under his breath. "Stupid nosy bitch."

Red-hot rage pulsed through her at his dismissal, slicing through the cold air surrounding them.

"Give me the keys. Now."

"What the hell—"

She seized his forearm and he fell silent. His gaze locked on hers as waves of despair and grief assaulted her. Impressions flew through her mind. Days and nights measured in empty bottles, the soul-stealing ache of loneliness, a little girl with pigtails looking back through the window of a fleeing SUV. She was crying. She needed someone.

"She needs her daddy," Vivian whispered.

Tears streamed down the man's face. He placed his free hand on top of hers and held her in a death grip. The gray haze surrounding him swirled and coalesced around their joined hands before disappearing beneath her skin.

"Her mama left me," he said, choking on a sob. "I haven't seen her in over a year. My baby girl...she was all I had and now she's gone."

"You won't see her ever again if you get in that car tonight. Go back inside and call a cab. Get yourself to an AA meeting tomorrow. You do it for her, you hear me? You do it for her."

She released him and stumbled under the weight of this stranger's burdens that had somehow seeped into her. He nodded before turning and walking back toward the bar on legs that seemed much steadier.

Vivian's legs were anything but steady as she watched him go, wondering how the hell she'd managed to see into the man's soul with just a touch of her hand.

And what the hell she'd do if it happened again.

CHAPTER FOUR

Mae was already asleep when Vivian got home from Bean's, so she sent Candi home early and crashed on the couch. Dazed, exhausted, and still smelling like bar, she watched the clouds blot out the stars through her skylights before sleep blocked everything else. After she woke with a jolt, her ears sought out any sound from Mae. Nothing there, but a noise from outside gave her pause. When she sat up and looked through one of the windows, she thought she caught a shadow darting across the deck. Was Ezra lurking out there?

Stretching, Vivian pulled her jeans back on, slipped into her sling-backs with a groan as her feet protested, and tiptoed over to peek out her back door window. Nothing. Leaving the chain latch in place, she cracked the door open to get a better look.

"Anyone out there?"

She received no answer, but thought she caught another movement in her periphery vision.

Okay, only an idiot would go skulking around outside in the dead of night after hearing a strange noise. She knew better, knew she should just get back inside the house instead of acting like one of those dumb girls in a horror flick. Yet the same overwhelming urge that had compelled her to stay with the dying man in the car, to stick around when Ezra showed up, and to intervene with the drunk from the parking lot warred with her good sense, compelling her to investigate now. The pull of that force won and she stepped out the back door into the night.

But not before she grabbed the Louisville slugger she kept beside the door.

"Hello?" she called, wishing she'd had the good sense to turn on the outside lights. "Ezra, is that you?"

God, when did the temperature drop? Shivering, she took a few more steps away from the door. "Hello? Who's there?"

"Good evening to you, Ms. Bedford," came a smooth voice from directly behind. She whirled around to face an unfamiliar man. He was dressed in a perfectly pressed white suit, a pale blue tie peeking out beneath his stiff collar the only dash of color adorning the blank canvas of his clothing. The man stood in stark contrast to the night all around. A shock of blond hair fell out below the brim of his Stetson hat, which matched his trimmed mustache. It too appeared almost silver in the ambient glow cast by the streetlamps. Lean, neat, and exuding an air of confidence, he was a handsome fellow by any standards. He smiled and bowed low. "Allow me to introduce myself. My name is Darkmore, Lazarus Darkmore. I apologize for giving you such a fright."

Something about this new late-night visitor felt oddly familiar. *Well, of course, idiot. He's the second weirdo to show up in your backyard in forty-eight hours.* "It's kind of late for company, and I didn't see you come up. Are you a friend of Ezra's?"

"Oh, you could call me an associate, I suppose. We have similar interests," he answered, the air around him chilling slightly.

"O...kay. Well, what can I do for you?"

"I won't ask anything of you, Ms. Bedford. You've been asked far too much as it is. No, ma'am, I came here to do for you. And it's about time, isn't it?"

Faint warning bells sounded in Vivian's brain, yet his words piqued her interest. She got a little lost in his icy, blue-eyed gaze, and after a moment the alarm faded to background noise. "What do you mean?"

"You've been saddled with your sister a long time, haven't you? Such a shame. A lovely young woman like you should be enjoying life. You were forced to make so many sacrifices during your formative years, weren't you? And now, just when you thought you finally had your chance at freedom, here she is again. Your own little cross to bear, isn't she?" His voice was a cool whisper, stinging the cuts of her aching life before numbing the pain.

He kept speaking with the steady cadence of gentle rain. "What's the worst part, Ms. Bedford, playing the martyr, being the good sister when you don't really mean it? You've wanted her gone for years. They could have sent her to a home, or she could have just done everyone a favor and departed this world. What's here for her anyway? It would be so much easier, so much more peaceful. You could just take a little longer to get there the next time she chokes. Or maybe slip a little extra medicine into her sweet tea? That would do the trick. No one would suspect a thing, and it would be better than swallowing those pills yourself."

"What the hell are you talking about? Who do you think you are, coming around in the middle of the night and sticking your nose in my business? Are you from the state?"

Vivian's mesmerism with this stranger in white battled with her anger and fear. His words cut deep, pulling her long-buried resentments right out in the open. They were a dagger and a balm all in one. *How does he know?*

"Oh no, dear lady. I'm not from the state. I am from an entirely different authority," he said as he moved closer. She hadn't the power to stop him or to run, couldn't even lift the bat in her hand. He smelled of autumn leaves covered with frost and his eyes glowed with the light of a harvest moon. "I can make it all go away."

"What?" she whispered with the air remaining in her lungs. Each step he took seemed to cool her breath as much as her body. She fought through the haze and tried to move away from him.

Shaking her head, she muttered, "No, no thanks, mister. I can manage. I promised...." She took a step back.

He smiled again, reaching out to grasp her arm. "Oh, don't rush to a decision just yet. I've got all the time in the world," he cooed as he pulled her close. His face hovered less than an inch from hers. He bent and caressed her cheek with his as his lips found her ear. "A living soul with your abilities could prove quite useful, and I could make it well worth your while."

"I d-don't know what you mean."

"Ah, but I think you do," he said, grasping her hand. His touch sent a cold rush through Vivian that reached her very core as a gray haze of light emanated from her skin. The same despair she'd tasted from the drunk in the parking lot flooded her, but then vanished as the light coalesced and entered the man in white.

"I can set you free, Ms. Bedford. You need only ask. And it would be far better to work with me than against me, I assure you. Think it over, will you?" he whispered. Her knees buckled and she collapsed in a puddle of cold terror. When she finally recovered, the man in white was gone.

A scream from Mae's room brought her back to her senses. Vivian ran in, registered her sister was choking, and grabbed her.

"Mae!" Vivian cried as she flipped her sister over onto her stomach. Mae's stiff body proved difficult to move. Vivian had broken her sister's arm once doing the same thing, and the memory pierced her now. She pounded on Mae's back, fighting her flailing limbs as she thrashed. Mae gasped for air and Vivian flew into a panic, grabbing the portable suction machine and turning it on. She turned her sister back over, supporting her head so she could maneuver the long tip into Mae's mouth.

"Goddamn it, I'm trying to help you!" Vivian screamed, still trying to get at the mass in her sister's throat before she choked on it. Mae bit her index finger and thumb hard enough to draw blood. Vivian rammed the probe in and accomplished her task, though Mae now screamed louder and coughed up blood. Releasing her, Vivian ran to the hall bathroom to clean her own wounds.

"Jesus Christ," she muttered, anger and resentment fueling the surging tide of panic. *I'm still so cold. Jesus, what the hell happened out there?* After wrapping her hand in a towel, she ran back to Mae's room, trying to block out screams and moans that never seemed to end.

The stench hit as soon as she entered, and Vivian didn't make it back to the bathroom before vomiting. Mae had soiled herself. Worse, her diaper failed to keep the contents in. She ignored her own mess and settled for wiping her mouth and taking a few deep breaths in order to recover. Grabbing more towels and fighting the urge to retch, Vivian froze, trying to regain her composure so she could decide where to begin. Shit covered the bed, floor, and her sister's hands. She kept screaming as Vivian began to clean her. Strength born from God only knew where brought her sister's thin arms crashing onto Vivian's face and body. Mae had given her bruises before, and white-hot anger filled Vivian at the memory.

She roughened her scrubbing.

"Be still, goddamn it! I have to get this shit off you before I can get to the rest of the fucking mess you made!" Mae wailed, crying out as Vivian slammed her to her side and yelled in her face. "And stop the damned crying! I can't take it anymore!"

Fury overtaking her, Vivian ran back to the hall bathroom and tossed the portable bath seat into the tub, cracking the fiberglass in the process.

"Fuck! Fuck! Fuck!" she wailed as she started the water then returned to her still flailing, screaming sister. She ripped off Mae's clothes and the soiled diaper, carried her to the bathroom, and dumped her into the seat, which agitated Mae even more. Vivian hosed her down with the handheld shower head then tossed a towel over her. Moving back to the bedroom, she yanked up the soiled linens with arms shaking with rage and disgust. Tossing them out onto the deck, she paused to ward off her nausea and returned to a shivering Mae.

Mae knocked Vivian in the forehead as she brought the towel to her sister's face, causing her to stumble backward and hit the edge of the vanity.

"Damn it, Mae!" she sobbed. The pain of the blow flooded her skull, which already throbbed with the dull ache of exhaustion and tears.

She stood, dizzy, and looked in the mirror as angry red marks welled on her cheek. Her hair was a tousled mess, her makeup running. A fresh wave of rage swelled in Vivian, and cold fury froze the blood in her veins even as hot blood seeped from the back of her head. Staggering, she limped back to Mae's room. Vivian managed to wipe down the mattress pad and put on a clean sheet before she had to sit down, tossing aside some of the knick-knacks she'd inherited along with the helpless creature that waited in the bathroom. She enfolded herself in a nearby blanket and wondered what was making her so damned cold.

A movement from the corner jolted her back to reality, but she saw nothing out of the ordinary when she turned her head. *Bad idea, Viv. Head-*

banging's out for now. Sheer force of will, and maybe a bit of fear, got her on her feet and helped her finish making the bed.

Moving back to the bathroom, Vivian turned her attention back to her sister and the urine dripping down her legs and into the tub. *Jesus Christ, can this get any worse?* Glancing back at the mirror, she startled at the flash of movement she swore she caught behind her. *What the hell?* When she peered out into the hallway and didn't see anything, she chalked it up to her imagination and turned her attention back to her sister. She hosed Mae off again, dried her, and put her into a fresh diaper and nightgown.

She didn't look into her sister's eyes as she carried her back to her room and placed her back in her bed, couldn't bear it after the way she'd treated her sister. *Please, oh please don't let her see what I've done. Don't let those eyes see the horror of her life.*

"Or the horror of yours, Ms. Bedford?"

Vivian whirled around and looked for the voice. She saw no one and nothing, and all she felt was a painful jab through her skull. And she still shivered with cold. What happened to the summer heat that had had her sweating when she'd walked outside? Mae screamed again and Vivian collapsed, clutching her head in her hands and rocking back and forth until the sickness in her stomach made her stop.

It didn't stop the ghosts of screams from long ago.

She rose, filled with hatred. Vivian grabbed one of her mother's angel figurines and swung it in Mae's direction. By some miracle the ceramic icon missed and shattered on the wooden bed rail.

Jesus, oh Jesus, what have I done?

Vivian staggered back as shame and horror flooded her, and then she turned to run.

As she fled, she heard laughter from the corner of her sister's room.

Vivian stumbled to the back door and ran into the darkness of night. She fell to the ground, tearing fistfuls of grass and beating on the hard earth until she was sure she'd broken both of her arms. The pain in her head, arms, and chest gripped her with such intensity she'd surely burst from the pressure. She screamed, and the high-pitched wail shattered the night but did nothing to relieve the waves of despair coursing through her shivering form.

Rolling over onto her back, she clutched her arms over her chest and tried to warm herself. When and how had the heat of summer vanished? It shouldn't be this cold. Something was very, very wrong. Trying to catch her breath, she became aware of two disturbing facts. The silence distressed her nearly as much as the chill. She heard no wind, no jar flies, or any other familiar night sounds. She only heard her own strangled gasps. Second, it was way too dark. Daring to lift her head, she saw neither the glow of her house lights nor illumination from neighborhood street lamps. Power outage?

She lifted herself to her knees. Crawling and fighting the terror that gnawed at her belly, she moved along the unfamiliar terrain. The grass crunched beneath her hands and knees, dry and frosty, not like the lush grass she had mowed only a few days back. The frigid air stung her nose and her lungs. Her head ached, and touching the wound unleashed a new wave of panic and guilt.

"Mae!" she called. "Oh God, you can't answer!"

She managed to rise and stumble through the blackness around her. The first whispers from her side made her jump. Desperate, urgent murmurs called out through the endless dark around her.

Then she ran.

The whispers followed, urging her, though she couldn't make out their meaning. She only stopped when her injured body slammed into something cold and hard. The something had arms. The something had an icy voice and sharp teeth.

The something made her scream.

"Hmm, that was so, so good," the cold voice crooned. "So very good."

Her voice stilled, as did her body, paralyzed in the grip of the voice's bearer. Cold seeped through her skin and she could barely breathe. Its hands clutched her shoulders. Surely this was Mister Death, and he'd come for her now. *Oh dear God, no! I have to get back to Mae...she was choking...she....*

The hands released her and the voice hissed. Vivian spun on her heels and ran away from the terrible unseen thing, its mocking laughter trailing behind her. The whispers bombarded her from all directions, but all she heard inside her head were Mae's moans and screams. Crippling terror mixed with dread. If she could run forever, she would. In the long days and nights of waiting, she'd considered getting in her car and leaving. She could just drive until the road ended and leave her heavy burdens behind. The laughing voice nipped at her back. It was gaining. It would catch her. Her legs cramped, her breath came in gasps, and she knew she'd soon collapse.

"Run, run, run, as fast as you can, you can't get away from the raggedy man," it mocked, using the old childhood rhyme.

She and her cousins used him to taunt and terrify one another during their shared youth. The raggedy man lurked in the woods, under beds, in dark corners. He lurked in the darkest depths of hearts and fed on the ugliness hidden there. He would feast on the darkness in Vivian Bedford's heart.

Unbidden images invaded her mind, scenes of her worst fears and atrocities she kept locked away deep within her subconscious. Choking the life out of her broken sister, slamming her against a wall, beating her with bare fists that pounded out a lifetime of rage and resentment. No escape. She fell to the ground. Waiting. Still. Surrendering. God, what she almost did to Mae, what she could have done. Only the sound of her ragged breathing filled the darkness surrounding her, that and the whispers, thousands of them, pleading.

They wanted out too, and they were begging her to take them away from this place.

The whispers stopped, and she became aware of heat nearby. She moved on instinct toward the heat. The warmth beckoned her and melted the shards of fear.

As she was lifted, she uttered, "Ezra?"

A lovely, deep voice answered. "No, but he sent me."

CHAPTER FIVE

Vivian woke with a jolt and bolted upright in her bed, which in and of itself was surprising in light of her last memory. Bolting upright wasn't such a good idea, as it turned out. She fought a wave of dizziness and a deep ache extending from the top of her head all the way down her neck and beyond. Steadying herself against the headboard, she reached up and felt the back of her head. An impressive knot, but no more blood, greeted her questing fingers. Touching her swollen cheek made her wince and set her wounded finger throbbing.

Eyes closed, she tried hard to remember the previous night. *Okay, I had a bad time with Mae and got knocked around. I knocked Mae around too. Oh dear God, what is wrong with me?* She'd hit her head a little too hard and hallucinated, or more likely dreamed, since what she remembered happening next couldn't possibly be real. Maybe she should go get an X-ray or CT scan. *Wait, how did I end up in my bed? What on Earth happened last night?*

Oh my God, where's Mae?

She pushed herself up and swung her legs over the bed's side. God, she hadn't even taken off her shoes before crawling into bed. She had the presence of mind to pause and catch her bearings before putting both feet on the ground, bracing herself before giving them her full weight.

As she stumbled out of her room and down the hall, her stereo poured out the sultry sounds of Sheryl Crow. Enticing aromas of sausage, eggs, and, God bless whoever was in there, *coffee* wafted from the kitchen. The home health aide must have let herself in and started fixing Mae's breakfast. The regulars often did on those rare mornings when Vivian indulged in a little extra sleep. While she certainly didn't expect or demand that Mae's caregivers feed her too, she always appreciated the folks who made coffee. She stood still for a moment and savored the aromas and the comforting sense of normalcy they conjured as she tried to reconcile what she thought she remembered from the night before with what must have actually happened.

"Need any help in there?" a male voice called from the kitchen.

She jumped and shrieked at the unexpected sound, her body slamming against the wall as she stumbled back.

"Sorry, didn't mean to scare you. You okay?"

Well, isn't that the question? Though it was vaguely familiar, she didn't immediately recognize the voice but assumed it belonged to a male nurse. The service often rotated staff members when someone called in sick. He was probably another newbie.

At least they hadn't sent Candi back.

"Sure you don't need any help?" His voice sounded friendly enough, even laced with a touch of concern.

Chiding herself for being paranoid, she replied, "Um, no thanks. I think I'll manage. Are you new? I was expecting Mary."

The voice answered with a hint of a chuckle. "I'm here at your service."

"Oh, okay," she answered, trying to stifle a yawn. As her mind caught up, she remembered more pressing matters. Swallowing hard, she asked, "Hey, how's Mae?"

"Mae's fine. Don't worry about her. She's still sleeping. Why don't you get cleaned up and come and grab a cup of coffee and breakfast?"

Shrugging, albeit painfully, she walked back to her bathroom and braved the mirror. Jesus, the black eye and bruises served as a vivid reminder of her unconscionable behavior. Vivian stripped and headed for the shower, letting the jets of warm water soothe her aching muscles. Too bad it couldn't soothe her aching soul or wash away her shame. A mild scrub of her scalp was all she could tolerate, but it got most of the grime out.

She toweled and finger-combed her hair before donning a T-shirt and jeans, brushing her teeth, and doing what she could to hide her mess of a face with makeup. Popping a couple of painkillers, she shuffled out of her room and to the kitchen.

A steaming cup of coffee sat on her kitchen table, flanked by a little cup of cream and a bowl of sugar. Her personal chef had parked a plate full of eggs, sausage, and pancakes on the table too, though he himself still remained out of sight. Vivian sat down and picked at her food, spending more time moving the contents of the plate around than actually eating. Still, she tried to make an effort, even though she knew she wasn't worthy of the gesture. It was just...no one ever cooked for her.

"Hey, thanks for breakfast. You didn't have to go to all that trouble, but I appreciate it," she called out, then muttered under her breath, "especially after last night."

"You're welcome," the disembodied voice replied. "What happened last night?"

She was surprised he caught that last part, and couldn't quite figure out where he'd gone. Maybe he was checking on Mae. She hoped so, since she wasn't ready to face her sister and the consequences of her actions. And she didn't quite trust herself around Mae.

Not yet. God, maybe not ever again.

No, damn it, *she* was the primary caregiver. She'd have to face up to what happened some time, starting with an explanation for the mess in Mae's room. God, she didn't want to talk about it, didn't want to think about it. But lying was the coward's way out.

Clearing her throat, Vivian spoke softly, "I, um...well, I had a rough time with my sister last night. She was choking and made a mess, so I had to clean her up and, things got...bad for us both. After that, well...." She wasn't quite sure how to continue, recalling her disturbing encounter with the man in white and the terrifying events in the cold dark that followed.

"What do you remember after that?"

"Um, I was just thinking about that. I think I must have passed out or had a bad dream because what I think happened couldn't possibly be real. I think I'll run by the ER later and get my head checked, if you'll be here a while to watch Mae."

"Well, you did pass out after I picked you up," he said.

"What? When? This morning? And where was I?" The first warning bells began to clang in her aching head, making the fine hairs on the nape of her neck stand on end.

"Not here," he answered.

The bad vibe that had visited her several times over the past few days put in another appearance. "Where was I? And speaking of, where are you right now? Why don't you come in here and sit down so we can have a real conversation?"

"I'd like to. A lot. But I'm not so sure that's such a good idea right now," said the voice. Where was he? She leaned forward and peered through the kitchen, checking the small space that doubled as pantry and laundry room. She didn't see him there either.

Wavering between irritation and a touch of fear, she asked, "Why not? It's pretty rude to yell at me from another room, you know. How about you come on out so we can talk face to face like normal people? I know I probably look like hell, but I did put on some clothes and makeup. And I don't bite."

Vivian leaned back as if to stretch and looked into the living room. The sofa and loveseat she'd inherited from her parents sat unoccupied. Some of the pictures on the mantle over her fireplace had been moved. Straightened piles of books and magazines she normally flung around sat neatly on the nearest end table. Coasters rested on her coffee table.

He'd cleaned?

"It's not that," he said with hesitation. "I'm afraid of what you might think of me. I just don't want to make you pass out again and fall out of your chair."

"Why would I pass out? Are you some knife-wielding serial killer? Or are you Quasimodo-ugly or something?" Irritation and a case of the jitters erased her Southern manners. And well-intentioned or not, he shouldn't have messed with her stuff.

He chuckled, though he sounded a little nervous. "No, not at all. But, if you don't mind, why don't you finish eating and go sit on the sofa? I promise I'll come out then and explain things. At least, I'll do my best with the things I can explain. You'll have to wait for Ezra to fill you in on the rest. I'm still kind of new."

"Ezra? How do you know Ezra?" Panic began to prickle up her spine.

"He sent me to you last night. I came as soon as I got word you needed help."

"It was you who found me outside," she whispered, the comforting timbre of his voice lifting the fog from her memory. "I remember you telling me he sent you. But how—how did he know I was in trouble?"

"He knows a lot."

Way too nervous to finish eating, she picked up her cup of coffee, along with a steak knife, and walked to the couch. She sat on the edge and waited for a few minutes, mentally gauging how fast she could get to the door and get out of the house. But what would she do about Mae?

"Hey, I'm on the couch now," she called out. With a touch of sarcasm she added, "Do you want me to close my eyes and count to ten?" *Just keep acting casual. Damn, I should have grabbed the phone!*

"That won't be necessary," said the voice from directly behind her. "Just try not to scream."

When she turned around, she let out a siren-sized wail and jumped clean off the sofa, dropping the knife in the process.

Vivian stared at the smiling face of a man who could not possibly be among the living. It was the face of the man from the car accident. A man she'd watched die. Same clothes, same mop of dark hair, same green-eyed gaze, this was no mistaken identity. Had he survived after all?

No, the paramedics had tried to reassure her, telling her he had a fighting chance, but she knew better. Ezra had even confirmed it. He'd died. He couldn't have survived that crash, and even if he had, he certainly wouldn't be walking now.

The man was dead.

The dead man continued to smile as she took three steps back, banging into the coffee table and falling down with a curse. She knocked one of the neat stacks of books off the table in the process and almost apologized before resuming the mother of all panic attacks. He crouched down and moved to her side, offering a hand to help her up as she balked, finally finding her voice.

"Oh my God, what in the hell *are* you? You, y-you...you're supposed to be dead."

"See, that's why I wanted you to sit down. I knew it would be a big shock, and I think you've had one too many tumbles in the past twenty-four hours," he said as he grabbed her arm. She pulled away and scooted the opposite direction.

"Jesus, oh Jesus what in the hell is happening?" she chanted as she continued to move away from the creature standing before her.

"Vivian, you need to calm down. I'm not going to hurt you. I promise." He held his palms up. "Put your head between your knees and take a few deep breaths. In through your nose, hold it for four seconds, and back out through your nose—"

"What? Breathing advice from a dead guy, a ghost, or an angel or...or... um, what the hell are you anyway?" She brought one hand to her mouth and gasped. "Oh...my...*God*! You're not a vampire are you?"

He rolled his eyes and leaned back to sit, heaving a deep sigh. When he spoke again, he slowly enunciated each word as though talking to a particularly petulant child. "What I am is someone who's trying to help you. Are you always this bull-headed?"

"Yes, Casper, I am! What do you expect, coming in here with your dead self and scaring the shit out of me?" Vivian shouted. Then she started muttering to herself. "I must be going crazy. I'm seriously going batshit fucking crazy, I'm hallucinating, I'm...oh God!"

She kept staring at him as the rational part of her addled brain pierced through panic. He seemed so...well, real. His body was solid, not transparent or immaterial. And he didn't feel cold either, like she'd expect from something dead. On the contrary, the flesh, sinew, and bones of his fingers, fingers that had gripped her, felt real enough. They exuded warmth and vitality. He wore ordinary-looking jeans and a blue shirt. She recognized the shirt, in fact, only this time it wasn't covered with blood.

She started to hyperventilate again.

"Are you going to breathe or do you just want to pass out and make me carry you back to your bed again?"

"I'm breathing, okay? I'm breathing! Why don't you explain yourself while I'm doing that?"

"Sure thing. Do you want to sit on the sofa?" he asked, offering her a hand.

"I can get up by myself," she said a little too sharply, pushing off the floor with her sore arms and wincing as she stood.

"You know what your problem is? You just don't know how to accept help," he said, shaking his head and having the nerve to look amused.

"Thanks, Freud," she quipped. "Been talking to my shrink? He says the same thing," she grumbled as she got up and dusted off her rear end. "Thinks he knows all about me and my life. You've been here all of a few hours and you're going to tell me my business?"

"Yeah, and you don't know how to ask for help either. Never have." His statement was cold fact, and boy did it ever piss her off.

"Okay, I don't care if you are a ghost, demon, or more likely than not just a hallucination, mister...what's your name anyway? Do you even have a name?" She rubbed her arms as she sat on the sofa, curling her legs underneath her body and wrapping her arms around her chest.

As fear dissipated, she drank in the form standing before her. He stood pretty tall, lean but not skinny. He had a broad chest and a pair of strong arms. Dark hair covered his head with waves that framed an alluring face. A few locks lay tousled above a pair of sharp green eyes. A small smile tugged at the corners of his mouth while he appeared to consider her questions. She stared at his mouth a little too long before dropping her gaze in mortification.

"My name is Ezekiel, but you can call me Zeke. And I'm not any of those things really. At least, I don't think I am," he said, seeming to give the matter some serious thought. "Like I said, I'm still sort of new at this."

"New at what, exactly?" she asked.

"Being a guardian spirit. I'm in charge of protecting the living, helping the dead move on, that sort of thing. Ezra's been teaching me," he replied with some hesitation. She didn't know if he was being evasive, or if he just wasn't so sure of the answer himself.

"Right. Listen, zombie boy, I don't know who or what you are, or exactly how you pulled off that little trick of appearing out of thin air, but

I'm not buying what you're selling. So how about you just get on out of my house before I call the cops."

"You said it yourself, I'm dead. And I've come back." He ran a hand through his hair and heaved a sigh. Then with a wicked grin and a gleam in his gaze, he lifted his hand and held it out between them. "I hate to have to do this, but it's the only way I'm going to convince you I am what I say I am."

His hand disappeared in a whirl of dust. From the wrist down, there was...nothing. No blood, no bone, just the end of an arm. All of a sudden, a burst of white light emerged from the stump and a swirl of particles rose and coalesced into a hand.

———

When consciousness returned, Vivian was flat on her back and fighting stars dancing behind her closed eyelids.

She opened her eyes slowly and sat up even slower, surprised to find Zeke, both hands intact, sitting across from her. He didn't move or try to touch her, but his gaze held both concern and that touch of mischief that made her want to slap him.

Still, his little ploy worked. She believed him now.

"So Ezra's dead too?" Vivian shook her head, realizing for about the third time that head-shaking was so not a good idea. "But you're both solid. Aren't spirits supposed to, you know, leave the body when people die, or is that just a myth?"

"Guardian spirits, soul brokers, have the power to assume corporeal form, at least for a time. It's necessary for our work, or so Ezra tells me."

"So you're his apprentice or something? If a bell rings do you get your angel wings?"

"Excuse me?" he asked while he seated himself on the loveseat across from her.

"Oh, come on! Haven't you ever seen *It's a Wonderful Life*? They show it every Christmas, for Pete's sake. You know, every time a bell rings, an angel gets his wings?" He hadn't been dead *that* long.

"Ezra didn't mention anything about wings." Zeke chuckled, and a wry smile decorated his face. Vivian had to fight not to return his smile with one of her own. "He just told me to look out for you. He thought the reaper might be calling on you soon."

"The reaper? You mean Darkmore? The guy in white?"

"Yeah, the reaper has a lot of names. I'm glad I was able to get you out of his realm," Zeke said in a very serious tone.

"His realm?"

"That cold place you went, where he took you, it's his realm. Well, he shares it with a lot of others, most of them not willing—"

She leaped out of her seat and slashed her hands through the air, cutting him off. "Whoa, whoa, whoa, back up there, mister. He took me to another *realm*? How the hell did he pull that off? I don't remember getting in a car—I just stumbled around my backyard for a while and then keeled over, right?"

"Maybe you should sit back down, Vivian. You look a little pale."

"Well *there's* a big surprise," she said, the volume of her voice rising with the pounding of her racing heart. "A dead man shows up in my kitchen and tells me I took a little trip to the Twilight Zone with some grim reaper in a cowboy hat and I have the audacity to blanch at the notion. Guardian spirits, soul brokers, reapers? Do you have any idea how crazy that sounds?"

"Yes, I do, and I wish we had more time to ease you into all of this. But Darkmore came after you sooner than we expected. You're just going to have to trust me on this," he said, leaning forward and gazing up at her with those mesmerizing green eyes that had lost none of the intensity she remembered from the night of his death.

The weight of his gaze more than anything else, including the quaking in her legs, compelled her to sit back down.

"Anyway, I'm supposed to keep an eye on you when Ezra's away, at least until we can figure out what the reaper wants with you and your sister."

She jolted back off the couch at that little revelation. "Wait a minute, he wants me *and* Mae? What is he and why would he want us? I mean, what did we ever do to him?"

"You didn't do anything at all, at least not intentionally. Darkmore and his kind, they're soul brokers like us—I mean, like me and like Ezra—only they work on the flip side. They hurt the living and rob the dead of peace. You caught a glimpse of where they take the souls they claim last night."

"Wait, what do you mean by *intentionally*?" In the confusing jumble of improbable statements he'd thrown at her, that particular word caught her attention and gave her a small shiver.

He blew out a breath and ran a hand through his thick head of dark hair. "I'm not sure how much I'm supposed to tell you," he muttered, seemingly lost in thought. After a moment, he snapped back to attention, capturing her with that intense gaze. "But I'm sure you can guess a few things."

"Such as?"

"Have you noticed anything, um, out of the ordinary lately?"

"Seriously? Where should I start?"

He snorted. "I meant besides me, Ezra, and Darkmore? Anything strange with yourself?"

"You mean the thing with my hand," she whispered.

"Seems you did more than save that man in the parking lot from a DUI last night."

Vivian stared at him while she struggled to wrap her mind around the impossible. "All I did was touch him, and it was like I could feel what he was feeling, see the thing that made him so miserable he could only forget it by drinking himself to death—"

Oh my God.

Zeke covered her trembling hand with his. "It was chilly, right?"

Unable to locate her voice, she nodded.

"The reaper was there, waiting to claim his soul. You got in the way."

"You mean he was going to die? But I didn't do it on purpose—wait, that didn't come out right. I mean, I'm glad he didn't die, but I had no idea he was supposed to die and I sure as hell had no idea that touching him would open up some sort of psychic hotline to salvation."

Zeke squeezed her hand and cupped her face with his other palm. "You did a good thing, believe me, and I want you to have absolute faith that the good you do will always work in your favor. I also want you to have absolute faith that I'm here to help and protect you."

She was taken aback by the fervor in his voice that came with the promise of help and protection. It was stupid, given her experience, but she really wanted to trust that promise. The intimacy of the moment made her more uncomfortable than the vow, but not because of him. She needed both, and need was dangerous.

Releasing his hand, she leaned back and asked, "Will that guy be okay?"

He scooted away, giving her some much-needed space. "That's up to him. Free will supersedes any other influence, be it from the living or from the spirit world. He has the chance to change his fate now, thanks to you."

"Yeah, but now I've got a reaper after me. Sounds more like a case of no good deed goes unpunished. I can understand why he'd be pissed off at me, but what does this have to do with my sister?"

"I don't know, but I promise you I'll do everything in my power to find out so we can stop him, and so will Ezra. He'll be back tonight, hopefully with some more answers."

"Wow, this all seems pretty out there. Hey, why do you have Biblical names? Ezra, Ezekiel, Lazarus, is it a job requirement for you to become a guardian, or whatever you are?" Her words almost kept pace with the thoughts tumbling out of her mouth.

"Nah." He laughed. "It's a coincidence, as far as I can tell. But you never know. I'll be sure and ask Job and Jeremiah when I get back to the office." He winked at her then.

"Just my luck to get a ghost of the smart-assed variety," she said with a snort and eye roll combo followed by a reluctant little grin.

"Luck has nothing to do with it," he said, dropping the smirk and growing serious. "I volunteered."

"You did?"

"Don't sound so surprised. You did me a great service the night I died."

"All I did was hold your hand," she muttered, looking down at her own pitiful hands, ugly hands that had done so much damage. She struggled against the waves of grief, horror, and helplessness as images of that night flooded her mind. She couldn't bear to face them any more than she could bear to face the fresh shame of last night's violence with Mae.

"Hey," he said. He moved a little closer, reaching out to hold her hand in his warm palm. "It's okay. It's over now."

"I'm sorry," she said. She looked back up into those green eyes.

"Don't be. I only wanted to say thank you." He gave her hand a light squeeze before switching gears and saying, "So, tell me a little about yourself."

"What?"

"I need to know about your life, your situation with your sister, stuff like that."

Oh God, she really didn't want to discuss her 'situation' right now.

Her reluctance must have shown in her gaze, or possibly her silence. He ran his thumb over her bruised knuckles, gently soothing. "I'm not prying. I just need to know so I can help."

"Oh, okay," she said, clearing her throat and digging for her strength. "Where do I start?"

"Why don't you tell me about Mae. How come you've got her? What about your folks? Or a home, you know?" Something about his tone gave her pause, but she figured she might as well be honest.

"Um, well, let's see," she began, fidgeting. "My parents died about six months ago."

"I'm sorry." When she looked up, he asked, "How did it happen?"

"They were on vacation in the Smoky Mountains, in one of those rented cabins. It was the first time they'd gone off on their own in years, since Mae's been, well...she's been pretty much the way she is now as long as I can remember. Her whole life, you know?"

Zeke nodded and bid her to continue.

"Our mother didn't like to leave her. It took Dad ages, but he finally just booked a little four-day getaway and made her go. Anyway, the place caught fire on the second night. Probably some electrical problem or some other freak one-in-a-million thing...." She paused, swallowing the hard lump lodged in her throat. She had an easier time explaining things than she did at first, but the loss was still fresh, as were her musings about the whys and the hows.

After a moment, he asked, "So you inherited Mae?"

"Yeah. I always promised I'd take care of her."

"On your own?" His eyes widened in apparent disbelief. He opened his mouth, and then closed it tight. He seemed to be lost in thought, and a flash of some emotion she couldn't identify crossed his fine features.

"Um, yeah. I'm her only sibling, her only family, so I'm all she's got. And...."

"And what?"

Oh, hell, might as well get the whole thing out. "I had someone." Boyfriend? Almost-fiancé? Coward? "He left when Mae came."

He didn't respond right away, but he looked as if someone had just slapped him across the face. Strange, but better than the look of pity. She changed the subject. "About last night...."

"Yes?"

The parts of her face that weren't black and blue must have been scarlet red by then, but she pressed on. "So after you found me and brought me back in, well...did anything else happen?"

They both jumped up as they heard a key enter the front door. "Uh oh," Vivian whispered. "That must be Mae's help for the day."

Zeke took her by the shoulders and bent to kiss her forehead. His kiss warmed her like Ezra's touch had a few nights back, only...more. The sensation reminded her of summer rain, and he carried the musky aroma of moss and oak, of good clean linen in her cedar chest. Linen that had been line-dried out in the sunshine.

"You're going to be a tough case, but I'm looking forward to it. Take care of yourself, Vivian. I'll see you soon."

"But how—"

She turned to glance over her shoulder at the uniformed nurse entering. When she turned back, Zeke was gone.

CHAPTER SIX

"Look, if you won't go to the hospital, will you at least call this number?" Mary asked, handing Vivian a card she'd pulled out of her binder.

"YMCA Crisis and Information Line?" Apparently, Vivian's feeble attempts at explaining the condition of her face hadn't convinced the concerned nurse.

"It's completely confidential. They have safe houses in Nashville and the surrounding counties. The scumbag who roughed you up won't be able to find you, I promise." She squared her shoulders and placed her hands on her hips, apparently unwilling to drop the subject. Beneath her five-foot-three frame, blonde curls, and pink scrubs, Nurse Mary was a pit bull in poodle's clothing.

"I appreciate your concern, but you've got it all wrong. I don't even have a boyfriend—haven't had one in a long time, and no man has or ever will raise a hand on me. It's like I told you, I had to clean up Mae last night and I forgot to duck. You've been here a while. You know she's stronger than she looks."

Mary didn't look convinced. "You could take Mae too, if that's what's worrying you. They wouldn't turn you away on account of your sister."

Shit. Any other day she'd be grateful that one of Mae's caregivers seemed determined to go the extra mile. Still, Mary might push the issue and report Vivian to the state if she thought there was a risk for violence in her home. Oh, she was right about the danger, but Vivian suspected no earthly hideout could keep them safe from the reaper. Telling the truth about him and her two guardians was absolutely out of the question, since it would most likely earn her a one-way ticket to the loony bin.

Right. Time to lie. "Look, I didn't want to say anything because it's kind of embarrassing, but the truth is that I was a little woozy last night because I took a sleeping pill." Okay, maybe not quite a lie, considering that particular scenario had happened before, but that worked in her favor. Adding in a dash of truth would make the story more convincing. "I've just been so stressed out these days, and I haven't been resting well. My doctor gave me something to take and last night was the first time I tried it. I guess it worked a little too well, since I woke up on the bathroom floor with a black eye and bruises. I must have I hit my head on the way down. Won't be taking those again."

Mary's expression changed from one of skepticism to pure compassion, "Oh honey, of course you're stressed out right now. It's called caregiver fatigue. I've seen it a lot in my line of work."

Mary set her binder down on the kitchen table and took both of Vivian's hands in hers before Vivian could pull away. She relaxed when the nurse didn't instantly recoil in pain and terror. And thankfully she wasn't assaulted with any unwanted impressions of private suffering.

"Go see your doctor just to make sure you don't have a concussion, then take the afternoon and go do something for you, okay? You need to take some breaks or you'll burn out, and I'm here to help."

"Wow, someone should nominate you for sainthood."

Mary chuckled. "I think you have to be dead first."

And speaking of dead.... "Hey, um, can I ask you something?"

"Sure."

"Do you believe in ghosts?"

Mary shrugged. "Don't know. I've never seen one. Why do you ask?"

"Oh, you know, just curious. I've got a little too much time on my hands and not enough *Law and Order* re-runs. Thought it might be fun to learn about something new and, um, a little off the wall. Ghosts, psychics, that sort of thing."

"You could always start with Google. It would be better than calling Miss Cleo, right? Not to mention cheaper. Or you could check out that ghost hunter show they have on the SyFy Channel, *after* you get back from the doctor."

"Yes, ma'am."

Donning a thick pair of sunglasses and a hat to hide her injuries, she grabbed her purse, laptop, and keys and drove along Nolensville Road, the suburban McMansion and chic condo communities that lined the outskirts of Davidson County abruptly shifting to the crowded, multinational Woodbine corridor. She cut past the Fairgrounds, taking Wedgewood to Belmont Boulevard, figuring she could grab lunch and do a bit of cyber-detective work before visiting the clinic.

She took a moment to savor the rich aromas filling Bongo Java, her favorite local coffee house and home of the world-famous NunBun. The celebrated confection had given Nashville a rather dubious fifteen minutes of fame from which most of Tennessee suffered. The pastry, made famous by bearing a striking resemblance to Mother Teresa, lent celebrity status to the city upon its appearance, and even more after someone stole it one Christmas morning. Had to love the local flavor.

Today's local flavors—a Café O'Lei paired with a Juanita Burrita. Sitting outside in spite of the heat, she fired up her laptop. Googling 'ghost' brought up all kinds of information on Wikipedia, just below the IMDb link for the Patrick Swayze flick. Vivian read with great interest, though the descriptions of wispy specters and poltergeists didn't exactly fit the bill. Her ghosts, for lack of a better term, weren't at all wispy. They were solid, strong, and seemed to exist at two different ends of the temperature spectrum. Ezra and Zeke, her guardian spirit guides she supposed, ran hot while being around Darkmore the reaper had chilled her to her very soul.

A search using 'corporeal spirit' yielded the usual undead suspects—vampires, zombies, ghouls, and specters, none of which described her otherworldly visitors. One article describing spirits as conscious energy forms, however, caught her attention. This source claimed that spirits were capable of channeling their energy to affect the physical world, and could help or harm human beings in the process.

Apparently, they also derived much of their energy from the physical world, including humans.

Figuring she had enough theories to mull over, Vivian packed up her laptop and drove past the immaculately groomed landscape of the Vanderbilt University campus until she arrived at the clinic, hoping they could work her in so she wouldn't have to fork over the cash for a visit to the emergency room. She'd spent more than enough time and money there with Mae over the past few months.

She exited the parking garage and walked across the street toward the clinic's entrance. A glance at her reflection in the sliding glass doors made her do a double take.

With a surge of alarm, she bolted through the lobby and ducked into a private restroom, removing her sunglasses and staring in the mirror with wide-eyed wonder at the state of her face. Her previously black eye had faded to a barely noticeable dull green streak, and the bruise that had marred her cheek had vanished completely. She hadn't noticed before, but a few quick flexes of her arm and leg muscles produced no residual aches.

"What the hell?"

She ran out of the bathroom so fast she nearly knocked over three nurses and a resident. She bumped into one of the nurses, her hand grazing bare skin, and sudden flashes of a woman stretched out on a hospital bed flooded her mind. Next came an image of that nurse scribbling notes in a chart and then going about her other duties with practiced efficiency, silent tears rolling down her cheeks before she squared her shoulders and scrubbed them away. That had been a little over an hour ago. Somehow, Vivian knew that.

Just as she knew the woman in that hospital bed was no longer among the living.

The temperature dipped, sending a shiver of alarm through Vivian's body that had nothing to do with the chill. The cold presence circled around her before moving in the direction of the stairwell. Every instinct she possessed screamed at her to run. But if the reaper was here, and not for her, since the chill had passed her by, then there could only be one other explanation for his appearance.

You caught a glimpse of where they take the souls they claim.

She had indeed, and it wasn't a fate she'd wish on her worst enemy.

Indecision gripped her. She should do something, needed to do something, but what? And what price would she pay for trying? The image of the dead woman flashed through her mind once more. Smooth skin, not yet ashen but pale, sightless eyes dulling from vibrant brown to opaque glassiness, the glint of a golden wedding band and one of those little birthstone necklaces, amethyst and emerald embedded in the bellies of two small charms.

Her mother had had a necklace like that, also with two charms, one for her and one for Mae.

She followed the lingering chill to the fourth floor, slipping past the nurse's station and rooms occupied by the living. Too bad her earlier vision hadn't included a room number. And in her not inconsiderable experience, hospitals tended to be cold, which made chasing an ephemeral nip in the air as irrational as it was risky.

But she'd be damned if she let that bastard take another soul.

She paused, passing through a sudden burst of warmth at her feet that emanated from beneath a closed door on her left. After a quick glance up and down the corridor, she opened the door and slipped inside the room. Bland eggshell walls and the standard-issue privacy curtain greeted her, along with the sting of medical grade disinfectant. No noise, though, thank God. She'd have a hard time accounting for an impromptu visit to a stranger's room, especially if she'd interrupted an exam.

Only one way to find out....

She peered around the corner. The corpse was covered with a thin sheet, arms resting on top like a morbid homage to sleeping beauty. She'd been quite attractive in life, no doubt. French-manicured fingernails, smooth, clear skin, and well-groomed blonde curls, the woman had clearly taken care of herself in life. Someone had removed her jewelry, hospital staff most likely.

She hoped it would find its way back to the family.

Unsure what else to do, she reached out and cupped the woman's cold hand in her palm. The flesh was still pliant, and dry. *Well, of course it is, idiot. She's not been gone that long.*

Nothing.

Feeling a bit foolish, not to mention desperate, Vivian closed her eyes and concentrated on their joined hands, the smooth surface of painted nails under her fingertips, the rough valley between thumb and forefinger. "Hey," she whispered, wishing she knew the woman's name, "are you still in there?"

Maybe she was too late. Maybe it only worked on the living, or the almost dead.

She hung her head, heavy with the weight of defeat.

"I'm sorry."

Releasing her hand, Vivian smoothed the woman's hair and wished her soul well. She'd hoped after Zeke...well, at least she'd been in time to help the man outside the bar. She stepped back from the bed, shook her head, and rammed her fist against the wall.

"It's never enough," she muttered, leaning against the wall and fighting to keep the tears at bay.

A blast of heat hit her from behind, coursing through her body with enough force to bring her to her knees. Images assaulted her, flashes of cream and baby blue ribbons on the table, wedding music, blonde waves swirling around a dark-haired handsome man in a tuxedo...lemon-scented furniture polish on fine oak, sunlight through a bay window, a small girl dancing in the garden while new life danced in her womb.

Then the cold crept in.

"No," she moaned. "No, I don't want to know, I don't want to see, please, no, pleasenopleasenopleaseno."

The bright-eyed baby boy laughing as he took his first steps, his dark hair flying in the wind...the lock of dark hair from his tender young scalp she clutched in her hands as they sealed his small coffin. Empty days, a cold bed, a little girl's pleas for Mama to get up, the dark-haired man screaming at her after his third bourbon. His '68 Mustang was in the garage, she just turned the key and sat in the garage, like going to sleep—

"Stop!"

She meant to scream, but the word came out as a strangled gasp. Not enough oxygen...choking on exhaust fumes...too tired. The woman thought it would be over soon, but Vivian knew better. This was just the beginning.

What's it going to be, Vivian? Is she yours, mine, or theirs?

The reaper's smooth voice cut through the chill and haze of the unwanted images and emotions roiling through her mind.

"I s-said s-t-top. Don't w-want to s-see anymore."

She didn't want to feel the pride of this stranger's first job or the rush of forbidden lust and shame during an encounter with a married colleague. The heartbreaking tenderness as an infant nuzzled soft flesh in search of warmth and nourishment ripped through her heart, and the calm with which manicured hands switched on the ignition and robbed the child of her mother, and a vast, hollow emptiness never to be filled again.

The crushing weight of the soul's memories left Vivian writhing on the floor, caught between burning fever and crippling chills.

What's the matter, my dear? You were so eager to save this one from my clutches only moments ago, rushing in with the blazing sword of self-right-eous zeal. Not so easy, is it? Gets rather messy, up close and personal.

Warmth, where was the warmth?

Oh, they're here as well, representatives from the other side, awaiting your decision.

"I d-don't understand."

You get to decide the fate of the recently deceased, of course. That's what you wanted.

"No."

Then you shouldn't have interfered. But that is irrelevant now. Choose, Vivian. Moneylender that you are, perhaps this will help. Think of it as a balance sheet, debt versus revenue in the currency of souls. Is our friend in the red or the black at the end of her life's work? Does motherly devotion trump the ultimate act of selfishness?

"Zeke...Ezra, help me...."

Oh, didn't they tell you? They aren't allowed to interfere once a soul's in play. In the interest of full disclosure, my associates and I are not permitted to interfere either.

"But you—"

And lest you mistake this little conversation as interference, I'm merely offering a brief treatise on your responsibility, and the price of your meddling.

The soul clung to her, desperate, fragile, confused, and asked, "Where am I? What's happening? Where do I go?"

"I don't know," she whispered.

Vivian pushed against it as more agony and ecstasy from its lifetime threatened to swallow her whole. To be connected so intimately, forced to see what secrets dwelled in the depths of another that no other soul should witness...it was a violation. She wanted to pound the corpse on the table for the ugliness of her sins and cradle it to her bosom to protect the tiny, damaged thing that once lived there.

The damaged thing had lingered for too long in its lifeless shell, trapped and seeking a way out.

She didn't have enough to fill it. The soul would devour her. She had to get away.

Another set of images fought for dominance against the unwanted invasion of the foreign soul, images more personal, more familiar...her own. Mae's soft skin under her touch, the comfort of warm water and clean cotton, a small, helpless body resting peacefully. The sobbing man staggering away from his car to call for help. A flash of green eyes, a blanket of warmth, gratitude.

"Give her peace," Vivian whispered.

In a burst of warmth and light, the soul let go of Vivian and vanished.

She rose on unsteady legs and ran a shaking hand through her hair. Light filtered through the window blinds, adding an eerie glow to the small room where she and the corpse remained, presumably alone. The hands of the wall clock had moved less than five minutes. God, it felt like hours had passed. She could slip away without being noticed, dragging her drained body and battered mind away from this unexpected battlefield.

She took one step toward the door when another burst of heat hit her, jolting her body with a rush of energy and invigorating her with euphoria, an alien sense of well-being and long-forgotten peace. And...power? My God, was that what she was experiencing? Vivian latched onto the sensation, gulping it in great swallows like cool water after a long, hot day's work.

Enjoy the taste of victory, my dear. You've earned it.

She froze. "Why are you still here?" she hissed in a voice she barely recognized. "I made my choice, freed her soul, so get out of here you wicked, torturing bastard!"

Laughter clanged through her subconscious before she pushed it back. It was too easy, and inspired a twinge of unease in the midst of triumph.

Oh, I'm never far away, Vivian.

She pushed back against the reaper's cool, calm whisper. It faded, but not before leaving her with one last thought.

The woman whose soul you just freed? She killed the boy. Thought you might like to know.

CHAPTER SEVEN

After letting Nurse Mary take off early, Vivian pulled off her sunglasses and the bandage she'd used to conceal her freshly healed cheek, then distracted herself with unnecessary housework while waiting for Ezra. Mary had already fed and bathed Mae before tucking her into bed, thank God. After last night, she didn't trust herself around her sister.

And after earlier, she didn't want to risk any more unwanted visions or damning whispers that hit far too close to home.

She killed the boy. Thought you might like to know.

Hiding underneath a blanket of numbness, she sleepwalked through the early evening and kept busy with light cleaning and baking. She poured herself a glass of iced tea and headed out to the deck just after sunset to wait for Ezra. On a whim, she went back inside and poured another glass for her guest. She didn't know if he could eat or drink, but it seemed only polite to offer some refreshment. Besides, between raw nerves and restlessness, she needed to maintain the illusion of normalcy.

Vivian arranged some slices of the marble loaf cake she'd baked on one of her nicer serving platters. After adding some napkins and a small vase, she carried the platter outside and placed it on her small bistro table.

Walking to the front of the house, she cut two purple irises from the small flowerbed beside the mailbox. She placed them in her vase, completing the presentation for her dessert offering. Ezra appeared as the last rays of daylight slipped away through the oaks and hickories, smiling and tipping his John Deere cap.

"Evening, Miss Vivian," he said as he seated himself on the deckchair beside hers. He carried with him the scents of tilled earth and freshly mowed grass. She offered him the glass of tea, which he took and downed with a hearty gulp. She laughed, ridiculously delighted by his enthusiasm, and he smiled in response.

"It's a nice thing, seeing you smile. And I thank you for the tea. Been a long, long time since I had a good old glass of sweet tea."

"You're welcome," she said, her calm voice masking the uneasy dread creeping up her spine in the presence of the spirit, friendly though he was. "Help yourself to some cake too."

"Don't mind if I do," he replied, placing a slice on one of her napkins and taking a big bite. He finished it in one more bite and grabbed a second helping, his contented grunt and beaming smile enough to let her know how much he enjoyed the hospitality.

"Zeke told me you'd be stopping by tonight," Vivian began. "I...I have about a million questions, but I really don't know where to start."

"Well now, I'd like to answer them, but it may take me a while, getting all the way through a million." He chuckled. "This is some mighty fine cake, by the way."

"Thank you," she replied.

After another appreciative groan, he finished chewing and spoke again. "I also know this is the time you keep for yourself. You need it, especially after this afternoon."

He knows. Of course he knows...but does he know I made the wrong choice? And, oh my God, at what cost?

She didn't know if he'd read her thoughts or her expression, but he reached over and patted her shoulder. "I don't reckon I'll take all of your free time. But it does get lonesome sometimes, I expect. And after what you've been through these past few days, I reckon you may not want to be left alone."

Too shaken to speak, she nodded.

"Then you wouldn't be minding some company?" he asked.

"No, I wouldn't," she said once she'd found her voice.

"Aw now, don't go getting scared. Child, you look like you seen a spook!" He burst out laughing, a breathy sound she might have welcomed on any other occasion. After he recovered, he took in her face. Chagrin replaced amusement.

"I don't mean you harm," he said, sliding off the chair and stooping beside her.

He grasped her hand, and it took all of the self-control she could muster not to flinch. But then the warmth surged through her, the same good, deep heat from before, and her tension and fears ebbed away under his touch. She wrapped her fingers around his and let the heat radiate through her.

He smiled up at her. "See, now you know. I don't mean you harm at all."

"Then why are you here?"

"To answer that, I'm of a mind to tell you my story, if you'll hear it. It is quite a tale, full of wonder and light." He faltered then, his eyes falling to her feet. "But full of dark things too. I'm sorry for that, but I got to tell it all."

She shivered, digging her nails into her palms. "I think I've had more tales of darkness than I can handle already."

He lifted his gaze to meet hers, hazel eyes intense and serious. "You're stronger than you think, else you wouldn't have made it through two run-ins with Darkmore."

"Is that why I'm a target, then? He likes the ones who can take a beating?"

"What you're really asking is, 'Why me,' and it's a fair question. We'll get to all that. It's part of the story—my story. And sharing it will help pass the time while we're looking out for you. I'm here to help, you know. So's Zeke."

She laughed then. "You mean, you're like a guardian angel, um, guardian ghost, or...what exactly are you, Ezra?"

"I'm a little bit of all them things, I reckon. If you like, you can think of me as sort of a special friend."

The day's tension finally caught up with her and she snapped, jumping out of her chair and pacing back and forth over the deck, pausing only to scan the neighboring yards. "Like an imaginary friend? Oh Christ, that's just great! Just what I need, letting the neighbors think I'm out at here at night talking to myself. And don't even get me started on the magical healing and psychic powers I've got going on. How am I supposed to explain all that?"

"Hey now." He stood and took her hand again, which she allowed after a gentle but persistent tug. "I can be seen by folks I choose to allow to see me. Or I can avoid being seen. I can make them miss seeing you too."

Between his warm, calming touch and earnest expression, confusion and anger yielded to rationality. She thought back to when she first noticed him on the night Zeke died. No one else who saw the car crash seemed to note his comings and goings.

"As far as the rest, well it wouldn't be right to leave you all banged up on account of working with us. That's why me and Zeke gave you a little boost on getting healed up."

"Fair enough, but what's going on with my hand? And how was I able to sense that dying woman at the hospital this afternoon and...and take a hold of her soul?"

"Well, I reckon you must've taken a little nip of my power a few nights back when I was crossing Zeke over."

"Your power? How?"

"You grabbed a hold of his hand while his spirit was departing the body. Some of my spirit light must've jumped right on into you. It happens sometimes."

Maybe those websites she'd surfed weren't far off the mark then. "Spirit light...that's what? Energy? Conscious energy?"

Ezra smiled, wrinkled face beaming with pride. "Been doing your homework, eh? Well, I reckon that's as good a name as any."

"Yeah, I'm a real star student," she muttered. "What exactly is this power? How does it work? What am I supposed to do with it? Darkmore said I earned whatever surge I got from the dead woman, but what does that—"

He reached out and touched her, the warmth from his hand slipping into her skin. Comfort, calm, reassurance, and that wonderful sensation of well-being filled her.

He smiled and sat down again. "Don't you worry about a thing tonight, except letting me bend your ear a bit. It may take a few nights to get it all out. Don't want to wear you out," he said with a wink. "You'll need all the strength you got for some hard times ahead. I expect you know that by now."

"Oh yes," Vivian whispered, thinking back to the awful events of the night before last and the horror of the afternoon. "I'm scared out of my mind, to tell you the truth. This is all a lot to take in, you know. The man in white, Zeke showing up, and you, well, so, you really are dead too, huh?"

"Well, yeah," he said. "But don't go feeling bad about that. It happened a while back, and I'm doing real well with my purpose now. Helping out good folks like you ain't a half-bad way to spend your afterlife."

"I don't know if I qualify as *good*," Vivian muttered, remembering her rage at Mae, the rage she now directed at herself for saving the soul of... God, she couldn't even bring herself to say it in her mind.

"Aw, now, I do," he said, looking at her with understanding. "I know. Come on and sit down, take a load off, why don't you?"

Vivian took a deep breath and sat next to the old spirit.

"I reckon I ought to start at the beginning, but first I got to give you a little bit of my history. I was born near here, in Murfreesboro, as a matter of fact, way back in 1905. My pa was a tobacco farmer, and I followed suit, being the eldest son. Life was pretty normal for me and my family, I guess. We got through the Depression and kept the land. My wife gave me six young 'uns, and four of them lived to make fine grown folks. I even had me a son go off to war in 1944, and I was even prouder when he come back alive and made something of himself. The others did just fine too."

"Were you in the war? I mean, is that how you, um...."

"Oh no, ma'am, I was too young to be in the first big war and too old for the second," he continued. "So that's not how I met my end at'll. I had me a good life for a long, long time before I got hurt real bad and was trapped."

"Trapped? What do you mean, Ezra?" Her gut clenched at his words, echoes of the tormented soul's cries wracking her mind.

"Let's see, I reckon I must've been about fifty-five years old when it happened. I had me a fine breakfast that day. Evelyn, my wife, stuffed me with a mess of biscuits and country ham. We had us some scrambled eggs fresh from the coop."

Vivian smiled at the image, grateful for the distraction from guilt and creeping fear. "And you covered your biscuits with a heaping helping of sausage gravy, I expect?"

"Well of course I did. There ain't no other way. I'm impressed, young lady!" He chuckled, slapping his knee.

"Well, I am a country girl at heart, though I don't really show it so much. But times have changed, you know. That stuff will kill you if you eat it every day. You'll keel over from a heart attack—" She stopped, looking sheepish.

"You're more right than you know," he said, his tone serious then. "But we had a lot of work to do that day, you see. We still had to harvest the tobacco leaves by hand in those days, me and my sons, before we could tie them up and start curing. Hard work, yes, ma'am. Tobacco makes good money, but it's a fussy old plant and you have to baby it. Plant them in seedbeds, put them out to field, keep an eye out for them dang bugs and weeds and blight. Then you got to fertilize, top, and sucker them. Hard work."

Vivian listened to the old man in his reverie, picturing him out in his bibs and cap as he labored in the fields. She'd seen enough farming in her youth to appreciate the work behind it, but even then there were machines around to do much of the heavy lifting.

"Aw, listen to me rambling on and on about growing tobacco when you probably just want me to get on with the tale," he said as he came back to the present. "Well, I was in the middle of grabbing me some leaves when I felt all numb and dizzy, just on my left side. I'd had me a bad headache all day, but I didn't think nothing much about it."

He stopped and took another long draw from his glass of tea. Vivian smiled as he pulled out an old-fashioned handkerchief to wipe his mouth. He chewed on a piece of ice and swallowed hard a couple of times.

"So anyhow," Ezra continued, "I stood still for a spell and waited for my head to quit aching so bad, but then things just got kind of blurry." He paused and took Vivian's hand again as she blanched. "Before things went black for a while, I saw old Darkmore for the first time. He was standing at the edge of my field, all dressed up in his whites looking like he was off to Sunday school, tipping his hat and grinning like a fool. Wasn't the last time I saw him, I'm sorry to say," he said.

His eyes turned dark, and for the first time Vivian saw the flash of power behind the facade of an old country grandpa. She got a sense of his anger and felt a twinge of fear. It was the same fear that had nagged at her gut since she'd had her first run-in with Darkmore.

"So, you died then, out there in your field?"

He looked at her with more than a little sadness. "Oh no, ma'am, Miss Vivian, I surely didn't. Would've been a blessing, but no. I hung around for quite a little spell. Wouldn't be sitting here bending your ear all night if my passing had been so easy, and I wouldn't have much of a story to tell you. But it's late and I think we ought to leave it there for now."

She opened her mouth to protest, but he held up a hand to still her.

"You've had enough for one night, child, and I believe I made you more scared than you was before. Now I don't want you to go worrying about nothing tonight. I'm just a shout away if you need me, and Zeke ain't too far off neither. You try to sleep. I'll be around in a few nights to check in and tell you some more."

"You mean you just want me to sit around and wait? Wait for Dark-more to come back?" Vivian balked. Seemed like all she'd done for the past months, maybe even years, was to sit on her hands and wait.

"I expect you'll find something to do in the meantime. Maybe even something helpful will come to mind, but don't worry too much about that. We're here. Zeke's a good boy and wants to help out too. You should let him, you know?" He smiled, stood up, and stretched, making clear that tonight's conversation was over and done.

"Am I safe tonight, do you think?"

"Look down yonder," he said, tilting his head toward the backyard. She walked to the rail and saw someone sitting on her stone wall, watching from the darkness. He stood up and waved to her, and Vivian smiled.

"You can come on in the house, if you want to, Zeke," she shouted. "The couch is pretty comfortable."

Turning back to Ezra, who was already ambling down the stairs, Vivian said, "Wait, Ezra. There's one thing I just don't get."

He stopped, but didn't turn around. "Just the one?"

"Fine, there's a lot I don't get yet, but this has to do with you."

"What's that, child?"

"Why did Darkmore come for you in the first place?"

He didn't turn around, but she still heard his soft reply. "Same reason he came for you, Miss Vivian. I cost him a soul."

CHAPTER EIGHT

Vivian wasn't used to having so many strangers in and out of her house, let alone those from the spirit world. But she had to admit she'd slept much better since Zeke spent the night on her couch. At least, she assumed he did. She wondered if he slept. She wondered if someone in Zeke's condition needed to sleep or eat. The latter was the real issue. A Southern girl was, at heart, a born hostess, and she couldn't abide having an uncomfortable guest. She had set her alarm for 6 a.m. the night before so she'd be up and at 'em to see to her guest. She stumbled out of bed, turned off said alarm, and made a quick run to the bathroom to freshen up. Then she crept out of her bedroom to peek in on Zeke.

She didn't see him, but she saw neatly folded blankets sitting atop the pillow she'd left him the night before. Fresh indentations in the couch cushions let her know he'd been there. Damn! Why in the hell did she have to get a *morning* guardian? She padded along to the kitchen and that's where she found him. The sight that greeted her inspired awe, disbelief, and, shortly after, a whole lot of belly laughs.

"Good morning to you too," he said, shaking his head as he turned away from the dusty mess of flour on the kitchen counter. Zeke was wearing Vivian's favorite apron, the one her mother had sewn for her. It was made of simple broadcloth with a pattern of frolicking felines of every hue and variety. A generous layer of flour dust covered the apron too, as well as a fair amount of Zeke.

"I was hoping to be finished before you got up. I'll clean up the mess," he offered with a sheepish smile.

"It's fine," Vivian said between gasping and giggles. "Really. I just want to know, though, what on Earth are you up to in here?"

"Well, I was trying to make biscuits, from scratch. It's harder than I thought it would be. The recipe didn't look all that bad," he said a bit defensively, brushing a dark lock from his forehead with a white finger. "Anyway, um, why don't I just put on some coffee and we'll figure out breakfast in a bit?"

"Sounds good. I think you really ought to stick with pancakes and eggs. Those were really good. Oh hey, I meant to ask, can you eat? Ezra drank a huge glass of tea last night and wolfed down some marble cake, so I figured you could. I mean, how functional is your, um, body, or whatever. How do you even have a body?" Her cheeks heated as she contemplated the functionality of Zeke's body. God, dry spell or no, she shouldn't be having those kinds of thoughts about a dead man.

"It's complicated, and even I don't understand all of the physics and magic behind it," Zeke said.

"Magic? Seriously, you expect me to believe magic brought you back?" she asked with a hint of sarcasm.

"Well, after all you've seen in the past few days, I think you'd be a little more open-minded," he shot back, wiping the flour from his hands on his jeans.

"Anyway, according to one of the others like me, I think he used to be a physicist, we are mostly energy. Conscious energy, or soul energy, if you prefer. Those of us who guard and guide have more energy than most spirits. We collect it, and we learn to control it. Believe me, it's a lot easier with someone there to teach you. We can use this energy to project from our realm to this one and others, and we can assume a physical form by manipulating the elements around us. That's his theory anyway."

"Sounds like some bullshit from an episode of *Star Trek* to me," she replied. "Though it fits with some stuff I read online." Not to mention what she'd experienced herself, assuming Ezra was right about her ability to borrow his powers.

"Well, like I said, it's only a theory. But think about it. What makes up your body, or mine, or anyone else's? Mostly water, some carbon, a few minerals. All of those elements are out there in the physical world. We can assemble those elements when we transport here, and disassemble them when we go back, like I showed you." He held up his hand and wiggled his flour-covered fingers.

"Earth to earth, ashes to ashes, dust to dust, and back again," she muttered to herself. "So what's the difference between you and a regular ghost?"

He quirked an eyebrow. "Regular ghost?"

"You know what I mean. The ones from all of those stories you hear about as a kid, or like the ones from haunted houses? Those wispy white things that just pass through walls or look like big balls of light? Or how about poltergeists?"

"They don't have as much energy." He shrugged. "There are also those who can't control it. They can only project as a light or a form without substance. Some of them can't even do that, but they can still move objects and manipulate the physical world."

"What about ghosts who haunt places and, you know, re-live the last moments of their lives?" Dangerous ground, but she needed to know, needed to believe the reprieve she'd offered the woman's soul hadn't been in vain. God, to murder one's own blood....

No, that hit too close to home, and she couldn't bear to face that judgment. Not yet.

"They're lost. We try to help them move on, but some just can't let go. Others, well...." Zeke paused. "They just aren't right."

"You mean they're crazy?"

"Something like that, yes. If you have enough baggage in this life, some of it's bound to carry over to the next," he replied softly.

The last gave Vivian considerable pause. Maybe hell wasn't the fiery pit described in tales from revivals past. Maybe hell was simple repetition, like the cosmic version of writing lines on a chalkboard during detention over and over again. She thought she'd read that somewhere.

It also reminded her of something else. "Those whispers I heard in Darkmore's realm, were those lost souls?"

"Some," he said. "He's acquired quite a few over time. Some don't have much energy to start with, and once they get there, well, you've seen it—all their energy goes to him or that other...thing, or to just surviving."

"Can anything be done for them?"

He furrowed his brows. "Well, supposedly they have a certain amount of time to serve there, but there's a backup in the exit queue. Seems to take almost as long to get out as it does to serve your sentence, at least from what I've seen. Bureaucratic bullshit even in the great beyond...who would've thought?"

Though he tried to disguise it with a light tone, she caught a flash of anxiety before the glint of wry amusement chased it away. The nosy part of her was tempted to press for an explanation, but then another thought interrupted her musings on the darker nature of the afterlife. "So, can anyone see you? What about psychics, or psychos? I mean, are all those weirdos you hear about talking to dead people really crazy?"

"I really couldn't say. So far I've only talked with you."

"Is that unusual?

"You'll have to ask Ezra, but I think we normally work behind the scenes, so to speak, keep a low profile. Maybe most of our living colleagues and charges have the good sense to do the same," he said with a wink.

"That's probably for the best. Enough people think I'm nucking futs as it is. Um, so, can you see the future?"

"Well, time is a little different on the other side," he said, shifting his eyes and running a hand through his hair.

"Oh, I get it, secret agent ghost-type stuff," she said, waving shaky hands in the air and making spooky sounds.

"Yeah, something like that."

"Well, what else can you do?"

"I know we can also possess the living. Some of us can enter their minds and control their thoughts, at least to an extent. Free will still rules, though we can sometimes sway our targets."

"Wait a minute," Vivian said, struggling to put the pieces together in her mind. "Darkmore said you aren't allowed to interfere when a soul's in play."

Zeke offered a sheepish grin. "Well, we aren't officially supposed to interfere, but there are ways to bend the rules a bit and push the soul in the right direction."

"Or suck the life out of a soul?"

His expression suddenly turned serious. "We only take energy from the dead or dying. Taking it from the living isn't possible for soul brokers. We're dead, so the transfer just works better that way. Our energy is pretty powerful. We pack a pretty mean punch, even in the world of the living. If we're strong enough, we can transport the living to our realm," he said, his gaze burning into hers. "You experienced that firsthand."

"Darkmore must be pretty strong then," Vivian said with a shudder. "But you are too. You brought me back."

Zeke gave her a sharp look. "That was dumb, damnable luck and a whole lot of help from Ezra." Vivian swore he sounded bitter. "I almost didn't make it back with you, and it cost me a lot of energy. It's a wonder I found you at all. Jesus, Vivian, what happened that night? I mean, Darkmore is ancient and very powerful, but it's still hard to take a human out of this world against her will."

The perceived accusation stung. "What? You think I wanted to go to that awful place?" She hadn't spent much time near Mae since the last night of hell, and the memory of rage directed at her helpless sister filled her with shame. She could have killed Mae, and if she had, would she have suffered the same fate as the woman in the hospital, or would someone have granted her a reprieve? Would he, or would Zeke, have turned away in disgust, abandoning her to eternal penance?

"Look, Darkmore showed up out of the blue and told me he could make all of my problems with Mae go away," she said as she turned her head away from him. "It's like he was able to look inside every dark corner of my mind and see things that I would never say out loud, secrets I don't ever let out into the light of day. Then I had the worst time with Mae, and I just wound up...wherever it is I went."

"It had to be more than that. I mean, from what I've been learning, it takes some real darkness to open those gates."

Darkness that made a person want to kill her helpless sibling, and herself, that's what he meant.

Darkness that could let the soul of a child-murderer go free?

"If you have something you want to accuse me of, by all means come right out and say it."

Zeke regarded her, appearing to weigh his options. Taking a deep and possibly unnecessary breath, he plunged right in. "Look, Vivian, don't take this the wrong way. I'm here to help, remember? I'm not the grand high inquisitor, but I do need to know what happened that night so we can figure out what's got Darkmore so interested in you and how we can keep him at bay."

"So you're still saying I did something to bring him here, right? I deserve all of this? Where the hell do you get off judging me, *Ezekiel?* You don't know me, you don't know what I've been through, what I've sacrificed—"

She stopped right there out of instinct and habit. Then a thought hit her. *Of course he's here to judge me. Surely that's what this was all about.* It was the same tired, old line she'd been fed since childhood. She was supposed to keep it all in—be the good and noble martyr. She wasn't supposed to complain. She was told to think of poor little Mae and how bad she had it. How many times had she heard someone say, "God never puts burdens on us without a reason, dear, and you must bear yours"?

The implication, of course, was that failure to bear the burden with grace made her evil.

The words of the reaper came back, stabbing her in the soft parts and leaving her raw and exposed. *You were so eager to save this one from my clutches only moments ago, rushing in with the blazing sword of self-righteous zeal. Not so easy, is it? Gets rather messy, up close and personal.*

"Vivian," he began again, a bit more gently this time. "I'm not saying anything of the sort—"

"Of course you are. Why else would you be here, throwing all of my sins back in my face? I have enough shit to deal with, in case you hadn't noticed!"

Near tears, she blinked them back fiercely and let the rage take hold. She'd be damned if she fed him her tears. "I'm sure you must have been some kind of saint or something, being chosen as a great guardian of a mere mortal like me, but what gives you the right—"

He moved in on her before she had the chance to blink, green eyes dilated almost full black with anger. He grabbed her shoulders and gripped her so tightly she winced.

"Don't think for one *second* that I'm some sort of saint! I'm not here serving the greater good. My sins have drained me dry more than once this side of the grave, and they'll do it again."

The same terror she'd experienced when she first encountered Darkmore slammed into her again. Only Zeke wasn't cold. He blazed hot, his skin burning hers as he released his grip from her shoulders and clutched both of her wrists. She dropped her gaze, but he grabbed her face and forced her to look at him.

"Never again accuse me of thinking myself higher than you," he said in a low, menacing tone. He released her with a rough shove and stepped back, scowling. "And since you asked, here's one more thing we guardians can do with our energy."

A burst of light shot from his outstretched hand and hit a nearby lamp, smashing it to pieces.

He staggered and she would've sworn he'd flickered, going momentarily transparent. "I have to go now. You can feed yourself, I'm sure. You'll see Ezra later. Call out if you need *him*."

Then he vanished.

CHAPTER NINE

Not having any help for the day, she spent the morning channeling her aggression with chores and cleaning, most of them unnecessary. Well, the kitchen actually *did* need a scrub-down, and she had to pick up the shards of broken lamp. Contrary to his earlier promise, Zeke didn't clean up his mess, the bastard.

Of course, she had a mess of her own to clean up too, didn't she? And she'd been avoiding it long enough.

She stood outside of Mae's room for a long time. A few soft groans let her know her sister was awake. She was probably hungry too, and wet. Vivian took a step inside and noticed the stack of neatly folded sheets on the nightstand. Someone must have cleaned them, along with the remnants of broken ceramic.

Zeke.

Pushing aside twinges of guilt and gratitude, she pulled out some fresh clothes, a pack of wipes, and a diaper, carrying them to Mae's bed. After changing Mae, she worked on removing her sister's nightgown, taking care when she coaxed those painfully thin, contorted arms out of the sleeves. She lifted Mae's body and leaned it forward, supporting her in an awkward embrace while she pulled the nightgown over her shoulders and head.

She saw an angry red scratch and some bruises running down Mae's back and she broke.

"Oh God, I'm so sorry." Vivian's choked sob pierced the quiet dark of the room as she rocked back and forth with her sister. "I'm so, so sorry."

After her tears ran their course, Vivian gently lowered Mae back down on the bed and stood, pausing to stretch and to wipe the tears from her eyes before getting back to work. Pulling the T-shirt over Mae's head proved a bit easier than getting the nightgown off had been, but she was still mindful of her sister's injuries when she stretched the soft fabric over her back.

"I can't take back what I've done," she said as she pulled the loose flannel pajama pants over Mae's legs. "But I can do right by you today, starting with breakfast."

After taking care of Mae's breakfast and showering, Vivian fought a fresh wave of restlessness by catching up on phone calls to concerned family and friends, which transformed residual anger into sadness. She had overcome the fresh grief at the loss of her parents. She'd had some time to heal, but the edges of the wounds remained ragged, tearing open and seeping fresh sorrow from time to time.

She took a nap, sleeping about two hours too long, and woke up feeling more miserable than she had before closing her eyes. Numbness turned to a dull ache, and she ran on autopilot while tending to Mae and deciding how to fill the remaining hours before darkness descended. She didn't want to think about how she would sleep without her guardian there, but she wouldn't call him. He'd recognized that bit of stubbornness in her and called her out on it, but she still had her pride, one of the bigger sins if memory served.

One of many she bore.

Maybe Ezra would stop by tonight. There, she could just hold on to that thought, any thought to keep the tears at bay.

Just as she began to contemplate the sad state of her refrigerator, she heard her doorbell, chiding herself as her heart leaped. Zeke didn't ring or knock. He just appeared. She opened the door and was greeted by a sight almost as welcome.

"Hey, girl!" Sue dropped her bags and threw her arms around Vivian's neck. "You look terrible. And you smell even worse. Ever heard of a shower?"

Vivian squeezed her friend tight, laughing through the tears. "Oh my God, Sue, you have no idea how glad I am to see you." She let her friend go and scooted aside so she could come in. "What's in the bag, babe?"

Sue laughed. "Well, you may be a weepy, stinky little thing, but at least you have your sense of humor. What I have is some Chinese takeout, some Godiva dark chocolate ice cream, and *Blue Collar Comedy* on DVD. Or, if you're not in the mood for Jeff Foxworthy and company, an assortment of chick flicks." She looked Vivian over and shook her head. "Okay, with the waterworks you got going on, I think we'll just skip the chick flicks."

"Good call," Vivian said, wiping her eyes. "What else you got?"

"My PJs and an overnight bag. You don't get to laugh at my mud mask, though, or I'm so out of here. Slumber party time! Now, please direct me to the booze stash, and get yourself under the shower and into your jammies so we can get this party started," Sue said, already on her way to the kitchen. Sue knew perfectly well where to find the good stuff at Vivian's house, or had at one time. How long had it been since she'd invited Sue over?

How long since she'd had anyone over?

She followed her friend's advice and felt about fifty percent better after a shower and her first drink. They enjoyed lo mein, spring rolls, and a few mojitos before settling into their sleeping bags on the sofa. Vivian sighed, wishing she could tell Sue all of her troubles. She wished for Zeke, in spite of still being pissed and, she admitted, guilty about their fight.

"Hey," Sue said, interrupting Vivian's reverie. "You okay?"

"I'm better than I was earlier."

"Well, hell, don't I have great timing? You know, I just had this feeling that I had to come and see you tonight. It kept bugging me, like an itch on my back I just couldn't reach, and so I grabbed my stuff and high-tailed it over here. Do you think we have some psychic connection or something?"

Vivian schooled her face to stillness. That was Zeke's doing. It had to be. Even though he'd been as angry with her as she'd been with him when he left, he'd known she would need a friend and sent one to her. He'd taken care of her. He really was her guardian.

"I don't know, Sue, but I'm sure glad you came by. I needed a friend tonight in the worst way."

"Well, next time I suggest you pick up the phone," she said, scooping Vivian up in a great big bear hug. "You may not always be able to depend on my ESP."

She settled in Sue's arms. "You know what? You're absolutely right. I, Vivian Margaret Bedford, do solemnly swear to stop being such a stubborn bitch by failing to call good friends or by pushing them away."

Sue smiled down at her and said, "Well, don't give it up entirely, the stubborn bitch part, that is. It's part of your charm."

While Sue popped in the next DVD and nuked some popcorn, Vivian made another silent vow. She would stop her whining, wallowing, and all of this goddamned waiting. Tomorrow she would take matters into her own hands and start finding out all she could about the man in white, and her other visitors too. If she could still breathe, she could move. If she could move, she could seek answers and take some action. *Time to get up off my ass and deal with this before I wind up dead. Or worse.*

Vivian preferred to fight, and resolved to start the battle in a place she'd run from most of her life, even though the very thought of setting foot in the place made her stomach churn. Though she'd long ago abandoned faith, her predicament probably did call for some divine intervention. Or, at the very least, some afterlife expertise.

Only one place to turn for that.

CHAPTER TEN

The history of Nashville was steeped in hymns, in spirituals, in the cadences of the fire and brimstone sermons of old-time tent revivals, and in the flow of backwoods creeks where the young are still born again into Jesus through the ritual of full-immersion baptism. A small yet thriving Jewish community and a growing, largely Iraqi Kurdish Islamic enclave flavored the city's healthy servings of spiritual nourishment. With a house of worship on every street corner, literally, any and all faith-based needs appeared to be covered here in the buckle of the Bible belt. In fact, church-shopping might very well be the official state pastime. While good for the average Evangelical, the listing of more than eight hundred places of worship left Vivian a bit overwhelmed.

After much hemming and hawing, she decided that if she was going to seek help, or at the very least information in the Christian tradition, she might as well start with the source. The Catholics seemed to have a great deal of insight into angels and demons based on pop culture. After making a few phone calls, however, Vivian figured getting an appointment with the friggin' governor might be easier than speaking with an actual priest.

Of course, there was one other way to go about it....

It could get her in some trouble, but maybe she could gather a bit of useful information before getting booted out.

And it was always easier to ask forgiveness than permission.

Taking advantage of Sue's generous offer to stay with Mae for a few hours, Vivian sat in the parking lot and stared up at the building, its Spanish mission-style architecture and red roof an odd contrast to the concrete and steel urban sprawl around it. *How very Nashville.* She'd seen enough during her years in the Music City not to be too surprised by anything that passed city planners. The place was riddled with double-wide trailers smack in the middle of McMansion-filled suburbs, kitschy little shops skirting run-down old homes on 12th South, not to mention the eyesore better known as the Hollywood 27 Theater. She'd spotted the lights on that damned building more than a few times while flying to and from her home city, back in the days before Mae. She could just see the postcard—"Welcome to Nashvegas! Have a nice day!"

Scanning the parking lot again and figuring she'd stalled long enough, she got out of her car and walked toward the cathedral. According to their website, confessions were heard all afternoon. Thankfully, she didn't burst into flames upon entering the sanctified space. Unfortunately, though, no one was available to point her in the right direction. The door to what she assumed was the confessional stood open, so she slid inside, closed the door, and sat down in front of the screen, struggling not to fidget. Guilt still tugged at her psyche, but then again, where better to indulge in self-flagellation? She had no one but herself to blame for this. If she'd kept her nasty temper in check instead of unleashing it on her guardian, she wouldn't need to sneak around and stalk members of the clergy, which was pathetic, not to mention just plain wrong.

A faint glow emanating from her fingertips served as a reminder to keep a tight leash on her temper, since apparently strong emotions served as a trigger for the psychic mojo she'd developed. Pushing aside thoughts of Zeke and her general discomfort, Vivian took a few deep breaths and willed her body and mind to calm. After a few moments, someone entered the other side. Though she couldn't see him very clearly in the dark, the soothing kindness of his voice calmed her as he uttered a short prayer.

"What sins have you to confess, my child?" The voice was warm, kind, and inviting.

"Probably too many to count, but that's not why I'm here."

"Oh?"

"Um," she stammered. "I'm not here for confession and I apologize for the false pretense, but I...well, I didn't know what else to do. The diocese secretary told me I couldn't make an appointment with a priest unless I was Catholic, but I really need some advice and I don't know where else to go."

He didn't answer, which she took as a bad sign.

"Look, I promise not to take up too much of your time. If you could just answer a few of my questions, I would be really, *really* grateful."

The uncomfortable silence stretched along with her growing sense of desperation. She kneeled down on the low bench in front of screen, bowing her head and closing her eyes, "Please, sir, I'm begging you. Just give me a few minutes of your time."

Eyes still closed, she heard him exit the confessional and open the door to her side. She braced herself for a reprimand. "I'm sorry," she muttered, not bothering to look up. "This was a bad idea. I'll go."

Gathering her purse, she stood and took a step to leave. The priest's hand on her arm stopped her.

"This is highly irregular, and frankly a new one for me. And considering how long I've been a man of the cloth, that's really saying something."

Vivian chanced a glance at the priest. The distinguished-looking older gentleman, whose salt and pepper hair complimented his blue-gray eyes, was dressed as she imagined, with the clerical collar, though she was surprised to see that he also wore jeans. His smile was as warm as his voice and held a hint of amusement that gave her hope.

"I'm Father Montgomery, by the way," he said, extending his hand.

Bracing herself and taking a deep breath, she accepted. Her efforts at keeping calm apparently paid off, since no unwelcome visions filled her consciousness upon contact. "Vivian Bedford. Pleased to meet you."

"So you have some questions for me? Well, I think I may have a few moments to spare," he said, chuckling and extending his arms toward the empty expanse of the cathedral. "Are you interested in converting, or are you a reporter, perhaps?"

Shit, maybe he found her visit suspicious. The Catholic Church hadn't exactly had a lot of good press in the past few years. Best to tread lightly.

"Neither, Father," she stated politely, though calling someone other than her dearly departed daddy "Father" seemed odd to Vivian. Must be a Protestant hang-up. "I have some questions regarding, um, for lack of a better word, the mystical aspects of the faith."

"I see," said Father Montgomery, rather seriously. "Could you be a little more specific? I can assure you that I'm not part of a grand conspiracy to conceal the truth of the Gnostic Gospel, nor am I set to take over the papacy, in spite of Mr. Brown's flights of fancy." He chuckled.

Here goes nothing. "Well, I'll admit that I did enjoy *The Da Vinci Code*, but I'm not interested in whether or not Jesus was married, Father. I was thinking more along the lines of the second book's topic, though, or title rather."

"Angels and demons, then?" He raised his eyebrows, "I can offer insight into theological interpretation, scripture, and prayer, but I'm afraid that we don't sanction many exorcisms, Ms. Bedford. The practice is somewhat outdated."

"Do you believe in angels, Father? Or demons?" She figured it would be best to understand his personal stance.

"Well, I can tell you the official position of the Church on angels. Most of it is based on St. Thomas's *Summa Theologica*. They are the spirits created by God before the physical world, and He endowed them with free will, just like men."

"And women," Vivian added. She couldn't help herself. The feminist streak normally rose when confronted with male authority figures, especially the religious types. She'd been irked by the story of Eve and the Fall of Man one too many times. "Though it seems to me that your church would like to endow us with less."

He chuckled again, which caught Vivian off guard. "Ms. Bedford, would you like a cup of coffee? It seems as though we may have quite a bit to talk about."

She smiled, in spite of her best effort to stop herself. "Fine, Padre," she said, palms up in mock surrender. "Truce and coffee. We can stick to the first topic, though, if you don't mind. It's a little more pressing for me at the moment. And you can call me Vivian, or Viv, if you like."

"As you wish," he said.

He led her to his office and invited her to sit while he fiddled with a small coffee maker. "So, you're interested in angels and demons. Any reason in particular?"

"Well, this is going to sound crazy, but I recently had what you might call a near-death experience." She cringed when saying the last bit aloud, but he simply smiled and nodded.

"Actually, they're quite common. Would you like to tell me about it?"

"Um, okay. It happened earlier this week when I got caught up in multi-car pileup. Luckily it was a near miss for me, but I watched a man die and since then I've been experiencing some strange...visions."

"Visions?"

"One might have been a dream," she muttered, the memory of her first encounter with Darkmore sending a shudder through her spine. Of course, the second remained all too vivid, but she could hardly tell the priest about it. God, what would she say? *Hi, you don't know me and I hate to bother you, but I seem to have become some sort of conduit between the living and the dead and I'm afraid I'm going to be carried off by the grim reaper to do his bidding. Think you can help?*

"It must have been quite some dream, judging from the look on your face," he said, placing a warm cup of coffee on the desk in front of her. "Are you sure you're all right?"

Vivian picked up the cup, working to still the slight tremor running through her hand. "Well, I wasn't injured, at least not physically."

She wondered where to begin and how much she could tell him without coming across as a nutjob. "What if, hypothetically mind you, someone gave you the choice between hurting other people in exchange for freedom from your own suffering or refusing and going someplace more terrible than the hell you were already living?"

"Sounds like the makings of great Mob film. That was a joke, by the way." Leaning back in his chair, he placed his tented fingertips under his chin. "Assuming this happened in your dream, perhaps it reflects a crisis of conscience you're experiencing, or perhaps a crisis of faith."

"Sounds very Freudian."

"Depends," he said, smiling. "While the desire to be free of one's burdens fits the Freudian notion of wish fulfillment, I'm guessing you have no desire to inflict harm upon others. Taking Jung's subjective approach, one might speculate that the dream is a manifestation of your shadow aspect—a representation of the least desirable parts of your personality that aren't embodied in your conscious life."

Well, that was unexpected. "Are you a priest or a shrink?"

"A bit of both, I suppose. Delving into the human psyche does come in handy in my line of work."

"So let me get this straight. If I buy into the whole interpretation of dreams thing, then deep down I'm just a dark, nasty person who should take the Devil up on his deal?"

And hadn't she already?

"Everyone has darkness and light within them, Vivian, and we're all tempted in our daily lives. It's a part of the human experience. We have at least two weapons against our baser natures, though—faith and free will."

Wasn't that a recurring theme? "I'm more willing to buy into the second notion than the first."

He chuckled. "Well at least we have someplace to start."

Two cups of coffee and an hour later, Vivian decided Father Montgomery was pretty cool for a clergyman, which was more than she'd expected. Though she still lacked a concrete solution for her unusual predicament, talking to him had eased her weary mind. Perhaps there was something to the whole confession-is-good-for-the-soul notion, after all. He even invited her to attend a service, or at the very least drop by sometime later if she had any more questions.

"Vivian, it's truly been a pleasure," he said, offering his hand as he walked her out. "I do hope I've been helpful."

"Oh, yes," she replied, smiling as she shook hands with the priest. "Very helpful. I appreciate your time, Father."

"Of course, I would be remiss in my duties as a man of the cloth if I didn't encourage you to join the fold, or attend a service at the very least."

"Fat chance, Padre."

"Well, then I suppose I shouldn't bother suggesting a suitable penance for your sins, which include sneaking into my confessional under false pretenses."

"Fat f...freakin' chance, Padre." Heat filled her cheeks at the near miss. *Nice save, Princess Potty-mouth.*

The priest chuckled. "At least I've had a positive influence on your vocabulary. Perhaps you'll drop by again sometime soon and tell me more about your interest in angels, demons, and spirits?" He winked, and the light gesture put her at ease. She wondered if all priests were as astute as Father Montgomery.

"I might take you up on it," she replied with a coy wink of her own. "Though you may be tempted to call the men in white coats to come and cart me off."

"Well, I'm sure it would be a very interesting story. I hope to see you again. Good day, Vivian. Go with God." He graced her with a warm smile as he made the sign of the cross.

"And to you too, Padre," she said, extending her hand. Unlike the first time, however, she received a few impressions when he accepted her hand-shake. He must have felt something as well, judging from his wide eyes and gasp.

"You know that doctor's visit you've been putting off, Padre? I think you'd be really wise to reconsider."

She released his hand and walked out of the cathedral before he had the chance to respond.

After dragging her laptop to Starbucks and spending more money than she should on a latte, Vivian spent half an hour scouring the Internet for information on Hell and Purgatory. On a whim, she scanned archived issues of *The Tennessean* for obituary listings. Nosy? Probably. Uncalled for? Perhaps not. He did, after all, put it out there by telling her he wasn't a saint.

Besides, he was dead. You couldn't stalk a dead guy.

She had to dig a little since she had nothing to go on other than his first name. Her search brought back unbidden memories of recent funeral arrangements, writing her parents' obits, and the prospect of doing it all over again for Mae. Angry, she forced herself to press on and eventually she hit pay dirt.

Ezekiel Nathaniel Longhollow, age 35 of Nashville. June 4. Visitation June 7, 4-6 p.m. Service June 8, 11 a.m. ....

He hadn't been much older than her when he died. He'd been married. He had a son.

Vivian dialed the funeral home number listed and found out where he was buried. She was naturally curious, she told herself as she packed up, grabbed her keys, and headed for Woodlawn Memorial Park, stopping to pick up some flowers along the way. Should be safer than a hospital, she thought. The dead in a cemetery had had time to settle the affairs of the recently deceased and leave. Or, extrapolating from Zeke's theory, if they lingered, they likely wouldn't have the energy to cause her any problems.

The cemetery itself was vast and immaculate. Unlike most cemeteries in the area, there were no upright headstones, which made navigating a bit more difficult. Its well-manicured lawn reminded her of the Governor's Club though, but Vivian thought a cemetery having its own radio broadcast was a bit morbid. It made sense, though, with the bones of folks like Johnny Paycheck, Webb Pierce, and Dan Seals resting in this hallowed ground in the heart of the Music City. She followed the map, driving slowly and looking around the gently sloping landscape peppered with bronze vases and the odd marble sculpture. She spotted his grave easily, still fresh with newly turned earth. The permanent bronze plate had yet to arrive, but a temporary marker bore his name, and she found a vase in which to deposit the bundle of calla lilies.

Vivian sighed. She'd expected to cry, but no tears came. How could you cry for someone you didn't even know? Or maybe she took comfort in knowing he was still around. Well, sort of around. Maybe he'd moved by now. After all, she'd given him no reason to stay.

Her vision blurred.

Nothing you can do for him here.

She decided to head home. It was getting late, and Sue would be itching to leave soon. Even if she wasn't, Vivian wasn't one to take advantage of a dear friend. She walked back to her car and gazed at her meager provisions, shaking her head. Assuming her guardians weren't coming back anytime soon, it seemed she would have to rely on her own wits and good old Ma Nature to keep the reaper and any other specters at bay.

Time to ghost-proof her house.

CHAPTER ELEVEN

By the time she finished setting up, the whole house smelled like a mixture of Thanksgiving and a forest fire. The stench was vile enough ward off the living. Whether or not it worked on the dead remained to be seen. At least she remembered to turn off the smoke detector first, both to keep Mae calm and to avoid a visit from the fire department.

"What in the blue blazes are you up to, child?"

Vivian shrieked, spun around, and nearly fell on top of Ezra.

"Jesus, you scared the hell out of me! Don't your kind ever knock?"

"Not generally, though in my defense, I ain't used to being seen." He eyed the burning bundle in her hand with obvious suspicion. "You ain't messing around with that there wacky weed, are you?"

Not since college.

"It's not marijuana, Ezra. It's sage, and smudging with it's supposed to ward off negative energy and rogue spirits. Though I'm guessing it doesn't work since *you're* still here," she said with an exasperated sigh. So much for the wisdom of Wikipedia.

He threw his head back and laughed. "Oh, that old wives' tale don't hold water, Miss Vivian. I could've told you that. It won't work on Darkmore either."

Yeah, there's plenty you could've told me by now. "Then I'm guessing the holy water I swiped earlier today won't do the trick then."

"Afraid not, darlin', but don't you worry. Me and Zeke got you covered."

"Good to know," she muttered.

"You thought we'd left you?"

She shrugged.

"I told you I can avoid being seen. I've been around, and so has Zeke. You've just got to learn to trust us. It's like your buddy the priest told you," he said with a wink. "Have a little faith."

She groaned and covered her eyes with her free hand. "Please tell me you didn't follow me *everywhere*."

"Well now, what kind of guardian would I be if I didn't tag along to make sure you stayed out of trouble?" At least he sounded a bit sheepish.

"Okay, okay. Just promise me you won't hang around when I'm changing or visiting the little girls' room and I'll give the whole faith thing another shot." She leveled her gaze at him and added, "And while we're on the subject, what kind of guardian leaves his charge in the dark about what she's up against? A little more information would be nice, you know."

Beet-red and obviously chagrined, Ezra said, "Fair enough. You got time to sit and listen to an old man tell some more of his tale?"

After extinguishing her burning pots of cedar and sage, Vivian joined Ezra on her back deck. She'd set out two plates with fresh, warm cobbler and two glasses of milk, remembering how much he enjoyed the cake on his last visit. And besides, if she sweetened the deal, maybe she'd finally get some answers about why she became a reaper target and a bona fide method for de-ghosting her home.

He gave her a broad grin. "Now that looks like a mighty fine pie, Miss Vivian," he said. "I believe I'll be all over that like a fly on a June bug."

"Help yourself." She laughed. "I have a whole pan, and I can't have it sitting around calling to me all night. I'll gain ten pounds."

"Well now, ain't a thing wrong with a little meat on your bones. Women ought to look like women. Y'all spend too much time worrying about a little extra here and there. Just eat up while I bend your ear in between bites."

"Okay. I'm glad you can still eat while you're here. Do you feel all the same things you could before? When you were alive?"

"Oh, we feel a lot. Sometimes we feel things much stronger than we used to when we walked this old world the first time around." He closed his eyes as he uttered the last, savoring the sweet confection. "Hmm, like this. Oh my. I don't know if it's on account of not having anything sweet for a spell, but I reckon this might be the finest pie I ever tasted. Smells good too. Just don't go telling my wife now, God rest her soul."

"Did you ever see her? On the other side?" The question popped out of her mouth before her mental filter could catch up.

A brief flash of pain and bitterness crossed his weathered old face. He hid it quickly, but not before she realized she'd said the wrong thing.

"No, ma'am," he said after a long pause. "That ain't allowed for us. We can travel with those we didn't know in our former lives, but not with our own, especially kinfolk. We can't help our own cross neither. It would be too much, too...." He struggled, searching for the words.

"Like a conflict of interest?"

"Just so," he said, giving her a broad grin that brought to mind a teacher beaming with pride at his star student. She wondered if his down-home demeanor was just an act. He was clearly very powerful, being able to maintain a corporeal form during his long visits. It followed that he must be wiser than he appeared. Maybe those of his kind just carried some parts of their former selves to the next place. Or maybe he'd donned the wholesome country grandpa mask to put her at ease. Maybe she could ask Zeke.

The thought of Zeke filled her with a pang of regret.

Ezra's rumbling voice brought her back to present concerns. "It's a hard thing to accept, parting from loved ones, at least at the first. But I don't let it trouble me now. Thessalonians tells us the dead in Christ will rise first. After that, those who are still alive will be caught up together with us folks in the clouds to meet the Lord in the sweet by and by."

"You really do believe that stuff, don't you?"

"You mean the Good Book?" He seemed astonished that she'd even ask. "Of course I do."

"Must be nice," she muttered. In spite of her cynicism, she had to admit, if only to herself, she sometimes envied the faithful. She often wished something out there could give her the sense of peace and purpose believers carried, even if it was just an illusion. Then again, she knew too many who just pretended to be on fire for the Lord for the sake of propriety, or for personal gain. Ezra didn't seem the sort to fake it, though. She could almost believe in him.

"It is nice, Miss Vivian. You got to have faith in something if you're going to make it in this weary old world."

Which begs the question.... "So have you ever lived without faith? Ever lost it?"

He quirked a bushy eyebrow and countered, "Ever hear about Paul on the road to Damascus?"

"Sure. I was raised by Bible-thumping Baptists....Oh, I get it! You've got the zeal of a convert, huh?"

"Something like that," he replied, a rueful smile ghosting his features. "After all I've seen and done in my walks of life, I had to hold on to something pretty strong."

"So you do believe you'll get to see her again someday? Your wife?" she asked, since he didn't seem to mind her questions.

"Well now, there's all manner of realms, so I reckon I might when my work's done in this one. The Word says so. 'For now we see through a glass, darkly; but then face to face: now I know in part; but then shall I know even as also I am known.'"

She hoped it was true, for the old spirit's sake. She also found the more pressing question rolling off her wayward tongue before she could stop it. "Have you seen my parents? Did they cross to a good place?" She looked him square in the face, hoping she hadn't angered him, but needing to know just the same.

He grimaced and shook his head. "Child, it ain't for me to go telling those things to you, much as it hurts me not to answer. If it was up to me, I'd take you to them, wherever they are."

"I'm sorry," Vivian said, feeling empty and alone. "I guess I'm not supposed to ask those kinds of questions."

"Oh, Miss Vivian," he sighed, taking her hand and filling her with his warmth. "It ain't wrong to wonder and worry about folks that have gone on.

It's human to want to know and to see what's over yonder. You just need to wait until it's time, that's all. You understand?"

"I don't like it, but I do understand. And I'll try to be patient," she said, feeling a bit less empty but still sad.

She braced herself before asking the difficult question, braced against despair and desperate hope. "Can you do...anything for Mae?"

Ezra squeezed her hand tighter and held her gaze, his filled with so much compassion and regret that she wanted to weep. "Child, I would give just about anything to heal little Mae and all those like her. But that's beyond what our kind can do. I know it ain't much comfort, but I can tell you she won't suffer like this in the next realm."

Vivian nodded, lowering her blurry gaze. Ezra patted her hand and gave her time and space to recover. After she heaved a deep sigh and wiped her eyes, he asked, "Everything else all right?"

After a long pause, she asked, "How's Zeke?"

He smiled at her and said, "Oh, he's just fine. Probably fretting as much about you as you are about him. You two need to ease up on each other." He chuckled. "But I reckon you'll break each other in directly. Don't you worry. He'll be here if you need him. You just have to call him."

I was afraid you'd say that.

She didn't want to call Zeke, didn't want to *have* to call him. Setting the issue aside, she asked, "Why don't you tell me some more of your story, Ezra?"

"Sure. Let's see, I left off at a real bad place as I recall," he mused, settling back in his chair and taking a long draw from his cup of milk. "I'd just passed out in the middle of my field. I found that out later, mind you, but at the time I thought I was a goner. I must have been out like a light for a good long spell. I still don't know how long, exactly, but I expect it was more than a few weeks. I woke up in a strange and awful sort of state, you see. I couldn't move much at all, but especially on my right side."

After another bite, he continued, "I wanted a drink, being powerful thirsty, and I knew I needed to get back into the field and tend to my chores, so I called out for my wife. She came directly, looking all scared and fussing over me like I was a little tot. I asked her for a drink, but all she did was start babbling in some nonsense talk. I asked again and again, the whole time just getting pretty bent out of shape. I wondered if the old bird didn't hear me. All she did was keep jabbering and jabbering and I couldn't make it out, so I grabbed a hold of her with my good arm. Boy, it must have been an iron grip because my gal just wailed and hollered until my oldest boy came a-running in. I was just about to tell him that his Ma done lost her mind when *he* started talking in the same nonsense."

Vivian gasped. He patted her hand and brought her back from the edge a bit.

"Now then," he said, still holding her hand to give her a beacon through the darkness. "I really knew I was in some kind of trouble when Ma *answered* Jake in the jabber talk, and he understood and answered back. It was the strangest thing, Miss Vivian, like watching them old clips of Hitler on the T.V. but without them English words at the bottom to tell you what they're talking about. I was just about to blow my top, thinking they was playing a trick on me. Boy, did I ever start cussing and fussing at them, I'm ashamed to say. I never did like using old sailor talk much, especially around my gal. But they just looked at me all sad and confused, like they didn't know what I was talking about. I was fighting and spitting mad by then, and I just got madder and madder until I jumped up and fell out of my bed."

"Oh, wow, Ezra," Vivian said. "How awful! What happened?"

"Well, by that time I reckon someone was able to run and get the doc who lived a ways up the road. That was back when a doc would make a house call. He came running in and they all helped get me back in bed, but dang it all if *he* wasn't talking that crazy nonsense too! That's when I started getting real scared. I tried to tell them I couldn't make out a thing they was saying, but I reckon they didn't understand me either. My missus just kept trying to pat my head and calm me down, like you would a little kid or a scared old dog. Well, after that, the damned doc stuck me in the ass with a big old needle and I was out like a light again before I knew it."

Ezra blushed. She took her turn patting his hand and offering reassurance.

"Well, anyhow," Ezra continued, "I woke up sometime later in a big old panic, remembering all the strange goings on. I didn't yell out, though, not right away. I just sat up, and that took some doing, let me tell you, and I reached around to grab the Almanac on my night table, the one I'd been reading on to plan for the harvest. Well, being a farmer, I followed my Almanac like a preacher follows his Word, so you can imagine my shock when I picked it up and couldn't make hide nor hair out of the gibberish writing. Boy, let me tell you, after that I hollered. Oh, did I holler and holler."

"Oh, Ezra...my God, what did you do?"

"I did the only thing I could do, Miss Vivian. I just laid there in my bed. I was pretty weak by then, so weak I couldn't sit up but a little bit at a time, and I sure couldn't walk none. I got to where I couldn't wash myself or feed myself, or do much anything else for myself," he added grimly. "I could scoot on over to the bedpan when my wife brought it, at least at first, but poor Evelyn had to tend to me just like I was a babe. I couldn't talk to anybody, or understand them either. Not until Darkmore showed up again. He could talk up a storm, but he wasn't the sort of company you really want to keep."

Vivian froze as the horror sunk in. "Ezra," she whispered. "What did he do to you?"

"Anything and everything he could to torment me, Miss Vivian. He used my broken body against me, he used my pride, he used my family...." He trailed off, but added at the end, "My Evelyn. He used her too."

"Why did he do it?"

"He wanted to break me, make me one of his. Oh, he tried all manner of promises first, to get me to give him my soul and reap the dead for him. But I held on, I fought the good fight, and I won."

"How?"

He paused, letting her take in his words and dab her eyes with the handkerchief he offered, and became very interested in her little pot of petunias sitting on her outdoor picnic table. "Child, I believe I done gave you enough frights for one evening. I'd best stop there. I hated to tell you, but it ain't bright and sunny, my story. Not for a good bit. It mostly gets darker."

"What?" she asked once she'd recovered, her voice hoarse with a mixture of pity, revulsion, and disbelief at the notion that he'd simply end his story then and there after all that buildup.

He held up a hand to stop her protest. "Like I told you, I hate to burden you with all this, but I promise it will help. The only reason I'm telling you all of this is to help, but you have to be patient and trust that I'll give you what you need when you need it."

Disbelief morphed into anger. "What do you mean you're stopping there tonight? You haven't given me anything! I need to know what to do to stop this grim reaper *now*, and you're telling me I have to wait for you to finish your little bedtime story?"

His friendly gaze hardened, eyes glowing with fury of his own. For the first time in their association, Vivian truly feared him.

"Oh, so you're going to get all high and mighty on me and start telling me my business? I've been doing this a lot longer than you and I know what I'm doing when it comes to protecting you and your sister. I—"

Vivian shot to her feet and sent sparks flying from her fingertips. Fear hadn't deserted her, but neither had stubbornness. Damned if she'd be bullied by anyone, dead or alive. "I'm not going to just sit back and wait for you to explain this in your own good time while I'm in danger! And what about Mae? If I'm gone, where does that leave her? Will the grim reaper come and claim her too?"

He remained seated, gaze still dark with anger, but also something that resembled grudging respect. She hoped so, at least. Otherwise, he'd probably burn her to bits. He nodded absently, as if coming to a decision.

"No," he began. "I don't reckon you'd be content to sit idle and wait, or to trust me either."

If he was waiting for her to disagree, he'd just have to keep right on waiting.

"There are things I can't tell you just yet, but I reckon there are few things you do need to know. First of all, I've been where you are, and I know what it's like to be scared out of your wits with newfangled powers you don't even understand. Do you believe me about that?"

The secrecy still rankled, but she nodded.

"And second of all, part of the way I beat him was working with the guardian spirits."

"Working with them how?"

He shrugged. "Nothing's for free in this old world, or the next. I had a lot of energy banked and I traded some for my freedom and staying on to help others instead of crossing over to the next place."

"Conscious energy, you mean? What you're using now to be...here, physically?"

He grinned. "Just so, Miss Vivian. We're all born with it, or start making it when we're still in the womb. Most living folks spend it up with the business of life. Near the end of a natural life, we slow down and store up more energy when we ain't using so much, or when something happens to stop normal life."

"So when you had your stroke..." Vivian paced, gathering her thoughts. "You stored up energy and Darkmore what, drained you?"

"He couldn't drain me while I was living. We ain't allowed that. But he did his best to speed up my trip to the great beyond."

"How?"

All of a sudden his hand shot out to grasp her wrist, and she froze as her mind filled with the dreadful sensations of paralyzing fear and complete helplessness. She couldn't move, couldn't speak, and couldn't scream in agony as some terrifying force tortured her essence, leaving her hollow and weak but painfully aware of life moving forward all around her. Bitter cold and darkness enveloped her, suffocating her soul with the knowledge that there would be no rest, no respite, no end.

Something slammed over her face, a pillow, choking off her fragile ties to life with the aid of one beloved above all others—a caregiver turned traitor.

And then, just as suddenly as they'd come, the images disappeared and she was once more herself.

When she came back to herself, Ezra appeared much older and worn with the weariness of ages, or perhaps she was just blinded by tears. He leveled her with his gaze and spoke in a low, hoarse whisper. "That's what Darkmore and his kind do, how they work. I would spare you from the same if I you'd let me. That's why I'm here."

"Oh God, I didn't...I had no idea..." *My Evelyn. He used her too.* Just like he'd used Vivian's darkness against Mae. She fought against the lump in her throat and continued. "What do you need me to do?"

He dropped his gaze. "You could maybe trust me a little."

She gave him a little nod. "I'll try, I promise. And I do appreciate every-thing you've done for me, Ezra. Honestly, I do." She thought of Zeke again and felt about two feet smaller. "I've been trying to find out some things too."

Because even if she could trust him, it just wasn't in her nature to sit and wait to be rescued—not by a man, angel, ghost, or otherwise. You did for yourself because no one else would—life lesson number one and the one she had carried with her since Mae and probably before.

Ezra stood, taking her hand and bringing her up to his level before speaking. "Oh child," he said with kindness and more than a little under-standing. "Always stuck between what you think you ought to do and what you want and need to do, ain't you?"

"How do you know all of that?" she asked. "I guess it's a rhetorical ques-tion. Zeke told me your kind could sometimes tell what the living think and feel."

"That's true, and it's a part of why I came to you." He smiled. "But have you not wondered if there's another reason why I understand? Maybe a higher purpose or plan?"

"I stopped believing a long time ago."

"Oh, that's all right!" He laughed, grabbing her and pulling her into a great big bear hug. His embrace filled her with the wonderful warmth and sense of well-being that emanated from the "good" spirits she'd met. "I believe in you, Miss Vivian. I surely do."

Releasing her, he chuckled and said, "Thank you kindly for the cobbler. You keep feeding me up like this, you might never be rid of me. And I thank you for listening to me rattle on. Now you keep right on doing what you're doing and we'll keep watch on our end. Between the three of us, we'll figure out what old Darkmore wants and how to get him moving on. And don't you fret 'bout nothing else. I'll be here as long as you need me."

But what about Zeke?

Since she didn't have the courage to actually ask Ezra about her other guardian, Vivian just nodded and turned to go inside, hoping that Ezra was right.

But then another thought occurred to her.

"Ezra?"

"Yes, ma'am?"

"You said you beat the reaper by working with the guardians," she began, turning slowly back to face him as dread gnawed at her gut. "And then you said that nothing's for free."

He didn't speak, and his expression remained unreadable.

Damn it, can't I get just one straight answer?

He didn't respond, so maybe he didn't make a habit of reading all of her thoughts. "So tell me, Ezra. What do I owe you?"

He gave her a wry smile. "I ain't saved you yet, child. As for what you may or may not owe me if and when I do, well...we'll get to all that."

He disappeared in a cloud of dust before she had the chance to protest.

In spite of her cryptic guardian spirit's sudden departure, Vivian took comfort in knowing he was nearby. She'd prefer having more answers, not to mention the means to protect herself and Mae, but it seemed she'd just have to bide her time and wait. That, or she could give the Internet another try, or hit a local New Age or occult bookstore.

Or she could ask Zeke.

She'd just have to swallow her pride and apologize first.

Well, that wasn't going to happen tonight. Better to get some much-needed rest and clear her head. Just before heading to bed, Vivian poked her head into Mae's room for a routine check.

The regular cadence of her breathing came as a relief, as did the peaceful aura filling the room. It made her wonder....

Taking a step inside, she whispered, "Ezra? Is that you?"

No one answered. Chiding herself, she turned to leave when she spotted a flash out of the corner of her eye. Spinning around, she scanned the room, her gaze coming to rest on Mae's sleeping figure. Though faint, wisps of light surrounded her sister, covering her body in a low cloud and swirling as if caught in some invisible vortex. Alarmed, she moved closer. The light swirled faster, spinning like a small tornado until a sudden shift sent it flying toward the corner of Mae's room just as she reached out, grazing the tail of it with her fingertips.

The sensation almost knocked her to the ground.

Her body seized, heat searing through her arm and filling her with a surge of raw power. An adrenaline surge and caffeine chaser mixed with

Prozac wouldn't even come close. How could something so intense feel so good? Scratch "good"—this was...indescribable. She shuddered as the intoxicating cocktail energy pulsed through her, followed by pulses of joy, contentment, and a sense of peace and comfort she'd never imagined, let alone experienced.

Wait, she had experienced it before, when she'd released the soul from the hospital.

And she'd only caught the tail end of that light.

Was Mae dying too? *Oh, please, dear God, no....*

When it was over, she stumbled back over to her sister's bed. Mae slumbered on, apparently unaffected by the tsunami that had just swirled above her. Her chest rose and fell with regular breaths. No rattling, no gasping, no jerks and struggles indicative of distress, only...peace. With trembling fingers, Vivian reached out and stroked her hair.

When something happens to stop normal life....

"My God, Mae, what was *that*?"

CHAPTER TWELVE

After another night of tossing and turning, Vivian finally decided to swallow her pride and reach out to Zeke. She'd been unusually restless in the wake of the mysterious energy surge, which had kept her wide-eyed and twitchy. Not sleeping had also left her plenty of time to replay their argument and realize her defensive overreaction stemmed from more her own guilt and shame than any accusation on his part.

God, the guardian showed up and rescued her from the cold pit of Hell, probably risking his own safety, and how did she repay him?

By yelling in his face.

She definitely owed him an apology, not to mention a thank you for sending Sue over to keep her company after their fight. Plus, he was her best bet for information since Ezra was hell-bent on taking his sweet time on doling it out. But more than that, she wanted to see him again. She only had one problem.

How was she supposed to get in touch with him?

Feeling ridiculous, but not knowing what else to do, she closed her eyes and said out loud, "Zeke? Are you there?"

She received no answer, so she tried again, a bit louder. "Zeke? It's Vivian. Can you hear me?"

Still no answer, and she felt a little anxious. Maybe he was still pissed off and didn't want to talk to her. Or was there some sort of formal call? It would be nice if these damned spirits would clue her in. "Ezekiel Nathaniel Longhollow, the mortal woman Vivian Margaret Bedford summons you from the spirit world. Hear me and heed my call, oh guardian!"

She startled enough to scream when she turned to find a pair of green eyes staring into her baby blues, eyebrows raised and a smile tugging at the corners of his lips.

"Nicely done, Vivian. If we ever institute a protocol for a summons, I think I'll suggest that one."

"Okay, smartass, I really need you spirit types to stop sneaking up on me. Didn't you hear me the first time?"

"Oh, I heard you loud and clear. I just wanted to make you sweat a little." He chuckled. "Besides, it was nice to hear my full name rolling off your tongue. Been checking up on me, have you?"

"Yes, I have," she said with defiance. "And if you want to be properly summoned, I'll have you know I *can* do it. I found a lot of information from the Internet at ghostvillage.com. I got all kinds of spells, charms, and warnings about evil spirits that can't be controlled. Maybe I should take the advice to heart when dealing with you."

"That's assuming I mean you harm," he said as he winked. "And I don't. And what's this about ghostvillage.com? I'll have to check the link out sometime myself, keep up with all the latest info and all. Now, what can I do for you?"

"You actually surf the net?" she asked, then remembered the reason she'd called him. "Oh, well, um, first I wanted to set things right between us." She lowered her gaze and held her breath. "I was a little defensive the other day."

She chanced a look up, and she saw him fighting not to smile.

"Yeah, okay, I got *really* defensive. You poked a sore spot and I got mad. I didn't mean to fly off the handle. I'm sorry, okay? I'll try to keep my temper in check from now on."

He regarded her, his face unreadable. The man must have been a great poker player in life. Her temper started rising again. What more did he want? Groveling? She was just about to voice some of her internal monologue when he placed one finger over her lips. "Shh," he whispered, then leaned down and pressed his warm lips to her cheek, brushing them softly over her skin. "Apology accepted."

Before she could find her voice to respond, Zeke stepped back, bowed his head, and took a deep breath before speaking. "I'm sorry too, for the record. I'll try to keep my temper in check as well. Oh, and we usually surf the Internet at night so we don't disturb the living. Sometimes we forget to close browsers or clear our histories, though, when we're done. Sorry, by the way. Now, is there anything else you need from me?"

After his tease of a kiss, she could think of a few things she would like from him. Blushing at the notion, she buried those less than appropriate thoughts deep in an unoccupied corner of her mind. Yes, he was attractive, and yes, she'd been deprived and lonely, but he was here as a protector and a...friend.

He's a ghost, for Christ's sake!

"Um, yeah, I would like to talk to you about some things, like you, and Darkmore, and this...situation. I want to know what I'm up against and how to fight it."

He heaved a heavy sigh and nodded. "I thought as much. Before we can understand why Darkmore is interested in you and Mae, I think I need to know a little more about your situation."

"Oh," she said. "Um, I thought we already covered all that."

"As I recall, we sort of got interrupted by your help last time we took up the subject."

God, I really don't want to have this conversation.

"Fine. What else do you want to know?"

"Vivian...."

"I told you already. Mom and Dad died. I got Mae. That's the situation."

"Why are you so angry?"

"I'm not." She turned away from him. "I just don't know what else you want me to say."

After a moment, he placed a gentle hand on her shoulder. "Has it always been hard for you?"

"Yes," she whispered, not meaning to answer out loud.

She held her breath and waited for more questions, more prodding, more of his unwelcome invasion of her life. He didn't speak, so she turned to look back at him. His gaze was soft, filled with understanding. Part of her wanted to fall into his gaze and bare her soul, but she'd closed and locked the door a long time ago. He'd have to work a lot harder to pry it from its hinges.

"May I meet your sister?"

Grateful to change the subject, she nodded in agreement. "Sure. She's awake. Follow me."

They walked down the hall and Vivian opened the door to Mae's room. She kept the lights low and the curtains drawn, since their mother swore that bright light agitated Mae. Vivian had done her best to recreate Mae's room from their parents' home. Her bed rested in the corner. The mattress sat high on top of the custom frame, making it easier for her caregivers to lift her in and out. A wooden rail encircled the mattress to keep Mae from rolling out and onto the floor. The wall space all around bore family photographs interspersed with posters, mostly of cartoon characters, kitties, and unicorns. Vivian had mounted a television on the wall facing Mae's headboard, which also displayed colorful cartoon characters. Mae's eyes were open at the moment and focused in the general direction of the television.

She led Zeke to her sister's bedside and cleared her throat. "This is my sister, Mae. Mae, meet Zeke Longhollow." Not quite sure what to do, she stepped back and made room so he could have a closer look.

He stood still for a while. When Vivian worked up the courage to look at him, he met her gaze and gestured to Mae, asking, "May I?"

"Um, sure. Go ahead."

He leaned over and placed his hand on Mae's forehead. The air surrounding him grew warmer, so she figured he was giving Mae the same comforting touch she'd received from Ezra. The gesture brought her to the verge of tears and she blinked and squeezed her eyes shut tight, hoping he wouldn't see.

As she turned to walk away, Zeke placed a warm palm on her shoulder. He gave her a gentle tug, bidding her to turn and face him. She resisted.

He tugged a little harder, so she turned toward him but kept her gaze on the floor. He lifted her chin and asked, "May I?"

When she nodded, he enfolded her in his arms. Warm waves of comfort and peace flowed from her guardian. The sensation reminded her of what she'd experienced the night before, only softer, more tender. She didn't even pull away when the tears came again. She doubted anything could have pulled her from his arms.

So he pulled her closer, tracing small patterns on her back and rocking her back and forth as she quietly sobbed. He smelled of a grassy meadow after a storm, his shoulders wide and his arms strong. No demands, no ridicule, no judgment, just...warmth.

He allowed her to drink her fill of his comfort. When she released him, she whispered, "Thank you."

"You're welcome. Now let's go see about some breakfast."

―――――

"Zeke?" she asked as they finished drying the dishes.

"Vivian?" he countered, inspiring her to thwack his fine ass with a dish towel. "Ow! That hurt!"

"Wuss," she teased, and they both dissolved into giggles. After she caught her breath, she asked, "Can you tell me about Darkmore now?"

"Yeah," he said, taking her cue and growing serious. "I still don't know everything about him. None of us do, not even Ezra. But we know some things that might help. I'll tell you what I can."

He seemed to be considering something, tilting his head a little to the left. *A musing spirit?* She stifled another chuckle and settled on a genuine smile. He smiled back, apparently having made up his mind. He held out his hand, and she accepted, gasping at the heat radiating from him.

"Oh, sorry," he said as the heat dissipated. "I still forget sometimes." Heat filled her cheeks when he ran his fingers over her ragged nails.

She wished she had nicer hands, but her old nervous habit returned roughly the first week she'd spent with Mae, and the constant scrubbing and cleaning didn't help.

She pulled her hand out of his grasp and shoved it and her other into the pockets of her jeans where they couldn't do any more damage, and where he couldn't see.

"So, between what you and Ezra told me, not to mention what I got from Darkmore," she said, shivering at the memory of the reaper's chill and his silken voice, "I'm a...a living soul broker, borrowing some of your powers and channeling conscious energy?"

He stared at her with that piercing gaze, but thankfully didn't try to take her hand again. "That's the gist of it. From what I understand it's rare, but it can and does happen from time to time, especially when the living person is close to death. You've experienced a good bit of loss recently, and your sister, well...."

His awkward slip tugged at her heartstrings. He didn't have to tiptoe around the issue. Anyone could see that Mae wasn't long for this world.

"But, if all it takes is being close to death, why aren't there more people like me? I mean, doctors, nurses, soldiers should be better candidates. What about people like Mae's caregivers, or nursing home staff? I mean, why me?"

He looked away then, and his reply was a low whisper. "It was my fault."

Gooseflesh erupted on her skin as a small ball of dread settled in the pit of her stomach. "What?"

He turned abruptly and started rummaging through her cabinets until he pulled out a small glass bowl. After filling it with water and testing the temperature, he placed it on the kitchen table and sat down, gesturing for her to join him. At a loss for what else to do, she pulled her hands out of her pockets and sat down next to him.

"May I?" he asked, reaching for her hands.

She shrank back, but he caught one wrist. His grip wasn't tight. She could get away if she chose, but he stroked the sensitive skin over her pulse and made soft sounds of reassurance. With the greatest gentleness, he ran his fingertips over her battered nails and placed her hand into the warm water before giving the same treatment to her other hand. The reverence and tender care made her eyes sting even as it unnerved her.

Then he cupped the bowl with both hands, now glowing with soft white light.

The stinging ache at her fingertips began to fade along with the redness. So awed was she by the sensations that she jumped a bit when he spoke again at last.

"You really should take better care of yourself. Such sensitive hands need attention, especially with all you do with them."

While grateful for the relief and reluctant to break the spell surrounding this unexpected intimate moment, she forced the issue at hand. "You said it was your fault."

"My soul was in play when you came to me, when you...touched me. The energy running through me, I think it opened a link between you and the spirit world. Maybe it's because you were in the crash and had a close call, or maybe there's something else about you that makes you more receptive, but I'm to blame for this," he said, drawing a small wisp of light from her index finger. A brief shock of heat ran through the finger in the beam's wake, taking with it the pain and redness.

"It's better," she said, awed.

"Yeah, figures you'd be a healer. Let's see if we can get the rest." He pulled beams of light from her fingertips, or did she release them? It didn't matter. By the time he'd finished, her hands were better. The nail beds remained ragged and ugly, but they didn't hurt anymore. Time would do the rest, if she let it.

"Wait, you said I'm a healer. But you did this," she said, staring at her fingers in wonder.

He shook his head. "No, it's your power. I just gave you a little boost to channel it."

Trying to unwind the knot of tangled thoughts rolling through her mind, she said, "So this power that I have, or borrowed, that's why Darkmore wants me? I don't understand. I mean, he can do what I do on his own, and much better than I can. I barely held onto that soul at the hospital, and I'm not even sure I sent her to the right place anyway."

"You don't think so?"

Something about his voice gave her pause. His gaze remained fixed on her hands, but it had turned dark and full of sorrow. The bitter tang of regret seeped from his flesh and made her take her hands from the bowl and grasp his.

"I'm not sorry," she said, willing him to meet her gaze. It wasn't just lip service. No matter what else had happened or what the woman had done, she didn't deserve to go with the reaper. "I'm not sorry I kept that soul from Darkmore, and I'm not sorry I came to you that night. God knows I'm not fit to be anyone's judge and jury."

She squeezed his hands and he tightened his grip, green eyes full of gratitude and pleading. But pleading for what? What did he need from her?

"God help me, I'm not sorry either," he whispered. "But I do swear I'll do everything in my power to help you stop him."

"Like what?"

He grabbed a towel and dried her hands, holding onto them a bit longer than necessary. Even without the heat and energy, his touch was warm and comforting. No demands, no pushing for something more intimate, just...there.

At last, he stood, gently pulling her from her seat. "Come on, let's go."

"Go where?"

"Outside," he said with a smile. "Until we know what Darkmore wants, you need protection. Might as well see what those hands of yours can really do."

————

"Again, see if you can hit that tree over there," Zeke said, pointing to her favorite maple.

Struggling for patience, not to mention breath, she wiped the sweat from her brow and said, "I've only managed one lame little lightning bolt so far, and it only went a few feet before fizzling out."

Zeke shrugged. "It's a start. You'll have to do better than that if you want to knock Darkmore out of his corporeal form."

She tried again, hoping her frustration with her guardian, who made it look so easy, would help her focus her powers. She got a few sparks to fly, but these didn't go any farther. And the effort left her weak-kneed and queasy.

"Screw it."

She plopped down on the ground and waited for Zeke to yell at her to get up off her ass and go another nine rounds. Instead, he sat down next to her and nudged her with his shoulder. "Tired?"

"Yeah."

"You need a boost. Here, let's try something else." He grabbed her hand and let loose a wave of white-hot light. She jerked, but he held firm. "Easy, don't fight it. Let it flow into you."

"It burns!"

"Just hold on a little longer."

"Fine," she said through gritted teeth. She looked away, hoping it would help if she didn't see the glow against her skin. "Is this what it feels like when you take in energy? Does it hurt?"

"No, not after the first time. But you're still alive, so I'm guessing that's why you're having issues. You've got real flesh and blood. I don't. And I've only ever transferred energy from the dead or dying when I've helped them cross. Still hurting?"

"Not as bad," she said, risking a look at their joined hands. "So you take energy from the dead and use it to send them to the great beyond?"

"Some of it."

God, this cryptic bullshit was getting old. "Okay, look, I get that some of this stuff is supposed to be top secret, but I'm getting sick of these half answers and subject changes. Give it to me straight or don't bother."

"Fine," he said, letting go of her hand and flopping back. He'd gone a little...dusty, and his skin was pale. His gaze, sharp as ever, caught hers and he gave her a rueful smile. "Don't worry. I'll recover. How do you feel?"

"Like I've had about ten energy drinks and a ton of caffeine, but I'm guessing I've just drained a good bit of *your* energy."

"You have. It takes a lot of energy to maintain corporeal form, and it takes even more to transfer a soul. We use what the soul can give us and then keep the rest."

Vivian stood, restless. Concentrating on the tree, she extended her hand and shot a burst of light that made it about halfway to the target and left a trail of smoke in its wake.

"Better. Try again."

She fired again and nearly sliced one branch clean off.

"Damn! I see why you want to hold onto this stuff. It's amazing!"

Zeke snorted. "Well, don't go too crazy. You'll use up my daily ration."

That gave her pause. "Ration? What does that mean? You have to give up the energy you take?"

"It's part of the deal. I take the energy and give it to Ezra, and he gives me my share." She must have given him a look because he furrowed his brows and hastily added, "It's not like it sounds. I mean, he takes most of the energy and uses it to help other souls and for the greater good."

She sent another blast, this one burning a small hole in the middle of another branch. "Wow, you didn't just swallow the Kool-Aid, you drank the whole pitcher."

The look he gave her could've burned a hole right through her heart, but he didn't deny it. She took another shot and made a clean, precise cut through the tree limb that sent it crashing to the ground. "Ezra told me Darkmore drains the energy out of the dead and dying, but from where I'm standing, seems like he isn't much better. You said you volunteered to work for him, to help me, but let me ask you something. Did he tell you about the fine print before or after?"

Zeke stood and started pacing, running a hand through his hair while he presumably gathered his thoughts. "Look, you have to understand, there's a bit of an energy crisis going on at the moment, and not just here on Earth. Exponential population growth, lots of lives in the balance, lots of souls in the queue or waiting to cross. Nice shot, by the way. Try it on me."

"Thanks, but first let's get back to this energy crisis. If each soul gives enough to cross with energy left over, why wouldn't there be enough?"

Zeke shook his head. "Probably the same as here on Earth. We've been using too much and not efficiently."

"Or maybe you guardians and reapers are getting greedy?"

"Maybe," he muttered.

No, definitely. It would explain a lot about Ezra's evasiveness and perhaps had something to do with why Ezra got recruited in the first place. Bracing herself, she sent a small, concentrated burst of light toward Zeke, nicking his right shoulder and sending dust flying. He staggered back, clutching his arm until it disappeared in a puff of smoke.

"God, I'm sorry," she yelped, rushing toward him and clutching what was left of his body against her.

"No," he said, voice hoarse but obviously pleased. "That was good. Aim that at the heart and you'd disable a corporeal reaper long enough to run away. Even if he doesn't build another body, he won't have enough energy to follow you fast. Hold on, let me just...."

He paled, straining under the effort of making his arm reappear in a swirl of debris.

"Take some of your energy back." She clung to him tighter, willing the light to flow back into him. "I know you said it was harder, but why not just take some energy from the living as an alternative?"

"I can't. The dead take from the dead and dying, not the living. The living use most of their energy, anyway. We wouldn't be allowed to drain them even if we were could. Ezra says there's a better way, but he hasn't told me how to do it yet."

"Shocking," she said dryly.

He didn't argue, but gripped her shoulder with his newly formed hand and leaned down, his gaze intense. "Two can play at that game, and since he isn't telling you everything, or me," the last part was muttered with a sharp note of contempt, "I suggest we keep this between the two of us. I'll keep pressing him for more information, and you keep practicing your skills and finding out what else you can do."

"Fair enough. But what about Darkmore? Do you suppose he has the same energy issues as you guardians do? Is that why all of those souls were trying to get out of his realm?"

"I think so. I'll keep working to find out. I've got to go now before I fall apart. When do you have help with Mae next?"

She cringed. "Two days from now, otherwise I'll have to pay extra."

"Then I'll see you in two days. Keep practicing. And Vivian?"

"Yeah?"

Before disappearing, he bent and placed a soft, reverent kiss on her hand. "Take care of yourself."

CHAPTER THIRTEEN

She wasn't surprised when Zeke materialized in her kitchen two days later. She also wasn't surprised that Ezra *hadn't* shown up, though it still stung. So much for trust.

Fortunately, the reaper hadn't shown up either. In spite of her practice sessions, she didn't think she had the skills to defend herself, and she needed more energy.

God, what if she had to drain Zeke again?

"So, what's on the agenda?" she asked, skipping the hey-how-are-you-doings and getting down to business.

"I've been...thinking, and I may know why Darkmore is so interested in you. How about we take a little walk? I can pack a picnic lunch if you like and we can go to Percy Warner."

"Why can't you just tell me here and now?"

"It may be a little uncomfortable and things could get messy," he answered, staring pointedly at the spot where a new lamp stood in place of the one he'd zapped.

Point taken. She nodded. "Sure, that would be nice. Let me get changed and check on Mae again. The caregiver should be here in about a half an hour. Do you want to, um, meet me there, or ride with me, or...." She trailed off, remembering the night she first encountered Zeke in his fragile, mortal form.

He smiled. "Go ahead and get changed. I'll drive us. Safely."

———

The drive west of the city was tranquil, though Vivian had to remind Zeke to stick with the speed limit. Belle Meade cops generally didn't have much to do except issue citations for speeding, loitering, or walking on the boulevard without reflective clothing. And being dead, she doubted he could produce a valid driver's license.

They walked along the paved path, trying as best they could to keep to the shade as the midday heat started to beat down on the land. The park was one of her favorites, hilly and high with tall trees skirted by ferns and a moss-covered low wall of stone that ran intermittently along one side of the paved path. The chatter of squirrels and the rapid-fire thunks of woodpeckers echoed down from tall trees along with harsh cries from chickadees and mockingbirds. Though it was too early in the day to spot deer, plenty of chipmunks scampered through the underbrush.

Zeke seemed to be taking in the beauty of their surroundings as well. He must have known this place well in life. When the silence became a little uncomfortable, she decided to break it.

"So, what can you tell me about Darkmore and what he wants with me and Mae?"

Zeke offered a wry smile, but did not turn to face her yet. "The last time we started this conversation, it didn't end so well."

"Yeah, well, I promised to try to keep my temper in check and remember you're here to help," she said, trying to hide her exasperation. Why did he keep putting her off? "And I'll do my best to keep that promise. So, I take it from what you said earlier that Darkmore was able to get to me because I was in a really dark place to begin with."

"That's my theory, yes." He schooled his features to stillness.

"Well, I think you're right," she continued, keeping her eyes fixed on her worn tennis shoes.

After a brief silence, she felt his warm hand take hers. He then spoke with a soft tenderness. "Why don't we have a seat on the blanket and eat our lunch while we talk, if you're ready?"

She nodded and they walked hand in hand to a lovely clearing near the end of the trail. She closed her eyes and breathed in the scent of the land, grass, trees, flowers, and earth. Opening her eyes, she let the utter beauty of this place fill her senses, the sounds of birds and wind meet her ears, the warmth of the day caress her skin. She focused on a cluster of buttercups and watched two bees perform feats of aerial acrobatics as they hopped from one flower to the next to gather nectar from the brilliant yellow blooms. Her fascination with such sights had not diminished over the years.

She turned to find her tall spirit smiling down at her. "You're a real nature girl."

"I guess I am. Always have been. It's peaceful. Places like this, they are what I always imagined Heaven must be like when I was smaller, when I believed in Heaven."

"Did you ever pray?"

"Well, yeah, I did sometimes. It gave me some comfort for a while. Did you, or do you?" she asked.

"I did from time to time when I was alive. Most people pray for the wrong things, you know. I did too. They want riches, but not the will and the means to earn it, or the drive. They want to be loved, but not the sacrifice and heartache that comes with caring for someone else more than themselves. They want happiness, but don't want to work to bring self-fulfillment and purpose. Fame without substance. Long life without meaning. To have all of their problems just disappear without any effort. All the wrong things."

With lost life comes great wisdom, she thought. "I guess it's just human nature, and nothing's ever going to change that."

"What about you, Vivian? What would you pray for?"

She gave him a teasing smile. "I thought you could hear the desperate voices of the masses?"

"I'm serious. What is it you would ask for in your prayers?" Apparently, he wasn't one to let things go.

"I told you, I gave up on praying and wishing a long time ago. Besides, 'if wishes were horses, beggars would ride,' according to my dearly departed mother, and no finer wisdom was ever doled out. Unless, of course, you count my other favorite saying."

"Which is?" he asked with a touch of the sardonic.

"Want in one hand, shit in the other and see which fills up faster."

He burst out laughing, a deep, reverberating sound as warm as his touch. "I'm not so sure that's true, but it feels that way some days. That was pretty good."

"Oh, I've got a million of them. My grandmother loved to tell us if we burned our asses, we still had to sit on them." She laughed.

"I'm sure you have loads of homespun wisdom. In fact, I'd be willing to bet it's a family trait, at least for the women. But for the sake of argument, what do you long for, dream of, desire in your heart of hearts?"

She sighed. "Peace, quiet, and an end to feeling alone. Is that so selfish?"

"Not at all. Those are very natural things for any human to want. What would it take to make that happen, do you suppose?"

"I don't know," she muttered.

"Of course you do."

He said it so softly that it took a moment for his words to sink in. "What are you talking about?"

"You know exactly what I'm talking about, Vivian. It's why the reaper came calling."

Dread knotted her stomach and she started to back away, but he caught her by the wrists and yanked her hard until she met his gaze, now devoid of warmth and compassion. Instead, he wore and expression of cold calculation, as though he might reach down into the darkest corner of her soul for the answers he sought.

"No," she said, knives of guilt and shame stabbing into her gut. She tried to wrench her arms free from his grip but he held tight, the heat of his grasp threatening to consume her.

"Answer me, Vivian. What would it take to set you free?"

She hesitated, and he grabbed her by the chin. "Quicker than that! Don't think, just answer. Now!"

"Mae gone! Dead and gone!" she cried out, then wrenched herself from his grip and stumbled away.

Walking away a few paces, she collapsed on the ground and let the pent-up anger, guilt, and sadness wash over her as hot tears flowed from her eyes. She shook, reliving the pain of that horrible night with Mae and began to wail. Vivian sensed his warmth before his arms enfolded her, lifting her and carrying her back to their blanket, just as he'd done on that dreadful night in the bitter cold. Settling her on his lap, he cradled her as his peace washed over her. She stayed in his arms for a long time before breaking the blessed silence.

"Darkmore knew how I felt. He came to me that night and was able to take me because I was full of hate, and I was so upset and tried to hit her and wanted her to go, and I...." She tried, but she couldn't finish.

"Shh," he whispered, stroking her cheek. "Shh. I know, Vivian. I know." She put her head back down on his chest and tried to relax. She felt a rumble when next he spoke. "I'm sorry I had to do that to you. I would not have had you relive that awful memory, but it was the only way."

"The only way?"

"The only way to fight the darkness is to acknowledge it and face it head on."

"Can he make me do bad things? Can he make me feel all of those awful, hateful things? All the rage?"

"I'm not sure he can make you feel anything you don't already, but he can make things happen to push you over the edge. He's driven by pain and suffering. He can't get enough of it. It's his sustenance. I think he chooses those who have the greatest capacity for suffering and tries to feed that suffering as much as he can. He wants to claim them as his own, but I think he has to make them want to be claimed."

"How can that be?" she asked. "All I wanted was to get out of there."

"You weren't there for very long. I don't know exactly how he does it, but maybe he makes things here in this realm so bad that you long for nothing other than darkness. Or maybe he makes you feel as though darkness is all you deserve."

Then she remembered, and a wave of guilt hit her like a punch in the gut. "Wait, that's why he...when I went to the hospital the other day and set that soul free before I knew...."

"She'd been stuck in a coma, trapped and suffering. Maybe that was punishment enough for whatever she'd done in life." He didn't press for details of the soul's sins, and she really didn't want to share the magnitude and risk his condemnation.

"Maybe...I don't know...." That wasn't true, though. She'd thought long and hard for days, weighing the sins of one soul against her own, the taking of a life against her near miss with Mae, how close she'd come. "Who am I to say? What does that make me?"

His lips formed something that resembled a smile, but it didn't reach his eyes. "It makes you human."

"Human frailty is one thing, but to even consider taking a life. She took her own life, and...someone else's too. You know, I thought about it. Killing myself."

"I know. But you didn't."

"Came close, but I couldn't do it. I needed to be there for Mae, and, well, I guess I'm maybe just too stubborn to give up."

He smiled for real then. "That's what made you strong enough to face Darkmore, strong enough to save the drunk driver, the soul of a killer, and... me. You're strong enough to look at the ugliness and see the pain beneath, and strong enough to forgive everyone but—"

"I barely survived and I was too scared to look away. If I hadn't been able to let go or run away...Oh God, if I didn't hit rock bottom on that night, what's left?"

He spoke, his voice just above a whisper. "You don't want to know. I hope you never have to know."

She wanted to ask him what he meant, but he rose and walked toward the picnic basket before she had the chance. "I don't think I'd be a very good guardian if I didn't feed you."

He handed her a sandwich and a thermos filled with sweet tea. She took a long draw and was delighted by the taste of mint and the hint of lemon. Apparently, Zeke had been poking around her herb garden. She only nibbled on her lunch, not having much of an appetite. She did appreciate his efforts to nourish her body as he had her mind and her heart. For his part, Zeke, much like Ezra, enjoyed his food and drink with the zeal of a man long deprived. She didn't blame him, she supposed. He hadn't been among the departed as long, but she believed she would ache for good food and drink if she walked in his shoes.

He quirked his brow at her. "Penny for your thoughts."

"I was just thinking about what it must be like for you, being here, but not really belonging here anymore—" She clapped her hand over her mouth. After a moment, she started again. "I'm so sorry, I didn't mean it like that. I just, um, I mean, I wondered if it's hard for you to be here with me and reminded of the life you just lost. Your family—"

The pained look that crossed his features stopped her again, and he looked away. When he looked back, his green eyes were intense and focused. She also saw the tenderness there, and traces of sorrow. He scooted closer to her and invited her to lean on him. Between his radiating warmth and her deep longing for someone to lean on, she obliged.

"I'm sorry, Zeke. I didn't mean to bring up things that hurt you," she said.

"Shh," he whispered. "No need to be sorry."

"If you need someone to lean on...." she began, half-convinced her foot would soon find its way into her too-often open mouth. "I mean, I don't know if guardians *need* much of anything, but I guess I just want you to know this works both ways. I mean...." She stammered, irritated with her inability to get find the right words. Finally, she sat up to face him again. "It should work both ways. I'm not just going to take and not give, even if you are supposed to comfort and protect me, and—"

He cupped his large hand over her mouth, grinning as her eyes widened in surprise and indignation. "First off, you *are* giving, whether you realize it or not. Second, you really need to learn when to shut up. You know that, right?" He held firm as she struggled.

Then, with only a moment's hesitation, he replaced his hand with his lips.

He teased her mouth with gentle, tentative brushes, and then probed more firmly as she relaxed. She moved her hands to his shoulders, then to his neck as she deepened the kiss, running her fingers through his thick hair and groaning with a strange mixture of immense satisfaction and growing hunger.

She stroked his lower lip with her tongue, and he responded to the invitation by opening his mouth to let her explore further. Her last coherent thought before sensation took over was to wonder if all spirits tasted this sumptuous, like the soft layer of crème brulee beneath a thick crust of sugar. Then she lost herself in his warmth, his strength, and his incredible mouth. It had been a while since she'd been kissed, and she had never, ever been kissed like this, or poured so much passion into a kiss as she did now.

They kissed for a long, long time, and she found herself on her back, blanket under her and Zeke cradling her from above. It pleased her to find his eyes closed when she peeked up at him, and she felt even more pleased to hear small groans of satisfaction rumbling from his chest. He stopped more abruptly than she expected, or liked for that matter, and regarded her as his fingers fanned her hair out along the blanket.

"If this is your way of changing the subject," she said, panting, "then I'd say you're pretty damned good at the art of conversation."

He stared back at her, and his silence became a little disconcerting, at least to Vivian. "I'd like to do that again, Vivian Bedford," he said. "I want that more than I've wanted anything for a very long time. I'd like to do a few other things. too."

So why don't you? She sighed, wondering what sort of hang-ups could stop a man, even a dead man, in the midst of passion.

Just my luck to get a would-be ghost lover with issues.

"I detect a 'but' coming up next, right?" She also wondered if she'd put her foot in her mouth again. What if he couldn't go further? His body wasn't exactly like a living man's.

He sighed as he brushed her cheek. "Not for the reasons you're probably thinking," he said with a wicked smile, bringing her hand between his legs, obviously delighted with her wide-eyed response. "I am capable, I assure you. At least, I feel fully capable."

"Well then, what's the issue? Is it against the rules or something?"

He quirked his head, then shook it. "You know, I didn't even think about it. It might be. It probably is. I mean, this hasn't exactly come up in my conversations with the others."

"So," she said as she gave him a sly smile, hoping her caresses would change his mind as she returned one hand to his chest and the other further south. "They say it's easier to ask for forgiveness than permission, you know?"

"Vivian, I'm supposed to protect you, not take advantage of you when you're hurting," he said, his voice deeper and gaze intense, earnest. "I may be a spirit, but I do have my limits, especially in this flesh."

"I'm counting on that," she whispered, placing light kisses along his jaw line, his neck, his lips. "What if I need this for my comfort? What if I need you? Would you deny me?"

He responded with another deep kiss, his hands moving over her belly and up to caress her breasts. She felt more heat, this time from within, and writhed in rhythm with the strokes of his tongue. Lost in sensation, she barely registered a sound from the trail above.

"Zeke?" A woman's voice spoke, not exactly a shriek, but pretty damned close. The sound was one of the most pitiable Vivian had ever heard, and her blood ran cold with fear.

CHAPTER FOURTEEN

"Is that you, Ezekiel? But...but it can't be you, can it?"

Quicker than humanly possible, Zeke wrapped himself fully around Vivian and she almost screamed as his searing heat intensified. The heat pulled her, spinning at an unnatural and painful speed down into an abyss. Blinding light streamed all around them in the spinning vortex. She couldn't breathe, couldn't think, and couldn't feel anything other than terror.

All that kept her anchored was the feeling of Zeke, his voice telling her with soothing tones to hold on, it would be done soon, just hold on. He was right. The pulling and spinning sensations ended, leaving her dizzy and disoriented, as she might be after getting off a high-speed, tortuous roller coaster.

His arms held her close, caressing her back and soothing her. She also knew on some primal level that he held her for his own comfort as well, his grip tight, his breath uneven, and his body trembling slightly. She moved her head, wanting to look at him and to see where he'd taken her, but he embraced her more tightly and pressed her head into the crook of his neck. To her amazement, she felt and tasted the damp saltiness of his tears.

"Don't look, Vivian! You aren't supposed to see this place, not until you cross over. I didn't know where else to go. Just hold on and keep your eyes shut until I can get us back. I have to wait," he muttered in despair. "I have to wait until it's safe, until she's gone...."

"Zeke," Vivian whispered. "Zeke, honey, it's okay. It's okay. I won't look, I promise. Who was she? She knew you. Is this bad? Are you in trouble?"

The only answer she received was his gasping breath.

"Zeke, you're scaring me. Tell me what's happening!"

He still didn't answer, and before she could protest a wave of nausea swept through her as she entered the vortex with him again. The bright light crept through her closed lids and her stomach dropped. A bit better prepared, she held onto her spirit guide with all of her might until they stopped.

"Is it safe? Can I open my eyes now?"

"Yes," he said, releasing her and stepping away.

When she opened her eyes, she found they'd landed back in the parking lot of the park, close to her car. But...it was full dark now. Vivian swore they'd only been gone for a few minutes, but instead of being mid-afternoon it was clearly well after nightfall.

"Oh my God, Zeke, what just happened?" One look at his aching form pushed her shock and fear aside, replacing it with worry over her guardian. She took a few deep breaths and steadied her mind and body. She moved toward him and took his hand, bringing him back to her. "Are you all right?"

"No," he answered, and she found a bit of strength in his honesty.

"You don't have to tell me about it right now," she said, bringing his hand to her lips. "But I do think we should go back home. I mean, to my home." She asked for the keys and together they drove off into the dark of night.

———

After dropping her off at her doorstep, Zeke disappeared without a word. She had endured a pretty long car ride in strained silence, leaving her with nothing but confusion and worry since he departed. She guessed that the woman from the park had known him well in life. What if she had been his girlfriend, or his wife?

Oh God, she saw us kissing!

She wasn't sure what or how to feel about the possibility, but refused to be sorry for what happened. She was sorry for the woman, and she was sorry she couldn't think of anything to help Zeke, though. He was hurting badly, and she'd been responsible for part of his pain. He'd come back from the grave to help her, and had to come back to close to where he'd once lived on account of her troubles. She wanted to call him to her, wanted that with every fiber of her being, her heart, and her body.

She just wasn't sure if she should.

She settled on busying herself with her nightly ritual. Mae had been fed, though the caregiver appeared none too thrilled with her late arrival home and made sure Vivian knew how she felt. Instead of becoming irritated, Vivian slipped her an extra twenty-five dollars and thanked her for her trouble. It wasn't bath night, but she decided to indulge her sister with a soak in lavender bubbles complete with a few lullabies. She massaged Mae's scalp between strokes with the hairbrush, speaking to her in low tones as she worked.

"Hey Mae-belle," she said. "I'm sorry about the other night, okay? I know you can't help how things are, and I should never have yelled at you and...roughed you up like I did." She didn't even try to stop the tears when they began to flow.

"We're all we've got now," she continued. "Well, unless you count our guardians. And you know what? I do count them. But I guess I just wanted to let you know I'm going to take care of you no matter what. I'm not going to let anything bad happen to you, I promise."

She'd been told time and again that Mae's reactions to stimuli were most likely involuntary. The doctors meant well, she was sure, not wanting to give them false hope. It didn't work for her mother, though. She happily believed that Mae heard her every word and felt her love and devotion. The rational part of Vivian believed the doctors. It was during quiet times like these, though, that she hoped against hope that her message had somehow gotten through. The heavy weight of guilt eased when she said the words aloud.

Perhaps that was enough.

After leaving her slumbering sister, she turned on the radio and stepped outside onto the deck. The thick, warm summer air of the dark night comforted her, and she hoped it would clear her head. She closed her eyes and let Patsy Cline carry her away as they went out walking after midnight, searching for a lover, pining after him on a warm country night.

When she opened her eyes, she saw him standing in the backyard, wrapped in the blanket they had shared during their picnic. With sure and steady steps, she walked toward him, took his hand, and led him back into the house. She closed the back door, dimmed the lights, and unwrapped him. Letting the blanket fall to the floor, she reached out and embraced him, holding him close as they swayed to the music. He opened himself to her scrutiny, and in his face and bleary gaze she found the rawness of sorrow, guilt, and beneath it a soul-deep longing.

Moving closer, she caressed his cheek, her face coming closer and closer, looking in his eyes all the while to ask permission. She met no resistance when her lips found his. She held him through the rest of the song, swaying to the music and gracing his lips with gentle kisses from time to time, then took his hand and led him to her room.

He hesitated at the threshold, and she looked back at him and watched his beautiful green eyes flicker with uncertainty.

She moved back to him and said, "Zeke, I want you to come and lie down with me. We don't have to do anything else, unless you want to."

He still seemed at a loss, so she tugged his hand a little harder and whispered, "Please."

He acquiesced, following her to the bed and reclining beside her. She rolled to face him, reaching out to stroke his face and his hair. He sighed. "I'm sorry," he said quietly. "I thought it would help, taking you to the park to talk. I should have known better than to risk going out in the open. I didn't think I'd see her again, my w-wife...I didn't th-think."

Wife.

She'd known, of course, from the obituary. He'd been married. Had a son. But knowing something and being confronted with it were two very different things. Especially given the anguish this confrontation had clearly caused her guardian. "You couldn't have known, right?"

He grimaced, but nodded after a moment.

"You can't go back to her and tell her you're...around?"

"No," he whispered. "That's not allowed. We normally get assigned somewhere else, or come back to where we once lived long after any connections are gone."

The full impact of his sacrifice hit her then. He'd endured all of the reminders of his life, including nearby loved ones, in order to protect her. Fighting the tightness in her throat, she said, "If it makes you feel any better, it did help. I'm just sorry it hurt you and...the woman who saw us." She couldn't bring herself to say "wife," but she ached to ease him none-theless, and to take comfort from him in turn.

"It does make me feel a little better. You make me feel better," he said, leaning in to rest his forehead on hers, battling his demons and himself. She stayed still, not forcing, just being there with him, for him.

He breathed deeply and stayed still for a moment, then groaned softly as he surrendered. His lips found hers once more, moving softly at first, then with more fervor as mutual hunger pulled at them both. He stopped long enough to remove both his shirt and hers, taking a moment to let his gaze roam over her body. She fought self-consciousness and allowed him to look his fill. Tentatively, she reached out to caress his chest, reveling in his response to her touch and in his peace-giving warmth. She anticipated much more heat, but checked her impatience.

This decision was his, as she had promised.

"Vivian," he whispered, moving his hands over her shoulders, down her arms, across her neck, down her sides, and over her belly. His hands roamed everywhere, except where she wanted them most. "Are you sure you want this? I don't want to push you, and I don't know what the consequences may be. I can't promise you anything beyond the time we're granted by powers that I don't even understand."

She considered, and decided she'd been denied and had denied herself one too many times.

"I want this, and I want you. No one knows how much time they have together. Believe me, I know. If I've learned anything from what life has thrown at me, it's that. But I do want to be with you tonight, tomorrow, as long as you're here."

He smiled at her, his gaze full of tenderness that soon clouded with uncertainty. "Even though you don't know who I was before, what I've done. I told you I wasn't a saint. I—"

"You can tell me later, or not. I don't care, and I certainly don't have the right to judge you or anyone else. I'm no saint myself."

He hesitated again, his desire to bare his soul apparently in conflict with his desire to satisfy other, more pressing needs. "I swear I will do everything in my power to keep you safe, and to stay with you as long as I am able. I *can* promise you I'll be here as long as you need me."

"Then that will have to be enough," she said, and kissed him again.

He kissed her back and continued to tease her body with light caresses, too light and not at all where she wanted and needed them most. She shifted, aching, seeking, yet he seemed determined to keep a slow and steady pace.

She moaned her frustration, and he met her with a deep and penetrating kiss. Much to her consternation, though, he stilled his hands. Deciding to give him a taste of his own medicine, she stroked his chest while carefully avoiding his smaller, masculine nipples. She moved one trembling hand down his abdomen, along the hollow of his hip. Though he lifted one leg in invitation, she settled on stroking his thighs.

He groaned. Neither granted the other mercy or quarter.

Finally, he broke the silence. "Will you undress for me?"

She gave him a broad smile filled with satisfaction, and another kiss, then stood and removed her simple white bra and slid off her blue jeans. Clad only in her panties, she wished she had something nicer to offer him. One look into her lover's eyes stopped the thought, and she discarded them and joined him in her bed.

"Touch me," she whispered, and he complied, eliciting a sharp intake of breath from her as his fingertips found her breasts. She wasn't sure how much came from his nature and how much came from her desire, but his fiery touch balanced on the razor's edge between pleasure and pain and left her aching for more.

He continued his soft caresses, leaning her back and replacing one hand with his tongue, kneading, stroking, and leaving her breathless and aching for more. He returned to her lips from time to time and let her body calm, only to begin his assault anew until her breath became shallow and she started to rock. He hummed in appreciation, and moved one hand down to part her and stroke her as she writhed.

"Zeke," she panted. "Zeke...more, please."

"Patience," he said, his voice husky. "Let me enjoy you for a while."

And he continued to touch and taste, setting a steady rhythm just shy of fast enough.

"Beautiful woman." He sighed as he drank in the sight of her quivering body, moved back up to kiss her mouth again and again.

"You've seen me naked before," she gasped, finding it increasingly difficult to think, let alone speak.

"Yes, but you weren't awake for me to tell you then. This is better," he whispered, stroking her again as she closed her eyes and furrowed her brow.

"Responsive..." he said with a kiss for one breast. "Alert...." She bit her lip and looked up at him with a silent plea, and then he drew her nipple into his warm mouth. "And open," he said against her sensitive skin as she opened her legs wider in invitation.

She let him tease and explore her for a while, and then gently pushed him away. He quirked a brow, a gesture that she had become quite fond of, and asked, "Is something wrong?"

"Nothing at all. It's just your turn now." She smiled, pushing again to put him on his back. It was his turn to gasp and moan as she caressed him with her hands and the tip of her tongue. She continued to tease, grudgingly impressed that he had yet to ask for more. After a while she was no longer able to wait. She took him fully into her mouth and got a strangled cry for her trouble.

As she continued to stroke and caress him with her tongue, he moved his hands to her head. Before she had the chance to freeze and brace for his grip, he pushed her hair away from her face and whispered, "Let me look at you while you love me." And she did.

She moved over him, meeting his gaze with a surge of warmth and confidence. His eyes shone with desire, but also with a tenderness that caused the high walls around her heart and soul to collapse.

"Take me inside you," he whispered, and she took him in her hand and guided him to her, pausing briefly to tease them both before she took him fully into her, stifling a cry of shock and pleasure as he filled her.

"Let go," he told her. "Don't hide anything from me."

They moved together, trying a few different rhythms and adjusting the angle and depth as they learned one another. Vivian found it most comforting. In spite of his otherness, these tender explorations remained very human. She moaned as one stroke from a shallow angle massaged her inside and out in all the right places. Zeke allowed her to lead as she found a pace that brought her closer to the edge, then joined her with deeper thrusts that caused her breathing to quicken and her eyes to fly open.

"Zeke! Oh God, oh—"

"Keep going," he gasped. He was close too. "Come for me, Vivian."

A few more strokes, and she flew over the edge, sobbing in the wake of a powerful release that coursed through her in waves. He soon followed, and the heat radiating from his body filled her with white-hot pleasure that bordered on pain. She opened her eyes to watch him and the brilliant light pouring out from his pores, his open mouth, and his eyes when they opened to meet hers. Pulling her close, he kissed her and filled her with his light in their union, not just a communion of the flesh, but of their very souls.

It left her spent, and for the first time in longer than she could recall, content. She made a valiant effort to hold onto consciousness while still joined with her lover, who held onto her so tightly his embrace threatened to suffocate her. After a time, he settled on stroking her hair and back, and she embraced him with trembling arms and wished she had words for all she felt. He placed soft kisses on her forehead, then on her eyes, her cheeks, and her lips when she lifted her face to meet his gaze.

She struggled to speak, but he stilled her with more kisses. "It's okay. I know," he said. "I feel it too."

When her eyelids grew heavy, Zeke separated them and moved her to her side. Enfolding her with his arms again, he whispered, "Rest, love. I'll stay with you, I promise."

"All night?" she murmured as she drifted toward oblivion.

"I'll hold you all night if that's what you want."

"And tomorrow?"

"I have to go back during the day, for a while, but I'll be here as soon as I can. Sleep now," Zeke said.

CHAPTER FIFTEEN

She woke with the lingering scent of Zeke all around her. Cedar and moss, the fresh notes of summer rain and rich earth, a hint of pine, and something else, deep and dark, something inherently masculine and protective filled her as she breathed him in. She closed her eyes once more and lost herself in the comforting smell, the memory of his arms enfolding her, the sound of his voice, etching the rare and wonderful experience into her memory and heart.

It was almost as good as waking up with him, though she still wished he could have stayed.

She opened one eye and peered at the alarm clock on her nightstand. It read 7:04 a.m. Mae should be awake soon. Listening to catch any groans of consciousness from her sister, she first heard the soft drone of the air conditioner fan running outside of her bedroom window. Beyond that, birdsong greeted her ears. The thrumming of a woodpecker came next. They liked the patch of woods that bordered her backyard, harvesting a bounty of squirming insects that filled the dead trees peppered in the strip of former farmland.

Funny, she hadn't noticed them in some time.

Closing her eyes, she concentrated on the sounds, tuning into a repetitive and grating noise above her. Did she have mice? She focused her attention and thought she heard squeaking, but decided it was just her imagination. Better find something else to focus on before she convinced herself a full-scale rodent invasion was underway.

The sound of a car engine registered when she shifted. It must be her neighbor leaving for work. More distant but still audible came the wail of a siren. Rolling on her side, she took time to focus once more on sounds within her home. The faucet in the kitchen was still dripping. She ought to get it fixed. The faint hum of chargers seemed to buzz all around.

"Well, I'm awake now," she said out loud, but not with her normal morning grumble. Riding the natural high brought on by lovemaking, she treated herself to a nice, long shower and scrubbed with one of the sweet-smelling body washes she'd been collecting. This one was supposed to energize her, not that she needed it. She figured if she got any more energized she'd be able to fly.

After toweling her hair and putting on some light makeup, she made her way to her sister's room. Mae was still asleep, breathing in a steady rhythm free of gasps and wheezes. She made another decision, a real treat for both of them. But she'd have to hurry. Mae wouldn't sleep much longer.

She went to the kitchen and got busy chopping onions, peppers, and mushrooms while the coffee brewed. By the time she'd whisked the eggs with a dollop of half-and-half and started them cooking in the shallow pan, she was able to enjoy her first cup. Veggies, ham, and cheese rounded out the omelet filling. She placed the bread in the toaster, planning to finish the rest after getting Mae out of bed and into her chair. Timing and multitasking made her sister's care and the routine easier, as she'd learned from watching their mother for years.

Mae stirred from her slumber when Vivian arrived and set about changing her diaper and clothing, cooing nonsense words and occasionally stroking her hair and face. If Mae noted any of this, she had no way to let Vivian know.

Vivian placed her into her wheelchair, mindful of her arms and the angle of her back. She parked Mae's chair near the bedroom window, then stripped the top layer of sheets, blankets, and the underlying protective padding from her bed. Aside from a few grunts and involuntary movements, her sister appeared calm and content. Still, Mae's rumbling stomach, not to mention her own, prompted Vivian to hurry. She took a moment to admire the brilliance of the morning sun and how it cast a lovely glow over Mae's face and hair. Perhaps this would be a good morning after all.

The routine continued after Vivian wheeled Mae into the kitchen, pausing only to offer Mae some diluted apple juice by way of a medicine dropper, and to take another sip of coffee. She then commenced preparation of Mae's breakfast. A deceptively simple practice in theory, but blending cooked food to the appropriate consistency was more art than science. She'd learned to be thorough, blending and adding small volumes of milk and water until she achieved the right balance. Too watery or too thick, and Mae could and would choke. The small chunks that the blender blades often missed posed a danger as well. Small portions could lodge in Mae's weakened lungs, creating conditions ripe for infection. Infection meant more choking, more medication that was difficult to administer, and more sleepless nights for them both. Mae's comfort and survival relied upon constant vigilance and attention to detail, at least for however long her caregivers could ward off the inevitable outcome of her frail condition.

Vivian timed the toaster to coincide with the last round of blending, adding chunks of torn toast to the macerated omelet and milk mixture and blending some more. She placed her own omelet and slice of toast onto a plate and carried it, plus her coffee, onto the deck. After she'd opened the parasol to shade a portion of the table, she carried Mae's blended breakfast and beverage outside. Mae in her wheelchair came next.

"Well Mae-belle, I hope you enjoy breakfast outdoors," Vivian said as she spooned the first bite into her sister's mouth. It went in on the first try, a small miracle. The first few times she'd fed her sister after becoming her primary caregiver had been an exercise in frustration for both, not to mention messy. Mae was a moving target. Vivian knew, rationally, that her spastic movements were beyond her control, though she often found the daily battles emotionally taxing.

Not today. Another small miracle. She'd take them wherever and whenever she could.

Vivian fed small spoonfuls to Mae and then shoveled forkfuls into her own mouth while Mae swallowed, or spit. It was the only way she got a hot meal short of eating before or after feedings. She didn't resent it this morning, not while sharing fresh air, a meal, and some of her newfound peace with her sister. All was well except for the brightness of the morning sun.

Vivian rose and shifted the umbrella in an effort to block the glare, but it didn't seem to help. After trying a few more angles, she gave up and went back inside to grab some sunglasses. She noticed the glow as soon as she stepped back outside.

What on Earth?

She stood frozen in fascination and disbelief as she stared at her sister. Thin strands of yellow light seemed to ebb and flow from her exposed skin, and Vivian swore she could even see a glow from beneath Mae's clothing.

She took a tentative step toward Mae's wheelchair, fearful, yet drawn to the light. Was it an aura? She'd always been under the impression that auras were more...uniform. This was more erratic, like sun flares, or the random currents and eddies through a little creek. It was like nothing she'd ever seen, with the exception of Zeke's light.

"Mae?" she asked, as if the light might somehow give her sister the gift of responsiveness. "Mae, can you hear me? What's going on with you?"

"It's her energy," said a voice from behind her. Vivian jumped and almost crashed into her guardian. "I'm just surprised you can see it."

"Have you *ever* heard of knocking?"

Zeke stifled a chuckle and pulled her into his arms, ignoring both her anger and her attempts to get away. "I'm sorry, Vivian, honestly. I—ouch! Watch it!" he said as he withdrew his arms in reaction to her kick. "Okay, okay! I surrender. I'll clear my throat or stomp my feet next time. You know, I still haven't gotten used to being invisible unless I choose to appear."

"You scared me half to death," she said, but with less force.

"I know, but I think you were already well on your way."

"Yeah," she muttered, sitting down. "I've been blindsided by too much weird stuff these days. Why is she glowing?"

He didn't answer her. He just kept staring. "Hello? Earth to Zeke?"

"Oh, sorry, I was still caught up in watching you with Mae. It was...interesting."

"Oh?" she asked, bidding him to continue as she motioned for him to take a seat.

"Well, you're so good with her and with all of this," he said, motioning to the food, the chair, the kitchen with his hands.

"No, I'm not," she said, looking away. "I've proven it more times than I care to remember."

She wasn't comfortable with praise in general, or praise of her treatment of Mae in particular. Admiration made her feel like a hypocrite since she'd never embraced the role of selfless caregiver. Instead, she resented the burden and she didn't always take to it with kindness. Resentment equaled failure. Today and the good days were penance and atonement.

"What did you mean about her energy?" Vivian asked.

"Changing the subject? I'm your guardian, remember? Full disclosure is key to a good working relationship." He uttered the words in a warm, sultry drawl dripping with innuendo.

"I'm serious." Heat began to pool low in her belly, though, in spite of her efforts to get an answer. "Tell me what's going on with Mae and the light, and then we can talk about whatever you want. Or not." Vivian could do sultry pretty well herself.

"I told you. Guardians, reapers, and other disembodied spirits are mostly energy, remember?"

When she nodded, he continued. "Well, spirit energy is encased in the bodies of the living too. It normally gets used while we're in the process of... well, living. Mae hasn't been doing much living, at least not what we would consider living. Her energy has been bottled up for a long time." He seemed to be lost in thought at the end.

"So what does that mean? Mae is suffering even more because her energy, or life force, or whatever, is stuck in there?" she asked, horrified at the notion.

God, like the soul from the hospital.

Or like Ezra.

He looked at her in silence for a few moments. Then he whispered, "That's what makes you good."

"What?"

"Vivian, your first thought just then, the first you voiced, the first thing that crossed your mind, was for Mae and what she might be enduring."

"So?" She shrugged. "I've had plenty of times where I've only thought of myself and how much I hate this." She could talk to Zeke with a bit more ease after last night, but she still wouldn't meet his gaze.

"I've thought about committing suicide more than once, you know, and I almost hurt Mae—badly—the night I first met the reaper. I could have done worse, too. Still think I'm such a model citizen?"

"You're still here. Courage isn't doing what's right when it's easy. It's doing what's right when all you want is to end yourself, someone else, or run the hell away. You don't have to like it. There's no glory in it, no gratitude, eternal or otherwise, no damned nobility about it. You just do it," he said. There was a note in his voice, an emotion she couldn't quite identify. She was getting ready to ask him about it but he started talking again.

"Now people like Mae, or with a similar condition, they have tremendous reservoirs of spirit energy and strength. We don't know exactly why. Maybe it's compensation for suffering in this realm, or perhaps they just don't use as much energy as folk we would consider normal. There probably is a link between spirit energy and the business of living life."

"So what happens when all of that energy is released?" she asked, fascinated.

"Something cosmic," he said. "Think volcanic eruptions, the biggest lightning strike you've ever seen, tornadoes straight out of the *Wizard of Oz.* Then multiply it by ten thousand."

"Wow," she whispered.

"You ain't just whistling Dixie."

"Wait, I've seen this once before," she said, remembering the night when she'd touched the vortex of light hovering over Mae's bed. The small taste of energy she'd consumed nearly knocked her out. She hadn't seen it since, though.

"Why can I see it now?"

"Maybe it's because you're her guardian."

She started to laugh, but something in his expression gave her pause. "Wait, you're serious, aren't you?"

He titled his head to the side and studied her. "Well, think about it. You've been caring for her for months, and you've protected her all of your life, you and your family. And you're a living soul broker."

"So?"

"So, if you can see her light, and if she's close to crossing," he said as he held up a hand to stop her protest, "that *might* mean her soul's in play. And if that's the case, you'd be in charge of her."

Even warmth from her guardian couldn't stop the cold chill of dread creeping up her spine. "But that's...no, she can't...wait, what do you mean her soul 'might' be in play? As in up for grabs in a guardian versus reaper grudge match? Wouldn't you know? Can't you tell?"

"Not always, at least for people in Mae's condition."

"But Mae's never done anything to deserve a visit from the reaper!"

Zeke sighed, brows furrowed in concentration. "That's no doubt true... which may mean that he's trying to—"

"Claim her through me!" she blurted, reaching out to grab his shoulders. "My God, that must be it! And if I'm her guardian, then he can't get to her if I don't let him. That's why he didn't just take her that night when he showed up. I can keep her safe!"

Zeke took her hands in his. "And I can keep you safe."

She smiled, touched by the solemn vow and relieved to finally have some answers. "And how did you come to know so much about all of this stuff all of a sudden? I thought you were a newbie."

"Oh, I've acquired more on-the-job experience. I told you, time is a bit different in our realm than it is here. There might be another reason you can perceive Mae's energy, you know. Maybe," he said, coming toward her, parting her legs so he could insinuate his body closer to hers, "it's because of me."

He placed light kisses along her collarbone and up her neck.

"Perhaps my presence, my influence, has opened your eyes and your senses?" More light kisses and caresses for her earlobe, and she marveled that she could still shiver while suffused with such heat.

"Maybe," she said, wrapping her arms around him. "But then again, maybe it's just a fluke. To be really, *really* sure, I think we'll have to extend your influence and see what happens."

"That can be arranged, Vivian," he said. After they returned Mae safely to her room, she found out that it could indeed.

———

"Zeke, where are you going?" she asked, stifling a yawn. She didn't want him to think she was clingy, but she couldn't help longing for the simple pleasure of falling asleep in his arms, secure in the knowledge that he'd still be there when she woke up.

"Sleep, love. I'll be back soon."

He conjured a shirt and smiled, no doubt amused by her reaction to the display of guardian magic. Refusing to be distracted, she sat up and said, "I asked you a question, and I'd like an answer."

He shrugged. "I've got to go to work."

"Work as in claiming a soul?"

His smile faltered and he dropped his gaze. "I don't *claim* souls, but yeah, I've been called to help a soul cross."

"Then take me with you." The demand burst out of her mouth at nearly the speed of thought, but she couldn't be bothered to worry about wisdom behind it, or complications, or ramifications. She had to do this.

Just as Zeke apparently felt compelled to argue. Dead or undead, he was still a typical male. "What? I can't do that!"

"Why not? I've done it before. And if I really am a living soul broker, then I'm supposed to be helping souls cross over." No point in pleading or whining about it. A direct not-taking-no-for-an-answer argument founded on logic and served with a side of stubbornness had a much better chance. Of course, he could pull an Ezra and disappear, so she flexed her fingers beneath the comforter, prepared to strike if necessary.

He might wind up wishing he hadn't taught her quite so well.

To his credit, he didn't up and disintegrate. Instead, he began to pace, running a hand through his mop of dark hair, no doubt thinking up some condescending argument against her participation. Something along the lines of how it wouldn't be "safe" for her. Well, screw that. Damned if she'd sit back and play damsel in distress. She hauled herself out of bed and began pulling on her jeans.

"Vivian, look—"

She cut him off while bending to grab her shirt. "Don't patronize me, Zeke. It won't work. And besides, you said it yourself. I need to learn how to use my powers so I can defend myself against the reaper. What better way to do that than helping you? Two birds, one stone."

He squared his shoulders and crossed his arms across his chest, leveling her with a stony gaze. "You didn't enjoy your first go around with the drunk driver. And you didn't want the responsibility with that other soul from the hospital."

"No," she answered honestly, pausing to rummage through her dresser for a brush and hair clip. "I didn't. But this time it's my choice. I've seen how the reaper works. I want to know what guardians do."

She had him, or so she thought until he spoke. "What about Mae? You're just going to leave her here by herself? You're her guardian, remember?"

Goddamn him, he was right. And she hated him for it.

Mirroring his stance, she met his stern gaze with her own. "I've left her before with caregivers. She's been safe. If I'm her guardian, she can't cross without me, right? And I'm guessing you can use some of that ghostly magic mojo to protect her while we're gone."

"First of all, we don't know for certain that you're her guardian, and second, I don't know if you're allowed to participate. Ezra—"

"Ezra isn't here!" She threw her hands up in the air before slamming a fist on the dresser. Sparks from her fingertips left a trail of scorch marks on the wood surface. She took a few deep breaths to rein in the rage and then started pacing. To his credit, Zeke remained silent, not to mention present, while she used the time and space to calm and collect her thoughts.

She stopped right in front of him and stood her ground. "Look, I understand it's a risk, and not just to me and Mae. I wouldn't put you in this position if I could help it, but you're all I've got."

She paused, sighed, and then met his gaze, pleading. "If it weren't for you, I'd be a sitting duck for the reaper. You've shown me my power and helped me find my purpose. All I need now is to unlock its potential. I'm asking you for the key. Please."

He cursed under his breath and turned away, rolling his shoulders as he started pacing. She held her breath and her tongue, returning the courtesy he'd shown her moments before, and waited. At last, he stopped in front of her and grabbed her chin, putting his face close enough for her to feel his hot breath as he spoke.

"You don't speak, you don't interfere, you don't *move* unless I tell you, and you stay hidden. I'll have to use some of my energy to make sure no other guardians know you're there, so make my job easier. We clear?"

She fought against the smile threatening to split her face and nodded. "Crystal."

He gave her a lopsided grin and shook his head. "All right then, tiger. Hold on tight and let's go save a soul."

CHAPTER SIXTEEN

She released the breath she'd been holding when they stumbled out of the swirling vortex and wished she'd thought to request an alternate means of transportation. Before she could get her bearings, Zeke grabbed her by the arm and shoved her into the corner of what appeared to be a hospital suite.

"God, why did it have to be another hospital?" she groaned.

Zeke's light hit her square in the chest and pushed her against the wall. She lifted her hands to defend herself, or maybe zap him the hell back. "What the—"

She choked on her reply when her arms slowly faded away before her eyes.

"I told you not to speak. It's going to be hard enough keeping you out of sight. Don't make me gag you too."

She bit off the smartass reply on the tip of her tongue and nodded. Wait, maybe he wouldn't get the message, since he'd apparently rendered her invisible. Weird. She didn't feel any different. Reaching out a tentative hand, which proved more difficult than she'd anticipated being unable to see where it was going, she tugged on the privacy curtain.

Zeke muttered a curse, his voice a low growl.

Sorry, she thought.

"Don't do it again. She's coming."

Who?

"The guardian who's helping me on this one."

Will she hear my thoughts?

"Maybe, but they'll probably just blend in with the background among other living souls in the hospital. But don't distract me, okay?"

Got it.

Vivian fought the near-irresistible urge to fidget while she checked out the room. The familiar sight of a narrow bed and countless monitors mingled with the scents of disinfectant, stale bed linens, and illness bringing on a sudden case of the cold sweats. The walls narrowed and her heart started racing.

Get a grip. You've done this before. You wanted to do this.

And this soul would be going someplace good since Zeke and another guardian were in charge. No chill eased the heat emanating from Zeke, so the reaper wouldn't be here. She was safe.

The air began to circulate in the room, swirling past her and around Zeke as white light burst and then coalesced, taking the shape of a woman. She emerged from the cloud of dust and stood tall, blonde curls shimmering as they caught rays of sunlight streaming through the half-open blinds of the small room's window. Shaking off the effects of her other-worldly journey, along with residual particles of earth from which she'd constructed her form, the guardian strode toward Zeke with grim purpose. He'd moved to the side of the bed and a lump formed in Vivian's throat as she took in her first sight of its small occupant.

That lump in her throat blocked a scream when her gaze moved to the female guardian's face.

The urge to bolt was almost as overwhelming as the urge to scream, but her legs refused to cooperate. Gripped by icy fear, she stood shivering as cold seeped into the room and filled her with a fresh wave of panic. Zeke stiffened before leveling his gaze in her direction, a look of mingled confusion and fury twisting his features as he mouthed the words, *Don't move!*

The other guardian whirled around with her arms at the ready, sparks shimmering from manicured fingertips.

"This one's ours," she whispered, low and menacing. Turning to Zeke, she said, "I was told there wouldn't be any interference."

Zeke shook his head. "There won't be. It's probably just lingering energy from another crossing."

The woman didn't look convinced, her wide-eyed gaze darting all around the room as if expecting the boogeyman to jump out any moment. "But it feels like fresh reaper." She shuddered. "I'd recognize that chill anywhere."

You would. You felt it yourself not so long ago.

So had Vivian, the day she'd set this very soul free.

The soul of the child-murderer, or so the reaper had claimed, now summoned to the bed of a dying child. God, it seemed so cruel, but then again, penance was meant to be painful, wasn't it? But what about the small girl swathed in white blankets and misery, writhing in a fitful state of semi-consciousness. She didn't deserve extra pain. Was it this so-called guardian's intention to bring more?

Fear morphed into anger and Vivian moved closer, hands raised and ready to strike.

A fresh wave of cold shot through the room, and Vivian realized with horror that *she* was the source.

No...nonononono not again....

The new guardian doubled over as light streamed out of her corporeal form and flowed into Vivian, assaulting her with another unwanted glimpse into the dead woman's soul.

———

She stood beside another hospital bed, trembling as tears streamed down her face. The small boy, face gaunt and contorted with pain, looked back at her, gaze pleading as she stroked the tender, bald head. God, he was thin, so terribly thin, and pale, swallowed by the tubes and wires delivering poisons to his tiny, battered body in an effort kill the cancer before it devoured him alive.

But the poisons were killing him instead.

"Mama, it hurts."

"I know, baby. I know."

"I don't want it to hurt anymore."

She hesitated before reaching into the pocket of her scrubs with a shaking hand to withdraw a syringe. The boy reached out his small hand, thin fingers tugging on his mother's sleeve. "When I die, do you think I'll get my hair back?"

With palpable effort, the woman choked back a sob. Clearing her throat, she said, "Yes, you will, baby. I know it."

He smiled through the tears streaming down his own little face and said, "Good. I've been cold since I lost it."

She hesitated. The boy tugged her sleeve harder, bringing the hand and syringe closer as the room grew warm, glowing with a light visible only to the boy.

And to Vivian.

"See, Mama," he said, his face alight with a brilliant smile. "It's already working."

Heaving a deep sigh, the woman squared her shoulders, uncapped the needle, and plunged the syringe into the boy's IV line. Then she fell to her knees and placed her head the boy's lap, shoulders quaking as he ran his fingers through her blonde hair.

"I love you, Mama."

———

When Vivian came back to herself, she was on the ground, clutching the corporeal guardian against her as the woman sobbed and trembled. Even more alarming, Vivian's now-visible hands glowed with a faint, reddish light. Unlike the peace and power that filled her when she'd first tasted this soul's burden, she experienced a strange sensation of fullness and...purpose.

"It's okay," Vivian whispered as she stroked the guardian's back.

The guardian stiffened and then pulled back from the embrace, sat up, and met Vivian's gaze. "I know you."

And I know you now, too.

She studied Vivian with an intensity that had her fighting not to squirm. "You're not a guardian. You're still alive. But you were the one who sent me to the guardians instead of...."

Unable to speak, Vivian simply nodded.

"What I did, it wasn't right," she said, then shook her head. "No, let me be clear. I'm not talking about my son. I don't regret that. He was suffering and we both knew he wasn't going to make it." Her direct gaze pierced Vivian, daring her to argue.

"I know," Vivian said. "I see that...now."

"But I don't understand. How could you save me from the reaper if you didn't know the why?"

Vivian regarded the spirit, wondering what to say. How could she explain without throwing out some trite little platitude? She'd heard so many of those in own her lifetime, the thought of casually tossing one out made her physically ill. She didn't have all of the answers. She wasn't certain she had *any* answers.

Heaving a sigh, she settled for the truth. "I couldn't do it. I just couldn't."

The guardian stared at her, eyes wide with expectation. Vivian threw her hands in the air, exasperated. "Look, what do you want me to say? Did I want your burdens? Did I come to you that day because I'm some damned hero? No. Did I know I was doing the right thing? Hell no! Guilt's been eating me alive ever since the reaper told me I let a child-killer go free!"

She paused mid-tirade to catch her breath, not daring to look at Zeke. "I don't know what I'm doing here, and I never wanted any of this. What more do you want from me?"

The guardian narrowed her gaze. "So you'd take it back, then, if you could?"

"No!"

"Even if you never knew the reason? Even if there was no reason?"

Wasn't that the million dollar question?

Taking a deep breath and a leap of faith, Vivian answered. "I wouldn't take it back, because...who am I to send you or anyone else to Hell? I've known some darkness of my own."

She paused, gathering her thoughts and spilling her heart's blood along with the awful truth.

"I looked into your soul, and I saw something of my own. I ran from the reaper when he came for me. Maybe it makes me a coward, and maybe I dodged what I deserved, but I'm no hypocrite," Vivian said. "I wouldn't put your soul in his keeping when I didn't let him keep my own. I'm not anyone's judge, jury, and executioner, and I...I thought you'd already suffered enough."

Zeke's warm hand landed on her shoulder, though she wasn't sure if he meant to comfort her or to stop her from breaking any more rules. At least it took the edge off of the residual chill she'd somehow generated. In fact, the room had turned downright balmy. Vivian turned her attention back to the girl on the bed. She'd apparently slept through the entire otherworldly exchange. In fact, she'd become quite still.

"Oh God, is she gone? Did I screw up her crossing?"

Zeke's gentle hold on her shoulder turned into a painful iron grip.

She jerked and looked over her shoulder, finally meeting his gaze. "What?"

Rather than a stern look of reproach or judgment, Zeke's expression seemed...haunted. Before she could ask why, his gaze went wide and he pointed to the corner of the room with a trembling hand. "This isn't supposed to happen."

A child's form materialized, cheeks full and ruddy under a mop of glossy dark hair. He smiled before turning his attention to the female guardian. "Hi, Mama."

The guardian leaped from the floor and captured the child in a fierce embrace, cradling his small body tight against her as the tears flowed. The energy within Vivian surged, the weight of the soul's burdens pulling her toward the tangle of mother and child as it struggled to break free. Then, all of a sudden, the light burst forth in a blinding blast of red that knocked Vivian flat on her back as the world went black.

———

She bolted upright, her bleary gaze darting frantically around the room in search of the guardian and the corporeal spirit of her child. A pair of strong hands caught her before the twin terrors of dizziness and nausea brought her crashing back to the hard floor.

Wait, she wasn't on the floor.

"Where are we?"

"Your place."

Vivian took a deep breath and struggled to get her bearings as she sat up slowly with Zeke's assistance. So, apparently he'd zapped them out of the hospital. But what about the soul they were supposed to help cross?

"What happened to the little girl?"

Zeke removed his hands from her shoulders and she immediately felt bereft of his warmth. "She's where we left her."

"But she was supposed to cross."

"Things changed." His flat tone scared her almost as much as the implications of her interference.

Vivian opened her eyes and found Zeke sitting across the room from her bed, back against the wall and head hanging low. God, what had she done? Clearing her throat and willing him to look at her, she said, "I don't know what happened back there, but I'm sorry if I—"

All of a sudden he looked up, piercing her with that green-eyed gaze. "Did you mean it?"

"Mean what?" Why was he keeping his distance? Judging from the palpable aura of desperation surrounding his corporeal form, he needed comfort as much as she did.

"You said you wouldn't take it back. You would've granted that soul's reprieve even if she couldn't justify what she'd done in life?"

She'd expected anger in the face of her monumental screw-up, for failure to follow his orders, for possibly throwing a monkey wrench of epic proportions into the afterlife management machinery. His question threw her for a loop. "What's going on, Zeke? And what happened to that guardian and her son?"

He slashed a hand through the air and spoke through gritted teeth. "Did you mean it?"

"Zeke, you're scaring me. What's going on here?" A fine tremor ran through his body, parts of which had begun to fade in a fine shimmer of dust.

She stood up on wobbly legs and made her way across the room, stopping just short of his hunched form. Wanting badly to take him in her arms, she held back for fear that she'd shatter him out of existence if she dared touch him. Instead, she sat down across from him and extended her hand, willing the light she still carried to bridge the gap between them.

To her dismay, he shrank back. "Don't."

"You need energy. You're fading."

She feared he would push her away or simply disappear. Instead, after a long moment's hesitation, he raised one trembling hand and accepted the light. His body resumed its normal healthy appearance, but the transfer did nothing to alter the heavy weight of unnamed despair he carried.

"Zeke, what's wrong? Talk to me. Are we in trouble here?"

He shook his head. When he met her gaze again, he'd donned a mask of bland calm. "Nothing's wrong. The girl's fine, it's...everything's fine. You don't worry about anything."

"But—"

He hauled himself up off the ground and walked past her. "I have to go."

Confusion gave way to anger and hurt. Damn it, he couldn't just leave like this. *Of course he can, you idiot. You just gave him an energy boost.* Using what little strength she had left, she got up and went after him. "Don't you even think about disappearing right now! Not until you tell me what the hell is going on."

He spun around to face her, waves of heat rolling off his body. "I told you, it's fine. I have some...things I've got to do, but I'll be back. I promise."

"I've heard that before." She'd meant to infuse the words with venom, but her voice emerged as a hoarse, choked whisper.

He grabbed her by the shoulders and shook her. "I *will* come back."

"Zeke, you've got to tell me what's going on. What happened to the guardian—"

"She's not a guardian anymore. She crossed. You did that."

"Wait, what? I can do that? But I—"

"You can and you did, but you need to keep it between us for now. I've got to report in and deliver energy from the crossing. Watch your back and look after Mae until I come back to you."

He pulled her into a fierce embrace before disappearing, leaving her clouded with confusion and the dust from which he'd come.

CHAPTER SEVENTEEN

"Viv? Hello, Vivian," Sue said as she waved her hand in front of her friend's face. "Earth calling. Anyone home?"

"Sorry," she muttered. "I'm just a little spacey today, that's all."

Three days holed up in her home and jumping at shadows left Vivian in desperate need of some normalcy. So after too much time spent pacing the floor and nearly blasting the walls with pent up energy, she'd agreed to meet Sue for an outing to the Country Music Hall of Fame while Zeke was off doing what she assumed was damage control on account of her unintended crossing.

Three days with no word, no sign, no indication of what she was meant to do.

No strong arms to comfort her.

She missed those arms.

"Mmm-hmm," said Sue. "I can see that. Your cheeks are about five shades redder, and I can also see the cat-that-ate-the-canary smile on your face too. You going to tell me his name?"

"What? No, it's no one, really," she said, trying to get a hold of herself. She couldn't very well tell Sue about Zeke the not-so-friendly ghost. "I'm just, you know, happy to be out and about with my best bud in downtown Nashvegas, that's all."

"Sure. Right."

"I mean it! It's good to get out of the house for a bit and hang out with you." Vivian tried her best to look sincere. "The rest is a little...complicated."

Sue gave her a look and a half. "Well, if you say so. I just can't believe you'd keep a secret like that from *me* of all people. But if you do have a little something going on right now, hypothetically speaking," she added quickly, in response to Vivian's balk, "keep it under the radar today. Jack's meeting us here and bringing one of his friends—"

"Oh, for God's sake, Sue!" Vivian threw up her hands in exasperation and stepped back a few paces. "I thought I told you, no more blind date ambushes." This was absolutely, positively the *last* thing she needed to deal with right now.

"Um, I seem to recall being asked to help get a certain sad-sack, hard-up redhead get a life not too long ago. Was that you, or some other lost cause I know?"

"Come on, you could have given me some warning at least!"

"No way! You'd just make some excuse and keep on living like a hermit." Vivian was on the verge of protest, but Sue happened to be right.

"Can you blame me?" Vivian shook her head in dismay. The last time she had an impromptu double date with Sue, Vivian spent nearly two hours being lectured on the benefits of an organic, all-vegan diet by a rather stuffy, pale chemistry professor from a local college.

Sue looked down, leaving Vivian perplexed and a little dismayed. *Bless her heart, she really does mean well.* After a moment, Sue sighed and said, "Look, don't go getting your panties in a wad. First of all, I just want you to be happy. You've been going through a lifetime's worth of hell, six months and counting, and I wanted to get you out of the house and into life. Second, Jack's a good guy. Do this for us, okay?"

Vivian eyed her friend in wonder. Sue had always been the good-time girl in their circle of friends, claiming zero interest in settling down anytime soon. Jack had been in and out of the picture for a while, hooking up with Sue whenever he happened to breeze through on a service call. Vivian liked him fine, but she didn't figure him for something special.

"Yeah, Jack is a good guy. He also lives half his life on the road. What gives?"

Sue took a deep breath and said, "Well, he's been looking at places here, you know.

"No, I didn't know. Now who's keeping big secrets, huh?"

"Hey, it was just talk. But then he made a deposit on a condo in Germantown. He says he's ready to put down some roots. Asked if I was interested."

"Are you?"

Vivian's shock was tempered by a bit of hurt and guilt. She'd been so wrapped up in her own troubles that she hadn't even noticed Sue's anxiety until now. How long had it been since Vivian asked about her life? She took her friend by the hand and pulled her over to the front steps. They sat in the shade of the awning that covered the entrance, its pattern mirroring the larger structure in homage to all of those honky tonk crooners who'd tickled the ivories over the industry's long history.

"Yes. No. Hell, I don't know," Sue began. "I think so when he's around, but then I start to fret when he's not. I mean, he's definitely a great guy. He's funny, he's a great kisser, and not a half-bad dancer." She smiled. "He's a terrible singer, though, but then again he is *really* great in the sack. He cooks, but doesn't clean—"

Vivian laughed. "What man does?" *Aside from the dead ones....*

Sue chuckled. "He makes me laugh," she said, her laughter dying and her tone taking a rare serious turn. "And we don't seem to run out of things to say."

"So what's the problem?" *At least he's alive.*

"Me, I guess. I don't know if I'm ready, but I don't want to lose him either. How's that for selfish?"

"Sounds like you're just scared. This is uncharted territory, after all," she teased.

"I guess you're right."

"Have you talked to Jack about this?"

Sue hesitated, which meant no. "Not really. I don't want to scare him off. But I don't want to lead him on either. I would feel awful if he moved here just for me and then, you know, we didn't work out."

"Well, I think you should talk it over with him. *Out* of bed!" Vivian said with mock sternness. "Just be honest with him, that's the best anyone can do. Life doesn't come with guarantees, but this sounds like a risk worth taking. Besides, I seem to recall getting a piece of good advice from a sassy blonde not too long ago. Something about life being too short to be on hold for too long? I think she was right."

"Okay," Sue replied. "I guess you're right. I'll talk to him. But...."

Here we go. "But what?"

"But you just *have* stick around with us today and keep Herb entertained, please, please promise me? I promised Jack I'd help him out with this guy. He's got lots of local contacts in the business that could really give Jack an edge in the market, you know?" Sue begged, grabbing both of Vivian's hands and squeezing them tight.

"Herb? His name is *Herb*?" Vivian rolled her eyes.

"Herbert, smartass! He just goes by Herb," Sue scolded.

"Well," Vivian said with a small smile of surrender, "it's better than Herbie, I guess."

"Hey, you never know," Sue said between giggles and snorts. "He just might turn out to be your love bug."

Herb wasn't such a bad guy, as it turned out. Had her life been less complicated, Vivian probably could've mustered some genuine interest. He wasn't very tall, certainly not as tall as Zeke, but he had broad shoulders, an easy smile, and a pretty cute rear view.

Plus, they both worked in finance and found common ground bemoaning interest rates and the ups and downs of the loan business. She enjoyed the novelty of talking to an ordinary man about the mundane, everyday topics she'd once taken for granted. Spending time with an ordinary, living man was pretty nice.

So why did she feel so damned guilty?

Because Zeke's been good to you and you're stepping out on him.

He *had* been so good to her, and not just in the bedroom. But he was dead. It wasn't as if they could ever just stroll around downtown Nashville, could they? *Maybe he could just go in disguise.* She wondered if guardians could change or even control their corporeal form. She took a deep breath and decided to relax and just enjoy the company and day without worrying about the unseen for a while.

The building that housed Music City's homage to the legends that made Nashville famous had a warehouse feel to it. Its open floor plan allowed for a central space between levels such that patrons on the upper and lower floors could see one another, not to mention overhead views of some impressive exhibits. She hadn't always been a big fan of country, but was soon engrossed in the history of the folksy music so intricately inter-twined with the history of her hometown.

Peppered throughout the staged displays of weathered instruments, old sheet music, and old-fashioned clothing, private booths stood and beckoned passersby to slip through their spirals and have a listen. Vivian took up the invitation and pressed the play button. The carpeted walls blocked out sounds from the outside and let the music fill her ears. She closed her eyes, surprised to find such a simple act heightened her sense of hearing.

As she listened, she swore she could feel vibrations from stringed instruments she could not even name through her fingertips. Individual notes floated from the speakers, and each one reverberated through her skin. She could almost feel the breath of the singer who'd crooned decades ago, fresh and hot. It was electric. She started to sway, hearing her voice as if from a distance as it sang along. Had she heard that old song before?

"Lady, you keep singing like that and someone's bound to offer you a record deal," said a smooth voice from behind.

"Oh!" Vivian whirled around to face her date. "I'm sorry. I didn't think I was so loud."

"Don't apologize," he replied with a sexy grin. "I was enjoying the show. You got a nice spring in your step too, if you don't mind my saying so."

Heat crept up her cheeks at the innuendo, but she accepted his hand when he offered it, willing herself to calm. Getting an unwanted flash from her date's psyche might prove downright awkward. Fortunately, the only flash she got was from his pearly whites as he bowed and brushed his lips over her knuckles. They slipped out of the booth and meandered past a few more displays, hand in hand. When they came across another booth, they shared a wicked grin, raced in together, and shared the next song.

The conversation flowed easily, and they shared a heap of laughs over Elvis Presley's tricked-out, 'solid gold' Cadillac and Webb Pierce's Silver Dollar convertible, complete with a saddle in the middle of the front seat, horseshoe pedals, and guns as door handles. The collection of garish costumes donned by the late Porter Wagoner were even more entertaining. Vivian could not help but wonder if his famous protégée, Miss Dolly, was talking about him when she said, "It costs a lot of money to look this cheap."

"Is it cold in here, or is it just me?" Vivian asked as they all walked into the rotunda. The chill surprised her since the high windows circling the room above the banner of the unbroken circle let in a lot of the summer sunlight.

"Must be you," said Herb. "I'm damned near boiling." He offered her his suit jacket, and Vivian accepted his good old-fashioned Southern chivalry with grace and gratitude.

The four of them split up temporarily to admire the various plaques. Vivian moved to the Benton mural, skimming through the visitor's guide to read about *The Sources of Country Music* before giving it the once-over. She nodded to one of the few other visitors exploring the rotunda. He seemed surprised, though he returned her nod. She might have easily missed him as he leaned against one of the granite supports flanking the display, immersed in the shadow. With his bushy brows, tousled gray hair, and unkempt mustache, he reminded Vivian a little of Mark Twain. She studied the mural, noting his stare out of the corner of her eye while doing her best to ignore it.

The weight of the man's gaze on her made her pretty uncomfortable. Plus, she'd been raised with the notion that staring was plain rude. Just as she was about to turn around and confront him, the man finally spoke.

"Well, what do you think?" he asked, stepping a little closer.

"It's colorful," she offered, and then decided perhaps she should try a little harder since her interrogator seemed less than impressed. "And comprehensive. Seems to cover the spectrum of the genre pretty well. The dulcimer's a nice touch. I always did like the sound, and a lot of country has roots in Celtic."

"Hmmfph," he grumbled. Then a loud snort echoed from the side opposite the grumpy old curmudgeon.

She turned on her heel when she heard the sound.

Where the hell did he come from?

Her new companion and the source of the snort had a dark mop of wavy hair, a beard and mustache, and a rather hairy chest in full view underneath a big gold medallion. She hadn't seen a look like his since Burt Reynolds in the 70s. He winked at her before turning his attention back to his guitar, and she warmed a little. Retro, sure, but he was easy on the eyes.

"Don't mind Guitar Guy," sneered the mean old coot. He then turned to address the other man. "Still hanging around here, hoping they'll finally let you in? Looks to me like you're driving this life away, too." He laughed as Guitar Guy shot him a withering look.

The old man turned back to Vivian with an expectant look.

Seriously, you want more?

She studied the mural again, struggling to remember what she had just read about it before the two men distracted her. She wasn't an art critic and wasn't particularly interested in the deeper meaning, but she decided to humor him, figuring he wouldn't leave until and unless she did.

"Well," she said, "it's realistic too. I like that. Not like all of the abstract industrial stuff that passes for art these days. I mean, you can still see all of the elements of the music, from the banjo player, the fiddler and square dancers, and the singers. It's pretty cool to see the train too. I half-expect Woody Guthrie to hop off with his guitar and bust out with some Okie blues."

"Pollack would disagree with you on the abstract, little lady." He chuckled, though he seemed pleased with her answer. "The damned train is what took the longest," he muttered. "I had to get the right engine, and they just couldn't send good photographs. But see Tex Ritter there in the foreground?" He pointed, and Vivian followed his finger. "He wasn't too bad. That part was easy. Still, this one was the death of me."

"Oh, so you painted it, huh?" she asked as she looked back, jumping clean out of her skin when she realized her companion had disappeared and had apparently taken Guitar Guy with him.

"Viv, you okay?" Herb's hand on her shoulder nearly gave her a coronary and she jerked away.

"Easy now," he said, grabbing her shoulders and turning her to face him. "Who were you talking to anyway?" he asked, brows furrowed with worry, looking around for anyone else in the room.

"Um, no one," she offered, stunned and dismayed, but at least having the good sense to keep her latest ghostly encounter to herself. "I was just looking at the mural. Must have gotten a little spooked."

"Oh yeah, I heard a funny story about that," Herb said. "The guy who painted it apparently keeled over from a heart attack right as he was finishing it up. Spooky, huh? No wonder you jumped like a jackrabbit."

"Yeah," Vivian muttered. "Spooky is right. Isn't it about closing time?"

Herb checked his watch. "Oh, dang, you're right. We better start heading down."

She made a monumental effort to hold herself together as they headed back to the lobby. Sue, Jack, and Herb were too engrossed in planning where to grab dinner to pay too much attention. Good thing too. She nearly fainted when a grinning Guitar Guy gave her another wink and a wave as they walked out the front door, then vanished into thin air.

CHAPTER EIGHTEEN

"I can't believe I just ate snail," Sue whispered after their waiter removed the appetizer dish.

"Like that's the worst thing you ever ate," Jack said with a chuckle. When she made a face at him, he slurped the last of the escargot with extra gusto.

"Do tell!" Herb chimed in.

"She's a real country girl, lemme tell y'all," Jack replied, leaning back, tugging on his belt buckle, and putting on his best redneck smirk. "We've had us some good eatin' with squirrel, jackrabbit, some rattlesnake and gator tail—"

"Oh good Lord, Jack! You want to get us thrown out?" Sue hissed. "Vivian, help me out, here. Hey, Earth to Vivian. What's gotten into you tonight anyhow?"

"I'm sorry, what was that?" Vivian replied. Maybe she should excuse herself and hightail it out of the restaurant or ask Sue if she had any Xanax. Or she could just have another cocktail.

"Take it easy. She's been spooked ever since we left the Hall of Fame," Herb said, patting her hand and giving it a quick squeeze.

"What, you see a ghost or something?" Jack teased.

"No!" Vivian said a little too quick and loud.

Sue looked at Vivian and asked, "Honey, you sure you're all right? You do look a little pale."

Before she had the chance to panic over being put on the spot, their entrees arrived. She did her best to forget about this disturbing turn of events and tried to focus on the food and the company. Sue got them into Germantown Café, one of those uber-modern eateries with décor that probably came straight out of some European catalog. Such ambiance normally spelled overpriced, watered-down drinks, snooty waiters, and not a lot of grub. The boys had groaned and Vivian had raised an eyebrow. Sue, as usual, proved them all wrong.

She thanked her lucky stars for the strong cocktails. It normally took at least two to get her going. Her first one from this bar calmed her down enough to stave off a major panic attack.

At least, it worked until she looked outside.

Their window-side table afforded the quartet a great view of down-town. The view also allowed Vivian to watch folks strolling around on the street below, and the sidewalk was littered with pedestrians. She reached out a shaky hand and downed the remainder of her drink.

More than a few of the people out there weren't walking in the same world.

The clothes gave some of them away. Top hats and bustles went out of fashion more than a hundred years back, and it wasn't exactly Halloween. She gasped as one authentic Southern belle all decked out in a hoop skirt collided with a living couple walking hand in hand. Well, she didn't really collide with them so much as walk right through them.

Vivian almost fell out of her chair.

"Girlfriend, you are so cut off," Sue scolded.

"Um, it's not that," Vivian said as she tried to regain her composure. "It's just...I left my cell phone in the car. I'd better go get it."

"Aw, just leave it for one night, Viv," Jack chimed in. "It'll do you some good. I'm surprised it's not growing out of your ear yet."

"Yeah, and your fish is getting cold," Sue added.

"What about Mae?" Though she hated to use her sister's disability as a crutch in this situation, it served as a handy excuse. No one offered to stop her again.

She slipped into the ladies' room first, hid in the stall, and took a few gulps of air to calm her raw nerves. She'd never make a very convincing actress, but she was going to have to get a grip before her friends got really worried. *Breathe, just breathe.* If she could breathe, she could move. If she could move, she could get through the rest of the night and then figure out what to do once back in the comfort and safety of her own home.

This shouldn't be such a surprise. She'd figured other spirits lurked around, unseen by the living. It made sense. Ezra had even told her so.

She just hadn't counted on seeing any other than her own personal guardians.

She didn't remember the walk to her car.

Vivian unlocked her car and opened the driver's side door with unsteady hands. She grabbed her phone and her bluetooth. After slamming the car door shut and clicking the lock button, she threw her shoulders back and did her best to keep a steady pace on her way back to the restaurant.

"Pardon me, ma'am," came a voice from behind.

She whirled around ready to strike. The bearer of the voice took a step back and looked at her with wide-eyed terror. She relaxed a hair when she realized he was just a homeless guy. Plenty roamed this part of downtown. His eyes were bloodshot, his hair and beard a dirty blond streaked with gray, and his grimy shirt and jacket had seen better days. He probably smelled like rotting wine too, by the look of him. Good thing she wasn't standing downwind.

"Good evening, sir," Vivian began. "What can I do for you?" She kept a polite tone but maintained a strong stance.

"I...I...need me some change. Gotta to call my girl," he stammered.

"I don't have any cash on me. Sorry, you'll have to go someplace else."

He didn't move. He just stood there and stared. She took two steps forward and said a little more loudly, "You heard what I said. I don't have any money. Get going."

"Nobody's answered me in so long. Please, ma'am, help me. You gotta to help me!"

"I *said* get going!"

"Move along, Charlie. You know you can't hold it anyway," came another voice.

She spun around again and came face to face with the man in white. The air chilled, freezing Vivian in terror.

"Don't mind Charlie, Ms. Bedford," the reaper said with some amusement in his voice. "You scared him more than he scared you I expect."

"I don't think that's possible," she whispered back.

"Oh, he'll ask for change 'til Kingdom come, but after so many years he never really expects an answer. I must say, it is truly a pleasure to see you again, and on such a fine evening. Did you enjoy your outing?"

"What do you want, Darkmore?"

"Tsk, tsk, dear lady. Where are your manners?" he asked, taking a step closer. "Since you seem determined to skip the pleasantries, however, let us proceed with business. Have you considered my offer?"

Vivian's breath caught. She'd been expecting the reaper, thought he'd turn up at her house or at the very least catch her alone. She never dreamed he'd be so bold as to appear in such a public place. Surely he wouldn't try to take her here?

"Why not? People disappear all the time. Honestly, how many people would miss you? Oh, I suppose your friends at the restaurant might call the police, file a missing person report. You might even make the local news for a night or two, but after that? You'd be lucky if your case was given more than a few weeks, a month at best. Then you'd be relegated to the cold case file, buried and forgotten. No family, few friends—you're so thoroughly cut off from life I would have no trouble at all claiming you."

The reaper spoke the cruel truth in a pleasant voice, smiling as though they were discussing the weather instead of the state of her life and the fate of her soul. His chill made her shudder, but she wasn't about to fall under whatever hypnotic spell he was throwing out. Not this time. She knew she didn't stand a chance, but she'd be damned if he would take her without a fight.

"I'm not yours to claim," she said. Then she reached out and latched onto his wrist with her right hand and sent a pulse of energy surging through him.

It was a gamble, but she let all of her grief, fear, and rage wash over her and willed it through their connection.

She wasn't sure it was working until Darkmore's eyes widened and she felt the slightest of tremors run through him. He looked from her face to their glowing hands and back again, disbelief and something that resembled awe taking over his expression. He pulled free of her grasp and kept staring at her as she stood still. She should run, but doubted her shaky legs would carry her far, which left her at the mercy of the reaper.

She was a dead woman.

"Now that certainly makes things more interesting," he said, a broad and deadly smile stretching across his face. "I'll see you soon, Vivian."

He winked and disappeared.

She screamed then and didn't stop.

———

Vivian held herself together until she made it home. After her encounter with the lost spirit and the reaper, her screams attracted the attention of some nearby living folk. They'd helped her back to her friends at the restaurant and she told them she'd been spooked by some random homeless guy. They bought her excuse, by some miracle.

Her terror was real enough.

Herb drove her home while Sue followed behind in her car. He even asked her for another date sometime. Either he was as crazy as she feared she was becoming or he liked a damsel in distress. Probably both. She passed him her phone number just to get rid of him, grabbed her keys from Sue, and then ran into her house.

She kicked off her shoes and made her way to her sofa, pulling her favorite blanket off the back to wrap around her shoulders. Tired, scared, and alone again. Naturally.

Then she became very, very warm.

"Who is he?" Zeke's voice asked, his tone neutral. She couldn't see him. She really, really wanted to see him.

"He's a friend of Sue's," Vivian replied, her head in her hands. When Zeke remained silent, she sighed. "His name is Herbert. Sue set me up on a blind date with him tonight. I didn't know anything about it beforehand."

He maintained his silence. She didn't know what else to say, and she didn't have any fight left in her anyway.

After a couple of minutes, he asked, "Is that all?"

"Yes!" she snapped. "What do you want from me? A confession signed in blood?"

She got more silence rather than an answer. Vivian dragged her hands through her hair and tugged hard. Her eyes burned even as she fought the tears. She started trembling.

"I think I should go," Zeke said quietly.

No, please don't go. You have no idea how much I don't want you to go. She couldn't find her voice. She began to shake.

"Vivian?"

She lifted her face from her hands and there he was, solid and real, suffusing her with his warmth and his nearness. He kneeled beside her and looked up, gaze filled with concern. She lost it then.

"Hey, hey," he murmured after she fell into his arms and buried her face in his chest. "What's wrong, Vivian?"

She couldn't answer. Instead, she tightened her embrace.

"I'm sorry," she whispered. She should've asked him where he'd been, what he'd been doing, if they were okay. She should've told him about all of the spirits she could suddenly see and about the reaper. But when she lifted her gaze to look at him, all she could manage was, "Don't go. Please."

He didn't speak. Instead, he lifted her, blanket and all, in his strong arms and carried her to her bed. He disappeared into the bathroom and left her to wait, still shaking and fighting tears. Then she heard running water and smelled cool, soothing mint.

Zeke emerged wearing jeans and nothing else. He pulled her to her feet and unwrapped her. Then he began to undress her.

"Zeke, I—"

"Shh."

"I'm not sure I feel like—"

"Trust me," he whispered, planting a kiss on her forehead. He picked her up again and brought her into the bathroom, filled with the warm, comforting glow of candlelight. Placing her before the mirror, he grabbed her brush and started fussing with her hair.

"Zeke, what are you—"

He shushed her and pinned her hair back. Then he turned her around to face him and wrapped his arms around her, massaging her back and shoulders until she relaxed. He placed another gentle kiss on her forehead, and another by her ear.

"I'm going to bathe you now," he whispered into the ear he'd kissed.

"Oh," she replied. She didn't feel so comfortable with the idea, but his tone and his insistent arms made it clear he wouldn't take no for an answer.

He helped her step into the water and bid her to sit. Once she'd immersed herself up to her shoulders, he fussed with the bath pillow and pressed gently against her shoulders until she complied and rested her head on its softness. The warmth of the water and of his hands made acquiescing much easier.

Easier, that was, until he grabbed her loofah and actually started bathing her.

"You know, this would be easier if you'd just sit back and relax," he said as he toweled his face off. She must have splashed him when she startled.

"I'm not sure I'm, ah...well...comfortable with this," she said, refusing to look up at him.

"With what?" he asked.

In truth, her discomfort came from the intimacy implied by such an act of care. Plus, no one had bathed her since her childhood. She couldn't even recall being bathed then.

"Look, I'm a grown woman," she said, shrinking back from him and covering herself with her arms. "I can wash myself." She still couldn't look at him.

"I know you can," he said. His gentle tone hadn't changed in spite of her raised voice. "You can do anything. You *do* everything. When's the last time you let someone do something for you?"

She started to argue, but stopped short. She thought about what he said. He was right. *She* was the caregiver. She fed, clothed, and, yes, even bathed Mae most days.

No one had fed her before Zeke, not for a long, long time.

"If you want me to stop, I will," he said quietly.

"It's not that," she answered. "I'm just not used to this."

Vivian looked at him then. His green eyes were wide and filled with determination. She also saw a trace of sadness, and longing.

"You really want to do this for me, don't you?"

"Yes, love. Let me care for you."

She leaned back, closed her eyes, and tried to relax as he washed her. He started with her back and shoulders, moving down her body and to her legs, and finally cleansed and massaged her feet. The sensations were incredible. With any other man, she would have thought such treatment was just a ploy to get her into bed. But while his touch was sensual, it didn't imply a desire for anything other than her comfort. Taking care to avoid any intimate areas, he finished by removing her makeup, massaging her scalp, and bidding her to relax in the warm water while he turned down the bed. Her fear and anxiety melted away in her guardian's presence and under his care.

Zeke returned with a warm towel and dried her. He made a point of dressing her in a simple cotton tank and shorts. She was floored. He really didn't expect anything from her.

Maybe he doesn't want you anymore.

She allowed him to lead her to her bed and tuck her in. He sat beside her, above the covers, and stroked her hair. She worried he might take his leave after she fell asleep.

"Aren't you tired?" he asked.

"Not really," she replied. "Aren't you going to join me?"

"Do you want me to?"

She let out an exasperated sigh, sat up, looked him square in the eye and said, "You honestly think I don't want you here?"

"You were gone all day," he said with his irritating calm. "And you returned accompanied by a man who's clearly interested in you."

"I told you, Sue blindsided me with a double date this evening. That's all."

"You were upset when you came back home and after I spoke to you," he continued. "I should have kept my presence a secret. I thought maybe I had upset you."

"You? No, it wasn't you, it was—" She stopped. It dawned on her then. She stared at him, dumbfounded. "Wait a minute, you're worried? You honestly don't know where you stand with me, do you?"

"What you've given me, what we've shared, we both needed. I'm your guardian and it's my duty to protect and care for you. I...I don't own you. You owe me nothing. If there's someone else you'd prefer, a living man, I won't stand in your way."

His expression, while not hostile, remained unreadable and his tone neutral. She was more accustomed to knock-down-drag-outs from her men, particularly in the face of jealousy. Maybe he wasn't jealous.

"So what are you saying? You were just doing your guardian duty in the park?"

"Vivian—"

"In my kitchen—"

"Vivian, listen—"

"On my bathroom floor—"

"Vivian! Stop it!"

And before she could continue her rant, he stopped her mouth with a rough kiss, pinning her down to the bed and searing her with intense heat. Words would not have convinced her. Zeke's actions did.

"Does this *feel* like just a duty?" he growled when he tore his lips from hers.

"No," she answered, gasping for breath herself. She reached down and grabbed him, making him groan louder. "Does this feel like pity?"

"No."

"Good. Now that we've got that straightened out, why don't you come to bed with me?"

"I'd love nothing better. But one thing first," he said as he looked down at her. "Tell me what had you so out of sorts when you came home."

"I had another run-in with Darkmore." When his brows furrowed and his temperature rose, she quickly added, "Don't worry—he didn't hurt me. I mean, it was scary, but he didn't force me to claim a soul or try to take me back to his realm."

"I should've been there," he murmured.

"It's not important," Vivian answered. "I was able to fend him off. Seems like all of that training you've been having me do is paying off."

He didn't look pleased, but nodded. "Good, but I still don't like you out there on your own, especially not knowing how much power you've got or how reliable it is."

"I'm fine. Besides, not to knock your masculine urges to be the fierce protector or anything, but I prefer to protect myself." She spoke lightly, but the statement remained true.

"I want to keep you safe," he whispered.

"You are. Nobody could've made me feel safer than you did tonight, and not just from mortal danger," she said, reaching up to caress his cheek. "We'll talk about it later. I promise. Right now, though," she said as she paused to place a tender kiss on his lips, "I need something more than talk."

She kissed him again and sank into blissful oblivion.

CHAPTER NINETEEN

She'd hoped the talk she'd promised Zeke wouldn't be necessary, so she'd put it off for days, almost a week.

She couldn't put it off any longer.

Vivian's father, God rest his soul, used to be fond of telling her, "If you run with the wolves, you're bound to start howling with them." What then, she wondered, came of running around with corporeal spirits?

Well, for starters, more spirits.

Unfortunately, the incident downtown hadn't been a fluke.

Aside from the surly artist and Guitar Guy from the Hall of Fame, not to mention poor Charlie and all the other spirits inhabiting downtown Nashville, she had a few more run-ins with folks only she could see. Those sightings complicated trips to the grocery store, the dry cleaner's, and the bank. Not to mention a few of the wispy specters who kept turning up at the most inconvenient times, like during her appointment with Human Resources to update them on the duration of her leave.

At least the display of genuine distress helped her get two more weeks of paid leave.

Then there was the issue of keener senses. She'd sometimes catch snippets of conversations between folks too far away for normal people to hear. More disturbing, she'd noticed that strange glow of light on people other than Mae. The elderly seemed brightest, though she caught flashes from younger folks on occasion.

More often than not, she absorbed those flashes. In fact, she seemed to draw in the energy, along with the unwanted burdens of the souls emitting it. Each transfer left her achy, restless, drawn as taut as a bowstring while simultaneously exhausted beyond measure.

And she was angry.

She still didn't know what had suddenly thrown open her connection to the larger spirit world, so how was she supposed to figure out how to close it?

She pondered this conundrum while waging war against the Bermuda grass that had insinuated itself into her back flower beds and choked out most of her creeping phlox, channeling her confusion and aggression into something marginally productive. Cursing mightily, she paused to wipe the sweat from her brow and then carefully tugged at another strand of the insidious creeping weed. It seemed simple in theory. Just grab the damned thing by the root and pull. Problem was, the runners put down roots as the plant spread and invaded. Miss one, and the weed just came right back. How was she supposed to get rid of something so pervasive and relentless once it had taken root?

She decided to quit for a while and grab a glass of lemonade, though she knew she really should keep going. Until her latest battle with Medicaid and the state itself were resolved, she would have less help with her sister's care and less time for household and lawn maintenance. Cutting out Mae's physical therapy had been a blow, but given the doctors' collective opinion on her prognosis, she could live with that. Cutting back the home care, however, was another matter entirely.

What kind of twisted logic made it easier to get benefits for your ailing kin by putting them in a nursing home rather than keeping them in their own home? She would keep fighting, even if she had to wheel her sister before a judge so he could see for himself. Most folks found it harder to ignore someone's plight when the someone was in your face. But for now she'd have to make do with no help at night.

Then again, she had Zeke, at least for now.

Ezra had yet to return, though, which was troubling. Darkmore's conspicuous absence made her just as uneasy. She hadn't seen him since their last run-in downtown but knew he still lurked close by the chill that hit her at unexpected moments. Flashes of white in her dreams had plagued her lately too.

Figuring weed wars and worry were becoming counterproductive, she gave up and headed inside for a shower. Stripping, she paused for a moment to regard her reflection, noting the small lines starting to creep from the corners of her eyes and deepening creases insinuating themselves around her mouth. She covered the grays. Had for years. But those sneaky, albeit barely visible, wrinkles had been giving her pause lately. Time marched on, and it was marching right across her face.

Where the hell was her life going? She wasn't old, but the prospect of youth's passage hit her now. She'd never thought much about a future plan, and had just put things off after her folks passed and until she could deal with Mae.

Or until she checked out. Of course, she'd stopped flirting with the idea of suicide after a taste of the darker side of the afterlife, not to mention the so-called lighter side. "Good guys" Zeke and Ezra weren't exactly enjoying an eternity filled with idle bliss.

Life wasn't always easy or pretty, but she shouldn't complain. She'd had some good times, had a good job, if and when she got back to it, a few friends and probably more to come if and when she got back to her life.

Maybe a move, a new house, a family.

She would never have any of that with Zeke.

"Damn it all to hell, girl, get a grip," she said to the mirror, half wondering what inspired all of this angst, half knowing all too well. She was falling hard for Zeke, and she shouldn't. After all, what sort of future could she hope for with a dead man?

As if on cue, a pair of hot arms enveloped her from behind. Though she didn't lift her gaze to meet his in the mirror, she gathered Zeke had appeared naked and was glad to see her from the feel of him. She leaned into him, letting his caresses ease the mess in her head as he showered her body with bliss. Determined not to speak and let that mess spoil the moment, she turned and looked at him, willing him to understand what she needed. That fierce, green-eyed gaze met and matched hers in intensity, though they flickered with uncertainty.

Well, if he couldn't or wouldn't read her mind, then she'd just have to show him.

Pulling his face down to hers, she assaulted his mouth with furious kisses and ran her hands over his face, shoulders, and arms, desperate to touch as much of his skin as she could. Her kisses and caresses were far from gentle, and she growled as she pulled him down to the ground with a force she didn't realize she possessed.

Pinning him down on the bath mat, she resisted his every effort to slow her. When he acquiesced, she straddled him and took him inside without prelude, rising and falling in a frenzy of need. She set a rapid pace as she clutched his arms, clinging to him with all of her strength as she rode him hard and fast. Her strangled cries mingled with his as he matched her desperate rhythm with his own thrusts. Release loomed on the horizon, but not close enough, and she screamed her frustration. Increasing the speed of their frantic coupling caused her already-sore muscles to spasm, yet she did not relent, even when he reached climax moments later. His light filled the room and filled her, though it did not complete her. Oh and she sorely needed completion. Forcing her body to the extreme, she kept going until she made it over the edge, wailing under the onslaught of more than the physical sensation.

And for a few sweet moments, she had peace.

She buried her face in his chest as she recovered. After a few deep breaths, she absently kissed his cheek while she disentangled herself from his body. She couldn't face him yet, but left the door open after turning on the shower. He accepted the silent invitation, and they enjoyed a lingering embrace before he washed her hair and her body. He got out first, giving her some much-needed solitude. After toweling off and donning her robe, she found him sitting on her bed. He patted the space beside him, bidding her to sit, which she did with more than a little reluctance.

He lifted her chin and said, "Not that I'm complaining, but would you like to tell me what that was all about?"

"It's nothing."

"Want to try that again?" His gaze was soft, but she saw the determination in his eyes. She'd have to explain whether she liked it or not.

"Look I'm sorry, okay—" she began before he raised his hand.

"I don't need an apology. Like I said, I'm not complaining," he repeated with a smile that eased her a bit. "I do need to know what's going on in here, though." He tapped her forehead with his index finger.

She let it out then. "Zeke, what are we doing? I mean, what am I to you? What happens when your 'assignment' is finished? What—"

He cut her off again, taking her hand. "You have no idea, do you? That is to say...what I mean is...I think...I love you, Vivian," he said, pausing to let his words sink in.

She'd heard those words before, but they were never spoken with such conviction, and never by someone she loved back.

Why does this have to be with someone I can't keep?

"But how can we make this work? And what kind of life can we have anyway? I don't regret a single moment I've spent with you. It was my choice, and I think I'm falling in love with you too. I just don't want to lose you. I want you to stay with me. I know it's selfish, but I want to keep you here with me and never let you go. It's just that...." She stopped, wringing her hands in frustration.

"Finish your thought, Vivian," he urged.

"Part of me wants to share you and show you off too. I want to take you out to dinner and go watch stupid, cheesy movies together. I want us to go on double dates with Sue, and I want to dream about weddings and babies and growing old together, all of the things I never cared about or just didn't have time to care about before. I want all of those things with you, but it just isn't possible, is it?" She finished with the awful, nagging question. The tears fell after, and with them came release and relief.

"You want a normal life." No anger, no judgment, no after-all-I've-given-you arguments. Just acknowledgment, and acceptance.

The latter made the tears fall harder.

"You do make me wish for a second chance, Vivian," he said quietly. "I love you and I am doing all I can to find a way to stay. But I don't want to stand in the way and keep you from living your life." He stood, moving to the bedroom window and basking in the glow of the afternoon sun.

Then he said, "I've been selfish too. I should give you some time and space."

He turned like he was about to leave, sending Vivian into a panic. "Wait! I don't want you to go," she pleaded, getting up and embracing him. "Just forget I said all that stuff and stay with me while you can, please?"

"I think I've turned out to be a pretty lousy guardian." Guilt and anguish strangled his voice. "I've been lousy at a lot of things in this world and the next."

"I don't know about before, but I know you've been a wonderful guardian, Zeke. What you've done for Mae, what you've been through with me." Her breath caught as she held him closer and continued. "No other person, friend or lover, has ever really been there *with* me."

He studied her and then smiled. "I think we need a night out."

"What?" she asked, wiping away fresh tears. She hadn't been expecting him to ask for a date. A date would be so normal.

"You know, a night out, an actual date? Dinner and a cheesy movie? Why not? We haven't had a real date, except for...." He faltered at the end, and she knew he was thinking of their last outing in the park.

She took his hand and said, "Don't worry, we can just stay in tonight, order some pizza. I don't have anyone to watch Mae until Saturday night anyway. Besides, I, um, I don't really want to go out right now anyway."

He cocked a brow and asked, "Why not?"

"It's nothing, really," she lied. She hoped she sounded convincing, but his expression said otherwise.

"It isn't nothing. Are you going to tell me, or do I have to go poking around in your mind myself?"

"You wouldn't *dare*," she challenged, grabbing him by the waist and pulling his body close in an effort to distract him. "Besides, I can think of a few other more interesting places for you to go poking around."

While his body responded, apparently his stubborn mind would not be persuaded. He turned and gently pushed her onto the bed. Once she was seated, he joined her, mindful to keep a healthy distance, before asking, "Tell me what's going on?"

Now wait just a damned minute.

"Oh, that's rich. You have the nerve to ask me what's going on? After shutting down and disappearing after I mediated my first soul crossing, you're honestly going to sit there and ask *me* what's going on?"

His gaze turned to stone and she braced for a fight. To her surprise, she was actually looking forward to a knock-down, drag-out fight with her guardian. God, what was wrong with her?

"You're right."

She could hardly believe her ears, not to mention Zeke's sudden shift in demeanor. Before she had the chance to voice one of the thousand-and-one thoughts careening through her brain, Zeke said, "I owe you an explanation for that. I owe you more than that."

He blew out a breath and leaned forward, scrubbing his face with rough hands. When he looked up again, his expression was haggard and his gaze raw. "I know it's not fair for me to ask you to go first, but if this," he waved his hand between the two of them as heat filled her cheeks, "has something to do with what's happening with your connection to the spirit realm, then I need to know about it, as your guardian and protector."

He covered her hands with his, letting the warmth flow and ease her.

She sighed, checking her temper. Guess now was as good a time as any to come clean. "Okay, here's the thing. I've been hearing and seeing things that no human should be able to see, including more spirits," she blurted out. "I mean, a *lot* more. It started a few weeks ago and sometimes I can't be sure when I'm talking to the living or the dead when I'm out. It's pretty scary. What's happening to me, Zeke?"

His brows furrowed. "You can speak with them, and they speak back? This is strange, Vivian. We aren't supposed to interact with the living unless absolutely necessary, and less powerful spirits shouldn't be able to do it at all. I don't understand."

"But I'm a soul broker, right? And I interact with you. Besides, I don't think they're all guardians," she answered.

"We *choose* to be seen by you. Wait, what do you mean they're not all guardians?" he asked, looking troubled.

"Well, they aren't all warm like you and Ezra. Some of them are cold. Some of them aren't all there either, you know, in the physical or other sense. Some are just wisps."

"You can see all of these manifestations?" He seemed incredulous. "That shouldn't be possible."

"Well, I saw Ezra the night you died, walking across the street plain as day," she retorted, probably a little more sharply than she intended. "Maybe you just aren't as good at hiding as you think you are."

He had her up and pinned to the bedroom wall at lightning speed, his hands sending searing heat through her arms as she cried out in shock and pain. "You saw Ezra that night, before you touched me? At the crash site... you *saw* Ezra?"

"Yes! He was in the crowd, for God's sake," she gasped, tears flooding her eyes. "Zeke, you're hurting me. Please let go."

His eyes looked wild, and she wasn't sure he'd heard her, so she gave him a powerful shove that flung him across the room with a brief flash of red light.

It left them both reeling with shock.

She stared down at her hands. She'd let loose a few sparks here and there when her temper had gotten the better of her, but she'd never lost control of the energy like that before. "I'm sorry! I didn't mean to do that." She met his gaze, pleading, "What's happening to me?"

He rose, wincing a bit. She'd knocked him pretty good, apparently. He ran his hand through his hair and over the back of his head before shaking it a little, and ran his other hand over his right arm, pausing at his elbow. When he lifted the hand, both he and Vivian saw the small streak of blood.

"Zeke," she said, walking to him and looking him over. "You're bleeding. I've never seen you bleed before? Is bleeding normal for a corporeal spirit?"

"No," he said absently. He closed his eyes for a moment as white light emanated from the wound, sealing it. "I haven't bled since the night I died. And healer or not, I also haven't heard of a mortal channeling this kind of energy." He shook his head as he paced back and forth, "I don't know what this means, Vivian."

She braced herself, knowing what they needed to do but anticipating a fight. "We need to talk to Ezra, Zeke. Now," she said with resolve.

"No," he muttered, still pacing. "I don't think that's a good idea."

"Zeke," she said, grabbing him by the shoulders to stop his damned pacing and to get him to look at her. "This is seriously freaking me out. We can't handle this on our own, we—"

"Vivian, you don't understand. You shouldn't have been able to see Ezra the night I died, not until after I opened the link when you touched me. No living person can see guardians or reapers until the end."

"The end? What are you talking about?"

"Until you die! I saw Ezra because my life was ending. He was there to help me cross."

His wide-eyed gaze was full of fear as he spoke, something Vivian hadn't seen in him since the night he died. "The only way you could have seen him when you did is if...." He struggled, appearing to disbelieve the conclusion he had reached. "Is if you were supposed to cross too."

"Wait," she said, panic washing over her like a bucket of ice water as realization dawned. "I was supposed to cross with Ezra? You mean I was supposed to *die*?" She started to pace then. "No, it can't be, can it? I mean—no, this is crazy. Ezra would have told me."

His reply was clipped and bitter. "Would he? We're very good at keeping secrets. Keeping ourselves hidden. I've kept us secret from the other guardians. But this, no, this isn't something he should have kept to himself. He should have at least told me. I am your guardian too."

Her head was spinning. She was lost at sea without a compass, and one of her two chief navigators was just as scared and confused. The other, it seemed, couldn't be trusted. Seeing spirits, throwing bursts of light across the room, being told she was, what? Dead? Dying? Supposed to die soon? *What's happening to me? Oh God, what's happening?* Trapped, helpless, all she wanted to do was run away someplace else, someplace safe.

She shut down, turning her focus inward. Her racing heart slowed, and she drew long and steady breaths until she found a frequency that allowed her to tune out her immediate surroundings and her fear.

She heard Zeke in the distance, trying to call her back as something pulled her away. Then, without warning, she experienced a familiar sensation, spinning through a vortex surrounded by streams of pale red light. Struggling to scream, she found she had no breath in her body and no solid surface on which to stand. It lasted for less than a minute, and then she plummeted back to the ground.

CHAPTER TWENTY

Once her stomach settled and she regained her balance, Vivian opened her eyes. *Where am I?* She was most certainly not in her bedroom anymore. She was not even indoors. She stood on a worn footpath in the middle of the woods.

She registered warmth all around, tempered by a cool breeze rustling through oaks, hickories, and dogwoods, the trees of her home and her childhood. They displayed their full green foliage, well past the blooms of spring but before the withering pre-autumn Southern heat beat them down. So she was in the year's prime then. That was the when.

But what about the where?

She jogged down the path, her direction guided by instinct. The trail widened a bit as she rounded a bend. Vivian found a delightful old springhouse, half concealed by thick vines. Running a little farther, she followed the bubbling babble of the lazy little creek that flowed left of the trail, her heart racing with anticipation and a wide smile splitting her face.

I've been here before. I know it! Are they still there?

Zigzagging around and over the tree roots along the path, she gasped with delight at the sight that greeted her. A makeshift bridge from a felled tree allowed her to exit the shaded wood and move over the water and into the clearing.

Just a little ways to go.

She was running, but not winded. The clear air filled her lungs and the clouds overhead billowed like cotton candy against the sky. Not pure blue sky, though. *No, that wouldn't be right. It has to be late afternoon.* The sky was painted in hues of pale blue punctuated by yellow and gold, and the clouds' shaded underbellies of gray faded in the slow descent of day.

She bounded across the log bridge. Realization dawned after she leaped off the bridge and into the grass. She was stark naked as a jaybird, and she laughed out loud. Great whoops of laughter brought her to the ground where she smelled fresh grass, good earth, and flowers. *Oh, they just have to be here!* She jumped up again and ran as fast as her bare feet would carry her. When she reached the spot and found them, she hollered at the top of her lungs with joy.

As far as her eyes could see, the rolling hills were bursting at the seams with black-eyed Susans. Their yellow petals waved to Vivian as if they remembered her. They must have, for this surely was a dream. This very sight had once greeted her eyes in her youth.

Well, perhaps now it carried the haze of nostalgia, or perhaps her dream state heightened the vision, but it was a heavenly vision.

She remembered when she had found this piece of paradise, spending an hour of pure rapture in this place, simply taking it all in, simply living, simply loving, simply *being*. Coming across the scene on an ordinary walk on a seemingly ordinary day, her feet had led her here to the unexpected extraordinary. She'd kept the memory locked in her mind and in her heart, fiercely guarding it as hers.

Now, to her amazement, she had returned.

Realizing the reason for her great need did not destroy her joy, but she ached to share this with the man she'd left behind. She closed her eyes and whispered, "Zeke, please, come here with me. You have to see this."

She turned around, expecting to see her guardian. Instead, she found herself alone in the field. She called him again. "Ezekiel Nathaniel Long-hollow, quit messing around and get over here right this minute!"

"He'll be along directly, child," came the familiar gravelly voice. "He just needs to recharge his battery, so to speak." The spirit associated with the voice was nowhere to be seen.

"Ezra?" Vivian cried, looking around. "Where are you?"

She suddenly remembered her nakedness and it filled her with shame. She shrank to the ground, pulling her knees up to her chest and wrapping her arms around her bare body as dread filled her. "Why are you here?"

"Don't be so scared now, Miss Vivian," his voice soothed. "I ain't looking anyway. But if it makes you feel better, why don't you grab that there blanket beside you."

She looked to her right and, sure enough, found the old worn quilt. She recognized it as her favorite blanket, hand-stitched by her great-grandmother. The double wedding band pattern had been made from scraps of fabric that held her heritage, from a time when nothing was wasted and all was cherished. Wrapping herself in the blanket warmed with the love and comfort of generations, she turned her attention back to the old spirit.

"What is this place, Ezra?"

"It's your place, Miss Vivian." He chuckled. "Only you weren't supposed to see it just yet. You went and jumped the gun just like a little kid sneaking up into the attic to take a peek at the Christmas goodies."

His light tone set her on edge even as his words brought the shock of discovery. And betrayal.

"Am I early, Ezra? I had a little talk with Zeke. He told me what seeing you that first night meant, that I only saw you because I was going to die."

"Child," he began, ambling toward her with hands up and palms out. "This wasn't the way things were supposed to happen, you being here now—"

"Was I supposed to die?" She gripped the old quilt's worn hem as if it were her only anchor to the present.

"Vivian...." Ezra muttered, trying to soothe.

"Yes or no?"

"Yes, child. You were meant to die in that crash."

He may as well have slapped her in the face. "Why didn't I die? Why didn't you tell me? How could you keep something like this from me?"

Ezra gave her a sad look and said, "Things like these, well they always happen for a reason, Miss Vivian. It ain't always for us to question—"

"Don't you *dare* try to get around me like that! I am not a little kid, I am not sneaking around, and we are not talking about a Christmas present. We are talking about my life...my death! Don't patronize me, and don't lie to me anymore. I trusted you. Zeke trusted you!" Tears fell in spite of her efforts to hold onto all of the bliss surrounding her.

"I am your guardian, and you were supposed to trust me. It was for the best, you not knowing, and I stand by that," Ezra said with an air of authority.

After they stared one another down for long minutes, the bastard shifted tactics and tried pleading with her. "Can't you never trust nobody, Miss Vivian? Why can't you leave well enough alone and let me do the worrying and the planning?"

"No, Ezra. Not anymore."

He sighed and shook his head. He'd always seemed old to Vivian, the burdens of his life's labors chiseled into the deep creases of his face. Now he seemed ancient, and weary beyond bearing.

Too bad.

"So were you just going to show up one night and carry me off without any warning? Why didn't you just take me away?" She sobbed with the pain of betrayal, the loss of faith she'd held onto by the smallest of threads. "You came to me, comforted me, brought me Zeke, and then you were going to take it all away? Is that it?"

He spoke with a low, sad voice. "Miss Vivian, I surely don't like to see you feeling so much hurt—"

"When were you going to tell me?"

"When the time was right. It's all a part of a higher plan—"

"When were you going to tell *me*, Ezra?" Zeke's voice arrived as his body began to materialize. A blinding white light swirled like a cyclone, followed by a flurry of fine particles that encased the light in a familiar form. He walked to her, apparently not bothered by his own nakedness, and helped her up as he wrapped his arms around her.

"Ezekiel." Ezra's voice changed from one of tenderness to one of admonition. "You ought to know better than to question your elders, boy. And you surely ought to have known better than to go and take the flesh of your charge. This trouble's on you and you know it!"

"Now wait just a damned minute," Vivian interrupted. "This was *my* choice. *Mine!* Do you hear me Ezra? I chose Zeke. I needed him and he was there for me. You sent him to me."

"To protect you, child, not to lead you astray. Spirits don't mix with the living. It ain't right. It ain't our way. This can only lead to suffering for you both, and it's led you away from your purpose. Zeke, take her back. Then you come on back home."

"Wait," she cried in despair. "I don't want to leave. I want to stay here," she pleaded, gripping Zeke's warm hand. "I want to stay here with you."

He held her face in his hands and her eyes in his fierce gaze. "We can't."

"But Ezra said this was my place. Is this my Heaven? Am I dead now?"

"This is the place that was prepared for you, but no, you're not dead," Zeke said. He sounded sure.

"Then how did I get here?" Vivian continued.

"Your forbidden union, I expect," Ezra said. "She has some of your guardian strength and power she ain't supposed to have. It'll leave you weak, Ezekiel. You weren't meant to share your light with the living."

"Ezra, please," came Zeke's voice, powerful yet reverent. "I'm begging you, let me stay with Vivian for a little while longer, take care of her."

"See her home now!" Ezra shouted.

A blinding white light more powerful than any Vivian had ever imagined followed Ezra's voice. Zeke held onto Vivian with all of his might as they fell into the vortex that spun them back to down to Earth.

CHAPTER TWENTY-ONE

She sat in the dreary emergency department waiting room, cloaked in the familiar blanket of thick dread. She had the room to herself. Seats previously occupied by the other lonely pilgrims now held magazines and empty food wrappers. With only the stale smell of coffee and the low hum of the corner television for company, the events of the past eight hours whirled through her weary mind in a jumbled cyclone of images.

After Zeke returned her from her latest accidental cosmic journey, Vivian ran inside her home and found Mae struggling to breathe. She'd flipped Mae over, first rubbing then tapping her back. She'd felt the ominous rattle in her sister's chest as Mae gasped and wheezed.

Think, think, think! Asthma attack?

She'd traveled back in time, twelve years old and Mama screaming for... something. *What does she need? Think! Mama wants the machine.* She'd grabbed the nebulizer, thankful she always kept it loaded with a cartridge, and plugged it in.

"Hold on, Mae-belle, baby, hold on," she'd whispered, as much to calm her own nerves as her sister's weak rasps. Vivian had turned her over, propped Mae up between her legs so she could sit, and flipped the switch. Mae moved her head away from the smoky mist flowing from the mouthpiece, but Vivian pushed her back. Mae coughed and spat, but she couldn't seem to catch her breath.

What next? Going through her checklist of possible causes, she'd tried suction next, first through Mae's nose and then through her throat. Vivian's breath had been labored and deep, as if she could will the extra air in her lungs to flow to her sister. It didn't help. The tube remained dry.

Her heart had clenched. Realization dawned on her when she knew her enemy.

Pneumonia.

Vivian panicked as Mae turned blue. Then she'd grabbed the phone.

The familiar parade of paramedics arrived, and she'd watched in numb helplessness as they attempted to aid her sister's failing lungs, then loaded her on the stretcher and into the cramped back of the ambulance. The sirens still clanged in her ears—the bright lights and glare of the sterile medical implements burned into her mind's eye. Two men had to hold Vivian back when they intubated Mae. She'd been certain the force of the invading tube would tear her sister's tiny throat.

Her thoughts returned to the present but offered little comfort.

Mae was dying.

An unwanted side effect of dabbling in the spirit world, her perception of death's slow and steady progression sent a jolt of panic through her heart and soul. No amount of planning and experience had prepared her for the full force of it. The past was full of close calls, false alarms, waiting for the inevitable. In those times and through those years, she had always shared the load with family. Now, no one bore the burden but Vivian.

She was alone, fighting a wave of sorrow that threatened to crush her.

With Mae's fate in the hands of the doctors, she was left with the void Zeke's absence. Even under the weight of her own pain, she'd been able to register his grief and sorrow at leaving her. He'd held her, kissed her, swearing he would find his way back to her.

She'd tried to understand, to forgive, and to keep the bitterness of resentment from overtaking her.

If this wasn't her hour of need, then when? Her guardian should be there to comfort and protect her, to give her something to hold on to and someone to hold her. Zeke should've been there with her. Because of Ezra, he'd been forced to forsake her.

And Ezra, her first guardian? The one who came to her in the guise of protector and guide? He had lied to her from the start.

I'm supposed to die too.

A slight drop in the temperature set off warning bells and her stomach clenched. A hospital wasn't the place to be when trying to avoid unwanted spirits. She was not alone.

She became aware of the commotion as she walked down the corridor toward one of the rooms—the frantic trauma team, transport staff, and accompanying police too distracted to notice her. The man on the gurney looked bad. Vivian caught clips of multiple conversations around her, picking out "multiple gunshot wounds" and "drive by." The shooter had apparently killed one bystander, maybe two.

The cold intensified as she moved closer to the trauma suite, causing her to shiver. The doors still stood open, and she walked just inside the room. She shouldn't have been there, and fully expected the staff to kick her out as soon as they spotted her. Yet something compelled her to witness whatever was to unfold in the room.

She watched with morbid fascination as the doctors and nurses worked on the man. Blood covered him. Gloved hands pushed down on his chest, poked, prodded, and stuck him with needles in an effort to ward off death. A familiar and frightening voice from the corner of the room grabbed her attention, freezing her with dread.

"Don't worry. It won't be much longer," Darkmore said.

He was speaking to the young man standing beside him. He placed a comforting hand on the man's shoulder. A younger girl stood on the other side of the man, tears streaming down her face as she clutched his hand. Darkmore turned to Vivian and gave her a friendly nod.

"They trying to save him," the man cried.

Vivian jumped, but the team continued working, undeterred by his protests.

"Him and his fool posse shot at me and Lindsey for no reason, and they trying to keep him alive? It ain't right!"

He lunged. Vivian screamed. No one else reacted, except Darkmore. In the silence that followed, she noticed the small smile turning up the corners of his full lips before shock overrode her senses.

Instead of crashing into the doctors and their patient, the young man passed right through them. He stumbled and fell to the ground, but not before knocking a few instruments off the tray on a nearby portable table. One nurse looked down at the mess, apparently startled, but then quickly returned her focus to the patient. The young man pulled himself up on shaky legs.

"What the hell?" he asked, turning to Darkmore. "What the hell's happening here?"

"We dead, Ty," came a reply, not from Darkmore, but from the girl now clinging to the man in white. "Can't nobody see us now."

"Girl, you done lost your mind!" He turned to Vivian. "She sees us."

"She dead too," said the girl.

"Oh no, my dear," Darkmore said, lowering himself to eye level with the girl. "She's not quite dead. She's just wavering between worlds right now. You're right about you and your brother though, I'm sorry to say." Had it been anyone else other than the creature before her, she'd have sworn she detected a note of genuine sorrow and...tenderness in his cool voice.

Ty walked back to his sister and Darkmore, avoiding the living and dying in the room this time as they ignored him. "For real?" he asked.

"I'm afraid so, Ty," Darkmore replied. "His bullets ended you both."

"No." Ty's eyes went wide with disbelief. "You crazy. You just some crazy freak trying to mess with me and my baby sis!"

Ty's fists balled as he spoke, his rage palpable. His energy wasn't cold, like Darkmore's presence, but red hot.

He took a swing.

Darkmore flashed out of the way and left Ty to stumble when his fist met nothing but air. Vivian shrieked as he fell through the floor and disappeared from view. Lindsey remained silent, and her heart ached for the girl. She walked over and stopped beside her. Reaching for her hand, she hesitated. What if it just passed through?

Closing her eyes and willing the connection, she touched the girl's hand, grateful for the warmth of the small palm in hers. She couldn't tell if

Lindsey took comfort from the touch, but she held on and squeezed in reassurance.

After a moment, Lindsey turned her large, dark eyes to Vivian and said, "They're back."

Vivian turned her gaze in the direction indicated by Lindsey's free hand and watched as Darkmore rose out of the solid floor with Ty in tow. Ty stood terrified as Darkmore drew a thin stream of light from him.

"Just a small taste," the reaper whispered to the man beside him, shuddering in his dark ecstasy. "That's enough. Thank you, Ty."

Vivian tried to stand in front of Lindsey to protect her, but the girl released her hand and walked to her brother.

Finally, Ty found his voice. "So you the reaper?"

"I am one of them, yes," said Darkmore. "But not for you two. For him."

"Then why we still here?" asked the girl.

"For justice," replied Darkmore.

They turned their attention back to the drama unfolding in the center of the suite. The prolonged electronic wail of the heart monitor held everyone's attention. Flatline. The medics administered more injections and tried a few more chest compressions, but the flatline persisted. A woman's detached voice called out, "Time of death, 11:47 p.m."

The medical team stood down and a few began cleaning up the mess around the deceased patient. He was gone. Vivian turned back to the others who watched and waited.

"Here he comes now," Darkmore said, patting the girl on her head. A form suddenly appeared beside the table. The spirit of the dead man, Vivian presumed. He looked around the room with wide-eyed confusion, his eyes falling on the trio in the corner opposite Vivian.

"What the fuck is this shit?" said the new man, eyes on Ty and Lindsey.

"You dead, motha fucka, that's what it is!" Ty screamed. He turned to Darkmore and cried, "Go on now and drag his ass to Hell!"

The reaper smiled and said, "With pleasure."

Darkmore reached out and took hold of the dead man, who froze in his grip, face filled with fear and agony. He turned to Lindsey and said, "Take your brother outside, child. They'll be waiting to see you home."

Then his icy blue gaze met Vivian's. "I'll be back soon, Ms. Bedford."

Tipping his hat with his free hand, he vanished, the screams of the soul he'd claimed echoing through the suite for those who could hear them.

They faded faster for Vivian, who turned and ran from the room.

CHAPTER TWENTY-TWO

Vivian slammed into Sue with enough force to knock both of them down.

When Sue recovered, she rose and rubbed her sore spots and then helped Vivian up. Sue appeared to be on the verge of giving her hell for being so careless, but the look on Vivian's face must have changed her mind.

"I came as soon as I heard. Why are you barreling down the hallway like that? Is it Mae? Is she...Oh, Viv," Sue said. She embraced Vivian, holding on to her for dear life as she shook her head.

"You're shaking like a leaf. Come on. Let's get you a chair and something to drink." Sue pulled her back to the waiting area. Once seated, Sue sat down and looked at Vivian, her face full of worry.

"Are you okay?"

Vivian tried to answer, but a strangled sob came out instead.

"You stay put. I'm going to get some help," Sue said before she darted off.

Vivian tried to pull herself together as she followed Sue's hushed conversation with a few women at the admitting desk. Apparently she'd landed back in the world of the living. Sue could see her. What had happened back there? She couldn't quite wrap her mind around the events she had just witnessed. She just needed some time to think.

Sue, accompanied by three nurses, interrupted her attempts.

"Vivian," Sue said in a soft, soothing voice. "Can you hear me, honey?"

Vivian stared at her. Sue turned to one of the nurses and asked, "Is there something you can give her? Bless her heart, she must be in shock."

Uh-oh. Medication wasn't a good idea. What if Darkmore came back?

"It's okay," Vivian managed to mutter, not quite certain where the strength in her voice came from. "I don't need anything, except maybe a good strong cup of coffee."

"You sure?" asked one of the nurses. "There's no shame in taking something for your nerves."

"No, I'll be okay," Vivian insisted. "I've got my best friend here now. She'll look after me."

Her answer seemed to satisfy, since Sue nodded to the nurses. "Thanks. Sorry to be a bother." Turning back to Vivian, she said, "You had me running scared for a minute. Looked like you might die of fright."

Vivian lowered her head and rubbed her aching temples with trembling fingers. "Sorry, Sue," she said. "I've just had one hell of a night." She then looked up and said with complete sincerity, "I'm really, really glad you're here."

"Me too," Sue replied, putting a hand on her shoulder. "Me too."

Vivian began to recount what she could of the night's turmoil for Sue, but was interrupted by news from the emergency department's attending doctor. Mae was breathing on her own, though just barely. They talked about a feeding tube. It was too risky feeding her the conventional way, not to mention the dangers her daily pill ration presented. The thought of liquid meals being squirted directly into Mae's stomach proved almost too much to bear. As far as she knew, tasting food was the only pleasure Mae might still experience, if she experienced anything at all.

They talked about "extraordinary measures," fancy doctor words for bringing someone back from the brink of death.

No, ma'am, Mae never had the faculties to leave a living will. Mama never wanted a DNR, and I never gave it much thought.

These were decisions Vivian felt wholly unqualified to make. Finally, they decided Vivian should take the rest of the night to mull over her options. They could keep Mae going on IV fluid for a few days, the doctor assured her.

Reading between the lines, she guessed she might not have to decide if Mae didn't last that long.

When Vivian returned to the lounge, Sue was still there and waiting for her. And she had coffee.

"Thanks," Vivian muttered, accepting the cup. "I could use something warm to drink. Why are hospitals always so cold?"

"It's partly to keep germs at bay," Sue said. "And partly because we're here."

"What?"

Sue winked and moved her hand to tip an imaginary hat. Realization dawned and Vivian's blood froze as Zeke's words replayed in her mind.

I know we can also possess the living.

"Let her go, Darkmore," she whispered, low and with remarkable calm.

Sue's voice chuckled. "I promise to release your friend after we have a little chat."

"Release her first and then we'll talk," Vivian countered.

Sue's voice cackled. "Making deals with the devil? I knew I liked you for a reason. But you aren't exactly in a position to make demands, Ms. Bedford."

"Besides," said the smiling thing that was once Sue Carlson, "This is safer. If the nurses see you talking out loud to someone who's invisible, they'll cart you off to the psych ward for sure.

"And," Sue's voice said as her gaze lowered, "I didn't expect you'd sit and chat with me any other way."

"It's me you want, not her," Vivian countered. *Oh dear God, not Sue.* "Please, just let her go and we'll talk. We can meet out on one of the court-yard benches, where no one else can see."

"You won't go running off on me will you?" the Sue creature asked with a twinkling smile and another wink. Even if she was foolish enough to try, Vivian knew he would get to her anyway.

She nodded and rose when the form of Sue stood. They began walking down the corridor that connected the emergency department to the general hospital and specialty clinics.

"Here," Sue's voice said as they ducked into the darkened alcove leading to what appeared to be some vacant offices. "We'll leave your friend here for now. You can come and pick her up after our little chat."

"Will she be okay?" Vivian asked.

"Of course," answered the Sue creature with a hint of indignation in her voice. "She'll just be a little sleepy. Won't remember a thing and she'll be none the worse for wear. I'll see you outside."

Sue's body sat down in one of the chairs and fell limp. Vivian straightened her as best she could so her friend wouldn't wake up with a cramp from slumping.

"I'm sorry," Vivian whispered, brushing Sue's hair out of her face. "I didn't mean for you to get mixed up in all of this. I'll be back soon."

Vivian walked down the rest of the dark corridor and out into the darker night. She saw Darkmore in his more familiar incarnation, beckoning her to sit next to him on a wooden bench, half-hidden by low tree branches. With a sense of falling, she walked toward the spirit and sat down. She didn't meet his gaze, and he didn't speak at first. She stared at her clasped hands resting on her lap. As much as she hated to admit it, being close to the cool spirit felt refreshing. Summer was at its peak, which meant the warmth didn't disappear with the daylight. The air hung heavy and muggy with no breeze blowing to ease the sweltering heat. She inhaled and caught the comforting scent of citrus.

Lemonade.

It was one of her favorite smells, as if the evil thing was trying to put her at ease.

"What happened to him?" she asked, still staring at her hands.

"To whom?"

"The man who died, the one whose soul you took," she clarified. "What happened to him?"

"I delivered him to the next realm," he said simply.

"To the cold, dark place you sent me?"

"I didn't send you anywhere, Ms. Bedford. You made it there on your own."

She faced him now, angry. "No, you just called the taxi to pick me up and drag me to Hell!"

"Hell? No, you weren't in Hell. At least not in the sense you probably understand it," he said with mild surprise.

"Then where was I, you demon, you, you...*devil?*"

"Calm down, dear lady." He laughed. "We may be outdoors, but your voice tends to carry when you're riled up. As for where you were, you were simply in another realm, one of the many planes of existence inhabited by the many forms of consciousness. And I'm not the devil."

"Then what are you?" she snapped. "And what do you want with me?"

"Always so black and white, you mortals," he mused. "Is this life so simple? Are the people you know all sinner or all saint? Think of our mutual friend from your last visit to this hospital. You and that unfortunate soul became rather well acquainted, as I recall. And from what I've heard, you met once more to settle the score, as it were."

That gave her pause. "Well, of course no one's purely good or evil," she answered, reply choked by irritation and lingering fear. So far he'd kept his word by releasing Sue, and he seemed content to talk. But she wasn't fool enough to think herself safe with the creature beside her.

Darkmore continued, apparently nonplussed by her outburst. "No, there are so many shades of gray. What makes you think the afterlife is any less complex? As for what I am, I am a guide, like your friends Ezra and Ezekiel."

"So you take the bad people off to a dark and frightening realm in the name of karmic justice or something?" She remembered Ezra's story. "But what about Ezra? Did you give him a stroke and leave him to rot just for shits and giggles? For your own amusement?"

Anger rose as she thought of the old man's suffering, of her sister's, of her own. "How is that justice?"

He sighed and paused before he spoke. "Always so black and white," he muttered again, shaking his head. "How much do you know about hyenas, or vultures, or jackals?"

"They're scavengers," she said. "They're like nature's garbage men."

"Yes, exactly. They serve their purpose, keeping nature in balance by taking out the trash, so to speak. This is what I, and those like me, do. Not always very pretty, but then again, neither are the hearts and actions that bring my kind calling on you."

"No, it isn't pretty." Vivian scowled. "That still doesn't explain Ezra, or all of the others you push over the edge with suffering and grief."

"Vivian," he began, with a patient smile. "May I call you Vivian?"

"Why not? If you're out to steal my soul, we may as well be on a first-name basis. I'll just call you Lazarus then."

"Lazarus is but one of my names," he answered. "But surely you can appreciate the significance. The risen man, cheater of death, one of only two winners in fate's cruel game, if you follow Biblical lore. I don't always win, mind you, but I do enjoy the game. You know, hyenas don't always scavenge for their meals. If the opportunity arises, they can be skilled predators. In the face of such delicious opportunities to explore the limits of human darkness a hungry reaper can hardly be blamed for feasting. It is our nature, our purpose."

"It's a hateful purpose," she said sharply. "To be an incubus, feeding from the pain of the living and the torment of the dead."

"Perhaps," he conceded. "But necessary all the same. As for Ezra, I did indeed taste his pain and found it delectable. You might want to ask him what brought me to his bedside. I'd be willing to bet he left that little detail out of the story. At any rate, he would have been quite a prize, yet he resisted. He hasn't told you how, has he?"

The reaper's words gave her pause. She wouldn't have given them a second thought yesterday, never would have dreamed the kind old spirit could deceive her so deeply, but now?

"He told me he made a deal with the guardians for his energy and then he went to work for them."

"And why, do you suppose, would they even bother with him? He was one of many mortals. Haven't you wondered what made him so special? What makes you special? No matter, it seems he still holds a grudge against me, even after all of these years and even though he got away in the end."

"The fact that he got away is very telling, I think," Vivian retorted. She didn't fully trust Ezra anymore, but she wasn't ready to take Darkmore at his word either. "Something good must be on his side, especially if he was able to save a soul from you."

"Oh, you mean *God*, Vivian?" he said, a flicker of surprise shining in his bright eyes. "I didn't figure you for a true believer, but then again, so many mortals take that path toward the end. Now your friend Ezra, he was a true believer through and through, even before I wound up in his field. He bowed to the God created in his own image, like the followers before him and those who've come after."

"What are you babbling about?" Couldn't he just get to the point?

Apparently, her mood and impatience mattered little to the reaper. He leaned back, made himself comfortable, and kept right on talking. "God of mercy and love, or God of justice and punishment? Righteous God or jealous God? Which is it? Your Jesus admonished his followers to turn the other cheek, but dear old Dad leveled entire civilizations on a whim. How does one reconcile these two sides of divinity?"

Her head ached, her heart hadn't stopped pounding since entering the trauma suite, and she really just wished he would get to whatever fucking point he was trying to make. For that reason as much as any other, Vivian answered. "Yeah, fine, I get it. People can be kind or cruel, caring or callous, naughty or nice, so you reason the duality of human nature is why we see God that way."

"Why does it have to be either one or the other? The Greeks and Romans had all manner of gods and goddesses to represent every facet of the human psyche and condition, and some of their notions made the preferred Almighty of this age seem downright tame. And don't even get me started on Norse mythology! The good, the bad, and the very ugly, to quote one of my favorite movies," he quipped.

"You like movies?"

"Oh indeed," he replied. "Especially westerns. I'm rather fond of Sergio Leone's works. Clint Eastwood too, but I digress. I get the feeling you're a little anxious, so let's get back on track, shall we? Now you mortals, in addition to benevolence and animosity, are equally capable of indifference. Consider your current situation, Vivian. Family? Friends? Who, other than your charming friend Susan, is here for you now?"

Tired, sad, and angry as she was, Darkmore's insistence on rubbing salt in her wounds left her beyond raw and weary. She shrugged and muttered, "Well, no one, other than you."

"Hmm." Darkmore sighed and waited. What, did he expect her to fall for the best buddy act?

"So I am. Ezra, however, is not. What does that tell you?"

"That he's pissed off at me for sleeping with Zeke and for throwing a monkey wrench in whatever plan he has for me."

She decided to leave out the part about the unexpected burst of spirit light. If she needed to use it to fight him, the element of surprise could come in handy.

"Well, if he's angry with you for such a small transgression, imagine how much he despises me," Darkmore said. "He even found a way to injure me and take his vengeance. That's what led me to you, you know. Your guardian has cost me what is mine on more than one occasion, much the same as you."

Vivian stared at the pale form in disbelief. "What?" Great God, did he mean...did he come that night to claim *her* soul? But she'd never—

Contemplated suicide? Hated your sister enough to lash out at her, maybe even kill—

"No," she whispered.

"I see you've worked out a few things on your own." He smiled. "So why don't you let me tell you the rest, and then we can get down to my proposal."

"Why should I trust you?"

"Why should you trust Ezra, or Ezekiel for that matter?"

"They came to help me, and to help Mae." She wasn't sure she believed her argument fully, but she would defend Zeke at the very least. Unlike Ezra, he'd always been honest.

"Ezra came to you," he said slowly, "because he was supposed to claim you for service as a guardian. Just as I was meant to take Mr. Longhollow."

His words sank in and filled Vivian with a cold terror. *Zeke* was supposed to cross to the dark place. Her Zeke. The spirit who'd held her, comforted and cared for her, the spirit who'd eased her burdens with Mae and loved her.

Darkmore had been sent to claim him that terrible night. How could that be?

He told you he was no saint.

"No, that's not possible," she said firmly. "I don't believe you. Zeke is a good spirit, so he must have been a good man."

"How much do you really know about your precious Zeke, Vivian?" he sneered. "He came to you, charmed you, *seduced* you, and now he's left you. Of course, you aren't the only one he abandoned—"

"Shut up! He didn't leave me. Ezra took him from me!"

"No, Ezra took him from me. He was *mine*!"

Darkmore stopped, closed his blue eyes and took a moment to calm. When he opened them again, he resumed his casual tone. "Seems Ezekiel can't behave himself even in the afterlife. He's much better suited for my line of work, but no matter now. What's done is done. However, Ezra owes me, and not just for his soul or the woman's soul you won him when last we met."

"What do you mean the soul I won him? I set her free!"

He shook his head and gave her a small, sad smile. "No, my dear, she's hardly free, or rather, she wasn't free until after your second meeting. You merely transferred her debt to the guardians. She was working for them, and not voluntarily."

Vivian stared at him, dumbfounded. "What are you saying? She was their slave?"

"Oh, Ezra and his kind would call their noble calling the true path to peace, but don't let them fool you. Her redemption came with the price of service. And since we're on the subject of debts and payments, Ezra's ledger remains in the red. He let you go that night in lieu of Zeke, and left you in limbo. I didn't get Zeke. That leaves you."

"You've got to be fucking kidding me!" she cried. "You want to just take me out in trade with Ezra?"

"My dear," he purred. "If I truly wanted to claim you as a prize, I could have done so by now. I doubt it would take much. I was quite close the night we met, as you may recall." She opened her mouth, prepared for round two, but the change in his expression and his open palms, held aloft in mock surrender, stilled her.

"But I confess, now that I've observed you more closely, you intrigue me. And believe me, it's been a very, very long time since any mortal has captured my interest. My kind tend to work alone, being more solitary by nature, but it's by no means a hard and fast rule. I offer you the chance to come with me as my partner."

Vivian stared at him, dumbstruck. "You think I would *choose* to come with you?"

"There are far worse ways to enter my realm," he said, steeling his gaze and lowering his smooth voice. "You would be my pupil, then my equal, perhaps even my better in time," he crooned, moving closer and wrapping her into his cool sphere.

Gooseflesh rose on her arms and shivers ran down her back while unwanted arousal awakened in other parts of her body. "Oh, the things I can show you, my Asherah, my Elath. How I would love to make you a goddess. We would reap the wicked and feast. You've been chained in this life. I can set you free in the next. Free will, Vivian. You have to admit, it's a better choice than Ezra offered."

Before she could stop him or protest, he leaned forward and placed his cool lips on hers, brushing softly and teasing. A spark similar to electricity jolted through her body as a thin stream of red light escaped his lips and entered her. His energy tasted powerful and raw, delicious and frightening. The essence of this creature intoxicated.

She still felt a good deal of fear, but she also felt a good many other things after Darkmore's lips left hers.

"I thought your kind dwelled in darkness," she whispered, "but your light...it's...."

"Like yours? Yes, my dear," he said, brushing her hair from her face. "Delicious, isn't it? All of the fury, the passion, I can teach you to how to channel it, how to use it, and how to *feed* it. You could unleash it instead of burying it deep inside. Power like yours shouldn't be wasted. It can be of great value and very useful. Think about it, Vivian. You need not fear the darkness when you know the way in, the way through, and the way out. I'll show you. Mine is but one realm, and there are those whose lot it is to dwell there, for a time of penance or for eternity. Your light, like mine, is the conduit. Use it."

"No," she sobbed. "It's not my light. It never was. It's Zeke's. I took it from him, I—"

He gave a soft little laugh and kissed her again before offering, "Hmm, seems you're a quick study indeed. You've already learned one way to feed it." He nuzzled her cheek before leaning back and rising. He offered her his hand, and she took it, unable to resist in the wake of his influence.

"You don't have to decide right this minute, Vivian, but soon. Think it over, will you?" He said in a voice thick with desire. "The guardians may have opened you as a conduit, but you control the energy. Do you have any idea how difficult it is to take energy from living souls? You can harness the burdens of the quick *and* the dead, my dear. Any reaper or guardian would covet such an ability, including your friend Ezra."

"What about Mae?" Vivian asked.

"Ah yes, your sister. What a prize she would be," he said, a wide smile gracing his chiseled features. "A lifetime locked in her shell. Her soul could unleash a powerful fury that would sustain us for millennia."

Powerful fury...a light to sustain the spirit world...like the energy she'd tasted from the woman's soul. Locked in a shell...trapped, Ezra had said he was trapped....

Another thought occurred to her, one that left her cold to the core.

"That's why you want me," she said, fighting the hurt she had no right to feel. "To get to her. It's always been about her." She whispered the last part so softly, she was sure only she had heard those words.

Zeke had told her that Mae and those like her were full of terrifying spirit power. So it followed, then, that such energy could be tapped. Was tapping such energy how those in the spirit realm fed their power? Oh God, poor Mae. To be trapped in this life and drained in the next.

"Oh no," Darkmore said, embracing her roughly. He felt like a crisp mountain stream. "Not for me it isn't. But maybe it is for them."

"What?" Vivian whispered, struggling against his hypnotic pull.

"They've been visiting you for quite some time, Vivian. Lingering near you and your sister while supposedly guarding you both and working to keep me at bay. Yet Ezra still hasn't finished telling you his little story, has he? Ah, I can see by the look on your face that you've been curious about the delay."

She nodded.

"Mae is the reason. Your guardian wants her too, and the bounty of energy she holds."

He disappeared with that.

CHAPTER TWENTY-THREE

Vivian stood rooted to the spot for a long time, weighing Darkmore's words before remembering Sue. She darted back inside and through the winding corridors, finding her friend tucked away exactly as she had left her. Filled with guilt, a familiar if not comfortable state, Vivian walked back the way she came and retrieved a thin, standard-issue hospital blanket from a lonely service cart. She wrapped Sue in the blanket, jotted a note apologizing for her absence, and left her friend to sleep. She didn't like leaving her there, but couldn't bring herself to wait. Honestly, she didn't want to explain to Sue what had happened either.

But she couldn't just walk away.

Using the courtesy phone, she made an anonymous report, figuring the nurses could check Sue out and make sure she was okay. Darkmore promised she would be, but Vivian still didn't trust him at his word.

That she didn't entirely distrust him seemed even more disturbing.

While wandering aimlessly down the abandoned hallway, the events of the night threatened to overwhelm her. Helplessness and vulnerability quickly shifted to anger, a simmering rage that intensified with each passing step. By the time she rounded the corner and slammed into the person walking in the opposite direction, she shook with fury.

"Jesus Christ, watch where you're fucking going!" she screamed from her place on the floor, the pain from the fall stoking the furnace of her rage.

"Forgive me, miss. I honestly didn't hear you coming. Please, allow me to help you up."

"Forget it. I've had just about all the help I can stand!" She pulled herself up, brushed her hair from her face, and was greeted by the calm face of Father Lloyd Montgomery.

"Vivian?" He seemed surprised, though she could not tell whether he was more surprised at running into her, literally, or by her violent reaction. He regarded her for a moment, and then said, "I'm surprised to see you here, and so late at night. Are you unwell?"

"Sorry, Padre," she muttered, shame-faced at her vulgarity-laden outburst in spite of her agitation. "I probably would have curbed the language, and the blasphemy too, if I'd known it was you."

He waved his hand. "Don't worry about it. You're quite obviously distressed. Would you care to grab a cup of coffee and sit for a while? My office is just upstairs."

"Office?"

"Yes, it's beside the hospital chapel. I'm on the pastoral care staff. I share the space with some other ministers, but we should have the place to ourselves at this late hour," he said as he pointed the way.

They walked in silence to the office, where Father Montgomery bid Vivian to sit in a well-worn armchair and relax while he set about brewing a fresh pot of coffee. Wrapped in its comfortable embrace, she began to succumb to exhaustion in the low light and ambience of the room.

Aside from religious symbols, exotic-looking trinkets and knickknacks peppered the office. One object in particular caught her attention—a piece of pottery, terra cotta in color and painted with brilliant shades of red and blue. The handles formed the arms, joined at the hips of the figure shaped from the clay and accentuated by the paint. The figure itself was female, as wide legs spread with primal pagan joy revealed. Now there was something she hadn't expected to see in a clergyman's office. Father Montgomery returned then. Rather than sitting in the chair behind the large desk, he surprised Vivian by sitting on the couch opposite her.

"I see you've found one of my favorite conversation pieces." He chuckled. "At least, it is a favorite among the laity. I don't think my fellow men of the cloth approve, especially the Baptists."

"I can see how it might raise a few hackles. Where did you get it?"

"Venezuela," he replied. "I did some mission work there many years ago, before Chavez, of course. I'm not surprised you were drawn to her. As I recall, you have a bit of a feminist streak," he said with a smile. "That was a joke, by the way. You look like you could use a bit of cheer. No hard feelings?"

"No, no hard feelings, Padre," Vivian replied absently. "Who is she?"

"The likeness is of the goddess Kuma, venerated by the Yaruro people as the creator of all things. Some claim she also receives the dead," the priest answered.

"Great, more grim reapers," she muttered.

"Excuse me?"

"Nothing, forget about it."

"I should thank you, by the way," he said. Her confusion must have shown on her face since he continued. "For encouraging me to visit my doctor the day we met, right before you left the Cathedral—I'm still not certain how you knew about that, but taking your advice probably saved my life."

"How so?" she whispered.

"I'd been putting off getting an angiogram. After your visit I called for an appointment and got in the next day. They found a major blockage."

"Are you okay now?"

"Yes, thanks to my new stent," he said, patting his chest. "Well, while we wait for our coffee, would you care to tell me what's troubling you so?"

"How much time you got?"

"As much as you need," he replied with complete sincerity.

"My sister's in the hospital, and she's probably not coming out," Vivian said. Seemed as good a place to start as any.

"I see," said Father Montgomery. "I'm sorry to hear that. Was this sudden?"

"No, she's been ill a long time, her whole life really. She's disabled," she said, struggling with the explanation. She'd had this conversation many times, the "explaining Mae" talk. The conversation never got easier.

"We never really knew what caused it. She was born with some problems. I mean, I remember wearing a surgical mask when I first got a look at her after my folks brought her home, but none of us knew how bad it would be. She did fine until she was about six months old or so. She could hold her head up and move around like normal babies back then."

The priest nodded, bidding her to continue. "Well, then she had surgery, and she was never the same after, at least that's what I was told later. I was pretty young. Maybe it was the anesthesia, or maybe she was always going to go downhill, who knows? At any rate, she's never been able to care for herself. She can't walk or talk, or feed herself, or do anything." She paused to gather her thoughts.

"Who cared for her?"

"My family. My mom did most of it, since Dad had to work. They died about six months ago. Since then...she's been mine," she said with a shrug.

"That's quite a burden to shoulder."

She waited, but he didn't offer further comment. He didn't avert his gaze either, which threw her for a loop. Vivian had grown accustomed to platitudes, well-intentioned advice, and uncomfortable pauses in these conversations. This man appeared to be inviting her to speak freely and at her leisure.

"Well, it's what I promised, and it's what I'll see through," she said, then added, "if I can." She dropped her head and rubbed her hands over her temples.

"Is there a reason you wouldn't be able to see this through?" Father Montgomery asked.

"I may not be around long enough," she replied, gaze still in her lap.

The priest sat silent for a moment, and then asked, "Vivian, are you unwell?"

She raised her head and caught the look of concern on his face.

Aw hell, he probably thinks I'm suicidal. How's that for irony?

She jumped out of her chair, grabbing her purse and headed toward the door, determined to leave before he called the psych ward.

"Look, it's not what you think, okay? Forget I said it. I'm not going to jump off a bridge or anything. It's just...there's just some other stuff I have to deal with. It's complicated." *Complicated? Talk about the understatement of the century.*

He stood and moved to block her access to the door. "Vivian, please sit down. I can assure you, whatever you are going through right now is not too complicated for you to work through with God's help."

She laughed out loud at that one. "God's help? Oh, like I haven't heard *that* before." Her frustration and rage found the perfect target in the form of the man in front of her. There he stood, dressed in his priestly raiment and spouting off the same empty words she'd heard since Mae's condition came to light.

"Let me guess. 'Trust in God—he'll see you through?' Or how about, 'You can get through anything, you just have to pray?' That's a personal favorite. Or maybe, 'Trust in the Lord with all thine heart and lean not unto thine own understanding?' Well, I don't think prayer is going to help me with this."

Closing her eyes and extending her hands, she tapped into her rage, terror, and trauma of the past several hours. Streams of red light burst from her fingertips and illuminated the room as they hit the wall, tearing through the sheetrock and even charring the cinderblock underneath.

The priest made the sign of the cross and turned toward her, his face frozen in terror. "Wh-wh-what are you?" he whispered.

"I'm dead!" she yelled. "Or dying, or somewhere in between. I was supposed to die weeks ago, but the spirit who came to get me took Zeke instead. All I did was stop at a car crash and hold his hand, and the guardians who took him instead of me left me with *this*." She waved her cursed hands, sending a few more sparks flying.

"I don't understand," he muttered as he backed himself against the wall. Confused and frightened, he muttered, "This isn't possible." Almost as an afterthought, he asked, "Who is Zeke?"

"Ezekiel Longhollow. He died in the crash, and Ezra took him to the spirit world instead of me. He was supposed to be carted off to hell, but Ezra took him. And now the reaper who was sent for Zeke is after me!"

"This doesn't make any sense," Father Montgomery said, maybe to himself and maybe to Vivian. She couldn't tell and remained too agitated to do anything but scream her plight to this man who was supposed to have the answers.

"I see ghosts and spirits everywhere, I've been shooting light out of my hands, and zapping in and out of this world and the next. The reaper apparently wants me to join up with him, and they all want Mae. She's all any of them want," she cried, her jumbled thoughts aligning as she gave voice to the awful truth.

"It's about her. It's always been about her. I put up with her being first all these years, and then I had to put my whole damned life on hold when my folks up and died and left me saddled with her, and now this!"

Father Montgomery stared at her. She'd shown him her darkness, all of it. If he had any words of comfort or acts of contrition, he didn't offer them. Not that she really blamed the man after what she'd shown him, though losing her one anchor this side of the grave left her aching and hollow.

"And now, *Father*, now I have to die," she whimpered, anger replaced by anguish. He just stared at her in disbelief.

"Did you hear me, Padre? I have to *die* and go straight to Hell for her, and bear the burdens of a host of lost souls right along with me."

She sobbed the last, and unable to continue she pushed the priest out of the way and ran out of his office.

CHAPTER TWENTY-FOUR

Vivian paced back and forth outside of the cathedral, debating over whether or not she was actually going to enter. The priest had some brass balls, she'd give him that. The last thing she had expected after her encounter with Father Montgomery was an invitation to Mass.

She had to replay the voicemail three times to convince herself the offer was genuine.

Of course, the only way to find out was to work up the nerve and go inside.

She'd waited in her car and scanned the parking lot for police or medical staff, thinking it might be a trap. Of course, telling any rational person what he had seen would make them question *his* sanity, but he probably still had the power to lock her up. She had no reason to trust him.

No reason but faith.

In the end she took a leap of faith, or rather a stumbling walk of faith, as she headed toward the building. She turned away from the door and walked halfway back to the parking lot before stopping and heading back. Finally, steeling her resolve, she walked inside.

It wasn't crowded. The sparse congregation put her a little more at ease, as did the fact that she hadn't accidentally set off a fireworks display from her fingers upon entering the place. Or been struck by lightning. Some stereotypes just got ingrained. She'd been working to gain control of the bursts of excess energy she'd harvested. Channeling that much power took a fair amount of concentration, but she'd gotten pretty good at hitting makeshift targets in the backyard, and even played around with the duration and intensity.

She didn't know how much energy she'd collected from the lost souls she'd encountered, from the living, from Zeke, or if he'd suffered at all from the transfer. Even more disturbing, she had no idea if and when she'd run out.

If she could reach him....

She wondered if she would ever see him again, but she set the thought aside in another corner of her mind to deal with later. She had enough on her plate at the moment.

She settled on a pew in the back corner, her preferred location when forced to spend time in religious venues. Made for an easy escape.

After communion, which she declined, Vivian caught the eye of Father Montgomery. He smiled at her and nodded. She hung back after the recessional hymn, approaching the priest only after the rest of the congregation had departed.

"Ah, Vivian," Father Montgomery said in greeting, shocking the hell out of her by taking her right hand in both of his own. His apparent lack of fear shocked her even more. "I'm so glad you could join us today. How is your sister?" he asked, as if addressing a perfectly normal person, not the sort of woman who went around blowing holes in office walls with ethereal spirit energy.

"Mae's stable. We decided to go ahead and put in the feeding tube. She's scheduled for surgery on Monday."

She regarded the priest for a moment before she blurted out, "Okay, let me just put this out there. I can't believe you called me after the other night. I must have scared the shi...shiitake mushrooms out of you, and, um, well, why did you call me?"

He laughed at her outburst, leaving her even more dismayed. After he recovered, he spoke again. "It was certainly an enlightening encounter, Vivian, and it left me with a great deal to consider. And after much prayer and meditation, I decided to act. God sent you to me for a reason, and I want to help you."

"That's nice of you, Padre, but I don't know what you could possibly do to get me out of this mess."

"Well, for starters, there's someone I would like you to meet. Two people, actually," he replied. "I asked them to wait for us in the Blessed Sacrament Chapel."

Well, that's certainly unexpected. "Who is it you want me to meet?"

"Better come along and see for yourself," he replied.

The priest extended his arm in invitation, so she followed his lead and walked with him. As they approached the chapel, he turned and said, "The people I would like you to meet are two of my parishioners, soon to be three."

They arrived at the alcove, illuminated by an ornate sanctuary lamp that provided a welcoming glow. Father Montgomery bowed before entering and bid Vivian to come in and take a seat across from two other occupants. She regarded them with mild curiosity. The woman looked to be about Vivian's age and was pretty, though she looked tired. Vivian imagined at least one source of her fatigue was the boy sitting next to her. He looked to be about four years old, and he didn't look at Vivian.

The other source of her fatigue resided in her swollen belly.

At least six months along, maybe more. Vivian couldn't tell since the woman sat slumped. She seemed like such a tiny little thing, though definitely all baby. *Must be hard on her.* Between carrying such a heavy load around and dealing with another kid, it was no wonder she had dark circles under her eyes. She gave Vivian a bright smile, however, which took her by surprise. The smile changed the woman's whole face and she looked younger and fresher.

She also seemed familiar.

"Hello," the woman offered. "I'm so very pleased to meet you. I can't believe Father Montgomery was able to track you down." She turned to the boy sitting next to her and coaxed him. "Zeb, honey, can you say hello?"

The boy, who had been rocking, didn't acknowledge his mother. Probably autistic. There had been some kids on the spectrum in Mae's classes when her sister had attended school, and this little guy reminded her of them. He didn't make any eye contact and seemed to be caught up in flapping and wringing his hands. Vivian kneeled down to his level and spoke without waiting for his attention.

"Hi there, Zeb. My name's Vivian. It's nice to meet you," she said, keeping a comfortable distance.

Zeb didn't react, so Vivian turned to his mother and asked, "Does he do high fives?" Vivian wanted to break the ice, but she didn't want to scare him, since a lot of kids with autism didn't do well with touch.

His mother's smile got a little brighter and touched Vivian's core. "Yes," she said. "Sometimes he will."

She turned back to the boy and held up a hand, palm out. "What do you say, Mister Zeb? Gimme a high five?"

The boy turned and slapped Vivian's hand. "That's cool! You do it like you mean it."

Zeb finally turned to face Vivian, giving her a glimpse at his striking gaze.

She froze, her heart sank, and her stomach lurched.

She knew those eyes.

CHAPTER TWENTY-FIVE

Father Montgomery finally spoke. "Vivian, I'd like you to meet Jennifer Longhollow and her son, Zeb. Jenn, this is Vivian Bedford. She was there the night your husband died."

Moving on autopilot, Vivian made her way back to her seat.

Zeke's wife.

So this was the woman who'd called out to Zeke on that awful day in the park. She had a split second of panic, but Jenn Longhollow didn't appear to recognize her, thank God. Pulling herself together, she cleared her throat and said, "Mrs. Longhollow, I am so very sorry for your loss."

She hoped her condolences sounded sincere, because they were. After all, Vivian understood. She'd lost him too.

"Thank you, Ms. Bedford. Please, call me Jenn," she replied. "The Father tells me you got to Zeke before the medics came. You were with him when he died?"

"It's Vivian, and yes, I was," she said. "I held his hand and tried to ease his suffering. I don't know if he was in a lot of pain, but the paramedics told me probably not. Shock, I guess...." she trailed off, not knowing what else to say.

"I'm glad he wasn't alone," Jenn said, her eyes watery.

Vivian bent back down to Zeb, granting his mother some space to pull herself together.

"Do you like puzzles?" she asked the boy as she fumbled around in her oversize bag. "I have something here that might tickle your fancy."

Vivian finally found the dusty old keychain Rubik's cube. The small square had traveled with her for a few decades and somehow always managed to survive the annual cleaning-of-the-purse spree. She placed the toy next to the seated child and backed away. After a few more rounds of hand-wringing, he picked it up and began to focus his efforts on aligning the colors, making her smile.

Father Montgomery touched Jennifer's shoulder. "Jenn, do you think Zeb would like to come to my office while you two chat?"

"That would be great," said Jenn, sounding as though she'd recovered. Vivian couldn't look at her just yet. "Zeb, honey, can you go with Father Montgomery? He's got those graham crackers you like."

The boy rose and walked with the Father, all the while focused on his Rubik's cube. Vivian returned to her seat, looked around the room, and waited for Jennifer Longhollow to speak. She didn't mind letting the woman take her time to get her bearings. Dealing with fresh grief herself, Vivian felt a strange kinship with the woman, odd as that seemed. She was more than a little uneasy about the whole situation, but was determined not to show it. The poor woman had been through enough, especially in her condition.

"Father Montgomery told me a little bit about your troubles with your sister," Jenn began. "I hope you don't mind. He thought it might make it easier to talk to you, you know...that you'd understand. I haven't talked about Zeke to anyone except Father Montgomery, and I...I'd like to talk to you about him, if you'll listen."

"I don't mind," Vivian said, steeling herself to meet Jenn's gaze. "I know it's rough losing someone you love all of a sudden. I lost my parents in a fire not so long ago. That's how I came have Mae. If you need to talk, I'll be happy to listen."

"I told you I was glad Zeke didn't die alone. I mean it some of the time, though I'm ashamed to admit that sometimes I do wish he'd suffered."

Vivian's face must have registered her shock at the statement, since

Jenn paused and looked away, waiting a bit before speaking again. Jenn still didn't meet her gaze, but stared off into the distance through the chapel door as she spoke in a flat, even tone.

"Zeke was leaving me that night."

Oh God, I can't hear this.

"They found his suitcase and a cashier's check that would have cleaned out a good bit of our nest egg. I mean, he didn't leave a note or anything, but I knew he was going for good."

When she was able to find her voice, Vivian whispered, "Why?"

Jenn shrugged. "We had to get married, you know what I mean?" She met Vivian's gaze and held it until Vivian nodded her understanding. Growing up around the South, Vivian was familiar with both proverbial and literal shotgun weddings.

"It wasn't too bad when Zeb was a baby. We tried to make it work, and I know in my heart of hearts he really *was* trying at the time. Even when we found out that Zeb was autistic, it was okay for a while...until I had to quit work and the bills came, and the trips to the specialists, and all of the worry."

"Yeah," Vivian murmured. "That's a lot to handle."

And it hit a little too close to home.

Jen nodded. "He provided for us, but I could tell he resented it. Zeke was a good-looking man, the kind women notice." She barked a bitter laugh. "I ought to know, since I was one of them. Anyway, one little fling is how we ended up where we did. He wasn't used to being tied down, let alone to a stay-at-home mom and a child with special needs. And I was so tired I...I didn't always have a lot left for him. I found my escape in support groups and cheap wine and, well, he coped in his way."

Jenn took a deep breath. "He started working late, or so he said, but I knew. It didn't take a genius to figure out he was stepping out on me. It hurt, but I figured I could handle anything as long as I could take care of my boy. He's my whole world. Maybe that bothered Zeke too. I never did ask."

Vivian bit back the bile that threatened to choke her.

"After Zeb turned three, something happened in Zeke. He started coming back home and spending time with us, even spending more time with me," she said, the hint of a blush rising in her cheeks. "He started taking us out with him in public, something he never did after Zeb started acting...off. He'd cook breakfast, bring me flowers, you know, little things. They go a long way."

"Sounds like he was trying to do right by you," Vivian offered. She really wanted to believe the best of Zeke, even though she figured this story would wind up about as bright as a black hole, kind of like Ezra's tale.

"Yeah, for a while," Jenn muttered. "I stopped drinking when I found out I was pregnant, got back to the church. And Zeke was excited about having another baby. He thought it might be nice to have a little girl." Her ghost of a smile made Vivian shudder.

"We got a few hints about Michelle on our first ultrasound. The doctor tried to reassure us, but we were pretty worried. It wasn't Down Syndrome, they said, but she just wasn't growing right. The waiting was hell. In the end, they still couldn't tell us exactly what to expect, but they told us she probably wouldn't be normal. I guess that's what did it for Zeke."

"What happened?" Vivian asked, feeling Jenn's heartache as if it were her own. She imagined how her own mother must have felt at the prospect of an unknown burden. She'd told Vivian, after she'd grown up of course, that she'd considered killing both herself and Mae at one point. At least her parents had leaned on one another. Bearing the burden alone was much worse, as Vivian had learned from experience.

"He shut down for a while. All of the interest he took in us didn't exactly end, but it was sour. He didn't step out on me again, as far as I know, but I could tell he was crushed. I also knew he was mad as hell. To his credit, he waited a few weeks before telling me we ought to get rid of the baby."

Vivian moved beside Jenn and took her hands. She might not have words, but she could listen and could share the load. She'd been on both sides, and she could share this woman's pain. It could be her gift to Jennifer Longhollow, the woman who'd loved Zeke in life.

"God help me, I thought about it," she continued through the tears. "Who wouldn't? But I just couldn't bear to kill a child, especially so late. It took so long to be sure, with all of the tests...." She trailed off.

"I wouldn't blame you if you did, and I don't blame you that you didn't. No one who's been there would. It would be a hell of a choice to make for anyone," Vivian said. She had often wondered if her own mother would have chosen to end Mae, had she known. She wondered what she would choose, knowing what she knew now.

She hoped she would never have to find out.

"Well, Zeke sure as hell blamed me."

Vivian steadied herself against the bitterness in Jenn's voice. She'd heard the same anguish that day in the park with Zeke. "We fought. He yelled, I screamed. I hit first. I'll own that. But then I wound up on the floor. Maybe he hoped I'd lose the baby, I don't know. But he was out of the house that morning and it was the last time I saw him alive. He must have spent the afternoon getting as much of our money as he could. I don't know where he was going, but he didn't make it far."

She held on to Jenn's hand as tight as she could. She knew now why Darkmore had been there to claim Zeke, and why Zeke had been so drawn to her. Maybe she was part of his penance, or perhaps he was part of hers. How often she'd considered doing exactly what Zeke had done—run away. What could be done for either of them?

Then, all of a sudden, she knew what to do. For Jenn, at least.

She wasn't sure it would work on command, but she had to try. She kept holding on to Jenn's hand, and she focused with all of her mind on the grieving woman. She connected to her hurt and anger, and tiny wisps of red light began streaming from Jenn into her, so faint that she doubted Jenn could see them. She hoped not. Terrible suffering and anguish poured into her along with the light, but it passed quickly and was not so hard to bear, being familiar. Placing the light deep inside of herself, she then embraced the woman beside her.

"Thanks for listening," Jenn said into Vivian's shoulder. "It helped."

"You're welcome," replied Vivian. "Now let's go see about your son."

———

Vivian bid Jennifer and Zeb Longhollow goodbye, having shared another few tear-laden hugs, information about state and federal resources for home care and other services available to children with special needs, and her own phone number. She let Zeb keep the Rubik's cube, since he seemed to enjoy it so much.

What she had received in return was far more valuable.

Father Montgomery bid her sit in his office, offering her a cup of Italian roast. He smiled at her and said, "Thank you for coming, Vivian. I can tell it helped Jennifer."

"It helped me too." She took a sip of her coffee, savoring it almost as much as the comfort offered by her unlikely ally. "What made you believe me?"

He smiled wryly, arching a brow. "You told me about Ezekiel."

She barked a wry laugh. "I told you a lot of things, Padre. Showed you a few too. I'm surprised you paid attention to that part."

"Well, I confess I was too shocked to register the connection at the time, but of course I knew the name. Jennifer came to me a few weeks earlier with a rather fantastic story about seeing her late husband's ghost. I dismissed the idea at first, given her condition and her state of mind, but after your display at the hospital, it didn't seem too far-fetched."

"Well, for what it's worth, I'm grateful you did," she said. "Does she have anyone to help her?"

"Zeke had good insurance, so they have some money. Her family is moving closer so they can help. The church will be there, myself included. She could use some good friends, I'm sure."

"I'm sure," Vivian replied, catching the hint.

Setting down his coffee cup with an air of finality, he leaned over the desk and asked, "What will you do now? And how may I be of service?"

"I think I know a way out," she said, after a few moments of musing. "Or at least a way through. There's something I should try...." The energy coursing through her from Jenn Longhollow's burdens had sparked her imagination as well as her fingertips. "I need to take care of a few things first, but will you meet me at the hospital later tonight?"

"Of course," said Father Montgomery, with a hint of caution. "I'll be on duty tonight anyway."

"Good. I'll see you later. Oh, by the way, try to remember to bring a warm jacket."

She got up and rushed out the door before he had a chance to protest.

CHAPTER TWENTY-SIX

The drive from the cathedral to the Country Music Hall of Fame didn't take long, and luckily traffic was light. Parking was another matter, as it always was downtown. Hoping she wouldn't have to pay admission, but willing to if necessary, Vivian entered the lobby, took a seat in the cafe, and waited.

While waiting, she found the perfect means to test her fledgling theory.

An elderly woman arrived in a wheelchair pushed by a daughter, or maybe a granddaughter. She was too frail to travel under her own power, and her slack jaw and vacant gaze suggested she wasn't exactly all there. Her chauffeur parked her at an adjacent table and skittered off to the ticket counter. The line wasn't long. Vivian would have to work fast.

Scooting her chair close to the woman, she cast her gaze quickly left and right. Then she took the woman's hand and willed the light to flow.

The woman's wrinkled hand jerked, likely an involuntary reaction to the heat. "Shh," Vivian whispered. "I know it's hot, but I need you to hold on. Please."

Nothing registered in the woman's gaze. Maybe a little more?

"Come on, come on," Vivian muttered, focusing on the echoes of misery, anger, and sorrow assaulting her senses. Jenn's burdens were heavy and weighed her down like an anchor, but a weight that held the comfort of familiarity. She heaved, channeling the pain of her own life as leverage and pulling the old woman's burdens from her soul so they could coalesce with hers. She took the energy and made something new.

Something she could give back to this lost soul.

Soft wisps of red light flowed from Vivian into the woman. Not the brilliant white of a guardian's nor the cold red of the reaper's, she gifted the energy forged from her own consciousness and will to the soul inside a decaying shell and bid it to take hold.

"Nana?"

Startled, Vivian let go of the woman's hand and raised her gaze to the caregiver. She sputtered an apology, hoping to avoid an ugly scene. "I'm sorry, I just...she reminds me of my sister, and I just wanted to let her know I was here. I *see* her."

The young woman didn't appear frightened. She smiled and nodded. "That's sweet of you. Her Alzheimer's is getting worse, but she still has good days." A flash of sorrow tightened the corners of her mouth, but she shook it off. "We don't always know when she'll come back to us, but music helps. The old timey stuff, you know, the stuff she heard when she was about my age. That's why I brought her here."

"I hope it helps," Vivian said, wishing she could do more. The old woman blinked, her gaze shifting for the first time, and turned to look up at her caregiver. "Lily?"

The caregiver smiled. "No, Nana, I'm Janice. Lily's daughter."

The old woman squinted while muttering something incomprehensible. But at least she'd shown some signs of awareness. Janice patted the woman's shoulder and said, "Come on, Nana. Let's go see if we can find you some Gene Autry."

All of a sudden, the woman stopped muttering and shook her head, blinking slowly a few times before looking up at her granddaughter with a wide-eyed gaze. Then a broad smile spread across the wrinkled face. "Why, Janice Peterson, I had no idea you knew about Gene Autry."

Janice's breath hitched. Then, with practiced caution, she said, "Yes, Nana. You told me about him. Remember when we used to watch his movies?"

"Well, of course I do, silly britches! You acted like you didn't care a bit about your Nana's old black and white picture shows. Didn't figure you were paying attention. Now what's all this talk about finding him?"

Janice smiled and shook her head in wonder. "I'll show you after we say goodbye to this nice lady you were talking to."

The woman turned to Vivian and nodded. "I thank you for keeping me such good company. Have a nice day now."

The old woman smiled, and as Janice wheeled her away, Vivian heard her hum a few notes from "Back in the Saddle Again." Something of the energy transfer seemed to have worked for this one woman. Could it work for a whole host of souls, or would her good intentions backfire?

Could it work for Mae?

She had more time to think about her situation while waiting, just as she'd had time in the car. The road to Hell was paved with good intentions, or so it was said, and hers certainly had been. She knew where the road was going to take her now. Closer to the point, the old saying told of the road's material and manufacture. But where did it all begin? Now seemed as good a time as any to reflect on this point.

And if she knew where it began, could she have avoided the on-ramp to oblivion, maybe the left turn leading to tragedy, or the one-way, dead-end street to sorrow?

It was easy to imagine the path's origin around the corner of some dark alleyway, or simply a deviation from the straight and narrow, like those Biblical admonitions about the broad path leading to destruction.

Well, there was the first problem.

The road was as broad as it was long. And there wasn't just one on-ramp, turn, or side street that led to damnation. It was no wonder so many followed it. So where did that leave everyone as they ambled along the highways and byways of life? The way seemed to leave a lot of good people stuck on a multi-lane interstate full of interchanges, connectors, and bypasses that all lead to perdition.

Too bad there wasn't an app for that. No one got the "avoid Hell" option on the GPS of life, and it probably couldn't be found on Google Maps either.

It didn't seem right.

Of course, all of this relied on the assumption that a whole lot of roads headed straight to disaster, versus a single, teeny-tiny little street leading to the opposite. What if just as many roads could get folks to Heaven, or closer to it, or to whatever existed in other faiths? Even heathens like Vivian hoped for a nice, sunny destination. And what about all of the little detours along the way? Maybe the roads to Paradise and Purgatory wound and intersected, like a network of interstates through the landscape of the afterlife. Nashville was a hub city with spokes going to and from pretty much anywhere. She had been back and forth, round and round, lost her way and found it again.

She wanted to believe in this kind of roadway between Heaven and Hell.

At least then she'd have a fighting chance.

Glancing at her watch, she noticed it was getting late. She wondered if she could just call him. Seemed worth a try.

She focused on his name, feeling grateful not to have to say the words out loud. He appeared on the stairwell, guitar slung across his shoulder, a small smile gracing his bearded face along with a quizzical look. She inclined her head toward the door, and he nodded. After meeting him out back, she did a quick scan of the area to make sure they were alone, since she hadn't quite figured out how to replicate the spiritual disappearing act.

"Didn't think I'd see you back here, ma'am," Guitar Guy said. "Though it's a nice surprise. I don't get too many visitors, you know?"

She grinned at the spirit. "It's nice to see you again. I'd love to chat for a while, but I kind of need a favor and I'm in an awfully big hurry."

"What can I do for you?"

"I need to get to Ezra. Do you know the way?"

He gave her a sidelong glance. "I do, but it's against the rules."

"I've broken more than a few already," she replied. He smirked, leading her to believe that this revelation didn't exactly come as a surprise.

When he didn't answer, she said. "Look, I understand if you don't want to help, but I'm going to zap out of this world and to the next with or without you. I've done it once before, but it sure would save me a lot of time and trouble if I knew the way. It's pretty important."

Vivian pulled out a box of sweet potato fries and a to-go cup full of tea from the cafe and passed them to the spirit. She figured bribery wouldn't hurt, and bribery appeared to work since his eyes lit up.

Guitar Guy looked surprised at first, but then his handsome face split into an ear-to-ear grin. He took a few bites, a giant swallow, and smiled at her again. "Yeah, you've been a hot topic among our kind these days. I reckon I can get you there."

He slid his guitar to his back by the strap, stacked the cup on top of the box, and took her hand with his free one. "But I plan on telling him you twisted my arm."

She closed her eyes and felt the familiar pull down the vortex and through streaming light. She didn't feel as sick this time. She must've been getting used to it.

She opened her eyes and held onto Guitar Guy until she got her bearings. Looking around she saw that they'd landed outside of an old farmhouse. It wasn't a fancy sort of place, save for some Victorian crown molding along the awning that sat just below the inverted V of the roof. A simple two-story floor plan with simple, narrow windows, simple columns holding up a modest front porch, and a friendly swing. Ezra sat in the swing, billows of smoke emanating from his honest-to-God corncob pipe. He didn't look happy to see her, but he didn't look too surprised either.

She marched right up and plopped right down next to him on the rickety old swing.

"Howdy, Ezra," she said in greeting. "How you doing? Nice place you got here, by the way."

"I'll do, Miss Vivian," he replied, looking dead ahead instead of at her. "You?"

"Oh, I've been keeping busy," she said. "Real busy."

"Is that a fact?" Ezra said, blowing a couple of smoke rings. He turned to Guitar Guy "Thank you kindly for escorting Miss Vivian to my place. I'll see her back directly."

"No problem, Ezra," Guitar Guy said, giving a little wave. "She wouldn't take no for an answer, you understand?"

"That sounds about right," Ezra said, nodding. Then he added, "Enjoy the fries." Taking his cue, Guitar Guy turned and disappeared in a swirling flash of light.

Vivian and Ezra sat a spell. She figured this was Ezra's special place, like her field of black-eyed Susans in the woods. The fields beyond the house were filled with tobacco and corn, and he even had a small garden growing okra, pole beans, and tomatoes. Seemed a little strange to see the tobacco, though, since she'd always figured Heaven to be a smoke-free zone. Still, she guessed it was Heaven for him, and it wasn't like smoking could kill a dead guy anyway.

This place suited him, the house and the surrounding land, and he seemed content. At least, he'd probably felt content until she showed up. She might have apologized for the intrusion had circumstances been a bit different.

Then again, she wasn't exactly in a gracious sort of mood.

"So, you plan on sitting there all day blowing smoke or are we going to talk?" she asked, waving her hands in front of her face. The smoke stank to high heaven, even in this realm. It stung her eyes, tickled her nose, and irked her something fierce. The old coot was probably doing it on purpose.

"Ain't got much to say right now, Miss Vivian. Besides, seems to me you're the one that's got a bee in her bonnet."

Oh, like that, is it?

Well, two could play at dueling with down-home expressions. "I do have a bone or two to pick with you, as a matter of fact, but that can wait." She leaned back, hands behind her head, and stretched, mimicking his posture.

"Maybe you'd like to hear a little story of mine? I'd be proud to tell it, and I'll just bet you can make the time for me," she said. "Turnabout's fair play, after all."

He kept on smoking and swinging, so she decided she would just keep right on talking. "Let's see, it's about a man who made some bad choices and hurt the ones he loved, so he was supposed to pay for it. Only it seems like he got a reprieve. Good for him, but seems it came with a pretty hefty price tag. Has to work off his debt, I hear."

"It's how we do. What better way to make amends than keeping others from making the same mistakes?"

"Fair enough, but I hear tell you're in the business of skimming off the top. But more to the point, it also seems that you forgot to pay the piper when you took his soul."

Ezra still didn't look at her, but he stopped the swing.

"Now, the way I figure, Zeke's beholden to you for getting him out of his time in Hell, or Purgatory, or whatever you want to call the bad realm. And maybe you even owe Darkmore a little something. As near as I can tell, if he comes calling, odds are his host has done something to earn a visit. He didn't just show up out of the blue when he came to your field that day, am I right?"

Ezra's brows dropped and his jaw ticked. He didn't answer her, but his expression told her enough.

"You don't want to fill in those little details you conveniently left out of your story? Fine. I'm guessing you figured out how to harness your own spirit energy by accident, kind of like I did. Maybe you had some help, maybe you didn't, but sitting around incapacitated for a time must have juiced you up enough that you were able to cross over, get away from Darkmore, and strike out on your own."

His gaze narrowed, but he didn't offer to contradict her conclusions, nor did he deign to tell her what he'd done to get on the reaper's radar in the first place. Didn't matter, she supposed, so long as they finished the business between them tonight.

"Now I'm guessing that by snatching Zeke instead of me, you got even with Darkmore and got yourself an apprentice in the bargain. Good for you. But you also got me into a heap of otherworldly trouble, so I figure you owe me, too. I'm here to settle up."

Ezra turned to face her.

Good, she finally had his attention.

He took another long draw from his pipe then said, "Seems like you've put a fair amount of thought into this. Think you got it all figured out? I ought to zap you right now for good measure, getting all high and mighty on me. And I surely ought to zap you again for carrying on like you did with Zeke—"

She whipped her hands out and let the sparks fly, shutting him down. "If anyone's going to be doing any zapping around here, old man, it's me."

His gaze narrowed, and while she didn't miss the sparks of light flashing from his palms, she braced herself and continued. "What happened with me and Zeke was perfectly natural. Any fool could have seen it was bound to happen, even a fool as old as you. Some wise man you turned out to be."

When he opened his mouth to protest, she cut him off again. "I'm not here for a lecture or judgment, and I'm sure as hell not here to apologize. I'm here with a proposition. You listening?"

"Fire away," he said.

"I want three things from you. I need to see Zeke again. That's the first thing. The second thing I want is for you to promise me you'll release him from his obligation to you and let him cross after I'm done with him."

"Now that's quite a tall order, missy," he said. "You got gumption, girl. I'll give you that." She swore if he slapped his knee she would haul off and hit him.

"We're talking about my soul here. You put it up for ransom, remember?"

"So you'll come serve in his stead?" he asked, sucking on his pipe.

Oh, hell no.

"And be beholden to you? That won't square you with Darkmore. I've got something a little different in mind."

"You'd sell yourself to Darkmore for Zeke, then?" he asked, his voice carefully neutral.

"I'll do what I have to do," Vivian said. Two could play that game.

"What's the third thing you want from me?"

"I want you to promise me a crossing for Mae. You don't touch her, and neither does Darkmore. She goes free when she passes, which won't be too long. You don't take one *drop* of her spirit light, energy, or whatever it is she's got that you and your kind are after. Take it or leave it." Vivian never did have a poker face, but she hoped with all of her might that the front she put on then would hold.

"And what makes you think I'll agree to any of this? What do I get in return?"

"Aside from the minor issue of getting the reaper off your back, I can offer you this." She grabbed his hand and willed her light into the old guardian, blending the force of her own burdens with those she'd reaped from Jen Longhollow and the old woman from the Hall of Fame into conscious energy.

Ezra's eyes went wide and he gripped her hand tight, drawing her energy out in great waves. "Well I'll be, Miss Vivian. You *have* been busy. I don't reckon I've ever come across that particular flavor before."

Breathing easier and feeling lighter after the release of her burdens, she took the gamble and said, "There's more where that came from. Much more. Probably enough to take care of your backlog and give you some to spare, if you meet my conditions."

"I could get more from your sister."

"Maybe, but you'll need me to do it, and I won't cooperate." She took a deep breath, closed her eyes, extended her hands, and hit Ezra with the full force of all the soul burdens she'd collected.

This blast was powerful enough to bring Ezra to his knees as he absorbed the concentrated energy she slammed into him. He gazed at her with wide-eyed awe and wonder as he flexed his fingers, struggling to contain the power. "Where did you get that?"

"From people."

He shook his head and stared as if stunned. "Living people? Not possible. Ain't none of us can channel energy from the living unless they're fixin' to cross over."

"I'm not one of you. Not really. I'm still alive," she said.

His eyes went wide. "You have no idea what this means, do you?"

"It means I'm pretty valuable. And that was only a taste. I have more, and I can get more, *if* you keep your end of the bargain."

He cocked his head to the side and considered for a moment, then nodded. "Where you want to meet up with Zeke?"

"My field, for starters," she replied. "He can take us where we need to go from there."

He rose from the porch swing and she followed. They spent a bit of time staring off into the horizon of Ezra's world. The sun was setting there, glowing over fields brimming with bounty in green and gold and bathing her in wondrous light. Zeke had told her time was a little different on the other side. She hoped he was right. She couldn't afford to lose any.

"So, Ezra, we got a deal here or don't we?"

"I reckon I can abide by what you offered. I sure do hope you can," he replied. "For what it's worth, I didn't mean for things to come to this."

"Well, you know what they say about the road to Hell and good intentions," she said. "Cheer up, Ezra. You can't win 'em all."

"I hope you know what you're doing. Go on now," he said, shooing her off his porch. "I'll get you started, but you know the way, I expect. Zeke'll be along directly."

She closed her eyes and focused her mind and heart on her place of peace, on yellow petals and gently bubbling streams, and the light began to swirl. Ezra sent his bright and gleaming light around her, and an extra beam or two into her. She smiled as she disappeared, the sound of his voice bidding her good luck filling her ears as she left her guardian.

CHAPTER TWENTY-SEVEN

Vivian sat beside the cool creek, soaking her feet and waiting for Zeke. She'd never learned how to skip stones, so she settled on picking a handful of Suzies and dropping the flower heads one by one into the water. *He loves me, he loves me not.* She hadn't dared pick a single flower when she'd found this place in life, but she figured this replica was hers to do with as she chose. Besides, she had the sneaking suspicion the flowers would be back where they belonged if and when she ever returned.

Watching the golden petals float on down the stream, Zeke's warmth engulfed her and she smiled. She waited, but she didn't feel him move closer. Instead, she felt an odd tingle running along her scalp and down over her temples.

"Trying to poke around in my skull isn't going to work, Zeke," she said with a touch of sternness. "If you have questions, you're just going to have to have a seat and talk to me." She patted the rock beside her, but didn't turn around to face him.

They both waited, and though Vivian ached to get up and go to him, she schooled herself to stillness. After a time, she heard his footfalls and breathed a sigh of relief. He sat beside her and stared at the water, at the woods beyond, anywhere but at her. Figuring he'd done the hard part, she grabbed his hand and squeezed.

He looked down at the ground and whispered, "I'm sorry."

He'd piqued Vivian's curiosity. "Why are you sorry, Zeke?"

"I couldn't be there for you when you needed me most," he said, squeezing her hand back. "It was hell having to leave you, and not being able to get back when you were hurting, and when Darkmore came for you."

"Wait," she said, jerking free of his hand and grabbing his face to turn it to hers. "You knew?"

"I am your guardian," he said simply.

"What else do you know?"

"That you found a way to get to Ezra. The rest is a little unclear."

"Oh yeah, I got to Ezra all right," she said bitterly. "He had the gall to be pissed off at me for it, but it seems like he's kept his end of the bargain. You're here with me now." She smiled at the last.

"So now what?"

She could think of a few things, but now was not the time. "We have to go," she answered, rising from her rock and bidding him to do the same.

"Where?" he asked, sporting a wry smile and a raised brow.

The ache deep in her chest made it hard to look at his face. She hated what she had to do, but the healing would outdo the hurt in time.

She hoped.

She reached up and gave him a long, deep kiss before asking, "Do you trust me?"

"Yes."

"Then hold on tight," she told him, taking his hands and focusing with all of her mind on two people as streams of white light spun them into the vortex. After a few moments, she felt solid ground beneath her feet, and Zeke's iron grip on her hands grew even tighter.

She knew she'd gotten it right then.

She opened her eyes and saw they'd landed at the foot of a driveway leading to an ordinary-looking suburban home, complete with an SUV and what she assumed had been Zeke's truck parked beside it. The landscaping looked a bit unkempt. Not too surprising, given the circumstances. If they'd had the time, she might have pulled a few weeds from the flowerbeds. Vivian chanced a glance at Zeke and she hurt right along with him.

She gathered him in her arms and held him close to her while he trembled.

When he let go, he met her gaze and said in an unsteady voice, "Why?"

"You have to face it, Zeke," she answered. She wouldn't let herself cry with him or for him right now. She would be his strength. "You have to face it, say goodbye, and then let go."

He stood there, dropping his gaze and staring at his feet. He seemed at a loss. She gave him a gentle tug and said, "Come on. You have to take us in and fix it so they can't see us. I'll be right here with you."

Reaching out and taking his face in her palms, she stroked his face and whispered, "You're not alone. I'm here."

The next thing she knew, they were standing inside a narrow hallway. Darkness filled the house in spite of the mid-afternoon daylight that lingered outside, and all was quiet within. She felt a surge of panic, wondering if they were even home. She hadn't thought of that. What if—

Zeke took her hand and led her to a room at the end of the hall. When they stepped inside, she recognized by the décor that they'd entered a young boy's room. The red and blue walls were neatly painted with friendly cartoon cars and trucks. He ran his free hand over these images as he walked in. Maybe he had painted them himself, before his life had fallen apart. Toys littered the floor, and there, asleep in a small toddler bed in the corner, was Zeb.

He let go of her hand and kneeled by the bed, whispering to the boy. She couldn't make out what he was saying, but the warmth and peace of his presence filled the room and enveloped her. He stroked his son's dark hair, wavy locks so like his own, and kissed his ample cheek. Then he held his hands over Zeb and filled the room and his son with his light while he filled Vivian with pride and love. Zeke lingered after the light faded, and Vivian moved to him, placing her hand on his shoulder to bring him back. Placing one more kiss on the boy's head, he rose with her and left the room.

They walked without words back into the hallway and toward another room. He turned to her and asked, "Would you mind waiting outside, love?"

She nodded and watched as Zeke opened the door. Before he shut it, she saw the sleeping form of his wife. Frankly, she felt relieved when he'd asked her to wait outside. She hadn't had a problem speaking with Jenn Longhollow face to face at the Cathedral, but the idea of seeing Zeke with Jenn had filled her with dread and a jealousy she had no right to feel. Of course, they weren't technically married anymore, given the whole "until death do you part" clause, but still...

Using the force of will and long experience, she clamped down on guilt and jealousy. Though her reaction was perfectly natural, tonight wasn't about her and her feelings. She'd deal with them later. Setting them aside, she focused her energy on Zeke.

She waited a long time while he took care of things, at least a long time from her perspective. She fidgeted and fought the urge to snoop. Although naturally curious about his former life, she refused to intrude on what Zeke had once shared with his family. He came out of the room and clicked the door closed behind him.

She studied him, noting the lack of tension in his posture, back straight, but no longer stiff, broad shoulders at ease, and softening of deep lines of strain etched into face. His aura seemed a bit lighter now, in spite of the tears running rivers down his fine features. He handed her a sealed envelope bearing his wife's name and their address, and she nodded her acceptance. She'd see it delivered. He no doubt wanted to give his wife closure, or perhaps reassurance, as a part of his atonement.

Whatever he'd written in the letter was between him and Jenn, and would remain so. She wiped his tears with her fingers and kissed his cheek. Taking her hands, they entered the vortex and left his old home, and she heard him whisper goodbye as they did.

When they arrived, she was surprised to see they had returned to her place. She'd figured he might take her to his paradise in this realm. If she and Ezra had one, didn't he? What did heaven mean for him?

Zeke smiled at her, discerning her thoughts, and said, "There wasn't a place ready for me when I arrived here."

"Oh," she replied, and remembered. Of course, there wouldn't have been...Then, voicing the subject she had been afraid to broach before, she said, "So you know what was supposed to happen that night, huh?"

"Yeah, I knew I wasn't meant for this place."

"Well, where do you stay?"

"Here and there," he said. She waited for him to elaborate. "It was nice to be able to crash at your house so often. I figured once I earned my stripes I'd get an office of sorts. But I swear I didn't know about the rest. As far as I was concerned, you were my charge to protect in the world of the living, and I—"

"Shh," she said, taking him in her arms, trying to quiet him.

"Vivian," he sighed. "What I did to them, to Jenn and the kids, what I was going to do...I'm not that man anymore."

"I know, baby, I know," she murmured.

"No, you don't," he continued. "You were my last sight that side of life on the night I died. I was already full of hate, fear, and regret. I knew I was dying and that my Hell would be to carry the awful guilt and shame with me for eternity. Even after Ezra, and after meeting you on this side, I've still carried it. But you made me face it tonight, face them, and it's given me some ease."

"I'm glad I could help you find peace."

"No," he said, and continued when he read the look of confusion on her face. "I'll not find peace yet. I don't *want* to find peace yet. I've done much that calls for atonement, and that's what I plan to do. I'll keep good faith with Ezra and with you and—"

"Shh," she said, cutting him off. "I know you will. I'll tell you what, though. I'm going to need someone to look after this place for me. You know, check my flowers, make sure no one's littering, that sort of thing. Think you can handle it?"

At least for a little while, baby, because you're going to a better place of your own soon.

"I can, Vivian. And I will guard you for the rest of your days. I swear I will. Ezra told me I'm free of him now, and I can choose my own assignments. Now we still have to work out a way around Darkmore. I was thinking—"

She stilled his lips with her fingers and whispered, "You really don't know when to shut up either, do you, Zeke Longhollow?" She kissed him then, long and slow, and he acquiesced. "This is our time, right here and right now, and right now all I want is you."

They made love on the grass in her field of gold and green. She savored every detail, the cool breeze, the smell of his skin, the deep blue of the sky and its billowing clouds, the sound of their shared breaths. Tucking these memories safe in her heart, she kissed a sleeping Zeke goodbye, taking the last flashes of his light with her. Grabbing her grandmother's quilt and his letter, she departed.

CHAPTER TWENTY-EIGHT

She sat next to her sister's hospital bed. It was strange. Mae seemed so much smaller in the sea of white sheets, supporting pillows, and her own plush blanket that Vivian had brought from their home. Hospital blankets were pitiful and thin, not enough to keep the chill at bay. Besides, it always felt nice to have a link to home when stuck in a strange place. Mae's features had grown thinner and paler, though Vivian would never had thought it possible. Her limbs no longer flailed with involuntary jerks and spasms. Her bones were prominent beneath sallow skin. The IV diet had taken its toll.

She brushed Mae's painfully beautiful hair and spoke to her in a quiet and soothing voice.

"We're all set, babe. All of my assets will cover your care as long as you need caring for, at least that's what the lawyers tell me. I did try to read through it once, but hell if I can make heads or tails of legalese. Ezra promised me you'd be okay if...well, after, so no worries. I can't imagine why on Earth or in the afterlife you'd ever be expected to serve time in their realm, but I didn't take any chances."

Setting the brush aside, she grabbed the bottle of hand cream and set to work on her sister's skin. The cold, dry air of the hospital had left it a bit flaky, so Vivian started with her hands and arms, still talking to her sister as she had when they were both smaller.

"So, I told you I have to go away in a little while. I'm leaving Father Montgomery here to look after you and to make sure Ezra keeps his word. He's pretty cool for a priest. I think you'll like him," she said as she rubbed her hands together to warm the lotion. She placed the blanket over her sister's upper body and began to work on her little legs.

"I want you to promise me you'll look after Zeke whenever you make it to the other side, if you see him there. I hope you will."

She would have told Mae to send her love to him, but he already knew. He'd be angry with her for a while, no doubt, but she'd made the right decision. If she had to give him up, she wanted him to be free and have peace. After she finished slathering lotion on her arms and torso, Vivian put a little balm on Mae's parched lips and imagined what those lips might tell her if they could.

She turned her head at the sound of a knock and was greeted by a somber Father Montgomery. She motioned for him to enter, and he came and stood beside the narrow bed. He seemed to be at a bit of a loss, though he did give her shoulder a squeeze.

"Padre, this is my little sister, Mae," she said, figuring introductions couldn't hurt. "Mae, this is Father Montgomery."

The priest took Mae's bent and withered right hand with gentle care and gave it a light shake as he said, "I'm very pleased to meet you, Ms. Mae Bedford. I'm Father Lloyd Montgomery." He stepped back, making the sign of the cross and muttering a small prayer before turning his attention to Vivian.

Vivian gave him a warm smile and said, "Can you give us just a minute?"

"Of course," the priest replied. "Shall I meet you in the chapel?"

Subtle, Padre, real subtle. "That would be fine."

Once the priest made his exit and shut the door behind him, she took a deep breath and focused all of her thoughts on Mae. She held her sister's hand and concentrated with all of her might. After a time, streams of a faint gray light began to seep from Mae, reminding Vivian of Ezra's smoke rings.

She braced herself as she took them into her, but was surprised to feel...nothing.

She didn't understand.

With Jenn and Zeke, as well as other folks she'd encountered during her hours spent in the hospital gathering burdens to store up energy, she'd been aware of the emotional essences that came with the light she'd learned to channel. The heavy weight of their guilt, the helpless rage behind it, and even the taste of the bitterness coursed through her. Each had a different flavor, but the base was familiar. Mae's light gave none of these sensations, and her soft glow remained intact. She had no idea what it meant, but she'd done all she could.

If she couldn't ease Mae in life, she'd make damned sure the spirits didn't rob her in death. With one last stroke of her sister's hair, the soft mass framing her small face, she bid Mae goodbye, picked up her bag, and left the room.

———

She took her time on the walk to Father Montgomery, stretching it out as long as she could. She didn't intend to stall. The decision was made, terms agreed upon, and Ezra had met half of his end. She would keep hers, and she used the extra time to shake off the sadness and shift into bitch-on-wheels mode to do the needful.

When she entered the chapel, the aroma of warm hazelnut brew delighted her. She sat down on the front pew beside the priest and grabbed her mug, closed her eyes, and savored the flavor as if it were her last.

It would be her last, come to think of it.

Opening her eyes, she looked around and let the comfort of silence and the soft glow of low light envelop her. A few panels of stained glass were illuminated on the back wall to give the illusion of windows. The requisite statue of Christ stood at the front of the chapel with his arms extended, ready to accept prayers for the sick and the dying, for the doctors, for miracles. She wondered what horrors and hopes had been offered to the stone man who could not possibly answer. Did these desperate pleas find their way someplace else? Did they feel the same as those she carried now?

"Mmm," she muttered at last. "Thanks for the coffee."

"You're welcome," he replied. Apparently not interested in idle chitchat, he asked, "What now?"

"Well, after I finish my coffee, I have an appointment to keep. I need you to look after Mae. If the room starts to get chilly, I want you to call out for Ezra. Trust me, things will definitely happen."

She picked up her sizable bag and dug around for a bit before producing a sweater and an envelope. "And I need you to make sure this gets to Jenn Longhollow. Anonymously," she said as she handed him Zeke's note.

If Father Montgomery found any of these requests odd, he didn't let it show. Must've been getting used to her world.

After placing the letter in his briefcase, he eyed her intently and said, "I can certainly honor your wishes, but can you give me some idea of what you're up to?"

"No can do, Padre," she said. "Just look after Mae for me. I have a plan. That'll have to do."

She almost believed it. At least she thought she sounded convincing enough as she pulled on the thick sweater. "If I'm truly meant to depart this world, I have no intention of leaving quietly or without a fight. I'll make it back home, too, if I can, or at least to a better place than the reaper has in mind."

"And you honestly think you can accomplish this all on your own?"

That's an excellent question, Padre, and one I can't afford to dwell on.

She didn't voice the fears weighing on her mind aloud, but the look she shot him probably spoke volumes. Instead, she decided to push through her fears and focus on getting where she needed to go before she lost her nerve.

She wrapped herself in her grandmother's blanket and closed her eyes. She tried to focus on rage, and dark, and cold. She heard the priest's voice, sounding as though it came from a great distance. Annoyed, she said, "Look, you're breaking my concentration here, Padre. Why don't you just go off and pray for me or something?"

As the rays of light began to swirl, she heard his voice again, much closer now. "I will pray for you, yes, but faith alone does not a mountain move."

She felt his grip too late.

CHAPTER TWENTY-NINE

Some things, like death and taxes, were universal. That's what conventional wisdom held. If she had any lingering doubt about another fundamental and universal truth the moment she landed back in Darkmore's realm, that doubt was erased. Men, no matter if they were alive, dead, or somewhere in between, just never, ever listened to a damned thing a woman said.

She hadn't come alone. Father Lloyd Montgomery had come with her. *Damn it! Damn it! Damn it!*

She looped her arm through his on instinct, holding him tight to keep him with her. She didn't know whether to hit him for burdening her with his presence here or hug him because he hadn't abandoned her. She only knew she needed to keep him close. She needed to keep him safe. Her sweater and blanket staved off some of the cold, but the darkness remained her primary concern. She took a tentative step, pulling the priest along with her, then another, and then another. The ground felt even, so she decided to save her light while they moved.

"You shouldn't have come here," she hissed the man beside her. "I told you to stay and watch Mae!"

"I couldn't let you go alone," he said, his soft voice slicing through the chilly air. "You were willing to sacrifice yourself, I could see that quite clearly. But I don't think you'll sacrifice me so easily. And I also think you'll want to get back to your sister even more now."

Clever bastard. He knew her weak spot all right. "Maybe you're right and maybe you're not, but it doesn't make it any more likely either of us will get out of here. Now let's move," she said, releasing his arm long enough to wrap the quilt around them both.

"Where are we going?"

"I don't know exactly, but I'm sure something will find us soon enough."

"Then why not stay put?"

"For starters, I didn't stay put last time I came here," she said. She was getting more irritated by standing still. "Second of all, it's about as cold as a witch's tit on the dark side of an iceberg out here, so let's just go, okay? Moving around will keep us a little warmer."

They started walking again, which calmed her a bit. They had been walking for about ten minutes, she reckoned, when the whispers began. She felt the priest stiffen, but he didn't speak immediately. He took a few deep breaths and began to pray as they walked.

"My Jesus, by the sorrows Thou didst suffer in Thine agony in the Garden, in Thy scourging and crowning with thorns, on the way to Calvary, in Thy crucifixion and death, have mercy on the souls in Purgatory, and especially on those that are most forsaken; do Thou deliver them from the terrible torments they endure; call them and admit them to Thy most sweet embrace in Paradise. Amen."

As the priest continued his chanted prayer, the area around them began to slowly illuminate. Father Montgomery kept his eyes closed tight, so Vivian witnessed this revelation first. They stood in the middle of a clearing surrounded by a dense forest, tropical perhaps, by the shape and length of the leaves, not to mention the damp heat. Strange, flat rock formations jutted out of the treeline in the distance, and a nearby river meandered through the landscape.

The scene might have been lovely if not for a thick, acrid layer of smoke and the stench of charred flesh, rot, decay.

The clearing must have held a small village once, yet all that remained were stunted stilts and fallen, partially burned thatch roofs. Several hammocks and baskets lay scattered across the clearing in disarray, dirty and stained red. Bits of broken pottery littered the ground as well.

"Dear God," Father Montgomery whispered from beside her. She should have told him to keep his eyes shut. She turned to him and was taken aback by his expression. It was more than shock—it was recognition. He knew where they were.

"What is this place?" she asked.

"It is the Warao village where I worked as a missionary when I was in Venezuela," he said. "But it shouldn't be like this, not burned, not desecrated, not—"

They were interrupted by a commotion in the surrounding forest. Things moved through the foliage, and they spoke as they moved. Ragged, inhuman voices gurgled and gasped words in a language unfamiliar to Vivian. But the priest seemed to understand.

He fell to the ground in terror, crossing himself and softly uttering, "No!" Over and over again. "No!"

Then, they came.

Putrid, rotting corpses emerged from the trees. Some appeared afflicted with disease, their bodies ravaged with oozing, pus-laden sores. Others were charred, skin peeling and bone exposed. More followed. What remained of their mutilated flesh was blue, and their voices were hoarse and guttural, as though they were choking. Unseeing eyes fixed on Vivian and Father Montgomery as rigid legs carried them ever closer and their wretched voices intoned in synchrony.

Karima, najamutuata jakutai,
Jiwai yatomanetekunarai.
Jirujuna rujanu rijana.
Najamutuata jiaobojona eku abaya.
Raina eku monukajase jiaobojona eku abakunarai.
Kanajoro ama saba jakutai taisi kamoau.
Kaisiko asiraja nonajakutai taisi kuare barinaka kaobojona bereaoko.
Taisi monuka kaobojona asirajasi kuare barinaka bere.
Kayakara minaka jau.
Tiarone asiraja arotuma amojekumo kejeronu.
Iji are Airamo tane rujakitane ja.

Iji are jijara taeraja.
Iji are Airamowitu.
Amén.

She couldn't understand the words, but the rhythm and cadence of the Lord's Prayer were familiar enough, and she understood all too well that whatever presence dwelled within this dark realm fed on pain. It brought them to this Godforsaken place to torment the priest with his sins and darkest fears.

The hideous creatures advancing upon him mocked and attacked what the priest held most dear—his faith.

She fought her own fear and the urge to run, focusing her energy on one of the creatures and filling her mind with the throngs of those long dead, infected and decimated by diseases borne by the Conquistadors of centuries past. Masses starved and murdered by invading waves of foreign occupiers, raped, ravaged, and burned for their land in the name of a God whose priests talked of mercy but whose practitioners knew only cruelty and injustice.

She caught flashes from the decaying minds as they approached. Missionaries bargaining with bags of rice for allegiance to their Bibles, women and children traded for crumbs from the tables of the invaders, villagers exiled in the wake of bulldozers and progress. She witnessed others falling prey to marauding guerrilla forces and drug traffickers, beholden to the whims of the corrupt and power-hungry who fed them with blood money. These specters raised their voices louder and louder, painful to the ears of the two living souls in their midst, and crushing to the man who cowered beside Vivian.

"Oh my God, I am heartily sorry for having offended Thee, and I detest all my sins because I dread the loss of Heaven and the pains of Hell; but most of all because they offend Thee, my God, Who art all-good and deserving of all my love. I firmly resolve, with the help of Thy grace, to confess my sins, to do penance, and to amend my life. Amen." These were the prayers of a desperate Father Montgomery as the corpses drew nearer, pointing their putrid fingers at him in accusation.

Soon he was reduced to uttering, "Forgive me, please, forgive me, I am so very sorry...forgive me forgive me forgive me...."

They needed to get out of there and fast, or she would lose the priest forever to his darkness.

"Get back and let him be!" she cried, picking up a piece of charred wood and waving it at the corpses. "You hear me? He's not for you!"

One of the creatures grabbed Vivian, digging into her flesh with its cold, bony fingers. She hit it with all of her might, slamming into its rib cage with a sickening crack, and still the dead thing gripped her. She hit it again and again, but it held on with single-minded relentlessness. Another clutched at her hair. She was surrounded. *They* were surrounded. A throng of the dead things had captured Father Montgomery, dragging him toward the river.

She screamed and then her light broke free.

"*Ya tira! Ya tira!*" the corpses hissed, releasing her.

She spun around, casting rays in all directions. She made her way to the priest, blasting the creatures that held him, and pulled him to his feet. The stunned corpses moved away, but they'd be back.

And she feared they'd bring more with them.

She spotted a dugout canoe on the nearby river's shore and dragged Father Montgomery with her. A short and ornately decorated figure in feathers and paint stood in the boat and beckoned them, shouting, "*Ho!*"

A large scarlet macaw with glowing eyes rested on the vessel's stern.

Father Montgomery resisted, stuttering, "No, we cannot go with him! He is *hoarotu*. He will drag us to *Hobeo*. We'll be eaten alive!"

"Can't be worse than this place."

She pushed him into the water toward the boat. The shaman was chanting in the strange language, and the corpses continued to scatter, fading into the tree line. Once Vivian and the priest were in the boat, the shaman uttered another cacophonous phrase and the boat moved of its own accord from the shore and traveled downstream. As they retreated, Vivian reached out with her mind and collected the horrors and suffering of the villagers in streams of light, collapsing from the effort. She still carried so much from the world of the living, and now the weight of these new burdens nearly crushed her.

But after choking on their rage, sorrow, and injustice that filled the frightening corpses, she couldn't abandon them to their torment.

The shaman regarded her, and in her current state she wondered if she should have heeded Father Montgomery's warning. She tried to tuck away all she had absorbed, but she was nearly bursting. He leaned down and studied her face and shivering form, the feathers of his headpiece tickling her cheek.

Her eyes went wide when he withdrew a knife.

"No!" Father Montgomery yelled, stumbling over in front of her and nearly tipping the boat in the process.

"*Yo no perjudicará el sol mujer. Ella necesita medicamento para luchar contra el mal espíritu,*" the small man said to the priest with a gentle tone that took her surprise.

"*Esto es una blasfemia! ¿Cómo podemos confiar en usted?*" the priest replied, still agitated.

Her head ached, her stomach clenched, and her breathing grew labored.

"He saved us, Padre," she whispered. "Maybe it's time for another leap of faith." She reached over and touched the shaman's forearm. Sensing no ill intention, she nodded.

The shaman chanted, singing in the same strange tongue he had used to aid the villagers' retreat. Strength infused her body and her spirit began to feel a little lighter. She wasn't fully herself, but it was enough.

"Thank you," she said.

He nodded, then took her hand, rolling up her sleeve to expose the flesh of her arm and bringing the knife down to pierce her. The priest started to protest, but Vivian interrupted. "No, it's fine. He needs the blood for his healings. And I think we need to give tribute for safe passage."

"Payment for the ferryman," Father Montgomery murmured.

"Something like that," she replied, and then turning to the shaman, she nodded. "Go ahead."

He cut quickly, and the sting wasn't as bad as she'd anticipated. He collected her blood in a small pouch then pressed some dried leaves into the wound, wrapping it in a bit of leather. They continued to move downstream, and she did her best to ignore the sounds and movements within the dense forest flanking the shore. The priest sat across from her and crossed himself with a trembling hand.

"Padre?" Vivian said. She had a few questions, but she also wanted to take his mind off their troubles. She needed to keep her mind occupied too.

"Yes," he replied. His voice still quavered, but he sounded stronger.

"When I lit up those, um, things, they shouted something at me. What did they say?"

"*Ya tira*," he said. "It means woman of the sun."

"Oh," she replied. "And, what is hor, horu, um—"

"*Hoarotu*," the priest said. "Him."

He pointed to the shaman who rescued them and the shaman nodded back. "He's one type of Warao shaman. And *Hoebo* is one of their gods of the underworld, who resides where the sun dies. It is said that he and the spirits of ancestral *hoaroa* are flesh-eaters. Living *hoarotu* must feed them."

"You learned all of this while you were a missionary?"

"Oh, yes," he said with a shudder. "We needed to know what our would-be flock believed so we could root it out of them. Heresy, blasphemy, that's what the Church was up against. Learn what they believe. Know their false prophets and their idols, and then destroy them to lead the poor souls to salvation."

He put his head in his hands, and Vivian could see they were still shaking.

She placed her hand on his shoulder and asked, "What happened, Father?"

Head still in hands, he sighed and then spoke. "I did as the Church wished. Oh, I helped build ramshackle schools, handed out food, brought them modern medicine from Doctors Without Borders, but there were strings of course. It was always more important to save their immortal souls. I wanted to help more...to give...and I did sometimes, but...."

"A bag of rice in one hand, a Bible in the other?" she asked, but gently.

"Worse," he said. "We made deals with some traders to help take us to the natives, and we introduced them, helped them earn the villagers' trust. We thought they could help bring the locals out of the shadows and into the light of God's Word and our world. Those traders were no better than the Conquistadors. *We* were no better. They cheated those people out of goods, land, women...brought in the evil of alcohol and drugs...."

"You didn't mean for all of that to happen," Vivian said, trying to soothe the priest.

"No, but I didn't stop it when it did. I didn't make it right either, and I've regretted it ever since. I will regret it forever. Those things back there, those souls, they came from out of darkness to remind me of my sins and to punish me for them."

He met her gaze then, his haunted and glazed. "We must be in Hell, Vivian, or close to it."

On that note, she decided to take a break from the questions and rest for the duration of their voyage. They sailed for a bit longer, and more of her strength returned. Good thing, since they soon stopped at another clearing.

The three of them hopped out of the boat and surveyed their surroundings. They were still in the rainforest, but beyond the clearing was nothing but darkness.

The shaman turned toward the priest and said, *"Te enfrentarás a más demonios. Camine por el sendero y no se detienen. Proteger a la sol mujer."* He pointed to a small trail cutting through the dense foliage.

The priest said, *"Sí. Vete en paz, hermano."*

They walked together toward the clearing, and Vivian offered a weak chuckle to ease her nerves and dread. "We aren't out of the woods yet, I take it?"

A grim Father Montgomery replied, "No, not yet. And I doubt my capability to be of much help after our first trial."

"If it's any consolation, I didn't do much better on my first little trip here," Vivian offered.

They kept moving into the bleak forest, its colors fading to shades of gray as the cold seeped in. Father Montgomery wrapped the blanket around Vivian's shoulders as they plodded along. Their footsteps were soon interrupted by a shift in the space around them. The sensation didn't feel the same as the vortex of light through which she'd traveled with the guardians, but it plummeted them someplace else nonetheless.

They were back in the darkness and the cold, where Father Montgomery stood frozen on the spot with fear. Vivian couldn't see him, but his raw terror and agony permeated the chilled air around them, raising the hairs on the back of her neck with its power. The presence in this place had shifted tactics.

The attack had become personal, and much more vicious.

Images from the Padre's mind flashed through Vivian's consciousness, a younger version of the priest, before he became a man of the cloth. A woman's voice called to him, over and over in a pitiful screech. "Lloyd!"

The ancient woman, a once-devoted mother now ravaged by senility, though her body and will remained very much intact. He had cared for her before giving himself over to the church, and he'd borne the burden alone.

She understood, and so did the demon responsible for conjuring this familiar brand of torment.

"Padre!" She shook him. "It isn't real. None of this is real. You have to come back to me now!"

The screeching woman, his tormentor, was pulling him to her, her incessant litany wearing down his resistance. Midnight wanderings, rooting through trashcans and dumpsters, soiled linens, furniture broken during bouts of rage born of confusion. These were the images and sounds that haunted his dreams, the Padre's own personal Hell to relive.

Mustering her resolve, she channeled his anguish. It took the form of a dull yellow light, which filtered out of the priest and into her.

So heavy, so very heavy.

"Vivian," Father Montgomery whispered first and then said loud and strong. "Vivian!"

She'd collapsed to the ground, a sense of resignation gaining ground over instincts to survive and to fight. She felt herself being pulled up by the priest, but she resisted.

No, I think I'll just stay here for a while. Just a little...longer.

Fatigue bore down on her, and she was overwrought with the burdens she'd collected. She was done.

A cool breeze flowed across her sweat-soaked forehead, carrying with it the perfume of mahogany and the pungency of withered lilies and carnations. Grave scents.

"Hello, Ms. Vivian," she heard Darkmore drawl.

CHAPTER THIRTY

"You didn't come alone?" Darkmore asked, his voice closer. She could've sworn she detected something akin to concern in that cool, smooth voice, but surely she'd imagined it.

"No," she whispered with a bit of irritation. "The Padre here hitched a ride."

"You should have called to me," Darkmore said, closer still. He must have kneeled down. Caressing her cheek with this hand, he sighed. "I would have brought you here with me, safely. You might have avoided the sorrow your mortal carried with him."

"Seems like I'm destined to reap the sorrows of the living anyhow," she snapped, pushing his hand away from her cheek in spite of the pleasant sensation it brought. "Not to mention the dead, so I might as well get used to it."

"Not like this," Darkmore said. Vivian opened her eyes and was taken aback. The man in white did, in fact, appear genuinely concerned, and more than a little alarmed. This was definitely not good.

What existed that could possibly frighten a reaper?

He turned to Father Montgomery and asked, "How long has she been like this?"

"It's been getting worse," the priest said, helping Darkmore to lift her to her feet. "She's been giving off and taking in a lot of light today, even before we arrived here."

"Oh, Vivian," Darkmore chided, albeit softly. "You should have waited. You should have called me, you—"

"You should've never dragged me into this!" Vivian hissed back at Darkmore. "You and Ezra and your damned reaper grudge-match."

"Perhaps that's true," Darkmore said. "But we can worry about it later. Come, I need to hide you both before he learns you're here."

"Before who knows?" Vivian and Father Montgomery asked simultaneously.

"Oh, you've met him once before," Darkmore whispered.

She shuddered, eyes widening at the memory of the dark, cold thing that held her in its grasp when she'd first entered Darkmore's realm. The raggedy man, the tormentor, the one whose lair this truly was.

"Let's go," she said.

The reaper illuminated the area around them, and he and the priest helped Vivian hobble along the uneven, rocky ground. Father Montgomery hesitated before stopping altogether. The priest turned his attention to Darkmore, sizing him up, or so it appeared to Vivian.

"Are you a force for good or for evil?" Father Montgomery asked.

"Neither one nor the other. Both." Darkmore answered.

"And what do you intend to do with Vivian?"

"I mean to keep her with me and teach her to channel her light for the harvest," he said, smiling at the incredulous look that graced Father Montgomery's face. "Come now, priest, a man of your calling must understand the necessity of our work."

"This is no place for her," he said. "If you require ransom for her soul, take mine instead."

The reaper surprised them both by laughing aloud, though he seemed to be fighting to keep his volume down. "Oh my, seems I've got two martyrs on my hands. What am I to do? Forgive me, Father, but I'm afraid your offer, generous as it is, simply won't do."

"So you'll send him back?" she asked, trying unsuccessfully to support her full weight.

"If you wish it, Vivian, I will see that he returns to the realm of the living unharmed," Darkmore replied with a small bow.

"But you can't stay here!" the priest cried.

"Shh, please keep your voice down and let's discuss this as we take a little stroll, shall we?" Darkmore said, tugging them along through the jumble of dirt, rocks, and jagged roots.

"Vivian came here of her own accord. Her own free will. As for what is to come, that is matter between the two of us—*alone*. Though I can assure you, Father, I will protect her so long as she is mine."

"Protect her from what, exactly? And what does it mean to be yours?" Father Montgomery asked, his tone dripping with contempt, and challenge.

Rather than answer, Darkmore froze, bringing them to a stop. Such was the power and presence of the man in white. His gaze grew colder, and his face contorted in a mask of rage.

Vivian was, at that moment, very frightened for Lloyd Montgomery.

The reaper snatched the priest's arm and pulled the helpless man closer until they stood nose to nose. "Shall I show you what it means?"

"Darkmore, *stop!*" she yelled.

She didn't dare touch either of them for fear of what she might absorb. Father Montgomery's eyes betrayed his terror. Yet to his credit, he didn't flinch. The reaper kept his cold energy focused on the priest, red light sparking from his fingertips and scorching the Padre's sleeve.

Oh dear God, he's not kidding.

She made one last appeal. "Lazarus, please, let him go now. Do it for me."

Shaking his head as though coming out of a trance, Darkmore released the priest. He didn't step back, though, and Vivian tensed, ready for a fight. But the reaper turned away then and took no further notice of Lloyd Montgomery. Instead, he blinked his blue eyes and the next thing Vivian knew, they were once more surrounded by more darkness.

"I moved us into the woods, and out of sight," Darkmore whispered. "He must know that you two are here. I'll have to go and meet him now."

He looked at Vivian, releasing enough illumination for her to see his face. "Stay here. If I don't come back within the hour, one of *your* hours, try to return to the realm of the living. I'll send help if I can."

He leaned in and kissed her softly on the lips. When he pulled back, she thought he was on the verge of speaking again, but he didn't. Instead, he disappeared, leaving Vivian and the priest alone in the darkness of his realm.

———

After about twenty minutes, she reckoned from her watch, though time seemed to be off in this realm, the priest suggested they leave. Vivian had to give him credit. In his position, she would probably have split in less than five. Tempting, to be sure. After another ten minutes, even more worry crept in, sending a stab of anxiety through her gut and clanging doubts through her mind. She wasn't certain whether to be comforted by the quiet around them or concerned by it.

Concern was definitely winning.

"Vivian?" The priest seemed to be afraid to speak to her. "I don't know what influence this being has over you, but I implore you to take us away from this place. Surely Ezra can protect you. I will do all I can as well."

"What do you know about Ezra?" she asked with a good bit of bitterness.

"I believe he must care for you a great deal since he's watching after your sister. He gave me his word he would protect and defend her, and that's why I came. We reasoned you wouldn't do anything too rash if you had a travel companion."

So Ezra had told the priest to come with her.

Sneaky old bastard.

"Betcha wish you hadn't come along right about now."

He didn't respond and she didn't pursue the matter since she wasn't sure she'd like the answer anyhow. After a few moments, Father Montgomery spoke again. "This Darkmore cannot be trusted, you know that."

"Well, for your information, neither can Ezra. In spite of what you guys teach in Sunday school, my so-called 'guardian angel' came to me in the guise of Heaven's little helper but sort of forgot to mention that he was supposed to haul me off into the afterlife. Which he didn't do. Which, if it didn't actually cause the mess I'm in right now, it sure as hell didn't help."

For the first time in their acquaintance, the priest actually sounded angry. "Listen, I don't pretend to have all of the answers, nor do I understand the mysteries of life, death, and God's plan. But I do trust in it—"

"Oh, I suppose you're going to quote from the book of Job now, huh? Dare I question God's glorious plan while the all-knowing Almighty intones 'Where were you when I made the world?' and all of that uplifting and oh-so-helpful crap?"

He waited a few beats before speaking in a quiet tone that permitted no interruption or argument. "Ms. Bedford, I can live with dissent and I can certainly participate in a civilized debate on matters of faith, but I will not tolerate mockery of my beliefs or presumptions about my intentions. I trust in God's plan, and even if you don't, I trust that you are a part of it. I trust in you, Vivian Bedford."

Well, didn't she feel like as ass now?

Swallowing her anger, and taking her foot out of her mouth, she took a deep breath and said, "Forgive me, Father Montgomery. I didn't mean to disrespect you. I am grateful you're here, but I'm really scared that I can't get you back."

"How were you going to get back before you knew I was tagging along? You said you had a plan, right?"

"I did," she said, steeling herself before letting rage and the festering mass of burdens she'd collected bubble to the surface. The first sparks started to sprinkle from the tips of her fingers, allowing Vivian to see the alarm on the priest's face. "I do have a plan to get you and everyone else trapped here out for good. Now's as good a time as any to see if it works. Stay put."

She allowed more and more light to filter through as she moved from the woods to the clearing beyond, pale pink and simmering pain morphing into all-out agony. She paused to retch, choking on the bitterness of grief and anguish. She heard Darkmore speaking words of supplication to whatever master he served, and she followed the sound.

The pressure bore down with such force that she could barely contain it. Aches with no salve, deep wounds with no sutures, grief no tears could wash away. All of this swelled within her being into a huge ball of fury. If she had to end this way, she would not go out with a whimper. No, she intended to go out with as big a bang as she could muster.

Vivian walked into the clearing and looked at Darkmore, who met her gaze with his wide-eyed, ice-blue stare. She turned and looked at the awful thing that faced him. With a deep breath, she commended her soul to the Fates and opened herself wide.

And let the fury go.

The red lights of rage lit up the dark realm as far as her mortal eyes could see, and God, did it burn!

CHAPTER THIRTY-ONE

Searing heat poured from her eyes, her mouth, and every pore, and the light that accompanied it left her blind. In the split second between the edge of the precipice and free fall stretching toward eternity, she saw many things too beautiful and terrible to behold.

Darkmore's look of awe was the first, captivated in worshipful reverence and terror, like staring down an incoming storm while frozen in the middle of its violent path.

The terrible faces of the damned in this realm would forever haunt her in this life, should she survive, or in the next if she didn't. They would creep out of darkened corners in the shade of sunny days and whisper to her through the soft wisps of gentle rains. Hungry ghost forms, savage and wretched, some among the throng surely belonged there forever and reveled in the depths of evil while others possessed the desperate hope for reprieve painted on their unseeing eyes.

She sensed every unquenchable desire and unfulfilled need these cursed creatures carried. Blistered and bare, some of the shivering masses hobbled toward the warmth she cast, pleading for shelter through chattering teeth. Others scattered through the flames and burned as their harpy shrieks echoed through the cold black far beyond the boundaries of the inferno. Still more were crushed in the chaos as hideous, nameless beasts consumed them raw.

Along the boundary of light and dark, others stood still, watching and waiting. She reached out to them, but they willingly bore the weight of their burdens, their longing for sight, and their hunger for lost pleasures. So many others, innumerable presences gathered in the circle of light and the surrounding darkness.

Some served willingly.

Vivian remained still as all feasted on despair, the fixed point in the madness surrounding her and engulfing the masses. She felt Darkmore's hands grasp her, heard his voice intone over the symphony of peril that he was with her. He would save her. She clung to the hope even as acrid smoke filled her lungs and obscured what little vision was left to her.

"The Padre!" she screamed. "Keep him out of this!"

Father Montgomery was fully mortal. He could never survive this. She didn't think she could either, not for much longer. "Lazarus, get him out *now*!"

"He's already out!" Darkmore cried. "Ezra—"

"He's gonna be just fine!" Ezra's voice boomed behind them from above. "And we're having ourselves one hell of a reckoning tonight!"

He bellowed from his fiery perch in a kind of manic rapture, arms spread out to the hellish congregation before and all around them. "Miss Vivian, you hold on tight now. She's coming. Lord have mercy she's coming and she's bringing some sweet manna to feed all these souls here tonight! Come on now, you old son of a gun," he commanded Darkmore. "You grab a hold of Miss Vivian now too, and don't you dare let her go!"

She beheld the power and might of the spirit and caught a glimpse of his true form, golden and glowing as pure light. Beneath the façade of good old country boy lurked the strength and fury of ages, the stuff of nightmares and the glory of legend.

He burned too.

Ezra grabbed her right hand and Darkmore her left as the fire raged with such heat it would surely consume the wicked and righteous all around. Then the presence of a fourth soul entered their sphere and enfolded them, sheltering Vivian from what she'd unleashed as she witnessed with unearthly eyes the rapturous redeemed leaving on white rays that streamed from their trinity.

The fourth was going with them, leading them. Vivian felt the pull of sweet oblivion luring her away, though she couldn't say where. Perhaps she too would move on to the other side, now that she'd finished her work.

Maybe I can go with Zeke.

The unseen presence touched her, a gentle caress on her cheek that reached to her very soul. Powerful, but this presence didn't fill her with awe or fear. Something about it seemed...personal. It carried with it beauty, light, forgiveness, and gratitude.

Did she deserve those things?

"Yes," it whispered. "I forgive you. I thank you. And I love you."

Vivian longed to fall into that presence and let it carry her home.

She almost surrendered, but then realized she had one more thing left to do.

"Lazarus!" she cried, even as Ezra enveloped her with him in his light. "Come with us!" She reached out to him with desperation bordering on panic. She couldn't leave him here. Not now, not after this.

Please....

The last thing she saw in that dark place was the reaper's face, still filled with awe and tenderness tempered with regret.

He shook his head and raised a hand to them and said, "No, Vivian... I'm already home."

Ezra departed and he carried her with him.

CHAPTER THIRTY-TWO

Vivian felt her bedroom before she saw it, felt it in all of the intangible ways that let you know you're home.

Maybe it was the familiar creak of the house frame, or the buzz of the air conditioner. It might have been the way her spot on the mattress molded to her body. She kept her eyes closed for a while, though conscious, and listened.

Relief washed over her as she heard Father Montgomery's soft prayers, and gratitude followed at the sound of Ezra's homespun wisdom and reassurance. She breathed deep and focused with all of her might, as though she could capture all she loved most in this place through the air. And she would hold onto all that had pained her most. A few tears prickled through her closed lashes.

Steeling herself, she opened her eyes and prepared to die.

"Good morning, Vivian," said the priest. "How are you feeling?"

"Like I've been to hell and back," she replied.

It was true. The deep aches that had remained dormant in her sleep now burned through her muscles. She groaned, but was determined to at least sit up and face the music with some dignity. Ezra helped ease her up. The old coot was pretty strong, she'd give him that. He was also gentle.

Vivian had the urge to reach up and put her arms around him for warmth and comfort, but her pride stopped her.

She'd almost forgiven him. Maybe crossing would help.

Business first? Probably best. "So, Ezra, what's the score now?"

"We're square now, me and Darkmore, and not just for Zeke," he said. He had the decency not to be coy.

Clearing his throat, Ezra continued. "You already know that I did a few things to earn a visit from him. And you figured out that he fed on my misery while I was trapped, as part of my sentence. But you were right. I found a way to tap into that energy and I got myself free with the help of the guardians, for a price. And for my service."

She still wondered what he'd done, not to mention how he wrangled a reprieve out of the guardians, but was too weary to push. He'd told her enough for now, and she appreciated his honesty.

And she wasn't so sure she really wanted to know. She'd had more than her fill of dark, soul-deep sins.

Speaking of dark souls.... "And what about Darkmore and his...souls? Are they okay? Is he okay or is he in some kind of trouble?" Vivian asked.

"Oh, after the feast of energy you gave to them that dwell in his realm, I figure he ought to be just fine and dandy, him and those that serve with him. And the one they serve."

She caught a faint tremor in his voice and swore he shivered at the mention of Darkmore's master. Not that she blamed him, having narrowly escaped the beast herself.

He gave his head a good shake and smiled. "You did real good, girl! I knew you had a plan, but I didn't figure it would work so damned good. All that energy you let loose set a whole host of souls free and helped 'em cross out of Darkmore's realm. Some of mine too. I'm proud of you."

"Thank you," she said, and meant it. In spite of everything, and to her surprise, she really meant it. She turned to the priest, who regarded her with compassion she hardly deserved. Her cheeks heated, being the focus of all of this praise and wonder. She hadn't done much at all, except take a big gamble, and she still couldn't quite wrap her head around the fact her gamble had actually paid off.

Heaving a deep sigh, she spoke to the priest. "You okay, Padre?" God, she hoped she hadn't completely destroyed the man's faith, even if she didn't share it. That would be a shame. The weary world needed a few more Father Montgomerys.

"I'm fine, Vivian," he replied. He moved to sit beside her on the bed and took her hand, his gaze filled with sorrow, and she wanted to weep for the damage she'd done by dragging him into all of this.

"You sure? I'm so sorry about everything—"

"Vivian, your sister—she's gone."

She stared at him. She'd expected Mae's demise. Expecting and accepting were two completely different things, though. What did she feel? Sad? Glad? Mad? All three rolled into one big lump lodged in her throat and her gut?

At the moment, what she felt most was alone.

"Child, she helped feed them, too," Ezra said. "And she made a fine crossing with as many lost souls as she could carry."

"It was Mae," Vivian whispered as realization dawned on her. *Oh, Mae-belle.* "She was the fourth? She did all of that?"

"Yes, ma'am," Ezra replied, beaming with pride. "She did, and she couldn't have done it without you."

"So she's in a better place?" Vivian asked in a small voice.

"Oh, Miss Vivian, she surely is." He sat on the other side of the bed and took her other hand in his. "I want you to know that she loved you something fierce. She still does. She thanks you. And she forgives you." She fell to weeping. Ezra was there to catch her with his warmth and comfort, along with the Padre, and she unleashed the grief of a lifetime as he held her close.

Mae did this, saved her, saved them all. She silently thanked her sister for the beautiful gift.

And Mae had forgiven her. Those simple, beautiful words filled her aching heart. *I forgive you. I thank you. I love you.*

Oh, Mae-belle. I love you too.

When she ran out of tears, she shook her head and met Ezra's gaze. "Well, I guess I'm ready now. Ready as I'll ever be."

"Ready for what?" he asked, brows furrowing in confusion.

"To go with you. Everything here is done, so it's time for you to finish your work and cross me over," she said.

"Is that what you want, Miss Vivian?" he asked. "You don't have to go just yet, you know."

"No, I don't know," she said. She'd had about enough surprises for a lifetime, but this one took the cake. Did he mean...she had a choice? She could choose life?

"Tell me."

"Well, I reckon I don't have a real deadline." He chuckled, but then had the grace to look sheepish. "Sorry about that. What I meant was, you've more than earned yourself some extra time here in this world, if you want it."

Did she want it? Mae wasn't there. She could have her life. But she was alone.

What do you do after something like this?

Her head started spinning and she sank back down in the bed.

"Aw, now, child, you don't have to decide right away. I can wait. You can call on me any time," he said. "You've earned that privilege too, I reckon."

Wow, feeling pretty generous, aren't we? she thought wryly. Then another thought occurred to her and she jumped up and sat nose to nose with the old spirit.

"What do you mean? I can still see you and your kind?"

"I can't do nothing about that," he said with a touch of sadness. "You still got ties with us, and those ties will bind until the end of your days. But," he chirped, looking suddenly much more spry, "I sure wouldn't mind the chance to come calling on you from time to time. You do make a mean cobbler."

She laughed. She couldn't help herself. She just laughed until she cried again. Then she slept, knowing the Padre and Ezra would be there when she woke again. Their presence made her feel a little less lonely. More than that, it gave a small measure of peace.

Small miracle, but maybe, just maybe, that feeling was worth the price she'd paid.

CHAPTER THIRTY-THREE

Six months later.

Vivian Bedford sat on her back deck and looked out over its wide expanse as far as her mortal eyes could see. It was one of those strange February days when Ma Nature forgot it was still winter and turned up the thermostat to seventy degrees. Even so, the nip in the air from the late-afternoon whistling wind inspired Vivian to pull out her grandmother's quilt and wrap it around her shoulders.

They'd been through a lot together.

She smiled, thinking of another who'd been through hell and back, and stuck with her in spite of it.

Father Lloyd Montgomery had presided over Mae Bedford's funeral. If any of the Baptist coalition in her family had a problem with her choice of clergymen, they'd had the good sense to keep silent. No one said a word about Vivian's decision to act as pallbearer for her sister either, even though women didn't normally perform such a service.

They'd all been decent, for the most part, and some had even been helpful.

Most swapped stories from happier times during shared childhood days after the funeral, when they'd gathered for the potluck back at Vivian's home. The Bedfords and McRoys hadn't always come through in a crisis, but they'd been at her side for Mae's goodbye and had stuck around since then. She'd grant them that, and she'd been making an effort to reconnect with a lot of them.

Family was family.

Mae Bedford's mortal remains were interred at Woodlawn Memorial Park in a spot that caught the warm rays of morning sun and stayed bright well into the afternoon. She thought Mae would approve. Whenever she visited, she would get a nod from the local spirits, and often enough a warm jolt from guardians passing through. Aside from that, most of the spirits she encountered left her alone, making her adjustment to this strange new reality a bit easier to bear.

She hadn't been able to bring herself to visit Zeke's plot yet. Maybe soon.

About two weeks after the funeral, she'd asked Father Montgomery to meet her at the hospital to "try something." He agreed with no questions. It wasn't possible to go through all of the things they'd faced together without forging some serious trust.

They'd made their way to the ICU and Vivian found she was able to go about unseen for a time, thanks to her connection to the spirit realm. The Padre could too, so long as she held his hand or his arm. She drew some light from one of the patients, tasted his suffering, and found she could stomach it. So they tried a few more. Later, the Father Montgomery invited her along to some of his visits to parishioners and to sit in on counseling sessions, unseen. She could take in their suffering too, and they came out better for it.

The effort left her weary, but she'd found a way to convert some of those burdens into raw energy, offloading some here and there to the lost and lonely specters she encountered or sometimes to other patients at the hospital whose time was drawing near. Hopefully it helped ease their crossings and gave them a little extra change for the proverbial tollbooth to the afterlife.

She'd been storing up the rest of the energy for herself, just in case. A newfound sense of purpose helped, but the ties binding her to life this side of the grave remained tenuous. They hadn't filled the hole in her soul left by loss and grief.

The New Year's celebrations came and went, and the cold of winter didn't do much to improve her outlook. Fortunately, Tennessee weather was fickle, and Jack Frost gave the land a respite on this particular February day. It was pleasant, and, save for the still-bare trees and the dormant brown grass, she might have mistaken it for April or May.

So she'd settled on her deck, enveloped in the twin comforts of blanket and coffee, determined to take a break from her search for answers to enjoy just...being.

She noticed them popping out around her stone wall, rushing the season as they often did. Little yellow and purple petals that might very well wind up covered by snow in a day or two lit up the bland landscape. For now, they were decorated with dewdrops, hanging like jewels along each petal, leaf, and short stem. Each dewdrop reflected the blue sky and clouds, the landscape, millions and millions of prisms bending each image so each was unique.

Many worlds, many possibilities.

Each drop held more wonder than her imagination could fathom if she looked close enough. Her crocuses had always made her smile, and today was no different. But today they made her think. Harbingers of spring, they lifted the blinders from her eyes and whispered to her of new beginnings.

It was the day that she decided to give life a try.

It put her in a temporary bind, but she left her firm for a smaller company. Fewer loans with more personalized service and recruitment of old clients got her well on her way to rebuilding her finances. And between re-growing her nest egg and rebuilding her life, she'd found time for her other work too.

Her first mission was working on a campaign to get Guitar Guy inducted into the Country Music Hall of Fame. She also started spending a fair amount of time with the Longhollows and found she enjoyed their company. Zeb bonded with her in his way, and baby Michelle seemed to be fine. They were taking life day by day. Vivian wasn't a half-bad babysitter either. Both Jenn and Father Montgomery seemed to enjoy their ongoing efforts to bring Vivian into the fold. Not happening, but the gesture touched her nonetheless.

She'd also been out on the town with Sue a lot, hitting Holland House, the hip and happening new bar tucked away in east Nashville. It was cozy, and its near-endless cocktail menu was almost as eclectic as its mustachioed and jovial Dutch proprietor. Sue had shacked up with Jack and they were doing just fine. She wasn't sure if wedding bells might ring in the future, but she wasn't counting it out. Sue suggested Vivian call Herb, especially since he'd been nice enough to show up at Mae's funeral.

They'd been out a few times, and that was going okay too.

Today, she was waiting for Ezra. He'd popped by at the hospital earlier in the week to let her know he'd be dropping by her place later. He had a few cases he thought might interest her. She realized then that her choices weren't going to be entirely her own after all, since she didn't think she wanted to cross him. Still, he had some brass balls to drop this on her. Instead of baking, she'd made some plain bologna sandwiches and picked up some Moon Pies just for spite.

But she'd also found it in her heart to make some sweet tea for him.

She was surprised when, instead of a dusty old John Deere cap, she spotted a white Stetson. The novelty of seeing Darkmore in the daylight floored her, since the reaper looked even more handsome. He smiled at her. She smiled inside and even on the outside, in spite of herself.

"Mind if I join you?" he called.

"I guess not, as long as you can play nice with Ezra when he gets here, or else hightail it out of here."

"Is that all the welcome I get?" He actually sounded offended.

"Well, hey there, Lazarus! How the hell are you? What's it been, six months? How's work? You must have been too busy dragging poor souls off to despair and darkness, I guess, or else you'd have stopped by sooner."

"I've missed you too, Vivian," he said with a wink.

She looked away, lest she fall for his charm. "Why are you here?"

"I came to do for you," he replied. Before she knew what hit her, he bent down and kissed her, soaking up the red light filled with the burdens she'd been gathering. Relief washed through her at the cleansing.

It was a great kiss too. She'd admit it. Later.

He stood up abruptly, looking immensely satisfied. So satisfied, in fact, he didn't speak for a few moments. Then again, neither did Vivian.

He tipped his hat and bowed before her. "Thank you, Ms. Vivian. See you around." And with a wink and a flash, he was gone. Vivian felt so good she decided to go back inside and bake some biscuits for Ezra after all.

She'd just pulled the biscuits out of the oven when she heard a knock at her back door. She turned and saw Ezra's face through the glass. He was smiling.

"Why don't you just come on inside?" she hollered. "It's not like you can't let yourself in."

He stood there, still smiling, but didn't offer to move.

Vivian walked to the door but didn't open it. Placing her hands on her hips, oven mitts and all, she looked at him and asked, "Well, what are you waiting on? The spirit to move you?"

She heard laughter behind her at the kitchen table and nearly fell down as she spun on her heels. At least he'd taken his hat off. But his dusty old boots were still on. "Well now, Miss Vivian, I didn't want to just waltz right in without an invite," he said in between snorts. "Hmm, the biscuits smell good, but I reckon the baloney and Moon Pies would've been enough, long as you got some RC Cola to go with them."

"Take whatever you like," she said, deciding not to take the bait. "And you can take the leftovers back to share too. I'm sure Guitar Guy wouldn't mind."

"Thank you kindly. Most days our buddy just takes a bite or two from the Hall of Fame cafe, so I reckon he'd enjoy something homemade. You best take care, Miss Vivian, else you'll have every guardian, reaper, and lost soul beating down your durned door for some home cooking. Who knows what else might show up?" he said with a grin.

She wasn't sure she cared to know what else lurked out there.

Ezra helped himself to some buttered biscuits, getting even more excited when Vivian set out some strawberry jelly her aunt had sent her. Watching him eat eased some of her irritation. There was just something gratifying about a man who enjoyed her cooking and wasn't shy about letting her know that he was in hog heaven. Vivian had her pride, just like any other woman.

She joined him at the table and nibbled on a biscuit, opting for coffee instead of tea. "So, let's get down to business. You want me to do some work for you?" she asked.

"I got a few folks who could use your help," he replied, wiping his mouth on a handkerchief he'd pulled out of the front pocket of his bibs.

"Do I have a choice?"

"You always got a choice, Miss Vivian," he replied. "You chose to stay here rather than move on someplace else. Could've been someplace better, you know? But you came back here and found yourself helping others that was left behind."

"I'm not so sure," she said. "I figured you were here to make me an offer I can't refuse. I mean, you seem to be like the Godfather of the guardians or something."

"Godfather?" He asked, scratching his head.

"You know? Al Pacino, Marlon Brando?" she asked with incredulity. "It's only one of the most famous films of all time. I thought all guys knew it by heart."

"Must have been after my time." He chuckled. "And I don't follow too many of them picture shows anyhow, except of course them with John Wayne. I sure did enjoy some of them with the missus."

What was it about spirits and westerns? "I can rent some for you, if you like," she said. "But back to the subject. What I mean is, if I say no to the things you want me to do, what are the consequences?"

"You afraid I'll go back on my word and cart you off to the next world? Make you serve there anyway?"

"Something like that."

"I won't go back on my word, Miss Vivian, but I can't exactly have you running around and using all that power you got without a little supervising and direction," Ezra said.

When she balked, he grabbed her hand and patted it as he continued. "Now don't go getting all riled up like you always do. I ain't here to stop you from doing the good works you been doing with your gift. But you have to understand, that's some mighty powerful stuff you're throwing around. You said it yourself. Channeling energy from the living makes you valuable. It also makes you a target for a whole lot of our kind out there. You need protection."

"And you need me to do some of your work for you," she said. Perhaps she was a touch snippy about it, but Vivian didn't like taking orders.

"It's what you'd have been doing if I'd collected you when I was supposed to," Ezra replied. His tone was neutral, but she guessed he was pretty well set on the terms. He could play dumb all he wanted, but this was sounding more and more like the ringleader of the underworld mafia to Vivian. Literally.

"We have our rules same as any other group," he went on. "Like a ball team, or a union, if you like. I'll look after you and coach you, and you can mostly choose the living you help, so long as you don't go interfering with any of my assignments or other guardians. You got a good nose for it."

"A union, huh?" she mused. "Do I get dental?"

"We don't have much use for it," he said, playing along.

"What about compensation?"

"You want to get paid, do you?" Ezra said more than asked. "Doing right by folks who need you ain't enough?"

"That was all well and good when this was strictly volunteer work," she began, squaring her shoulders for a fight. "But now that it's mandatory, I suppose I should get something extra for my trouble. I still have to pay the bills and keep you and all the other strays I seem to be collecting fed and watered."

"I suppose you do," he conceded. "And I sure wouldn't want you skimping on the vittles. Can't waste a good cook. I'll see to it you're never short on what you need."

"You do that. And remember I didn't take a vow of poverty either."

"Anything else?"

"Vacation time?"

"We work as we're needed, but you're still human," he said, eyes skyward and hands behind his head. He seemed to be working out a few things in his head. After a while, he nodded. "Yeah, I reckon you can have scheduled time off. You'll be needing it later."

"What is that supposed to mean?"

"You still got to live your life, Miss Vivian," he said with a tender smile. "I don't plan on taking that joy away from you. After all you been through and done for Miss Mae, you've more than earned some joy."

The old spirit probably knew more than he was saying about her future, though she didn't press him. Wouldn't do much good, she figured, since

Zeke hadn't been willing to talk about that part of their world. Of course, thinking of Zeke made the future look gray and shady rather than warm and sunny. She missed him so much that sometimes she thought she really couldn't go on. But then, her stubbornness got the better of her. Her wonder at the mysteries of life did as well. She owed it to Zeke and Mae and all those others who didn't get a second chance to grab life and live it to the fullest.

"What about the Padre?"

"I called on him," Ezra drawled. "He likes the idea of us working together. Between the two of us, we ought to be able to keep an eye on you most of the time."

"That's not exactly comforting."

"Depends on how you choose to see it," he said. "Most things depend on how you look at them. I'll bet dollars to doughnuts you're thinking this gift you've been given might just wind up costing you too much in the end. Am I right?"

"Yup, that sounds like the long and the short of it."

"Well, did you ever stop to consider maybe that's why it's worth so much? It's kind of like its owner that way," he said with a big grin.

Thus sayeth the hillbilly Yoda. "Hey, about your tale...."

"Yeah?"

"You never did fill in those details for me. You didn't finish it either."

"Nope, I reckon I didn't. Then again, you found a way to get the job done without hearing the ending. Like I said, you definitely got gumption, girl!"

"I'd really like to hear the rest some time."

Then, taking a deep breath, she worked up the nerve to ask the most important question, the one that had been burning her mind, heart, and soul for the past half-year. "And I'd like to know something else. Did you know things would work out like this? Was this your plan all along?"

"We'll get to all that," Ezra said. Seemed like that was as good as she was going to get for the time being, though she was wise enough to draw her own conclusions.

So that left one more question.

Would she take it back if she could?

Vivian chatted with Ezra a bit longer and they reached a tentative working agreement. She figured she'd leave out her other agreement with Darkmore. Ezra might think he had her right where he wanted her, but it never did hurt to have an ace in the hole.

Afterward, she picked up her flowers and headed out to the cemetery. Her drive along Nashville's winding interstates took her through a couple of interchanges, as most routes in the city would. A detour here, a curve around some obstacle there, the occasional exchange with other travelers was sometimes a little wave of thanks for making room or a honk and the finger on a bad day. Changing lanes and circling around to get on the right road was just what you did to get anywhere around here, even when you were on your way to commune with the dead.

It was just what you had to do to get by.

Cold as it was getting, she still liked to go to Woodlawn at sunset. The cemetery always looked prettier then, out of the glare of the winter sun. Mae got some sweet-smelling pink roses. Taking a deep breath, she made the trek to Zeke's plot. It was easy to find, as it was the only spot of green on the property.

The neat rectangular plot was bordered on all sides with dormant grass, straw-colored and crisp, devoid of life. The interior of the plot was a striking green. She smiled at the small miracle before her, knowing no Earthly force could make green grass grow in the dead of winter. Her smile broadened as she walked closer and discerned spots of yellow with brown in the center sprouting out of the green. No Earthly force made those Suzies sprout this time of year either. A message? A thank you? She didn't know for sure, but she hoped it meant he'd crossed over to a better place.

That he was home.

"No, love, I wouldn't take it back."

As she bent down to trace the letters forming his name, the aches she'd been ignoring since she came back from the dead began to take their toll. Tears rolled and stung her cheeks as the temperature fell, but they didn't worry her this time. It was the weather, not evil spirits. She often took comfort in the ordinary these days.

Depositing her flowers among his, she stood and straightened her jacket, wiped her eyes with gloved hands, and looked around. The dead were present, of course. They always were. Some familiars waved while others nodded. A few stood motionless and paid her no mind. Most new spirits didn't pay her any mind until they realized she could see them.

She was getting used to her new reality.

Whispering to the earth below her, she stood for a moment longer, then turned and walked away from the waking dead and back to the land of the living.

THE END

Thank you for reading! Did you enjoy?

Please Add Your Review! And don't miss the Soul Broker novels with book 2, RAISING THE DEAD. Turn the page for a sneak peek!

SNEAK PEEK OF RAISING THE DEAD

The woman appeared on her deck.

He'd been watching her for a long time, at least by mortal standards. Flesh was such a limiting state. The departed reckoned time a bit differently than the living. It was one advantage—or disadvantage—of their eternal natures.

Of course, time had never worked in his favor on either side of eternity.

Hidden in the nearby tree line, he stared up at the back door to her home, the white of its recently painted frame eerie as it glowed in the moonlight. Deck chairs and a small table cast long shadows as a gust sent a shiver of ripples through the fabric of a large umbrella. Empty a heartbeat before, and then all of a sudden, there she stood.

She took his breath away. Always had.

She didn't step out of the back door, nor did she casually stroll up the stairs. She materialized, as if she'd conjured her body out of thin air.

Not possible for ordinary mortals, of course. She was still technically among the living. Only powerful incorporeal guardian and reaper spirits could conjure a corporeal form from the elements. But this almost-mortal woman had learned a few of their tricks, including some she hadn't bothered to share with the guardians for whom she worked.

Her auburn curls whipped in the wind as it howled through the dark night. She fought to push the rogue strands out of her face while she waited for her dark guest, or so he suspected.

She hadn't told her guardian supervisors about *him,* either. His fists clenched as emotion exploded through his body, which threatened to shatter into the dust from which it came.

Rage to be sure, and jealousy, perhaps—or, more accurately, a deep sense of betrayal—nearly consumed him, but he struggled for calm. He was here to observe, not to intervene. That would come later, and only if he caught her in the act.

Playing both sides was a dangerous game, and one that came with the risk of dire consequences.

He'd learned that lesson from a rather unpleasant personal experience.

He half-hoped he was wrong about her. The heart he now possessed longed for it.

Vivian Bedford had intrigued him ever since he'd been assigned to monitor the rare mortal soul broker. Nearly broken under the weight of an unbearable burden, she'd proven tenacious, fiercely protective of those she loved, and surprisingly cunning in her dealings with afterlife management. She'd taken the hard road, clinging to mortal life in spite of being forever bound to the world of spirits. Death would have been the much simpler choice, if less courageous.

Pride mingled with anger and jealousy.

He'd had a hand in shaping her into the formidable soul broker she'd become, and he'd paid a heavy price. But it seemed she was seeking guidance from another mentor now. Right on cue, the man in white appeared, and she welcomed the reaper with a brief but passionate kiss.

With that one act, she'd given him the ammunition he needed. Now, he only had to pick the right moment to pull the trigger.

If he could.

———

Don't stop now. Keep reading with your copy of RAISING THE DEAD available now. And sign up for the City Owl Press newsletter to receive notice of all book releases!

Don't miss Soul Broker novels with book 2, RAISING THE DEAD available now! And find more from D. B. Sieders at www.dbsieders.com

———

Afterlife management is a tricky business, especially for a living soul broker.

Juggling normal life with her otherworldly responsibilities—like helping departed souls cross to the other side while collecting grief from the living through her empathetic connection—just got a whole lot more complicated. Her guardian spirit bosses, who make the mafia look tame, don't like the side jobs she's been taking to help living souls in peril.

But they don't know the half of it.

She's been working in secret with Lazarus Darkmore, a grim reaper and unlikely ally against the guardians' hold on her. When a rogue guardian sends an ominous message that threatens to expose the alliance unless she stops, she has no choice but to put her trust in the reaper. But can a creature as dark and terrifying as Darkmore keep her safe, or will his appetite for cruelty and terror be her undoing?

With a spirit world energy crisis looming and guardian spirits closing in, Vivian must choose—toe the line with the guardians, plunge into darkness with the reaper, or join a rebellion that could unleash hell on earth.

———

Please sign up for the City Owl Press newsletter for chances to win special subscriber-only contests and giveaways as well as receiving information on upcoming releases and special excerpts.

All reviews are **welcome** and **appreciated**. Please consider leaving one on your favorite social media and book buying sites.

For books in the world of romance and speculative fiction that embody Innovation, Creativity, and Affordability, check out City Owl Press at www.cityowlpress.com.

ACKNOWLEDGMENTS

Though not the first I published, this is the first novel I wrote and is the book of my heart. The journey began around 2008. One night while sitting on my back deck and staring out over the landscape, I wondered, "What would happen if a ghost came strolling out of the tree line?" (There may or may not have been a few glasses of wine involved). I thought, "Why would he be strolling out in the open? Is he looking for someone? Does he have a story to tell? What is his story?"

That was the birth of Ezra, Vivian, and the birth of my writing career, though I didn't know that at the time. I thought I'd write a short story. It turned out to be much, much more than that, and I am grateful.

Since this has been a long journey, I have quite a few people to thank— first and foremost, my friends Stephanie Moore and Ronald Wuister. They were there from the beginning, read the first drafts, and gave me a wealth of great advice and encouragement. I also received support in those days from a cyber pal who I only know as Green Jewels. I also need to thank members of the Amazon Breakthrough Novel Award Competition Class of 2012, including Jeff Lee, Bob Simms, Jenny Milchman, Thomas Knight, Jeffrey Getzin, Jeff Fielder, Sheryl Dunn, Gae Polisner, Hart Johnson, Rodney Walther, Hart Johnson, Dwight Okita, Janet Oakley, Blackie Noir, Claire

Chilton, Patrick Frievald, Cal Noble, Erica Olsen, Nichole Elizabeth, Christopher Ledbetter, Alison Deluca, John Aragon, Mary Walters, Sophia Samatar, Lisa Grintals-McClellan, and a host of other now lifelong writer friends who kept me going on the contest circuit.

From there (and after many edits with the help of Alice Sullivan, Trish Milburn, Dee Burks, Liz Ragland, and Abby Rose), I was guided by my writing mentor, Bente Gallagher, to Romance Writers of America by way of Music City Romance Writers. I learned and honed my craft with the help of my MCRW sisters and brothers, all the while editing, revising, and refining this particular story that just wouldn't let me go. It got better—good enough to final in the Grace Notes Books 2011 Discovering the Undiscovered Competition in Book Length Fiction, the 2012 William Faulkner-William Wisdom Creative Writing Competition in Novels and Narrative Non-fiction, and the Georgia Romance Writers 2015 Unpublished Maggie Contest. After many rounds of mostly kind rejections from publishers and literary agents, I was fortunate enough to meet agents Victoria Lea and Natalia Aponte at the Killer Nashville Writer's conference in 2012 and signed with them shortly after.

Other beta readers who helped include Mary Bruss, owner of the much beloved and sorely missed Mysteries and More Booksellers in Nashville. She read a very early draft and was quite kind in her assessment. She also introduced me to the amazing Nashville Writer Community. Thanks also to Maggie Young, Jennifer Merritt, Deborah Wilbrink, Debbie Herbert, AJ Scudiere, Eli Jackson, Rebecca Cook, Karen Strunk Riley, Jody Wallace, and Josephine Carr for beta reads.

In the meantime, I completed and published other projects and while Natalia and Victoria shopped around *Waking the Dead*. Publishing is, I've found, a rather slow process. But all good things to those who wait, and after a long wait and many close-but-not-quite deals, this book found a wonderful home at City Owl Press.

I am eternally grateful for Victoria and Natalia for believing in this project and bringing it to publication. Thanks to Yelena Casale and Tina Moss of City Owl Press for the wonderful opportunity, as well as to Amanda Roberts for her fantastic edits! Shout out to Olivia of MiblArt for the gorgeous cover art!

And most importantly, I thank my family. They are my biggest supporters, fans, and greatest source of inspiration.

ABOUT THE AUTHOR

Award-winning author D.B. Sieders was born and raised in East Tennessee and spent her childhood hiking in the Great Smoky Mountains and chasing salamanders, fish, and frogs. She loved to tell stories while sitting around the campfire.

She is a working scientist by day, but never lost her love of telling stories. Now, she's a purveyor of unconventional fantasy romance featuring strong heroines and the heroes who strive to match them. Her heroes and heroines face a healthy dose of angst as they strive for redemption and a happily ever after, which everyone deserves.

www.dbsieders.com

facebook.com/DBSieders

twitter.com/DBSieders

goodreads.com/dbsieders

amazon.com/D.B.-Sieders/B00D18ZPOY

ABOUT THE PUBLISHER

City Owl Press is a cutting edge indie publishing company, bringing the world of romance and speculative fiction to discerning readers.

www.cityowlpress.com